Letters
to a
Stranger

Letters to a Stranger

MERCEDES PINTO MALDONADO

TRANSLATED BY JENNIE ERIKSON

LAKE UNION
PUBLISHING

This is a work of fiction. Names, characters, organizations, places, events, and incidents are either products of the author's imagination or are used fictitiously. Any resemblance to actual persons, living or dead, or actual events is purely coincidental.

Text copyright © 2015 by Mercedes Pinto Maldonado
Translation copyright © 2019 by Jennie Erikson
All rights reserved.

No part of this book may be reproduced, or stored in a retrieval system, or transmitted in any form or by any means, electronic, mechanical, photocopying, recording, or otherwise, without express written permission of the publisher.

Previously published as *Cartas a una Extraña* by Amazon Publishing in Luxembourg in 2016. Translated from Spanish by Jennie Erikson. First published in English by Lake Union Publishing in collaboration with Amazon Crossing in 2019.

Published by Lake Union Publishing, in collaboration with Amazon Crossing, Seattle.

www.apub.com

Amazon, the Amazon logo, Lake Union Publishing and Amazon Crossing are trademarks of Amazon.com, Inc., or its affiliates.

ISBN-13: 9781542007306
ISBN-10: 1542007305

Cover design by Lisa Horton

Printed in the United States of America

First edition

To my mother, a model of perseverance, who has given everything for her family. She is the antithesis of Doña Alberta, the mother of the protagonist in this story.

*At that time, I found a strange refuge. By chance,
as they say. But coincidences like that don't exist. If
you need something desperately and find it, this is
not a coincidence; your own need and desire lead
you to it.*

Hermann Hesse, Demian

Chapter 1

Wednesday, 11 June 2014

After a gap of fifteen years, most people would feel quite emotional, returning to the house where they were born and grew up. The simple act of opening the front door after so much time and coming face to face with such a significant section of their past – years in which their personality developed and shaped the rest of their life – would be enough to make the majority of folk take a deep breath before stepping through.

Well, not so far as I was concerned. I crossed that threshold with blinding indifference, as if it were nothing more than heading into the supermarket to pick up a sandwich on a night off from the restaurant. I was just annoyed at the interruption to my life and the inconvenience of going away right now, just before the peak tourist season in London: my business needed all employees on hand and my absence was a problem.

The news came and I didn't have time to stop and think – the preparations for such an unexpected trip kept me busy right through to the last minute, but once on board the plane, with two hours of inactivity stretching ahead, my mind suddenly cleared. The seat to my right was unoccupied, and the novel I'd been glued to for the past three nights lay forgotten on the bedside table back home in my London flat. I didn't fly often, and take-off always makes my stomach lurch, so I tried to keep my mind busy, which felt strange, alien, more from the enforced idleness than from the unusual situation. I was used to managing every moment of my day with meticulous efficiency, making best use of my time, and having nothing to do made me anxious. I searched for distraction on the other side of the window, but London and all of its magnificence lay hidden beneath a dense blanket of endless dreary grey.

◆ ◆ ◆

She had died . . . My mother had left this world less than forty-eight hours earlier and I felt nothing, only irritation because this was not the best time to head off travelling, and especially to Spain, absolutely the last place I wanted to go. The burial had taken place this morning. Condolences had been offered and the mourning clothes returned to the back of the wardrobe, so the only task that remained now was to deal with her belongings, half of which suddenly belonged to me. Teresa, the woman who had kept our house throughout my mother's marriage, had told me on the phone that my sister Yolanda had been living for some time in Australia and was unable to come to Madrid. And so it fell to me to put in an appearance and handle all the usual matters in such times – choosing which goods and personal items of the deceased, my mother, the 'distinguished' Doña Alberta, should be thrown away, and which should be sold or kept, so the property could be put on the market as soon as possible. This was going to be enormously unpleasant, but that was all.

I'd never had the slightest desire to return, or even been tempted to call. Any curiosity as to what might be taking place in the house where I grew up had been non-existent since my departure. In my first months of freedom I hadn't even dared answer my phone, in case my sister or mother had somehow got hold of my number. At that point in my life my only priority was to forget. I'd left because I was suffocating, convinced I would go mad if I stayed even one more day.

I climbed out of the taxi with my single suitcase. I didn't think I was going to be staying any longer than absolutely necessary, and at the start of summer light clothes were all I needed. Teresa was waiting for me and she opened the door right away, having heard the sound of the car. She was exactly the same as I remembered, and, although a few white strands were beginning to appear at the temples, her hair still shone black, clean and silky, tied back in a low bun, which looked as though it hadn't moved in all the years gone by. She still wore a delicate flowered scarf knotted around her neck, the two ends resting gently on her chest like the wings of a butterfly on a flower. Her lips remained slightly pink, looking as moist and cool as I remembered them. She still wore the woollen jumper, dark knee-length skirt and shoes of a nun . . . And her gaze even now was deep and steady, the gaze of someone whose heart shines out through their eyes. Teresa was one of those rare souls who can hug you without even touching you. I had told her a thousand times over that the only source of kindness in Alberta's house was the person who stood in her own black-laced shoes. My words had always upset her though, because they betrayed the deep contempt I felt for my mother and sister. I was always mystified by the devotion and respect she showed to her mistress, in whose service she had slaved for forty years. For me Teresa wasn't only the woman who kept our house in order; she was the closest thing I had to a mother.

I had thought that during the fifteen years I'd spent in London I'd been reborn, reinvented, and that nothing from the past still survived in me. But before I could hug my beloved Teresa, as soon as I stepped on the welcome mat – and it wasn't a welcome sight, I thought – I automatically started maniacally wiping the soles of my shoes: five times on each side. Either you did it, or you didn't come in at all. That was how my mother was – she had to remind you who was in charge in that pristine house before you'd even set foot inside. One, two, three . . . OK, that was enough. It didn't matter any more. I broke off the doormat ritual to hug Teresa.

'My darling, how wonderful to have you home again! My little Berta . . .' she said, standing on tiptoe to kiss me. 'Let me look at you.' She stepped back for a closer inspection. 'You're so slim, elegant and beautiful, and—'

'Yes, Teresa, I'm the same, just older. But I'm so very glad to see that you're exactly how I remember you.'

'Come in, come in, I've made you something to eat. After all this time I expect you eat early like the English. It's really so good that you're here, I can't tell you how much I've missed you and your sister in these last few days. It's truly such a joy, my dear,' she repeated, walking into the house.

I set my suitcase down next to the door and prepared to follow her in. So far I'd only seen this one loving face from my past: Teresa. Standing at the entrance to the dreaded hallway, I congratulated myself on having had the strength to get past the first hurdle.

Then, all of a sudden, I was hit by a shock wave, held paralysed in the centre of the doorway, in full sight of the sitting room, both of its doors flung open wide. My hand flew to my heart as Teresa, in high spirits, headed off to the kitchen. I heard her telling me what was for dinner but the words seemed to come from far, far away, and I could neither move nor answer her questions. I searched desperately for something to hold on to. I couldn't breathe – it felt as though a ball of rotten straw had stuck in my throat. When at last I took a deep breath, the source of my crippling anxiety became clear and I leaned against the nearest wall, sliding down until I was sitting on the floor. Just then Teresa came along with a tray in her hands and almost tripped over my feet.

'Oh, darling! You're white as a sheet, love. What's wrong?' she asked worriedly, setting the tray of tapas down on the sideboard.

'It was her scent, Teresa . . .' I managed to say, gasping for air. 'It got inside me and almost choked me.'

'Oh dear, no! Come on, put your head between your legs. You're cold as ice,' she said, massaging my temples gently. 'I'll fetch you a glass of water. Goodness gracious, you gave me quite a turn.'

She returned a few seconds later. 'Drink up, love. Is that any better? Your colour's coming back now. Yes, this is all still too recent for you. Let's step outdoors again for a while.'

As soon as I'd recovered a little, I took Teresa's arm and we went out into the garden together, where I discovered that it was a particularly lovely afternoon. I knew it was time to face up to the reason for my return, but neither of us dared break the silence.

'I see some things haven't changed,' Teresa said finally. 'Her perfume still upsets you.'

'I can't believe how much the house still smells of her. But it's not just the smell, it's everything it represents – it's like breathing the very *essence* of her, along with all my worst memories.'

'I've made up your room . . . I suppose you'll be sleeping here?' she said, rapidly changing the subject. She didn't like it when I criticised my mother.

'That was the general idea, though now I'm not so sure I want to stay . . .'

'You'll see your room is exactly how you left it.'

'OK. Oh, your Russian salad is delicious, not to mention the croquettes . . . Mmm . . .'

'Tell me, sweetheart, what have you been doing with yourself all these years? Are you married? Do you have a boyfriend? It's been so long since I heard from you . . .'

'Well, I started washing dishes in a restaurant, worked my way up and now I own it. That's my job: I manage one of the best restaurants in London – Berta's Kitchen. And no, no boyfriend, no husband, no children . . . I live alone in a flat and my life revolves around my work.'

'I'm glad you've been doing so well, and there's me dreaming up all these stories in my head . . . Do you want to know how it happened then?'

I wanted to know as soon as possible, though more out of a sense of duty than of interest. 'What can I say, Teresa. Do I need to know?'

'Yes, you do. Have a little bit more, won't you?'

'More? I stopped growing a long time ago. You know what, I think I'll have a whisky – that might help me relax and take in what you're about to tell me. By the way, this garden is still the most beautiful in the whole of Madrid. I never could understand how you managed to keep all these flowers alive, even in winter,' I told her, looking around.

'Oh, you just have to spend a little time at it every day. Plants appreciate it when you take care of them. I'll go and see what there is in the drinks cabinet in the sitting room. She was the only one here who enjoyed a drink, as you know . . . Well, we'll see.'

With the first sip warming my blood, I felt more able to listen, and at last Teresa started to tell me everything that I, as the deceased's daughter, was honour-bound to know.

'I left her when she was eating her pudding . . . I went to the chemist's to get her blood pressure medication before they shut and . . . when I got back she was dead – her head in the remains of the watermelon. I think she'd only just died, because she fell to the floor as I was coming into the sitting room. Darling, it was all so . . . so sudden . . . I can't get that image out of my head.'

Tears welled up in her eyes and slid down her cheeks. I was shocked to see her cry. I honestly never thought anyone would grieve her loss, not even Teresa.

'So I guess there isn't really much more to tell, because it all happened so fast. On second thought, even the way she died was lucky – how many people would love to meet their maker like that?' I said sarcastically, choosing to ignore how much it pained her to remember the scene.

She seemed upset at my attitude, and decided she'd done her duty for the day and it was time for her to leave.

'I've got to go, love – I don't want to miss the ten o'clock bus. I've left information about the solicitor by the phone, along with the address. Don't forget he's expecting you in his office tomorrow morning at nine. Would you like me to come along?'

'It's all right, don't worry about it.'

'I'll stop by tomorrow in case you need anything.'

Before she walked through the front gate, I said what I knew she was hoping to hear: 'Teresa . . .'

'Yes?'

'I'm so sorry you had to go through all that on your own.'

'I'll see you tomorrow. Get some rest, sweetheart.'

It was a little unfeeling, my behaviour in the face of her sorrow, but my mind simply refused to adopt the role of the grieving daughter who had just lost her darling mother. More than anything, the moment I came back I felt the same visceral sense of rejection I'd always experienced in that house.

I poured myself another glass and stayed out a little longer in the fading light, enjoying the scents of the garden. Everything beautiful that surrounded me was Teresa's doing, the woman who had worked for us for forty years. My mother had never pulled a single weed. She never cared about anything or anyone except herself.

◆ ◆ ◆

I was dying to go to the loo, but to get there I had to cross the space where her stale scent still lingered. I'd thought those years were long forgotten, like all the junk you only remember when you're clearing out the corners of the attic, but I hadn't counted on the fact that the very essence of a person is carried in their smell and there's no way to shut that out like we do unwanted goods. It clings to everything and has the power to open doors in your subconscious, releasing all your loveliest as well as most painful memories.

Holding my breath, I ran to the guest toilet, which she never used. It smelled clean and of no one at all.

Then I crossed through the sitting room, dragging my suitcase, without breathing or looking around me. In the main corridor I turned my back on my mother's bedroom door so I could open my own in safety. Everything was neat and orderly, just as it was then, almost sterile. She never allowed me a single poster of my favourite singer of the day on the wall; in fact, she never allowed me to have a favourite singer at all. She didn't even let me decorate my bed with the cuddly toys my friends gave me for my birthdays. Everything had to be bare, with no personality. Anything that revealed my character or personal taste was ruthlessly edited from my room, and the same went for my sister. Our mother's determination to quash our dreams and desires forced us to lead double lives where our true selves remained hidden and stifled, while the selves we showed to the world were so perfect as to be almost artificial. Maybe that's why it was so easy for me to start my life over; because I'd never actually *lived* anywhere before that. I could finally just be myself, the real me, with no punishment or criticism of who I was.

Setting my suitcase down by the desk, I found a piece of paper with the Wi-Fi password written on it. It would be great to have internet access during my stay here, to keep in touch with Harry, my friends and the chef at the restaurant. I took a quick shower and then logged on to my laptop. I meant to go on Facebook and chat a bit with Mary and Emily, but after answering some urgent emails I felt absolutely exhausted. I waited in bed for the drowsiness to take hold and send me off to sleep, but despite my tiredness the opposite happened, and I suddenly felt with cold clarity precisely where I was and why. A chaotic swarm of vivid memories from my time in this house now buzzed furiously in my mind.

What had I been thinking . . . ? I'd convinced myself that I was a new person, a complete stranger to the naive girl who'd lived in Madrid, now long since dead and buried. I never contemplated that my return would merge these two selves together. If anything, I'd imagined a simple encounter between two women meeting for the first time, each unaffected by the other's life, because there was nothing to connect them any more. The truth was, however, that we both shared the same skin. After a lot of time and space, and seeing other worlds freer and more authentic than the one in which I'd grown up, I'd wrested control of my own life and the opportunity to be the only star of my story. The memories that assaulted me now seemed like impossible nightmares. How could a young girl endure such subjugation, live in such terror of making a mistake? How could anyone survive a life of such absolute coldness and lack of love? It was all thanks to Teresa, who had provided the delicate pulse of light and warmth that crept into that house every day.

I remembered how my friends' mothers had displayed the pictures their daughters had drawn at school on the door of the fridge, along with their favourite poems or crowning achievements in their spelling tests, and I marvelled at this with an envy so strong that it hurt. My mother, Doña Alberta, merely kept a long list on her fridge with all the things Yolanda and I might conceivably do wrong on the left, and the corresponding penalty on the right. Get up late and you had to clean the bathroom; come home late, clean both bathrooms; switch your bedroom light off after midnight, pull weeds in the garden; raise your voice and you were grounded for the weekend; tell a lie and it was a double punishment: clean the bathrooms as well as be grounded. This last punishment was sheer hypocrisy, because I have no memory of the biggest liar in the house, my mother, ever cleaning a bathroom. The endless list only grew larger as Yolanda and I got older, engineered with precision to keep the two of us at home doing chores most weekends. My sister, rather cleverer and bolder than I was, often managed to wriggle out of her duties, so while I was living here the work almost always fell on Teresa and me. In my life story there were two Cinderellas, a vile stepsister and a heartless mother.

Living under a prisonlike regime turned me into a submissive child, while Yolanda became more and more out for herself and whatever she could get, Machiavellian and sly – pretty much like our mother, in fact, only cheekier and more daring . . . plus she was the more attractive of the two in terms of looks. Her style of beauty was bewitching but perverse.

The drowsiness that had carried me to bed, the product of whisky and fatigue, vanished entirely as I tossed and turned on the freshly laundered sheets, desperate for sleep to come. Unable to quit my thoughts, finally I stopped trying, seeking instead to banish the nightmares of my past through reliving my fondest memories. Teresa featured in every one of them – my enigmatic, loyal and attentive Teresa. I recalled the years when she lived with us, when my world became brighter and more bearable – and how she would sing to me while giving me a bath, or those nights when unbeknownst to my mother she would read me stories to help me sleep. Doña Alberta would get angry with her, berating Teresa for undermining her in front of her daughters and breaking the rules. Whenever she scolded her, it made me anxious that Teresa might get the sack, or end up punished like Yolanda and me. Teresa would always wait until my mother was out of sight and then whisper soothingly in my ear, 'Don't worry, darling, she can't punish me – I never go out at the weekend in any case and I simply love cleaning bathrooms!' Then she'd smile and wink at me.

I remembered the afternoons when my mother would go shopping or went out to see friends, and Teresa could spoil us as much as she liked. She'd make us chocolate cake and we'd be free to laugh out loud, playing ludo and cheating on purpose. Sometimes she even made us forget that our mother might come home at any moment. I remembered also special times in Marbella during the summer holidays. My mother couldn't stand the sun, so it was Teresa who took us down to the beach. She'd wake before dawn to finish her housework and cook a splendid lunch to leave at home for Mother so she'd allow us to enjoy our day by the sea. What freedom – and all because my mother wasn't there, and we knew she wouldn't be showing up any time soon. We'd play openly with other kids at the beach and splash about, laughing in the water with no fear of being told off over and over again. During those wonderful sessions at the beach, we could just be children.

Comforted by that rosy vision, full of laughter, sun, water and salt, I finally managed to doze off.

Chapter 2

Thursday, 12 June 2014

I awoke many times in the night, although Morpheus lured me back without too much trouble. It was hard to get up in the morning; the alarm went off at seven, but I snoozed on for another fifteen minutes or so.

Madrid held several surprises in store for me that day. The first came right away in the form of a cat, who looked nearly the size of a tiger, staring defiantly up at me from its cosy nest in my open suitcase, among the very clothes I'd meant to wear that morning.

My morning grogginess evaporated in an instant at this unexpected vision. I'll admit that I've never been that fond of pets, particularly cats, probably in large part because I don't remember ever seeing my mother without the company of her treasured Califa, a surly cat who enjoyed all the caresses that Doña Alberta should have been lavishing upon her daughters. When she died, shortly before I left for London, it was the first time I ever saw her mistress cry. She and I, we knew to keep our distance, never getting too close to each other, but this cat now resting on my luggage was apparently not aware of the rules.

I swatted in its direction and the creature ran out of my room, but I found him again in the kitchen, next to two bowls: one empty and the other holding a measure of dirty water. He stared at me intently, now openly and with more confidence. I tried to ignore him, not having time to make new friends right then, and started rifling through cupboards and drawers after supplies for making coffee. The cat remained motionless, doing his excellent impression of a plump cuddly toy glued to the floor. The only sign of life was in his eyes, which were as expressive as the Madrid sunrise.

◆ ◆ ◆

Tiring of blindly throwing open and slamming shut the cupboard doors, I paused for a moment to take a proper look inside and was suddenly overcome by a strange fatigue, along with a slight vertigo that made me slide down to the floor alongside the cat – the same symptoms I'd experienced the day before on first returning to the house. Everything was just so bloody neat and tidy, and it felt like coming face to face with her cold and empty soul. The plates and glasses were neatly lined up, identical, sparkling, as if brand new; cutlery lay in its proper sections, each knife, fork and spoon neatly stacked one on top of the other, exactly twelve of each; the saucepans shone like mirrors, all arranged to perfection; in identical little piles, separated by colour, the tea towels were folded so crisply they could have been done by machine; the cups sat face down on their saucers, perfectly centred, a dozen for *café con leche* and another dozen for plain coffee. It looked like the work of a psychopath, but it wasn't: it was all done by Teresa – on the orders of a psychopath, of course.

Ever since I was old enough to have common sense, I'd tried to understand why my mother never once tucked me into bed, or tied my scarf on cold school mornings. I remembered so many years when, night after night, I would squeeze my eyes tight shut, hoping and believing that tonight my dreams would come true and she would come to kiss me goodnight. Sometimes I thought I felt something brush my forehead, like the soft petal of a flower, and then I'd squeeze my eyes shut even more tightly until they hurt, so I wouldn't accidentally open them and realise it was nothing more than the phantom sensation of my own wishes, or once again the soft tip of Teresa's flowery scarf. I so dearly wanted the kiss to be from her, even though I knew she'd handed over all the duties of motherhood to her housekeeper – even the goodnight kiss.

Now, at thirty-four years old, I'd fallen in love many times. I know these men loved me, but I could never say how much I loved them back. Both of them left me because they were lonely, just as I had always felt with my mother – lost and empty. I feared that I'd inherited her worst traits: her indifference to the pain of others and her inability to feel anything properly as others did . . . Out of everything I'd been through with her, that was the hardest thing to forgive.

On the other hand, I certainly had not inherited one bit of her orderliness, nor her iron discipline, which had been beaten into me along with a pervasive sense of failure and not being good enough. Nor had I inherited her self-control and elegance, which only life among the English had finally taught me. In all the time I had spent with her in this house, over nineteen long and bitter years, she had given me only one thing: an impenetrable hole in my heart where all the joyous love and affection she had denied me should have lived. And that could never be forgiven. Nor could I forgive her for refusing to tell a soul the truth about my real father. Even I grew up believing that he was a friend of the family, a distant relative who'd visit to lend a hand with those issues that a widow with two daughters couldn't handle on her own. Not to mention the obvious preference she had for my sister – only because, as she told me constantly, Yolanda was smarter and more graceful, more beautiful and more . . . more everything, and so like herself in every way. I was always made to feel like the ugly duckling. No child should know loneliness until they're ready to seek it consciously and through their own will, to then embrace it wholeheartedly when they find it. Although by then, of course, they're no longer a child.

Outside the house everyone respected and even admired her. At parents' evenings, she was always the best: the most beautiful, the best educated, the best dressed . . . the perfect mother indeed. In those moments I was proud to be her daughter and loved it when my friends told me how beautiful she was. But going home, the pride faded and the respect was overtaken once more by fear.

I still remember the last time Grandmother Rosa came to the house to visit her granddaughters. I couldn't have been more than ten years old. I don't know what they talked about, closeted away in the sitting room, but I will never forget what she said to my mother the last time we ever saw her: 'You're as unscrupulous and arrogant as your father was all his miserable life.' Unscrupulous and arrogant . . . I'd immediately run to look those words up in the dictionary, so I could try to understand my mother better and know more about her. I didn't understand the definitions that the dictionary gave me, so I checked my thesaurus anxiously and found the following words: haughty, brazen, conceited, proud, narcissistic, pretentious . . . Her own mother had described her in that way! I could not forgive her for robbing me of my grandmother, nor for having to find out on my own two years later that she had died. Teresa told me, to be kept as a secret between the two of us. Yes, my mother was certainly hard-hearted.

When I finally left home, I went without a single word. I left because if I'd stayed on any longer among all the lies I would have gone mad. Now that I thought of it, there were so many things I could not forgive and forget – among other reasons, because she never once sought my forgiveness.

I recalled our last conversation, which took place on a rainy Tuesday in February, shortly after my sister announced her bizarre marriage. My mother and I were eating lunch in silence. Light filtered in through the dark, dense, gloomy green of the late-winter garden, casting our shadows against the wall, stiff as strangers. The table was set beautifully, of course, with each item of cutlery in its rightful place, the bread to the left, the glasses in front, and napkins on our laps . . . Our spines were glued so straight to the backs of our chairs that in spite of all the years of practice, we could barely lift our spoons to our mouths without spilling our soup. Everything was done according to protocol, as though we were dining in the presence of the King.

'I'm leaving, Mama,' I announced, breaking the dense silence.

She didn't respond.

'I'm moving to London. I'm going to share a flat with Clara and a few other friends. She's found me a job at a restaurant.'

My mother, quite unruffled, continued spooning her soup elegantly into her mouth.

'My plane leaves tomorrow at eleven o'clock.'

'Tell Teresa to help you pack or you'll forget all the essential items, like you usually do,' was the one thing my mother said – a sentence seared in my memory for all time.

Like a volcano that has bubbled and seethed over ageless aeons, the vast molten seas of my rage and disappointment could hold back no longer, but burst out as I stood up to my mother for the first and last time in my life. 'Great – it finally turns out we have something in common! You also have the regrettable habit of forgetting the little essentials, don't you think? You've done it your whole miserable life. You've forgotten how to smile, how to answer when your children want to know something, how to hug us, play with us, how to care about a single tiny thing we might be feeling . . . You've forgotten how to love us – and that's the only thing that truly matters! But then how could someone as vile as you ever claim to love another person besides yourself . . . ?'

She didn't even flinch. In any other situation she'd have lashed out with some unreasonable and hefty punishment, but right at that moment she knew she'd lost all control over me and, as I'd heard her say on many previous occasions, she did everything she could to rid herself of her enemies. Because anyone who wasn't under her power immediately became her enemy.

The next day neither she nor my sister was around to say goodbye. Only Teresa was there. She never failed us, any of us. She was the only one who cared that I was leaving.

As soon as I set foot in London, I swore always to be honest with myself and with the rest of the world – all the hypocrisy, lying and secrets were things of the past. I knew that if I wanted a fresh start I had to be true to myself. I see now that with my utter lack of trust, it took me a long time and a great deal of solitude to adjust to life in this new city and among its people. Up until then, I'd always believed that every single person in the world lied and had ulterior motives. At work I was polite and efficient, but never truly open with my colleagues. I couldn't let anyone hurt me again. My clumsiness with the language was a good cover for my habitual silence. By then there were three guys and a girl working at the restaurant. Two of them were waiters and the rest of us did everything else from sweeping the floors to keeping the kitchen clean. Most often I was put in charge of the washing up. They'd invite me to their parties and get-togethers, and tried hard to welcome me into their group, but I'd refuse even to go for a coffee. I simply needed to survive while I tried to get my life together.

It was a long and painful process, but my soul healed bit by bit and I began to adapt. Within two years my metamorphosis was complete. I was young but responsible so before too long the manager promoted me, partly because I didn't get distracted like the others did. I was always focused on my work, punctual as clockwork, and forever ready to lend a hand as the situation called for it. I followed the restaurant owner's orders like a robot, and the hours passed, then the days, and then the months . . . glued to the dishwasher, concentrating on loading and unloading plates, glasses and cutlery, repressing any thought that might lead to my past and to her. I worked until I was so tired I could barely stand. I passed two years like this, earning the maximum possible and spending as little as I could. It was like a long hard trek across the desert of my soul.

Given all this effort I received one promotion after the other, demonstrating to my workmates and myself that I had incredible reserves of energy and an extraordinarily strong work ethic. I tapped into the anger that had built up over so many years with her. Slowly but surely I turned into a woman in control of her own future, and won the respect and admiration of my colleagues. My progress was relentless, as I became an essential part of the business. Next I decided to go to night school to educate myself so nothing could stand in my way. I gave it my all, and it bore fruit when the owner of the restaurant offered me half of the business so he could pay off his debts – after a few more years in London I ended up owning the whole restaurant. From that moment on I began to have confidence in myself, to connect with the people at work, to travel, to make friends, to have boyfriends . . . If my mother could have seen this new Berta, she would have been green with envy. She must have been the only mother in the world to be jealous enough of her own daughter to smother her in her own shadow, in an effort to make sure I would never surpass her own achievements. All on my own, I had managed to become the last thing my mother would have wanted: infinitely better as a person and as a woman, and more elegant even than she was. Take that, Doña Alberta!

Within a few months, people told me I had blossomed, and that I was well liked but with an aura of mystery that gave me a certain appeal, so there were often blokes buzzing around, hoping to get together with me. Sometimes I took them up on it, more for the company and the sex than for any real romantic interest. I was never really head over heels with anyone, and as soon as each relationship got too serious I'd leave without a second thought. I only ever really let my guard down with one man, Harry, and that went terribly wrong, although I know it was thanks to him and his uncontrollable, non-stop verbal diarrhoea that I finally mastered English. I also had a half-hearted flirtation with Brandon, my chef and right-hand man at the restaurant, which didn't go far because I knew he was genuinely interested in me, but it didn't seem right to toy with the affections of a family man. As soon as I told him I didn't want to get heavy, he drew a line with me that he never again tried to cross, although I know he still wanted me. I think his devotion arose from his admiration of my ability to survive all alone in London and grow to be the owner of one of the best restaurants in the city. Yes, against all the odds I'd become loved and respected, and I'd also grown to care about the people around me.

Flushed with the memories of what I'd achieved, I felt better already and heaved myself to my feet, full of energy and determination to finish up in the kitchen. The echo as the cupboard doors slammed shut rang out in the silence of the early morning, shattering it like glass of the finest crystal. My feline companion stirred in his corner and meowed softly, restoring my sense of calm. I remembered having spotted a glass jar of dry cat food under the sink and felt sorry for him. On the side of one of his dishes I read the name 'Aristotle'.

'Ah, so you're Aristotle, are you? I'll call you Aris. Nice kitty, Aris!' I said to him, while he waited patiently for me to fill his dish.

I desperately needed caffeine and a shower, so I left Aris to his breakfast and returned to my mission, this time leaving traces of my progress wherever I hunted in the cupboards – shifting glasses, cutlery and jars, moving awkwardly, letting the ground coffee spill on the worktops and the sugar go everywhere. I dug through the heap of tea towels in my hunt for a napkin until I found one. 'Ooh, you have no idea how long I've wanted to do that,' I mumbled to myself.

After jumping in the shower and then rearranging the bottles and bath towels to my liking, I dressed and left in a hurry, grabbing a biscuit for my breakfast on the way out. Aris saw me off at the door with the most adorable expression on his little face. 'Cheers, Aris. You're a clever boy – yes, you are. I reckon we're going to be friends!' I said, dashing past.

◆ ◆ ◆

Although I'd left the house at quarter past eight, I found that Ramón Soler had already been waiting for me for some time. A sexy young secretary led me through to his office. *Way too flashy for such a formal job*, I thought. The solicitor, a man of high standing in the community, was seated at his desk, a forced smile on his lips, choking back his annoyance at being made to wait. At his side sat an older woman with a look on her face that said, *I know the day has only just begun, but I simply cannot wait to go home.* They were extremely chic in both clothing and demeanour, with the effortless style that comes naturally to those who have to dress well on account of their profession.

Ramón rose to his feet to greet me. 'Señorita Berta de Castro?' he asked, holding out his hand.

'That's right. Pleased to meet you, Señor Soler.'

'Please, call me Ramón.'

'I'm so sorry I'm late, but it's been years since I was last in Madrid,' I apologised, as he squeezed my fingers in the perfect handshake – three firm yet steady pumps – with the confidence of someone who shook hands dozens of times every day.

'I'd like to introduce Julia Peralta,' he said, referring to his colleague alongside him, who had also now risen to her feet. 'She will act as your sister's proxy and together with the attorney will handle the other half of the inheritance. As you are aware, we've worked very quickly to set up this first appointment. Teresa told us yesterday that you have only a few days over here to wrap this up.'

'I'm so sorry for your loss,' Señora Peralta said by way of greeting, holding out her arthritic claw.

'Mother would appreciate that, wherever she may be. You're probably the only person to feel genuinely sorry that she's gone.'

They'd been there at the funeral the previous day. Both were rendered speechless for a few seconds, although the corners of the solicitor's mouth turned up in a slow dry smile. He'd been dealing with my mother for years, and I imagined that he wanted to show his support without making it obvious to the person working alongside him on this inheritance case.

Ramón gave an excellent summary of my legal situation regarding the inheritance, while the sexy girl stalked in and out of the office with the photocopies her boss requested over the intercom.

'Well,' he began, 'Julia just sent me this information through yesterday, so I haven't had much time to—'

'I haven't spoken to my sister in fifteen years,' I said, surprising him again.

Knowing my mother as I did, I was sure she would never have entrusted him with anything remotely personal.

'I understand . . . And that's why I'm here, to help sort out your affairs relating to your mother's estate. It consists of two properties – the house in Villaviciosa de Odón, here in Madrid, and the one in Marbella – as well as her savings, which amount to some four hundred and twenty-two thousand euros. According to the most recent valuation, that should give us a rough figure of . . .' He nodded at his colleague and she handed over the documents. 'Right, according to the valuation . . . Ah yes, the house in Madrid, which will need a new valuation at current prices, is estimated to be worth around seven hundred and fifty thousand euros, and the one in Marbella around four hundred and seventy thousand. On behalf of your sister, her proxy here is authorised to make the proposal that she waive her rights to the properties in exchange for your mother's savings. As you can see, that represents very favourable terms on your side. Naturally, all the legal fees would be split between the two of you . . .'

'Well . . . yes, that does seem quite generous on my behalf. Do you have any idea why my sister would have made this decision?'

'I'm not party to that information. Why don't you ask her direct—?'

'No, no, it's fine,' I interrupted.

His colleague now took charge of the proceedings. 'Señorita Berta, this process will take time. We have quite a bit of paperwork to fill out and we'll need your signature on a lot of it. You may go now and return when we need you, or give power of attorney to a lawyer of your choice, as your sister did.'

'For the time being I'll remain in Madrid – for the next few days at least – but I won't rule out the possibility of hiring a lawyer to represent me if it proves necessary.'

'Of course,' Señor Soler responded. 'You will find copies of all the documentation in this file.' He handed me a folder with the name of the firm stamped in gold letters on a crimson background. 'When you've decided whether or not to stay on, and we've settled any outstanding business, then we can talk more specifically about the legal details of the agreement,' he said, standing up to say goodbye. He was clearly in a hurry – perhaps my tardiness had made him late for an appointment with his next client. 'I wish you a pleasant stay in Madrid, Señorita Berta.'

He hurried out after another handshake, and then Julia did the same.

I left the law firm feeling more relaxed. Everything had been so much easier and more profitable than I had hoped, although I didn't fully understand the significance of what I had just learned. I didn't trust Yolanda at all, and was sure that her generous offer wasn't made freely but rather that some underhand motive lay behind it. Or did she just have so much money these days that her share in the properties meant nothing to her? What would keep her away at a time like this?

It was a marvellous morning in which to be out and about. It had been so long since I'd last experienced this much warmth and sunlight . . . I decided to stroll through Madrid with my folder, and become reacquainted with the city I'd grown up in without ever really getting to know it. I fancied taking my time and strolling wherever the whim took me, which I never did in London, because right now I had the time and suddenly I wasn't worried about money. The inheritance would come in handy for the changes I proposed to make to my restaurant – I needed a new kitchen and new fittings in the dining room. It felt good not to have to worry about paying my creditors or settling the staff wages. Business was good, but I constantly had to balance the books so as not to end up in the red. For once, something connected to Doña Alberta was actually making me happy.

I stopped in front of the shop windows where the latest fashions were on display for the summer season: dresses, shoes and handbags . . . All the clothes seemed so much more festive and uninhibited than what the London shops had to offer, so I bought a few shirts and some expensive sandals, which were unlikely to find use more than a couple of times a year back home. Next I went into a department store and bought myself a Kindle. Bloody hell, I was a millionaire all of a sudden, and I'd been wanting a Kindle for such a long time! I decided to hail a taxi to take me home as well, now that I could afford it. Being rich certainly had its advantages.

Because I was out of the habit, I suddenly realised I'd forgotten to take the keys from the sideboard. Previously when I'd lived here, I'd always had to ask for the keys from my mother; Yolanda and I had never had our own set. I called Teresa from the taxi to ask if a neighbour might have a key, or if there was one hidden under a flowerpot like in the movies. She told me she'd come to the house and wait there for me.

◆ ◆ ◆

So there I was, watching as she came up the little path to the front gate, a pair of neatly folded pyjamas on her arm for me, as though no time had passed at all.

When I left, she was the only thing I missed out of the whole world I'd abandoned. I would have called her, but Teresa was still so close to my mother and sister. Staying in contact with her would have meant staying in touch with her environment – my former home – and I wanted to eradicate every little thing connected with the past from my life. Losing Teresa had been heartbreaking but inevitable.

The visit to the solicitor's office had made my trip over a little easier, and I was happy and in the mood to celebrate. 'For goodness' sake, Teresa, you don't have to do that for me any more. Come on, put it down – I'm taking you out for lunch at the best restaurant in Madrid.'

'Oh sure, love, and where would you take an old woman like me . . . ?'

'Come on, come with me – let me spoil you for once! I'll just put down my bags, nip to the loo, and then we'll go. The taxi's waiting.' I looked at her for a moment. 'You look fantastic – you always look perfect.'

The taxi driver brought us to Santceloni on the Castellana – the best in all Madrid, he told us. Clearly uncomfortable, Teresa spent the entire ride trying to smooth down her hair.

A veal terrine with foie gras now set in front of me, I began to tell her about my visit to the law firm.

'I'm rich, Teresa,' I said simply, even though I couldn't be too sure until I'd signed all the paperwork. 'Don't ask me why, but Yolanda's given me her share of the houses in Madrid and Marbella, while she gets our mother's savings. Any idea why she'd have chosen to do this?'

'Me? Don't be silly, darling – the very idea . . . I honestly don't know how long it's been since I last saw your sister. I don't know, maybe the money was simply enough for her and she didn't think it was worth travelling all the way over here. Who knows where she might be or what she's doing these days. She always was so restless—'

'There has to be something else though,' I said, interrupting, then took a sip of the Ribera del Duero. The wine blew me away – it was the best I'd ever tasted. I made a mental note to order some in for my restaurant. 'From what I remember, there was no end to my sister's greed. This is a lot of money we're talking about.'

'Well . . . I wonder if . . .'

'Go on.'

'I guess Bodo must have left her a fortune.'

'And what? I've already thought of that.'

'Darling, Bodo was your father. You must've thought about what you'd stand to inherit if you established paternity – it would be a lot more than what your mother left you.'

'I hadn't thought of that . . . It's true, of course . . . Maybe that's it.' Teresa's logic surprised me as it made so much sense. Then it dawned on me that this wasn't just a simple hunch on her part – she knew far more than she was letting on. 'I don't want anything from him. As far as I'm concerned, I have no father, and I don't think he thought of me as his daughter either. Well, moving on, tell me everything I've missed while I've been away.'

Teresa fiddled with the ends of her scarf, then tentatively began to speak. 'There's so much to say – it's been so long since we've been in touch . . . Your mother's death was such a shock . . .' For a moment her eyes shone with tears. 'She was still so young – it was so sudden, you know? At least she didn't suffer . . .'

'And what about my sister? Tell me about when she got married,' I said, changing the subject as I had no desire to talk about my mother.

Teresa tensed up and the natural candour in her eyes vanished. I knew I wasn't going to like what she had to tell me. But what else was new? I didn't much want to know what had gone on in that house since I left.

'Well . . . Yolanda . . . Well, you know how your sister was . . .'

'Won't you have a sip of this excellent wine with me? It'll make you feel better.'

'Certainly not, sweetheart. I don't think—'

'Come on, Teresa, just this once . . .'

It did her the power of good and she resumed her account looking rather more confident and relaxed.

'Around twelve years ago, I can't remember exactly when, your sister fell in love with a young man more her own age – I think he was employed as the gardener at the house in Marbella. She was married to Bodo and they were spending a lot of time over there by then. With this young man, though, it was like one of those grand passions you see in the cinema.'

I wondered blankly if she was talking about someone else, because my sister wasn't capable of falling in love, no matter how much time had passed. But I didn't want to interrupt Teresa's flow.

'I suppose it was only to be expected, because she hadn't exactly married Bodo for love. The poor lad – the gardener I'm talking about now – was crazy about her, you know? The fact is that . . . Go on, give me another sip.'

I passed her the glass. It made me extremely nervous that she needed more alcohol to be able to go on.

'Well, the thing is, from the looks of it he loved her with all his heart and, well, he just couldn't cope with having to share her with her husband.' Teresa cleared her throat and went on. 'Not that I judge him for it, heaven forbid, I'm just telling you what I heard. Anyway, to cut a long story short, your sister's husband disappeared one night and according to the police, all the evidence pointed to foul play by her lover.'

I couldn't even blink. It sounded like the plot of a B-film, the ones that play on TV on Saturday afternoons.

'The truth is, we don't know for sure if he's dead, because the body was never found . . . At first, the police suspected the pair of them. They even thought for a while that it was all your sister's doing, but, based on the clues and witnesses that turned up, it had to have been him,' she explained, with a strange expression I'd never seen on her face before. 'You can't imagine the commotion it caused. It was all over the papers and even on TV – you know how popular Bodo was in Marbella.'

'Yes, I remember – that had to have been a mighty big shock. It's just that . . . I can hardly believe what you're telling me.'

'Your mother didn't want anything to do with it. It was weeks before she could watch TV again . . . Yolanda came back a few times after that, but it was horrible for your mother and she didn't want to talk about it . . . One time she had a long discussion with one of the police officers who came over to question her. You know how secretive your mother was about her personal life . . .' Teresa trailed off, trying to calm herself. She couldn't even talk about my mother without getting emotional. 'She just wasn't herself after that. She stopped seeing her friends, couldn't stand being around them . . . Whatever the case, the scandal truly hit her hard.' She smoothed her hair nervously, knowing that her words were painful for me.

'Oh yes, I know . . . the honour of the high and mighty Doña Alberta being questioned by her friends,' I said, as nonchalantly as though we were just gossiping about a neighbour. In fact I felt quite removed from all of this and was almost enjoying it, savouring the sweet revenge that fate had thrown at my mother, although I then tried immediately to rise above the feeling, which felt beneath my dignity.

'She'd tried so hard to make people think she'd not been with any other man since she was widowed. No one ever imagined that you and Yolanda had different fathers, and much less that—'

'That my sister married my mother's lover out of pure greed? And that my sister's husband turned out to be my father?'

I wanted to help Teresa confirm these statements by framing them as questions. I refused to play the same game we always used to, where none of us could talk out loud about the family's disgrace – the way my mother had acted. Her efforts at leading a double life, hidden away from her family, friends and neighbours, had tortured me since my earliest childhood, leaving me profoundly traumatised so that I was unable to express myself with the ease and spontaneity that came so naturally to other people of my age. It was true: my father had been my mother's lover for many years, even before she was widowed. My sister, five years older than me, was the product of the honourable marriage of Señor and Señora de Castro. When Fabián, my sister's father, disappeared, my mother was already pregnant with me, although no one knew that the child in her belly was not that of her husband. The father was the man who had bought the houses in Madrid and Marbella – Bodo, the German fellow who came to see us once in a while, passing himself off as a friend of the family. Over time, the relationship between my parents, Alberta and Bodo, had cooled. I remember that Bodo continued coming to the house, but was treated almost as an unwelcome guest. He was a man of considerable power, with a lot of money, and when my sister grew up she demonstrated quite openly that he offered the one thing she wanted: access to the finer things in life. She spared no thought for his being my father, or what this would mean for me and our mother. Yolanda never cared about anything but herself.

'Teresa, you could make a good thriller out of my family story all right, but trust me – it wasn't this marriage that ruined my life. The whole thing was one sordid, selfish struggle.'

'I think your mother came to love Bodo in her own way . . .'

'More than she loved herself? Oh, Teresa, after everything you witnessed in that house, how could you imagine my mother ever loved anyone else her whole life long?'

Now I was looking at her close up across the table, I noticed how tired she appeared. She'd no doubt remained in vigil beside the coffin all night before the funeral. She shifted in her chair, stretched her skirt out over her knees, and went on with her story.

'When the young gardener finally found out that all the evidence pointed to him being responsible for Bodo's disappearance, he ran away. The authorities issued an arrest warrant, and a little later, when the charges had been dropped against her, Yolanda left too. Sometimes I wonder if they actually made a life together in Australia . . . I don't know.'

'Well, I reckon I can tell you the answer to that: I doubt very much that Yolanda's in Australia, and you can bet your bottom dollar she's not living with that guy. She's never been honest about a thing in her life. As soon as she learned to speak, anything she said was designed to manipulate. You honestly think she'd risk giving up her privileged lifestyle for someone on the run from the law? I simply can't see her doing that . . .'

'How cynical you've become, darling.'

'Yes, it's taken me a long time, but as you can see . . . But you've stayed the same as ever, Teresa, always ready to forgive the unforgivable. I don't know how you've managed to live among so many lies!'

The food was spectacular, but overall it was a sad and uncomfortable meal. She'd much rather have chatted about light-hearted matters, like the times we'd shared when my mother was away, or my life in London, which she really did want to hear about. But that was impossible. It was all too fresh and, although she tried to hide it, I could see just how much recent events had hurt her.

I didn't much feel like spending the afternoon at Doña Alberta's house, but the wine had affected me and I was dizzy. Aris was waiting for me just inside the house, a good distance from the door so he was safe. He watched me with a certain quiet dignity, as though seeking my approval. And, well, I did need a bit of company . . .

He knew I was glad to see him and drew a little closer, until he was nuzzling against my ankles.

'I like you, Aris. I never thought I'd say it, but you're the best part of my trip home,' I told him, stroking him carefully, since it was the first time I'd ever willingly touched an animal.

Aris was like a snowy ball of fluff with streaks of bright reddish-brown. His ears and nose were like those of a mink, and his eyes were the clearest green. The best thing about him was his gaze: calm, forthright, incandescent . . . It made you want to float along, to go through life in peace and tranquillity, silent and mysterious.

I answered a few emails, poked about online and made some calls to the restaurant, where they assured me that everything was running smoothly, then looked up some books on Amazon to download on to my Kindle, and finally lay down on my bed to read. I'd left all the windows in the house wide open because the lingering musk of her perfume was killing me. I'd thought about parking myself on the sofa in the sitting room to read, but couldn't stay long enough even to sit down: the stench in there was overpowering.

It was impossible to concentrate on what I was reading because right then my own life resembled the course of a thriller, far more intense than anything someone else might dream up. I wondered, in fact, how often reality does overshadow fiction?

Aris lay at my side on the floor, and now and then I reached down with my arm to pet his fluffy, silken fur. He liked this and before long was lying on the bed alongside me.

Finally I gave up, put the Kindle down on the bedside table, and surrendered to the thoughts occupying my mind until the memories floated away like the last clouds of a storm, and Aris and I slept.

I awoke disorientated and it took a good few seconds before I knew where I was. Pouring myself a glass of tonic water, I decided it was high time to inspect every room of the house – my house. At last I could look through all the places that had been off limits when I had lived here before. I fed Aris, not sure how often a cat might expect its next meal, and then set off on my personal tour through the museum of horrors, though not before changing into more comfortable clothing as the underwire of my bra was digging into my flesh.

I started at the beginning, in the hallway. I'd already walked through it several times since my arrival, although I hadn't paid close attention to it. It looked the same as always with its walnut furniture and the matching mirror, umbrella stand, coat rack and chair. I went through the drawers of the sideboard, one on each side at the top, and found a set of keys, more keys, some receipts, a shoehorn, a letter opener, torch, small sewing kit, notebook and a few pens. Below the drawers was a cupboard with two doors concealing the shoe rack, which held three pairs of house shoes, some gardening boots and a pair of cream-coloured sandals. Everything was so goddamn neat and sterile . . .

I passed by the kitchen on my left and the small cloakroom to the right, and then came to the sitting room. It was just as I remembered it, typical of any upper-middle-class family, nothing special, with an enormous mirrored cabinet holding the fine china reserved for special occasions that never came, six chairs around a sturdy table, a small table for the phone and two immaculate floral-patterned sofas in front of the TV. The smell of this room where she'd spent so much time was so intense that I could almost see it taking shape, outlining my mother's silhouette on the sofa, watching the screen or flicking through her gossip magazines. Yes, I could see her so very clearly with her shirt buttoned just high enough to hint at her fulsome breasts; her nails perfectly painted in a pearly pink; the bracelet with a single lucky charm on it, a gold die; her make-up subtle yet deliberate. I never once saw her go without her glossy mauve lipstick and her spectacles with their golden frames, set off by her long, ash-blonde hair, not a strand out of place . . . A chill ran down my spine, but I forced myself to go on. I needed to finish my search. There was nothing unexpected in the cabinet: silver cutlery, crockery and glassware from Bohemia, custom-made hand-embroidered tablecloths . . . She always chose traditional things with established value and never took a risk. Everything of the highest quality, of course.

I went down the main corridor. My room was on the left and five steps ahead was Yolanda's. It was exactly like mine with a desk, bed, chair and wardrobe. She liked to show off what a fair-minded mother she was, making no distinctions between us, but everything was done to keep up appearances – all of it! I returned to my room and threw open my own wardrobe doors and . . . nothing! Two dozen wooden clothes hangers hung from the bar like naked skeletons, all identical. The cupboards, too, were empty and the drawers as barren as the rest of it. I hadn't had time since I'd arrived to inspect the furniture in my room, and had assumed it would be full of things I hadn't been able to take with me, or things I hadn't wanted in the first place.

Nothing – there was absolutely nothing in the room in which I'd cherished my most intimate secrets and desires for nineteen years. She had erased me from her life without hesitation, just as she did with everything else, without feeling or compassion, cold and ruthless. My room was no longer mine; it was empty like a room in a modern hotel chain, clean and practical. I wondered what she'd done with my journals, my poems, my box of keepsakes, my photo albums . . . my doll – the only one I'd managed to hang on to, thanks to Teresa.

On my eleventh birthday my mother decided that I was too old to play with dolls and that there were children who needed my toys more than I did – as if she ever knew anything about what a child needs.

I remember how I felt when I came home from school that day to find the garden full of cardboard boxes, one with the word 'Dolls' written on the top. I was sure that Neca was inside with the rest of them – my friend, who'd comforted me as I wept in the long nights when I lay awake, terrified of the dark, convinced that a horrible man was watching from outside the window. I sat down on the steps to the verandah without taking my eyes off that box, and with a deep, raw sorrow began to cry silently.

'So much drama over a tatty old piece of cloth and rubber? Where did I go wrong with you, Berta? You're such a spoiled and moody girl, and not on my account. I'm more and more convinced that I've placed far too much trust in Teresa. Now stop that ridiculous snivelling and lay the table!'

I adored Neca with a passion, quite as though she were a real person. For years I had wanted to love and be loved so badly that I'd projected all my feelings on to her, so when I went indoors, wiping my tears away and leaving her out there, shut up in the dark in a cardboard box, I felt a mixture of hatred – for my mother as well as for myself; one a monster and the other a coward – and an emptiness that tore my insides apart.

'Coming, Mama,' I answered. That was all I said to her.

And I swallowed my tears, which burned like fire in my throat. After clearing the table, I shut myself in my room where my silent tears fell freely. I knew I'd be punished if she heard me.

A short while later, I heard a soft knock at the door and figured it would be Teresa telling me it was time to do my homework. It was indeed her, with a bag in her hand.

'Don't cry, sweetheart,' she said, drying my tears with her flowery handkerchief. 'Look who I've got.' She took Neca out of the bag. 'It's a secret, right?' she whispered. 'Hide her well or we'll both be sent away.'

It was like coming back to life, as though I'd been forgiven a huge sin and offered another chance to love and be loved.

When I made the break from home, I'd needed to be realistic and take only things that were absolutely necessary. Everything else I packed carefully in neat boxes properly labelled, hoping that Teresa would see to their storage. Neca was in one of them, and I'd labelled that box with big clear red letters: 'Property of Berta. Personal and important.' I assumed that when Alberta realised I wasn't coming back, she'd give away most of my clothes and belongings, all the handbags, jewellery and belts, but as for my personal items . . . As Yolanda and I got older she stopped poking about in our things; she believed that, just as she had her own private space, so her daughters too should enjoy the same right – provided, of course, that nothing went beyond the wardrobe or the table, everything was kept immaculate and there was no decoration on the furniture, bed or walls. And she was never one to snoop either – her respect for other people's things lay beyond question. There had to be one good trait in her warped personality, although in her any quality was a double-edged sword.

And now nothing was left. It was as if I'd imagined that whole world of my childhood.

I ate dinner in the kitchen with my new friend, Aris – just an apple and some yoghurt because lunch had been so filling. Then I went to my room to read until I managed to fall asleep.

Chapter 3

Friday, 13 June 2014

I was pleasantly surprised to discover it was past eleven o'clock when I woke up the next morning. I had thought I wouldn't be able to sleep past eight, like the good adopted Englishwoman that I was. Wide awake now, I listened as Teresa bustled about the house and garden, wanting to luxuriate in bed for just a little longer.

When eventually I got up to go to the loo, I smelled coffee. She was always a step ahead of what anyone thought of or needed. I wandered into the kitchen and she came in through the other door, the one leading out to the garden.

'Good morning, love. Did you sleep well?'

'You have no idea – I slept like the dead. Morning, Teresa.'

'I'm so glad to hear it. Coffee is ready, and everything's all laid out for you to make toast, if you fancy it. I'll be done in a flash and then I have to rush out. I need to run a few errands.'

'No problem – you do your thing. Aris will keep me company, won't you?' I said, looking at the cat, fluffy as a cuddly toy, who gazed right back at me as though in answer.

'Oh, so he's called Aris now, is he? I like that better than the longer name . . .'

'Me too.'

She finished watering the plants as I ate my leisurely breakfast; back in London it was already almost lunchtime. Between sips of aromatic coffee and bites of toast, I decided that later this afternoon, as soon as I was alone, I would finally venture into the most difficult room of all: my mother's bedroom. It wasn't long before Teresa left, saying she would see me tomorrow, and thanking me again for inviting her to lunch at such a wonderful restaurant the day before. She always had a grateful word on her lips.

The door was partially open and I pushed it gently, afraid to look inside, and then... Suddenly I couldn't take another step, as if there were an invisible wall blocking the entrance. It was that same powerful scent, making my throat constrict. I broke out in a sweat and my heart started racing. It felt as though I were at the top of a great height and about to jump to my death, an irrational fear – I knew that – but the sensation was so vivid that it terrified me. Looking down to pull myself together, I met Aris's penetrating gaze, which appeared to say, *Are we going in or not?* Placing my hand over my thumping heart, I took the first step.

Two folders lay on the bed, one labelled 'House and Contents' and the other 'Insurance and Receipts'. Teresa had probably had to go through them to prepare for the funeral, or to give the solicitor something he needed. I opened the wardrobe cautiously, since that seemed to be the source of the unbearable stench and, holding my breath, quickly scanned its contents. Everything was displayed as neatly as in a shop window, so tidy it was shocking. I needed to breathe and the smell made me so dizzy I had to sit down. From the foot of the bed, the gaping wardrobe reminded me of a madwoman screaming out her confession.

After a moment I felt a little better and approached the chest of drawers, opening its drawers one by one. The contents were just like everything else: knickers, tights, handkerchiefs, all folded as tidily as the miniatures in a doll's house. One of the drawers was locked and I guessed that was where she kept her jewellery. I must remember to ask Teresa.

Next, I peered into the en suite from the doorway. My mother only used it at night, because it didn't have a bathtub. She loved hot baths so always preferred the main bathroom, which also had better lighting for applying her make-up. Next door to her en suite was her true sanctuary – a small sitting room for her personal use, which could only be accessed from her bedroom. It was the most sacrosanct space in the whole house, and until now I'd never been in it, at least not that I could remember. Once Yolanda had dared me to sneak in, demanding I go with her in a way that was not her usual style, as though she were afraid to enter alone. Knowing how daring and reckless she was, I'd been surprised. In the end, the little room was locked so we'd searched the wardrobe instead. I must have been really young because I have only the vaguest memories of this event. I don't remember what I saw, only the unshakeable feeling that my sister was as much afraid of that room as she was strongly drawn to it, as though she had been there before and experienced something traumatic. Despite the haziness of that memory, it must have scarred me deeply and was doubtless the reason for the hideous fear I'd felt ever since. From then on and for years afterwards, I was convinced that all the ghoulies and ghosties lived there, kept locked up by my mother, and that when she went to bed at night she opened the door to give them full rein over the house and garden.

The room wasn't locked now. I had to turn on the light because there wasn't even a window in there to see by. She must have done that intentionally when the house was built, or maybe later for some strange reason that I had always suspected my sister was in on. It didn't make any sense, because one of the walls faced the garden and the room would have had a lovely view of the jasmine, not to mention its fragrant scent in summertime. Instead there was an air conditioner. I couldn't help thinking how much the dark room resembled my mother – at first glance you wouldn't know anything was amiss with its round table, the squishy brown-leather easy chair, stereo system, TV set and shelves full of old opera records and magazines. One of said magazines lay open on the table at the crossword, alongside a pen and a small laptop. It seemed extraordinary that she'd been up to date with the latest technologies, but I guess that explained why the house was connected to the internet.

I didn't touch a thing but felt deeply disappointed – I'd expected a whole lot more from the room where she'd spent so many hours locked away. I don't know . . . I guess I'd thought I'd find slanderous letters, photo albums exposing a secret past – which surely she must have – pornographic films . . . All I knew was that there must be something in here important enough to be locked away, to arouse so much dread and curiosity in Yolanda. We knew that when our mother went to her room after dinner she didn't go to bed right away but sat in that little room for hours, because we saw the light under her door, filtering out into the main bedroom, and heard the music echoing long into the night. She never slept well. Every morning she would greet us with the same words: 'Morning, girls. What a dreadful night that was.' Then we knew she'd be in a bad mood and have a headache later on that day – the same as every day.

In my imagination, she had possessed some minute fragments of a heart at some point and kept them protected within those four walls. Sometimes I wondered if she was locking herself away to grieve for a lost love or to atone for her sins: her evident contempt for the world and for her daughters. Knowing that the self she kept hidden away was simply listening to old records and doing crossword puzzles was a huge disappointment and one more to add to the list. The more I saw of her life, the darker and emptier it looked. I walked all around the table, searching in every corner, but didn't find a single bloody clue to shed light on the dark secret I'd imagined she'd had to lock up in that windowless chamber. A sharp stab of pain jabbed in my head – the lack of explanations was making me sick.

I'd come back to Madrid thinking nothing I could find here would affect me, but now my memories were plaguing me more cruelly than ever. When I first got to London it was easy to bury my past with my extreme change in circumstances, the gruelling days at work, hope and the unfamiliar sensation of freedom – along with the distance. I'd thought the pain would just go away all by itself, but, no, it was still alive deep within me, and now I was once more bringing it to the surface. Aris had stopped just outside the door; he'd come into the bedroom but wouldn't set foot in this room. Maybe he didn't realise yet that he no longer had to obey the absurd orders of his mistress.

Feeling faint, I cut short my tour. In any case, my phone was ringing insistently in my pocket. It was Emily, my business accountant and now my good friend; she just wanted to know how I was doing in Spain and to reassure me that everything was fine at the restaurant. 'It's getting better and better, Berta – fourteen tables booked for tonight. That's not bad at all,' she told me, before saying goodbye in her peculiar attempt at Spanish. I was relieved everything was going so well in my absence.

I left my mother's bedroom, passing the main bathroom on the right and the staircase that led to the attic on the upper floor. That would have to wait for another time. For now, I was completely mentally drained.

It was already past lunchtime in Spain, while in England families would already be preparing their dinner, but I wasn't hungry: I'd had a late breakfast and my stomach was unsettled. To pass the time I fetched my laptop and sat out in the garden. I needed to answer a few emails from suppliers, but couldn't concentrate and decided just to forward them on to Brandon.

Someone nearby was listening to dreamy boleros, so I let myself be swept along with the music, falling into a peaceful, drowsy haze. The afternoon was passing very pleasantly, slow and calm, keeping pace with my mind, allowing me to finally think clearly again.

◆ ◆ ◆

I had not yet processed everything I'd learned since my arrival: my mother was dead, I would soon own the two houses I'd grown up in, and my father – my sister's husband – had probably been killed by his wife's young lover. Anyone would be horrified at such a tale, but all the more so if it happened within the bosom of their family. At first, listening to the awful story Teresa was telling me, it felt as though she was talking about something completely unrelated, something that was none of my business, but in the few hours I'd spent in my mother's house it was all brought home to me with startling clarity – it could not affect my life any more closely. And I didn't know if I was strong enough.

Rocking in one of the hammocks, I stared up at the sky. With some difficulty, I tried to put my thoughts in order while I mulled it all over. The news that Yolanda was going to marry Bodo, who would always be a stranger to me, had hit the family like a nuclear bomb. I'm sure there were other more shocking things in our family history, but those I hadn't experienced personally.

Over the years I had never understand Bodo's role in the family. I couldn't understand how Fabián, my mother's husband, had never recognised the truth about her relationship with the property developer. Maybe he was too heavily medicated and just didn't notice, or maybe his poor memory and the disorientation resulting from his illness had put him out of touch with reality. I'd never understood how he could disappear so suddenly, however unhinged he had become towards the end – it was so peculiar that he should have gone out for a walk one day and just never come back . . . Sometimes I heard the neighbours talking about how it was such a shame that he was gone, especially since he was about to be a father for the second time, and above all since he and my mother had had the perfect marriage. But when Alberta talked to us about him – when at the time I thought he was my father too – she claimed he'd been a tyrant and a bully, surely to justify her illicit relationship with Bodo.

The German fellow showed up at the house at unexpected moments, on the pretext of advising my mother on legal issues concerning her property, or to wish her a happy birthday; sometimes he simply came by to say hello. I was never clear on whether he was a distant relative or a friend of the family. But Yolanda had always known he was sleeping with our mother. He owned property in Marbella and was one of the investors who had developed the neighbourhood where our holiday home was located. When we were on holiday we saw a lot more of him. Some afternoons, when the sun was starting to set, he'd visit us for no reason at all and stay until dinnertime, when Teresa would be forced to serve him begrudgingly. He and my mother spent hours discussing politics, the weather, issues put in front of the city council . . . but they never went any deeper than idle chit-chat, like two old pensioners gossiping as they threw crumbs to the pigeons, even though they were both still young.

He spoke fluent Spanish, although his native tongue left him with a strong German accent. A tall, strong, decent-looking man with perfect manners, his hair was always immaculately combed and done up with pomade, his shirts impeccably ironed and his shoes gleaming. Despite his heaviness he looked more Latin than German, with his dark eyes and hair and his light tan. He sweated a lot in the summer, and became quite obsessed with constantly pinching the fabric of his shirt to hold it away from his chest and get a breeze on his skin. The compulsion was so bad that he even did it in winter. I didn't like him at all. In photos he could appear almost handsome, even intriguing, but in real life he seemed ugly and untrustworthy. He was a vain fellow, in fact, who thought too highly of himself because in reality his only value came from his appearance and his bank account. Furthermore, the paltry displays of affection shown to my sister and me were fake and I could tell he didn't mean them. He'd look at us so oddly too, as though devouring us with his eyes. When he arrived, he'd stand uncomfortably close to us as he came up for a kiss, so my sister and I always ran away from his gestures of 'affection', much as we might do from a bucket of iced water.

The day I found out who he was to me, I felt the greatest betrayal and disappointment of my life – he was absolutely the very last person I would have picked as a father. More than anything I wanted to imagine I was Fabián's daughter and to think of him as the best father in the world, whom heaven had cruelly taken away from me, even if my mother insisted on vilifying him.

I was about nine years old when Yolanda told me during one of our sisterly arguments. 'Berta, you're so stupid you don't even realise that Bodo is your father.'

'Liar, you're just saying that to hurt me – you're so mean!' I repeated over and over.

'It's true. I heard him and Mother talking about it – just ask Teresa.'

And it was true. Teresa couldn't deny it. I never talked to my mother about it. She knew that I knew but she never brought it up. She never admitted her mistakes to anyone.

How many times had I looked in the mirror and deluded myself, thinking that Bodo and I didn't look a bit alike, but the truth was I did take after him a little; physically I had equal parts of him and Alberta. Like my sister, I was lucky to inherit my mother's eyes (from the nose up, the three of us were carbon copies of each other), because I hated the German man's sly, mocking, sunken eyes.

I hated Bodo more with every passing month. Teresa strongly disapproved of him and didn't bother to hide it, which the lady of the house ignored. One day, coming out of the cinema, I found out by chance that he had a family. My first instinct was to feign ignorance, just like he did, but Yolanda, always bolder and more inquisitive than me, went straight up to him and Bodo was forced to introduce us to his two sons, aged six and four, and his extremely young wife. They were my brothers . . . and they didn't even know it. A torrent of anguish flooded my heart. By then I was about ten years old and my sister around fifteen. Yolanda had become a mean and selfish teenager, with a particular gift for finding weakness in others and using it to her benefit. Amused at the encounter, she always acted in a suggestive and provocative way around Bodo. I think even then she had plans for him. She was always cleverer than me, and not only because she was five years older. She'd understood from a young age that any attempt to get affection from our mother was useless, and had fixed on devoting her considerable energies to more lucrative endeavours. I, on the other hand, never gave up – I struggled to be loved until I left home, and it cost me dearly, because it made me the weakest person in the family.

◆ ◆ ◆

I couldn't believe how much Alberta would let slide with her elder daughter. Yolanda was certainly old enough to come and go as she pleased, but that was no reason for our mother to relax the iron tyranny of her reign. She'd made us into completely dependent women, with no initiative, little education and nothing to offer the world. If we wanted to keep on enjoying the comfortable lifestyle to which we were accustomed, we had to abide by her rules. Yolanda began spending nights away from home, openly refusing to take her punishments and getting away with murder. At the time I wondered if she had some ace up her sleeve, but I never would have imagined the hand she was hiding! I suspected something was up after a few weeks, because my mother didn't even blink at Yolanda's shameless behaviour. I think my sister, for some reason I didn't know then and still don't now, was blackmailing her and that's how she got away with so much. Or maybe the two of them had unfinished business that my mother didn't want to tackle. Perhaps she thought Yolanda would settle back into the way she was before and never have to deal with it. But that wasn't the case; in fact, she took it to an extreme that Alberta never could have imagined.

I remember that day as though it were yesterday. It was past nine o'clock at night and Mother and I were eating an omelette and salad. Some meals stick in your mind no matter how much you want to forget them. Suddenly we heard the click of the front door and Yolanda burst into the room like a tornado.

'Good evening, family.'

'I suppose,' my mother answered. 'If you want any dinner you'll have to make something yourself.'

'Relax, Mother. I only have a minute to tell you my news: I'm getting married!'

'Don't talk nonsense, Yolanda. Are you quite crazy?' my mother asked, putting down her fork. She'd gone terribly pale.

'Nonsense? And why is it nonsense?'

I wasn't too surprised. She'd probably found the perfect victim and wanted to trap him before he could get away. She'd always wanted a man who would pay for all her expensive whims, and over the last few months she'd been surrounded by a few too many luxuries. But I really didn't care one way or the other.

'We haven't even met him, and a wedding takes a lot of work and preparation . . .'

'Don't worry, Mother.' *Mother.* For Yolanda that word was synonymous with contempt. Whenever she wanted to get on her good side, always with some ulterior motive, she called her 'Mama'. 'You already know him perfectly well. I'm getting married to Bodo.'

Alberta froze and seemed unable to breathe. For once she let her mask drop and I could see her hands shaking. She picked up the napkin from her lap, a clear sign that dinner was over, took a deep breath and said wildly: 'That's madness! Bodo is a married man with children!'

'He's left Noelia – incredible, isn't it? I guess it's just my amazing powers of seduction.'

I listened to all this in shock. Yolanda was standing in front of us. From where I was sitting she looked more diabolically tall and lovely than I'd ever seen her before, with her shining long mane of chestnut-red hair, worn loose down to the middle of her back. She was wearing an expensive brown leather jacket, a flattering sky-blue blouse and perfectly cut designer jeans, showing off her flawless body. Yolanda had a striking figure, and she knew it.

'Get out of here, Berta, leave us alone!' my mother ordered, beside herself.

'Don't bother, sister, I'm leaving. They're waiting for me . . .'

'I told you to leave us alone!' my mother shouted again, getting more and more enraged and taking it out on me.

I got up, left the table and shut myself in my room. They were talking heatedly but keeping their voices down so no one would hear, and it was impossible to make out at first what they were saying until they lost control and the insults, abuse and threats floated in to my bedroom with perfect clarity.

'This is just another of your reckless impulses, Yolanda. This wedding can't go ahead. Bodo is more than twenty years older than you and . . . he's like one of the family. Wait to fall in love with someone your own age . . .'

'Mother, Mother, Mother . . . I can hardly believe you would use such a stupid trick on me. Fall in love? Ha! Me, fall in love . . . You know very well that I'm incapable of love – just like you, I never learned how. Bodo has everything I need to be happy and to get out of this damn house: money. Mountains of the stuff – more money than even I know what to do with! What more could I want?'

'The stupid man!' my mother retorted, her voice growing even more shrill as though she'd taken leave of her senses, overwhelmed with helplessness at not being able to control such a serious situation, which threatened to ruin her own virtuous standing in society. 'How has he let himself get so tangled up?'

'Isn't it obvious? This is the third time he's done it that we know of. The poor dear just doesn't learn – a woman barely has to look at him and he opens his wallet.'

'You don't know anything about Bodo! He's not the man for you,' Mother insisted, now fully yelling.

I was no longer bothered about the neighbours overhearing, although they'd surely be shocked to hear Alberta's voice screaming quite so loudly.

'Oh, I don't, is that it? I'm telling you I know him and I know all about him, because he's been in and out of this house since I was five years old. I can assure you I know him better than you think – I know him better than you ever did. You'll see – he'll never leave me for someone else, but I have to marry him to make sure. I'm afraid

I definitely stand a better chance than you do, because I'm not the one committing adultery. I don't need to hide my "love". And yes, he is absolutely the perfect man for me.'

'That was a long time ago. You can't hold that over my head forever.'

'But of course I can. So long as you care more about what people say than you do about your own daughters, I will continue to use it against you. Can you imagine your friends finding out that your daughter Yolanda is marrying her sister's father?'

'Shut up, shut up!'

'You refused to give up your position as a respectable widow so you lied to the whole world, telling them that Papa had died, leaving the seed of his second daughter in your womb . . . You know, I wasn't that young – some images stand out perfectly clear in my mind . . . I've always wondered why—'

'Shut up or I won't be responsible for what happens!' Mother screamed.

I didn't understand my sister's last words, nor what she meant when she mentioned the images in her head or what it was she had wondered.

'Nothing has ever been good enough for you – you always want more, more, more . . . You had it all planned out, didn't you? You know exactly what I'm talking about . . . Why do I even bother asking? Of course you planned it all along, and I know how – you never leave a loose end, except for this one. Ha ha ha! I can't deny that it feels good to finally take my revenge.'

'Are you really going to marry your sister's father?' our mother asked then in a low voice, sounding almost resigned. There must have been something really serious I didn't know about, preventing my mother from challenging her openly.

'Yes. What difference does it make, so long as no one knows . . . ? Isn't that the only thing that matters? Don't worry, I'll keep your secret – this one and the other one too.'

I summoned all my courage and left my room. I stepped timidly into the sitting room, but the rage inside was burning me up.

'You can't marry my father, Yoli.'

'Of course I can, little sister, of course I can. He's your father, not mine, and he's never acted like one in any case. Besides, no one knows anyway so what's the problem? Oh dear, I just realised I'll be your stepmother soon. Isn't that funny?'

'You'd be the perfect stepmother,' I replied, not caring about the consequences of what I was saying. But she was too happy to bother firing back with one of her sarcastic remarks.

'Yeah, whatever . . . All right then, I'm off. I'll come round tomorrow to pick up some of my things. Bodo's rented a beautiful flat in Salamanca and we're moving in. Poor dear, he's been waiting for me for nearly an hour – he must be so fed up.'

'He's outside?' asked my mother, who was apparently going from one state of shock to another.

'Yes, I didn't think it was quite appropriate for him to come in with me when I gave you the news. See you tomorrow, my darlings.'

My mother and I were left staring at one another, speechless, although she remained sitting on her high horse and here I was, challenging her openly for the first time. The moment seemed to stretch on forever.

Finally I ventured: 'I don't know if I can ever forgive you for all the lies, all your greed and arrogance, for such coldness . . . I really don't think I can. Before I found out who my real father was, I could still live under the illusion that Fabián went missing before I was born and that he would have really loved me, but after this . . . You didn't even have the basic dignity to sit me down and tell me yourself. I would say not to worry about me, as I honestly don't give a stuff about this wedding, but I don't need to – right now I know you're just thinking about yourself, like you always do.'

'So you're going to torment me too, are you? You have no idea what I've been through. I could have aborted you, but—'

'Well, I don't know if I should thank you or wish that you had, given how much I've suffered, having you as my mother. Knowing you, I bet you went on with the pregnancy for some reason that had absolutely nothing to do with me.'

No apology, no hug, not even a tear . . . She rose from the chair and before leaving the room said, 'Don't forget to clear the table and clean up the kitchen.'

For once I refused to obey orders, but stalked off to slam the door of my room before shutting myself away. Amazingly enough, this was one time when I wasn't afraid of her.

◆ ◆ ◆

Night had crept in among the ivy, bougainvillea and jasmine. There was no moon that night and my eyes drank in the twinkling points of the stars in the vast sky overhead. The darkness and silence that enveloped me were warm, sweet and serene. Aris was sharing the hammock with me, merging peacefully into the surroundings, purring as I stroked him. I thought about how far I had come since my escape from this house fifteen years ago. Since then I had done the impossible – learned to appreciate and respect others, and to accept appreciation and respect myself.

I had let myself be carried away by the pleasantness of this moment, however, my mind lighting upon disjointed thoughts and memories – of my childhood, my trip, my life in London and my friends, Harry, my first years of independence . . . It had been so long since I'd given myself time to think, and I savoured it now like a little one with her first sweet. Jumbled parts of my life crowded chaotically through my head, my mind everything and nothing like a child's random drawing – impossible to make sense of but full of meaning. After a while, my contemplations took shape and led me once more to the gruesome thought that my biological father had possibly been murdered by my sister's lover. I was convinced that Yolanda was merely playing the innocent party as far as this episode was concerned. Searching through my memories, I realised she'd always been behind anything questionable that happened at home, yet was always the one who came out of it unscathed. I wanted to be wrong, if only just this once, but that wouldn't have been typical of my sister – the Machiavellian, cold and selfish Yolanda. I was fascinated to know how it had all come about, but saw it more like the events in a crime novel rather than something with any bearing on my own life.

My sister, so in love with a man that she would scheme to get rid of Bodo in order to be with him . . . How I wished that might be true. It might have redeemed her because there's a certain dignity in a crime of passion, but that just wasn't her style. No, if she was in any way connected with this crime, then it had to be about money. It also seemed impossible for anyone to worship her so much they would murder her husband, but then perhaps love really is blind.

I tried to imagine what married life could have been like for Yolanda and Bodo, and it just seemed utterly crazy. He'd known her since she was less than five years old, at least since my mother got pregnant with me, or maybe even before . . . I didn't know exactly when his romance with her had started. The German property developer had watched Yolanda grow up, become a woman, all the while sleeping with her mother . . . although I guess I don't know exactly what kind of relationship they had, or what their rules were. What kind of demented pervert was Bodo? What rubbish . . . I was losing all objectivity.

Bodo, as always, was no more than a puppet in the hands of a young and beautiful woman. He was so vain it was laughable, accustomed to having the best of everything without putting in any effort, and even though all his relationships with women had been superficial and part of the insincere sham of his life, each one a link in the long chain of his failed love affairs, in the professional world he had worked towards success from a very young age, or so we all thought judging from his standard of living. Almost certainly, the corrupt participant in that absurd relationship had been Yolanda, just as it had been our mother before her. Looking at it from the outside, they weren't that odd a pair – she young and beautiful, with elegant and expensive tastes, and he a successful businessman with plenty of money to fund the most extravagant whim. Yolanda was one of those – a whim that had apparently cost him his life. Furthermore, an age difference of twenty years in such cases is hardly unusual. It was everything that lay behind it that was less common in this particular story.

I nibbled on some leftovers, took a shower and climbed into bed with my Kindle.

Falling asleep, I mused over the realisation that for the first time in years I had no plans for the next day. The lack of routine, away from all my usual daily tasks, left me somewhat adrift.

Chapter 4

Saturday, 14 June 2014

I slept restlessly, waking, I think, at least four times in the night. Well into the morning a flood of sunlight shone in through the window, almost blinding me when I tried to open my eyes. Still groggy and half-asleep, I leapt out of bed, startled and bewildered, thinking I was back in my flat in London and that I was late for work, before I realised that such glorious light could only mean I was in Spain.

After feeding Aris, with a *café con leche* and several biscuits set out in front of me, I tried to plan my day. The kitchen door stood open to the garden and the scent of flowers wafted in on the warm breeze. I've always savoured the beauty of the morning, before the air grows heavy with cooking smells and people start coming and going.

Just then my phone rang.

'Harry, hi! How's it going?' I was glad to hear his voice. 'I can always count on you to call at the worst time. I was just about to take a shower.'

'Oh! Sorry, my darling . . .' Even though our relationship had been purely physical for a long time now, he still called me 'my darling'. He switched languages and explained in Spanish, 'I'm sorry, but I was at the restaurant and they told me your mother had died and you were in Madrid. I'm sorry I didn't call sooner . . . How are you?'

'Good . . . tired but good.'

'When are you coming home?'

'I don't know. I might stay a few weeks.'

'OK, I'll call you again. Talk soon, my darling.'

'Talk soon.'

And, thinking about Harry, I went on with my day. He was my first and my last before I left London, although ours was an on-off relationship and I'd had other flings in the meantime. I had to admit that as a lover he had no equal, but as a boyfriend he was a complete disaster. During the months we'd tried living together, not a day went by that we didn't fight. Sometimes these rows were caused by my fits of jealousy, which even I didn't understand – not because they weren't justified, but because I don't think I was ever really in love with him. He truly was a hopeless rascal. Living together was a dreadful idea that we hit on one night after a few drinks, but before too long we were back in our own flats. Deep down we both knew it wouldn't work out, so we'd rented a small furnished flat between his workplace and mine, and never got rid of our individual homes. When we were back to being single, at first we called each other every day, because we'd promised to keep in touch as friends, but soon we returned to sharing the one thing that really brought us together: sex – only once or twice a week, of course, and then we'd each go back to our own beds. The fact is that when we stopped living together I missed more than his lovemaking – among other things, his sense of humour, his vitality, his ability to calm me down when I came home tired and fed up after a long night at the restaurant . . . But I never told him. I know we had an emotional connection that went beyond just the physical and that's why we tried it, but we were simply incompatible living together and I never lost hope of finding a man who would fall madly in love with me. Harry said that I was chasing a fantasy, that such a man didn't exist. Harry certainly wasn't Mr Right as far as I was concerned.

I took a shower and decided to investigate the only room I hadn't yet searched in the house: the attic.

◆ ◆ ◆

I climbed the stairs leading up to the top floor like someone nervous of running into a sadistic killer: slowly, very tense and with all five senses heightened in case I had to turn and run. In our house, the attic was like the ghost town of a once-great city. It wasn't just the abandoned bits and pieces up there – something in that space was much more mysterious and less childish. The attic was where my mother hid the most shameful family secrets; the old junk she got rid of without any problem.

All lives have a public display and also a back room that they don't want other people to see, either now or ever. Between these rooms is a passage through which we come and go, in a neverending attempt to find a balance between the two. Our attic wasn't that particular passageway, nor was it just the repository of all the things we were probably never going to use again but which had sentimental value and couldn't be thrown out. Our attic was hell itself, where Alberta cast out her sins and weaknesses; only they didn't burn up or crumble to ashes, but instead wandered forever in a closed, dark space with no way out, more like a state of purgatory. Virtually no one went up to the attic, and she did least of all. Only Teresa went once in a while, to check for rodents. No one else ventured up there: we girls were forbidden to, and the lady of the house, the only person allowed to poke about up there, had no desire to dig up the detritus of her past.

Standing at the top step of the steep staircase, my heart pounded desperately in my chest, as though in warning that I was getting too close to something dangerous – but the door facing me was locked. I should have known. Suddenly I felt a hand on my shoulder and my nerves seemed to shatter into a million tiny pieces. For a moment, I crossed the veil between life and death.

'Oh my heavens, Berta – what's the matter? Not again! Say something, sweetheart!' Teresa shouted in despair, afraid this would end with the two of us tumbling down the staircase. 'You must be ill, my love – this is the second time this has happened.'

Somehow, we ended up sitting on the top step, which acted as a small landing.

'It's locked,' I said finally. 'Do you know where the key is?'

'I think so, but this is no time for that. Come on, let's go into the kitchen and I'll make you something. You're far too thin, my darling,' she said, helping me down the steps and keeping hold of my waist.

'Find me that key, Teresa,' I babbled, still dizzy and confused.

'Yes, yes, forget about the blessed key now – there's plenty of time to look for it. Careful, dear, let's just make sure we don't both break our necks.'

'Don't worry, it's passed now. I'm feeling much better. I don't know what the hell is wrong with this house . . .'

'Nothing's wrong with this house – you're just weak, that's all. I bet in England all you do is work and you don't even remember to eat.'

'I work in a restaurant with one of the best chefs in the world, remember?' I argued, forcing myself to smile to reassure her as we came down from hell, which in this case seemed to be up in the direction where heaven should be.

We reached the last steps to find Aris staring at us as though he knew what had happened.

◆ ◆ ◆

I took sips of my soothing lemon balm infusion while my pulse settled, and Teresa grilled a steak for me along with a light salad.

'Please find me that key, Teresa,' I insisted.

'Yes, yes, darling, later,' she answered, without looking up from the pan. 'Right now you need to eat something. You need vitamins.'

She decided to let me eat lunch on my own and disappeared off into the depths of the house, returning some time later.

'I can't find it, love,' she said at last, standing in the doorway to the kitchen.

'I wouldn't be surprised if she swallowed it before she died. She probably choked to death on it,' I answered sharply.

'Goodness, dear, the things you say . . .'

'We'll call a locksmith. I have to get in there somehow. If the attic is locked, there has to be a reason. Teresa . . .'

'What?' she answered solemnly. She didn't like it when I talked about my mother that way.

'Are you sure you don't know where the key is? I remember you used to go in the attic.'

'Come on, love, stop seeing ghosts everywhere. There's nothing but old stuff up there that nobody wants. Your mother would give me the key every now and then to make sure everything was OK – it really could be anywhere. Now, I'm going to clean up the kitchen and then head home. I have a lot of ironing to do.'

'Don't worry, I'll do it.'

'Are you sure? Are you feeling better then?'

'I feel perfect, thank you – your lunch worked wonders. Don't you worry about me.'

'All right then, I'm going. I think I'll stop off at the grocer's first. Need anything?'

'I need you to call a locksmith.'

'Fine, I'll call them tomorrow, dear. My, you can be persistent,' she added impatiently.

◆ ◆ ◆

Lying in the hammock in the garden with Aris at my feet, I returned some calls. I had two messages from Brandon concerning a few business matters and my lack of communication since I'd been in Spain. He couldn't believe that the responsible and perfectionist Berta wasn't calling three or four times a day to manage the one thing she cared about most: her restaurant, Berta's Kitchen.

In fact, it had taken only a few days for me to completely disconnect from my life in London. When I first arrived, I had very quickly developed an obsessive personality; the shy and apathetic Berta, who had previously only watched the days drift by as a mere observer, began to get involved with life, to have goals and go after them. I was so determined to be an active participant in the world that I didn't give myself a single moment to mull over my past. Here in Madrid, after stepping back into my old environment, the London Berta suddenly felt very far away. In truth, I'd been living in a bubble and I realised now that the old Berta had never really left at all. Brandon was confused by my attitude, most of all when I told him that I trusted him completely to make decisions without my approval, if he thought it made sense. Before hanging up he wished me well, convinced that something serious must be going on.

I read for a little while under the willow tree in the garden. The sun was sinking in the sky, slowly and peacefully, and the temperature was perfect. Now and then I stroked my hand through

Aris's thick fur. Before long I set the Kindle down, and turned on my side in the hammock to look at the little tiger as I petted him. Tickling him under the chin, I realised that the spot where his collar fastened looked somehow bulkier than it should. Yes, there was something there. It was probably his ID tag, in case he got lost. I undid the buckle and . . . I couldn't believe it: something fell on to the fabric of the hammock. It was a key! It had to be the key to the attic. That's how dark and twisted my mother was. Maybe she hid it in Aris's collar because she didn't even trust Teresa. I was strongly tempted to go up there immediately, but it was getting dark and this was no time to embark on a task that required a clear mind, time and daylight. I knew the next day was going to be intense. Right now I didn't even have the strength to crawl up those stairs.

I put the key back where I'd found it – it was a hard place to forget and it wouldn't get lost – then let myself be enveloped in the falling dusk and its mantle of stars. Allowing myself the time to enjoy the clear luminous sky was sheer delight after so many years in London. Watching the sky before going to bed was becoming a pleasant and comforting habit.

Chapter 5

Sunday, 15 June 2014

It was my fifth day in Spain and the fourth time I'd woken up in glorious sunlight. A loud noise from the kitchen served as my alarm call. I was scared at first, but then thought it surely must just be Teresa.

Aris lay on the bed near my feet, staring at me. I sat up, stroked his back and said, 'Well, my friend, we have something important to do today, but let's grab some breakfast first.'

I headed to the bathroom and then strolled into the kitchen.

'Morning, Teresa. Goodness, don't you even take Sundays off?'

'And a very good morning to you too, my love. Dear me, no – a bit of light sweeping and watering plants isn't work. How are you feeling today?'

'Not bad, thank you. I had a hard time falling asleep, but then slept six or seven hours solid,' I answered, hunting in the cupboard for Aris's food. 'You won't believe this, but . . .'

'Believe what? Don't be so mysterious.'

'You'll be pleased when I tell you.'

'Oh dear, will I?'

'I found the key to the attic. At least, I think I did . . .'

'Well, you'll get to save some money. You have no idea what locksmiths charge around here these days.'

'You'll never guess where it was.'

Teresa ignored what I said and asked, in a totally unrelated question: 'Would you like me to make you some *pan con tomate*?'

'Hang on a minute . . . No way . . . You knew the key was on Aris's collar, didn't you?'

'Oh, my dear, that's utter nonsense. How would I know a thing like that? I'd have told you.'

I didn't believe her – and moreover, I was now starting to be suspicious of Teresa. After all, she knew much more about my family than she was letting on.

'What are you doing today?' she asked. 'I saw a car out by the gate. You have no excuse to stay shut up in here. It's a marvellous day outside – why don't you get out of the house?'

'Maybe I'll go out later this afternoon, but I want to go up to the attic this morning.'

'Oh dear, you certainly are fixated on that attic. Do you want me to stay with you in case you have another of your fainting fits? I go cold with fright every time I think about it,' she said, as the coffee maker whistled behind her, downplaying the importance of the subject.

'I appreciate it, but I'd rather do it alone – it's a personal thing. But don't worry, I feel fine.'

Teresa turned off the hob and bent down to fumble around Aris's neck.

'Here, have it,' she said, putting the key in my hand.

'Were you thinking of taking it with you so I wouldn't find it? What's up there exactly in that attic?'

'Oh dear, no, that certainly wasn't what I was . . . Your mother didn't trust anyone by the end – she hid it in the cat's collar, but I pet him once in a while too and came across it . . .'

'My mother didn't even trust you any more? There has to be a reason why she hid the attic key . . . You will tell me another time, won't you?'

'Honestly, this girl . . . I'm not even sure what's up there, it's been so long since I went in. It's just that yesterday you looked so poorly there on the staircase . . . Well, I just didn't think it was a good time to give you the key.'

'Teresa, I have the strangest feeling you're trying to protect me from something. I'm a grown woman, you know. I grew up in this house. I'm ready for anything I'm going to find.'

'Of course I want to protect you – from getting dizzy and tumbling down those awful stairs, all on your own here . . . No, no, I don't even want to think about it.'

'I know.'

'Well, go on then, eat your breakfast and do what you have to do. I'll be here a bit longer, tidying up in the garden.'

While I ate, I gave Teresa the third degree.

'You know, yesterday I was thinking that you've been with us my whole life, and I don't know a single thing about you. It's strange – you've never talked about your own life, or at least not with me.'

'There's not much to tell, love – my life is pretty simple.'

'Yes, but you had to come from somewhere. Everyone has a family,' I said, starting with a theme I thought she'd feel most comfortable with.

'I've known no family but yours since I was a girl. My mother worked for Fabián's parents from a very young age, then she married a boy from Valladolid who worked in construction and they moved into their own house. Ten years after I was born, my father died of cancer. Just think,' she said with a sigh, 'my mother was left with nothing but a daughter she had to feed and clothe. Your grandmother Loreto was so generous and kind to us, back in those days . . . What a woman she was!' she said, sighing again but with more feeling this time, while I was thinking that this certainly didn't sound like the grandmother I could recall. 'Anyway, my mother went back to work for them and the family let us both live with them. Your grandparents had a beautiful, enormous house, one of the finest in Valladolid – I can remember the garden well . . . At the time, Fabián was twenty-three years old and had just finished his studies. Soon afterwards, he met your mother, and after a few years of back and forth, they got married. I had just turned eighteen and finished school a long time before . . . It wasn't my thing, sweetheart. Anyway, I was old enough and had started to work in other houses, so Fabián talked to my mother to ask if I could work for his family after the wedding, and she thought it would be a blessing for her daughter to work in the home of this gentleman whom she loved like a son. Fabián was such a good man . . .'

'My mother didn't think so. She was always telling us how he was a tyrant, and a mean and miserly man . . .'

'Anyhow, all I've done since then is take care of your sister and then you too,' she continued, as though she hadn't heard me at all. 'When you and Yolanda grew older, I bought a little place in Leganés – you know that – but I've been at your mother's side right up to the end,' she added. Stirred by memories, her eyes shimmered with tears.

'Haven't you ever had a boyfriend or friends of your own?'

'Darling, when your daily bread comes from taking care of other people, you forget all about yourself. I'm not complaining – I've always had food and a roof over my head, and I even managed to save up enough to buy my own house. With my savings and the hours I spend working for your mother's friends, I have enough to live on and I don't need much more than that.'

'That sounds so sad to me.'

'Sweetheart, it's a lot like your life: solitude and work. I'm just older than you . . .'

'I guess that's true.'

Her last comment felt like a low blow, but I realised immediately that it wasn't in Teresa's nature to say something rude; she had simply said it without thinking.

'I've been through a lot, just like everyone else, but sad . . . no. I've known so many people with more than me who have suffered so much more.' I know she said the last part intentionally, although again without any malice. 'I've so enjoyed watching you and your sister grow up, and I've loved you as though you were my own daughters. I've even spent summers in Marbella, like the rich people do. No, I'm certainly not complaining. Well, I need to tidy up the kitchen a little now and finish off in the garden. If you need anything, I'll be here a little while longer.'

She was right, after all. My family's life, despite having everything we could need in the world, was so much sadder than hers.

'Teresa . . .'

'Yes?' she answered, without turning away from the sink, thereby signalling that the conversation was over.

'You've been working for me for five days. Before I leave, you'll have to tell me what I owe you.'

She spun to face me. 'Everything I can do for you is more than paid, and, even if it wasn't, I would do it gladly. I've told you, darling – you're like my family. Come on, let's get on with things now. I want to cut some roses and take them to your mother's grave before I go home.'

'Did she like roses?'

'Of course, darling – who doesn't?' she said, finally terminating the conversation and turning back to the sink again.

I sat there for a few more minutes, watching her, petting Aris, who by then had been bold enough to jump up on to my lap. She knew I was watching, but kept on with what she was doing. She was attractive and had a lovely sweetness about her, and looked great for a woman of almost sixty. She was quite refined in the way she carried herself, acquired maybe from the various ladies she had worked for. I found it hard to believe that she had never had her own life, her own family. She had such an enormous capacity for love, was honest and loyal . . . It was strange that such a good woman had always lived in our family's shadow. Suddenly I had the feeling there was a whole different side to Teresa, one I knew nothing about.

◆ ◆ ◆

This morning I climbed the staircase to the attic a little more confidently, carrying Aris in my arms to keep me company. Yes, the key fitted. The door was painted white but looked like solid iron. I pushed it cautiously, in case any local wildlife happened to be wandering around in that lonely place, and then stepped inside. The first thing that hit me was the intense whiff of stale dust. The room was very dark – although there were two large windows, the blinds were completely closed and only a few feeble rays of light stole in through the slats. After a few moments, my eyes adjusted to the darkness and I began to make out details of the large space. Over in the left-hand corner, all the way at the back, there were a few dozen boxes of various sizes, all carefully stacked. Covering part of one of the windows and pushed up against the wall stood the silhouette of an old chest of drawers and, to its right, the outline of an enormous coat stand that looked like something out of Dante's *Inferno*. I was still standing in the doorway and couldn't see the details too well, but it looked as if it was still fulfilling its duty during this period of exile, still draped with a few items of clothing, a number of hats and some walking sticks.

Putting Aris down on the floor, I took a step forward. He was very suspicious, and for the moment stayed put exactly where I'd set him, which at least reassured me that there weren't any rodents up here. I walked in further and the musty stench got even stronger, almost enough to make me gag. I pulled myself together and continued my investigation. Against the wall to the right was a wardrobe and next to it a pile of rubbish. To the left stood an old armchair and a couple of trunks, as well as various boxes and bundles strewn about in a seemingly random arrangement. The centre of the room was quite clear. A stack of picture frames leaned against the wall next to the door to my right, with boxes and yet more boxes on the other side of me.

I had two options if I wanted to examine everything in here properly and in comfort: open the blinds or turn on the light. I searched for the light switch without success, so decided to try the more accessible window, only to find that the cord of the blind was jammed. It seemed that my exploration was thwarted before it had even begun. I tried the blind on the other window and had better luck – although most of the area was covered by the chest of drawers, light suddenly poured into half of the attic at least. Walking away, I almost fell flat on my face, stumbling over a chandelier that looked centuries old.

Arriving at the boxes, I saw they were sealed and labelled, the contents of each one written on the side: 'Documents', 'Textbooks', 'Schoolwork' . . . My heart leapt with emotion. Here were all the things Yolanda and I had made at school and brought home excitedly, eager to show them to Teresa, who was the only one who made a fuss over them, and they had all ended up in the attic . . . I had always thought they'd been thrown out by our mother. I wanted to open a box and go through it, but restrained myself – there would be plenty of time for that.

The unexpected discovery made me wonder if there was more than I'd hoped for in the attic of Alberta's mansion. I kept looking, still thinking about the surprising find I'd made so far. More boxes of documents – there was enough here to represent the historical archive of a long and illustrious dynasty. And . . . one of them said, in big red letters, 'Property of Berta. Personal and important'. My heart pounded in my chest once more. Was it possible that Neca was still closed up in there? Again, I was overcome with the temptation to sit down and open the box, but first I wanted to take stock of everything up there, which all belonged to me now. Yolanda had given me her half, and my mother could no longer stop me from going anywhere in this house that was now mine. Or could she? For a split second I felt there was someone behind me. I whirled around, startled: it was Aris. He'd decided to sniff around. The label on one box was old and worn, but I finally deciphered it: 'Fabián's Tin Soldiers'. The more I explored, the more surprises came to light.

I left the corner with all the boxes and very carefully, checking each step I took, made my way over to the chest of drawers. There were six drawers, three on each side. It was a wonderful piece of antique furniture that, apart from the layers of dust, looked in perfect condition. I thought it might be Empire style, from the early nineteenth century, with gold inlay that shone brightly against the beautiful mahogany wood. On top lay a handful of picture frames, two of them face up: one showed a soldier in sepia tone, and the other a young woman wrapped in yellow lace. I didn't recognise either of them, although maybe the man . . . Yes, he did look a little like Yolanda.

I started opening the drawers, one by one. Time and humidity had left their mark on the wood and they stuck on their runners. In the first drawer I found sewing equipment, including a few interesting items such as a pincushion embroidered with a pastoral scene that must have been hundreds of years old, an embroidery frame that would have delighted any needlewoman, some darning eggs for mending socks and stockings, a tape measure, a little box of needles and another full of silk stockings. Which industrious woman had this all belonged to? Certainly not my mother. In the second drawer I found a complete silver vanity set, which needed cleaning but was still lovely, embossed all over with small flowers. The next drawer down was full of jewellery – necklaces, bracelets, rings, watches that no longer told the time . . . I assumed none of it was too valuable, or else it wouldn't have been left there. Amongst the jewellery was a leather box holding a pocket watch. I opened it and my grandmother Rosa, no more than twenty years old or so in the picture, gazed back at me sweetly. For a moment it looked just like my mother, but no – the features were almost identical, but my mother's face would never have been blessed with that same warm and loving expression. I went on to the three drawers on the right. The first one was jammed, so I left it for last. The other two held ties, opera glasses, a shoe cleaning kit and a couple of men's wallets. I tried the first drawer again but it wouldn't budge. After working on it for a moment, I realised it must be locked. All the drawers had keyholes, but only this first one on the right had actually been locked. I tried one more time to force it open, but it definitely was not simply stuck or warped by humidity. Just then Teresa came in.

'I'm leaving for the day, sweetheart.'

'Teresa, you scared me!'

'Oh dear, I'm sorry, darling, how careless of me. You were so focused on what you were up to . . .'

'I've just been trying to open this wretched drawer, but I reckon she must have locked it. There must be something important in there – Mother only locked up stuff she didn't want to share, not even with you. I don't suppose you know where this particular key is, do you?' I asked sarcastically, making it clear that I no longer trusted her answers.

'I really don't know, dear. I haven't been up here in such a long time. I'll try to think where it might be, but—'

'Well, think hard or I'll have to break the lock,' I said, not sure I believed her. 'I need to know what's inside.'

'I have to go,' she said, completely ignoring my words, 'and I won't be back until tomorrow. I've left you some lunch in the kitchen. You need to eat – you're all skin and bones. Do you want me to buy you anything special? I'm off to the market tomorrow.'

'No, I'm fine. I might go for a walk this afternoon and head into town.'

'You know I'm happy to get whatever you need for you.'

'Of course I know that, Teresa,' I told her, and went over to kiss her cheek, which made her smile.

'Why don't you stop all this? It can't be good for you to spend time in this nasty place. There's nothing up here but old rubbish. You'll have time to go through it little by little . . .'

'I don't think so. As soon as I wrap things up with the solicitor I'm going back to London. I'll have to come back a few more times at least, just for the essential things. Nowadays you can do most of it online. I'd like to leave next week and I want to have gone through all this stuff by then. I have to know what needs saving and what needs throwing away before putting the house up for sale. Don't you see? This place is full of mysteries. No, I'm not selling without going through every last inch of this attic. So far, it's proving to be very interesting.'

My last words left her speechless. I'm not sure why, but I think she'd have preferred me to leave everything for the future owners to throw away.

'Teresa,' I said, pointing to the label on the box of dolls, 'do you think Neca could be in there?'

'I think she must,' she said quietly, seemingly lost in thought.

'Thank you,' I said, smiling, convinced that Neca had only survived the last fifteen years without me because of Teresa's protection.

'You're welcome, sweetheart. I'll see you tomorrow then. I want to stop by the cemetery and I'm in a bit of a hurry.'

She bent down to pet Aris and then left.

It seemed like a good time to take a break. My mouth was dry from all the dust.

My journey to the past had roused my appetite, and I grew even hungrier as I made my way down the stairs. It smelled just the same as when I used to come home from school! The lunches that Teresa made were by far the thing I looked forward to most when coming home. I enjoyed her delicious food no matter what else was happening around the table; certain pleasures were just too good to be ruined. I think that's why the restaurant industry always appealed to me, and I think also that my restaurant had become so popular due in large part to the expert palate I'd developed thanks to our family housekeeper – no dish got the green light until approved by my taste buds. In fact, some of the recipes I featured on the menu were directly inspired by Teresa's home cooking. This time she had left me sofrito in a pan. All it needed was some rice thrown in, which she'd left on the counter in a small glass. If only for her culinary skills, I know my mother would have kept Teresa on for the rest of her life; she loved to eat well, but was far too much of a lady to work in the kitchen herself.

I dined like a queen. The 'rice with dead chicken', as she called it when we asked her what there was to eat, was delicious. I was proud that I'd managed to imitate some of her dishes in my restaurant, but when I tasted the first mouthful . . . Wow, there was nothing like Teresa's food! If she had a restaurant in London, it would have no competition.

After making myself some coffee and answering a few emails, I went back up to the attic and headed straight for the box that I was most focused on.

There, in amongst about thirty dolls of various styles and periods, was my Neca, carefully wrapped in tissue paper. I'd been sure that after my departure, my mother had ordered Teresa to throw out all the boxes of personal items I'd left in my wardrobe, and our housekeeper, before going through with it, had saved my most precious childhood belongings. My old doll was bald, with a foam rubber body and a face that was a poor imitation of a newborn, but dressed in her pink pyjamas and little woollen hat she looked so sweet. She was my dearest possession in the world – the recipient of all my childhood dreams, so much sadness and longing. Even Teresa had not been entrusted with so many of my secret thoughts and emotions. I owed my sanity to Neca. As crazy as it may seem, children do sometimes tap into their emotions in a genuine, albeit one-sided, relationship with an inanimate object. I was one of those children with an invisible friend, only this particular friend lived inside a handful of foam rubber. Adults are surprised when they see their child talking to themselves and becoming so attached to something they view only as a hollow shell. But a child who chooses to interact with an imaginary friend is someone who feels that no one understands them, and whose fundamental need for contact forces them to invent someone who will listen.

I clutched her now to my chest, just as I used to in all those moments when . . . Those very many times when I had felt so alone! Hugging her, I was catapulted straight back into my childhood, overwhelmed by the familiar feeling of protection she gave me. Perched here on a vintage trunk with the ghosts of the past crowding in from all corners of this desolate chamber, the old wound within me ripped open and bled more intensely than ever. Reliving the past as the stitches of time unravelled seemed even more painful than going through it in the first place. How true it is that when you live in a constricted environment, you assume that all the sorrows surrounding you are simply part of life, intrinsic to existence – and that everyone else experiences the same. You swallow every bitter pill with resignation, believing quite simply that that's all life has to offer. When you finally come across other ways of living and experience the good and healthy things in life, such as freedom, independence and respect for others . . . then you understand that there's so much more to existence than your own misery and that you've simply been living under a rule of tyranny. It was extraordinary how greatly I'd suffered! I felt like a child again, the little Berta who would hug her doll . . . though right now it hurt so much more than before. But only for a moment – I don't know if I could have stood it for another second. When I tore myself out of the past and returned to reality, my tears started to flow, moved by compassion for the innocent little girl who had spent so many years afraid. Remembrance was a bitter purgative, and now I was throwing up all the rotten memories and that took its time, because I could no longer suppress the sobs that demanded release. It was the long, silent and healing weeping of a woman who had begun to face herself and what lay behind her. I no longer needed Neca these days, but the very sight of her made my heart full. Still clutching on to her, I stood up and, with some difficulty because of the rusting locks and hinges, opened up the trunk on which I'd been sitting.

The heavy stench of foetid mothballs hit me like a slap in the face, and a mass of yellowed tulle poked out from the aged wood. Trapped in the murky darkness for so many years, the fabric seemed to shimmer as though with little gold lights hidden in its folds. At first glance, it looked like a bridal veil. Carefully, I reached out my hand to touch the filmy amber material, afraid it might disintegrate like the dry wings of a butterfly, melting away with the softest of breaths. I wasn't too far off. The garment was a little rough to the touch and I noticed a faint rustling between my fingers as I handled it. I sat Neca on the chest of drawers and picked up the fabric. I could see now that it clearly was a bridal veil. The dress lay underneath, along with a picture frame and a beautiful mother-of-pearl box containing a gold chain with a clear raindrop pendant and earrings to match. Whoever had cut those stones was a master of his art. I couldn't help thinking that such wonderful things didn't deserve to languish there and that, if this trunk remained unlocked, what treasure must still remain hidden in that drawer in my mother's bedroom? I left everything just as I'd found it – if it had survived so many decades, then surely it could stay there another day. There was also a pearl bracelet, a diamond solitaire ring and a pair of cufflinks engraved with the initials F and C. In a larger cardboard box I found a pair of shoes lined with the softest silk.

For a long time I'd wondered whether my mother was in fact ever really married to Fabián, because at home I'd never seen a single photo or memento of what is supposed to be the happiest day of a woman's life. It was as if she wanted to bury all the years she had shared with him, which was complete nonsense. If her image as a respectable widow was so important to her, why had she hidden away anything that reminded her of her wedding? As was so often the case with her, there were more questions than answers. But here was the final proof. The photos confirmed their marriage: a terribly beautiful young woman posing with a serious expression on her face next to her new husband, a little older than her, a little less attractive, but with a huge smile on his face. I didn't need to know much about photography to know what had taken place on the day of that wedding. It was a simple financial arrangement: a rather plain man, older and from a good family, proud of his young sweetheart – a girl as beautiful as she was ambitious. I put it all back inside and closed the trunk, then moved on to inspect the contents of the box next to it, which was smaller and in better condition.

It was filled to the brim with letters, postcards and notes of congratulation. I was surprised to see that Alberta had saved sentimental stuff like this. I had always thought she'd systematically got rid of everything connecting her with her past. Could Teresa be responsible for this too – saving everything so I would find it one day? It seemed very likely.

Perhaps there was a part of my mother that nobody knew. With a handful of yellowing letters, I sat back down on the trunk holding all her memories from her wedding to Fabián. Aris, who had been watching me alertly and cautiously from across the room, came closer. He circled me twice and then sprawled out at my feet, as if he knew I wouldn't be moving for a while. He didn't need to talk or even communicate; he could simply read my thoughts.

My mind felt strewn with debris as though a hurricane had blown through, littered with all the little pieces of my life. I felt drained and empty, scarcely in touch with reality, somehow quite separate from this person shut up in the attic.

My shaking hands started to drop the cards and letters on to the dusty floor and on Aris's back, until there was only one left between my fingers. I stared at the return address on the envelope: 'Loreto Medina Ávila, Number 48, Cánovas del Castillo Street, Valladolid'. It had been sliced open carefully, as though with a very fine letter opener. Hastily I drew out the sheet of paper inside. The name Loreto didn't even ring a bell with me for a moment, because I'd forgotten that Teresa had mentioned her to me earlier that same day, but when I saw that the letter was addressed to Alberta, my curiosity was deeply aroused. It was written in pen, in a very neat, exquisite hand.

Valladolid
15 January 1980

Dear Alberta,

I can imagine how surprised you'll be to get this letter. I would have called you, but I haven't been able to get your phone number. I know we haven't spoken in a long time, and I'm guessing you won't be happy to hear from me. I never wanted you for my son (it's absurd to deny it after all this time). I saw how much of a stranger my only son became to the whole family after a while, and I couldn't stand that. He, who had always been so kind, loving and generous with everyone, suddenly cut us all out of his life, particularly me. You're a mother, so you must understand how that felt.

I don't want your forgiveness – I don't think you'd give it to me anyway. What I need is your compassion: for you to take pity on a mother whose heart is broken because she doesn't know where her son is. I have read and reread the medical and police reports, and I cannot believe that Fabián just left, or that he lost his memory. Honestly, I don't think he was ever actually mentally ill in the first place. Before he married you, he was vigorously healthy in every way, and every other member of the family has always led a long and healthy life. He only became so ill-tempered once he started seeing you. His coldness and hostility to everyone who loved him were quite strange, and I can't help believing that you're responsible for them. But for him to disappear off the face of the earth without trace – well, he never would have done that. I know he would never have abandoned his daughter. He adores her, and wherever he is, if he's still alive, he would do anything to get in touch with Yolanda.

Alberta, take pity on me – you more than anyone must be able to put yourself in my place, with your second child about to be born. If you know anything about Fabián or what happened to him, please tell me, I beg you. I don't want anything he might have left to you – I swear on all that's dearest to me, you can have it all. I just need to know where and how my son is.

Give Yolanda a kiss from her loving grandmother. She is always in my heart.

Loreto Medina Ávila

I was shocked. My mother had always told us that Fabián, the man I'd thought for nine years was my father, was a selfish person, sharp and distant with his family, and that he had made it hard for his wife to live with him. She made us believe that if it weren't for her, he would have squandered all his inheritance in ridiculous investments and yet was miserly towards her and their daughter. I grew up convinced that Alberta's bad temper was partly due to the miserable years she had lived with Fabián, who with each passing day had stripped away the illusions of her youth. But this letter from Loreto held information I'd never heard before: what medical report was she talking about? Did he really adore Yolanda? Alberta had always told us he'd treated her like a nuisance. How much of the de Castro inheritance had he left to my mother? No, this wasn't the Fabián she had described to my sister and me over all those years.

This was the letter of a broken-hearted mother, desperate, unashamedly honest, a woman convinced that her cruel daughter-in-law was hiding the truth. I wondered how much Alberta had taken with her to the grave, and if I was really ready to find out the answers. Teresa must know something – she'd been in the house the whole time and must have suspected that my mother had something to do with Fabián's disappearance. I would have to talk to her about this tomorrow.

I opened the trunk again and was about to take out another letter, keep uncovering secrets, then realised that my mental strength was fading, and knew I'd done more than enough for today. I put away all the letters that were on the floor and slammed the trunk shut, feeling angry and sick. It would have been so different if I'd found adoring letters, people who were affectionate with each other, a past brimming over with love and delight . . .

I picked up Aris and quickly left that chamber of horrors, in desperate need of fresh air. But before closing the door, I turned back and retraced my footsteps: this was no place for Neca, and, besides, I needed her. The sight of my childhood friend, propped up in a halo of dust glowing with the light from the window, made me shudder.

My sorrow started to fade as the murky water flowed into the drain of the shower, washing the dust from my body. There was a huge gulf of fifteen years between me and the stuff in the attic; it was all in the past now. I poured myself a whisky and went out into the garden to enjoy the evening with Aris and Neca, the only two friends I could be sure of in Spain. *It's all so sad*, I thought.

I regretted having opened Pandora's box since my return. I hadn't needed to – I could just have dealt with the necessary legal matters and nothing else. In the past few days, my mother's evil spirit had once again trapped me in her clutches. I'd felt so strong when the aeroplane took off, so sure that the past was now behind me and that once she was dead, she couldn't hurt me any more. What absolute nonsense! We are the sum of our experiences: every day, every moment shapes and conditions us, for better or for worse. When memories are painful, we bury them like dead leaves in the darkest corners of our souls. Sometimes if we're lucky, they stay there, dormant, for the rest of our lives, even though they've already changed us and become part of who we are. At other times they awaken when you least expect it, to leave their hiding places and shake everything up. They make us relive the past, suffer it all over again . . . But the fact remains that their sudden reappearance is also an opportunity to process and to forgive, and that maybe, once we do that, we can really start over without looking back.

I couldn't enjoy that evening. As soon as I lay down in the hammock, I realised that not everything had gone down the drain along with the dust from the attic. A black hole seemed to loom in my chest, ready to swallow me alive. Trying to rid myself of the feeling, I breathed in slowly and deeply in an effort to relax. I had then the idea of studying my pain from another perspective, stepping outside my own head to analyse myself as a psychologist might have done. True, I'd been an innocent victim of unparalleled tyranny throughout my childhood and teenage years, but things had changed – I'd grown and matured and was proud of myself for that. Deep down I must have the strength I needed to overcome the cruellest monster any person can face: their past. I think the pain I was going through was caused more by the thought of the deceptions than by the memories themselves. I wasn't as strong as I thought. I'd fallen right back into playing the role of a victim – a weakness I despised in other people and wouldn't tolerate in my employees at the restaurant – and had only myself to blame for that. My mother wasn't here any more, so I was battling ghosts. In that moment I knew that victory would only come with understanding and reconciliation. I had to reach into the depths of it and bear the pain until the end, even if it killed me. I would come out of it free or I would be lost forever.

A few doors down, children were playing in their garden. Their laughter was delightful and sincere . . . How I envied them and wished that my own childhood had been like that! I didn't recall ever having played or laughed in our own garden. We weren't allowed to disturb the neighbours: it was rude to interrupt other people's silence with laughter and shouting. As a neighbour to these kids now, I didn't feel remotely bothered. Actually I was grateful to be reminded that beyond my own heartache, happiness and innocence went on. These kids had no ghosts to struggle with, and the possibility of growing into adults with happy and fulfilling lives lay well within their grasp.

I poured myself another tumblerful of whisky. I needed to forget. Slowly I drifted into another dimension where there was little room for thought. All I could do was float like a cloud among the stars that enveloped me. A couple of hours later and feeling much calmer, I decided it was time to eat something.

A couple of good-sized tomatoes sat on a plate on the kitchen counter, and they smelled divine. I sliced them up for dinner, seasoning them with oil and salt. Teresa's culinary genius extended even to her trips to the market – where had she found such delicious tomatoes? After wolfing them down, I mopped up the juices with a hunk of bread. I guess the whisky had made me hungry.

I should have gone to bed then, but instead went back out into the garden, afraid that even passing the door to the sitting room would rob me of the peace I'd struggled to find all evening.

◆ ◆ ◆

I woke at dawn, shivering in the humid darkness of the night, my shirt soaked with dew, and cursed myself for my stupidity and for having allowed myself a third tumbler of the good stuff. Through my confusion and my aching head, I thought how funny it was that I'd happened to catch the first cold night of the year in the middle of June in Spain. Clumsily I stripped off my clothes and fell into bed. Aris lay curled up at the foot of the bed; with more sense than me, he must have been there for hours.

Chapter 6

Monday, 16 June 2014

Sometime after eleven o'clock, the ringing of my mobile roused me from a deep sleep. It was Brandon, calling to bring me up to date on the restaurant's bills and orders. Like the good English lad that he was, he didn't ask me anything personal, even though he must have heard from the tone of my voice that I'd just woken up. He greeted me politely and then filled me in on what was happening at the restaurant. It's a good thing he couldn't see me – with a cat on one side and a doll on the other – or else he'd have properly worried and would definitely have been asking questions. It was a relief that everything was going well at the restaurant without me, but I admit it did bother me a little that I was so expendable: after so many years of working myself to the bone, day in, day out, never taking a day off, bringing work home on my nights off, sleeping just enough so I'd be able to stay on my feet, only now to discover that everything worked just fine without me. I consoled myself with the thought that it was only because of all the groundwork I'd put in place.

The kitchen door was open on to the garden, and a moment later Teresa came in with the bottle of whisky in one hand and my glass in the other.

'Morning, Teresa – why didn't you wake me? I wanted to go into town to do some shopping . . .'

'Morning, darling. Well, what's the rush? You have plenty of time – the stores don't close until ten at night. You slept in because you needed it.'

'I guess so. It's hard to remember how much free time I have here. Will you have a coffee with me?'

'Of course. I'll put on a pot.'

Sitting in the kitchen with our coffee cups in our hands, I told her what I'd found the day before. 'Yesterday I came across an old trunk full of letters and cards up there.'

'Well, there could be just about anything in that old attic,' she answered, sounding a little nervous.

'I can well believe it. I had no idea there'd be so much or that it would be so interesting. I only read one letter at random, and it gave me quite a turn.'

'Oh my dear, I knew it – I should never have left you . . .'

'No, it wasn't like that – I just meant that the letter really surprised me,' I said to reassure her, although I don't think it worked. She still seemed just as worried about what I might have read.

'Sweetheart, why don't you forget about all this – it's not worth all the dust. It's filthy up there, and—'

'Yes, I couldn't have said it better myself. It's all filth up there.'

'Well then, forget about it. I'm sure you have better things to think about.'

'I'd like to forget it, Teresa, but I can't. I came back here ready to put my past with my mother behind me and get back to my life as soon as possible, but you see there's no way to escape her clutches, alive or dead. There is one thing . . .'

'Oh come on now, that's all just nonsense. Listen, you've become a beautiful, independent woman and you've done it all on your own. Of course you escaped – I can tell just by looking at you.'

Teresa was trying to convince me to leave the past behind, minimising everything I'd suffered within these walls, but her insistence, which she was unable to hide, made me think she knew much more than she was letting on.

'What was Fabián like? You knew him well – you practically saw him grow up,' I asked her without preamble.

'No, don't be silly – when I knew him I was just a child and he was already finishing his law degree. Later on, when I worked for him and your mother . . . Well, he wasn't a very good man and . . . He was always a smart boy, that's what they said about him at home. In fact, his mother never stopped saying it. What else can I say?'

'OK, but what was he like?' I pressed.

'He was just a normal man, Berta.' She'd done the same thing she always did when I was little and she was annoyed with me: she stopped using her endearments when talking to me. Clearly she was unhappy, and I could tell she didn't like talking about the subject. 'He split his days between the university and his studies, and . . .'

'And what?'

'And I think he was seeing the daughter of some friends of the family.'

'Go on.'

'That's it, love. He finished his degree with good grades, started working in his father's firm, and shortly after that he got married. That's how things were back then.'

'So he had another wife before marrying my mother? I didn't know that. Well, I don't really know anything. I guess he was widowed?'

'No, they never married.'

'Well, no need to say any more – I'm guessing Alberta came between them.'

'It's not that simple, dear.'

'You're telling me! Was anything in my mother's life simple?'

'These things just happen. They fell in love – Fabián was head over heels for your mother. You have no idea how beautiful she was . . .' Her eyes lit up.

'I saw a photograph of their wedding in the attic, and yes, she was pretty, unbelievably so. So what happened next?' I was dying to hear the interesting part, and could see she was ready to spill the beans.

'The marriage wasn't easy for them. Loreto never accepted your mother, and since Manuel died shortly after his only son's marriage, the two of them decided to move to Madrid. They didn't like it in Valladolid any more. Then Fabián got sick and . . . well, you know the rest.'

'How did Fabián die?'

'A brain tumour – you know that already,' she answered, and I could tell she was done with talking. She'd been quite relaxed until I asked the last question.

'Don't lie to me, Teresa. I'm not a child any more. Tell me the truth.'

'He lost his mind. One day he went out for a walk and he never came back, that's all. Your mother preferred to tell everyone he'd died so no one would gossip. She said that people respect the dead more than they respect people who go missing . . . She also thought it would be easier for Yolanda.'

'Of course, and, by the way, she also told people the tragedy had happened while she was pregnant. It was all so well done. Do you know that her mother-in-law never believed at all that her son had simply wandered off and disappeared?'

'Well, that's normal. What mother would want to believe it?' Teresa answered, toying nervously with her flowery scarf.

'No, Teresa, none of this is normal – nothing that happened in my mother's life is normal. She was a dreadful woman and an unscrupulous predator. No, I don't believe for one moment that he disappeared, just like I don't believe anything she told me her whole life. It was all one big sham.'

'Sweetheart . . . you're really starting to upset me. It's all water under the bridge now,' she said a little more kindly, in another attempt to persuade me to drop it.

'Well, apparently some of the water is flowing right on back again. Here we are fifteen years later trying to figure out if there's any truth in this family at all.'

'But that's all there is. Why keep looking?'

'That's all there is? There's something about your story that just doesn't feel quite right, Teresa – there's something missing. Let me guess. Let's see if my version makes more sense than yours.'

'Another time, darling, I have so much work to do . . .'

'Wait, it'll only take a second. You see, I think it happened like this—'

'My dear, I don't like you talking this way. We've only just buried your mother and I hate hearing you talk about her like this.'

'I'm sorry. But please, don't leave yet – listen to how I think the story goes . . .'

Looking more closely now at her sad face, I thought twice about telling her my version. I didn't want to hurt her, but on the other hand I needed her to know that my suspicions were more logical than her weak arguments. I needed her to stop sugar-coating the truth and hiding information from me.

'OK then, this is how I reckon it really went. Fabián's a well-to-do chap about to marry his long-term girlfriend, when he's swept off his feet by Señorita Alberta, who's expecting more than a comfortable life. Her mother-in-law twigs that her son's new wife isn't entirely pure in her motivation, so she tries to sabotage their life together. The beautiful Mrs de Castro consequently decides to put some distance between them, and convinces her husband to move to Madrid, where they'll no longer be under his mother's thumb. *Inexplicably*, for some strange reason, Fabián starts having mental problems, and his wife makes sure he's incapacitated while handling his father's inheritance. Then, once more *inexplicably*,' I said, emphasising the last word as Teresa's expression changed, 'he disappears for good. And the best part is that she already has a younger and more handsome lover in place, just dumb enough not to think things through too carefully and with even more wads of cash than her husband had.'

'That's only your version,' Teresa interjected, looking more and more uncomfortable. 'It all depends on how you look at it, but you're assuming too much, especially considering you weren't even born yet. I never meddled in your mother's business – you know how private she was with her personal affairs. All I know is that Fabián started ranting and raving and every day he was a little odder, and that wasn't the first time he'd gone missing. Once a neighbour had to bring him home, so it wasn't too much of a stretch to think that one day he wouldn't come home at all. He even got lost out in the garden . . . Anyway, I need to go.'

'Teresa, you know that at first I planned to stay here only for a week and return to my life as soon as possible. I promise you, that sounds like a better scenario than all of this. But I've decided now that I can't leave until I've tidied up every corner of my past. I know you can help me settle this as soon as possible. It's your decision.'

She didn't say anything else; she didn't even say goodbye. She took off her apron and, without going back to the garden to gather the tools she'd been using, simply left the house, slamming the door in a way that was not like her at all.

I decided to get ready and eat in town before doing my shopping. There was a call on the landline just as I was about to leave. It was someone from the hospital where my mother had been brought, already dead, reminding the family to pick up the patient's belongings, even though she hadn't really been a patient since she'd arrived at the hospital and been taken straight to the mortuary. I only survived the stench in the corner where the phone was because it took a mere ten seconds for them to give me the message.

The hospital was on my way into town, so I stopped by and played my role as the 'good daughter'. They gave me a black bag, tied with a clumsy knot. If there'd been a rubbish bin on my way to the car, I would have thrown it out in a second.

◆ ◆ ◆

It felt good to walk through town and distract myself with all the shop windows and pedestrians. Watching them, I imagined their lives, each as distinct as they were normal. People with straightforward lives: a job, a family, a mortgage . . . I was sure that, however unspeakable their secrets, they could never compare with those that Alberta had taken with her to the grave. As I walked through the heart of old Madrid, I knew that I'd come back to fulfil a mission and couldn't leave without victory.

I felt the stares of everyone I passed on the street. I'd said as much to Teresa: something about me was different and London had marked me in some way that was obvious to the people of Madrid. I wore comfortable clothes, carefully chosen but nothing special (so no one in the city would recognise me). I'd learned to make the most of myself and take care of my body. Even my haircut enhanced and showed off my features. The overall effect might come across as informal, as though I'd just tossed my clothes on in the morning, but no. It was the result of years of effort to hide the dull, chubby girl I used to be. I was wearing jeans that fitted perfectly, the result of trying on dozens in my favourite store in London. My best friend Mary had excellent taste and the patience of a saint, and she always came along with me. To go with my jeans

I wore a basic white cotton shirt, a subtle black print vest, blue trainers and a belt that accentuated my slender waist. The most important aspect was that I felt confident in the way I looked.

I ate lunch at the Corte Inglés. While they served me, I took the opportunity to write emails to Harry, Mary and Emily, whom I missed a lot during these moments of leisure and window-shopping. Three trivial messages:

Hi, how's everything going? It's all going fine over here . . .

I didn't want to share with them anything I was going through in Madrid; my mother was my dirty laundry, which I didn't want anyone else to see. I'd never lied to them, but I hadn't been totally honest either, partly because even I didn't know the truth about her. To my friends, acquaintances and employees, I was just a young Spanish girl who'd settled in London after coming over to look for work, end of story. I thought about my relationship with Mary, who I knew absolutely everything about and who I still didn't trust with anything important about my own past.

I was lost in such thoughts when my phone rang. It was Señor Soler, informing me that the paperwork was going to be held up another few days for bureaucratic reasons; apparently the fact my sister lived so far away was complicating things. 'I'm sorry to delay your return to London, Señorita Berta. We're doing everything we can to hurry it along. I'll keep you informed,' he said in closing. I wasn't too bothered – I'd already accepted that I would be spending more time in Madrid than I'd planned.

After lunch I did some shopping and then headed home. I was surprised by just how excited I was at the thought that Aris would be waiting for me at the house. I happened to be passing through the pet food aisle at the market, so bought him some special tins to make him happy.

◆ ◆ ◆

I parked at the front of the house and took all my bags from the boot, including the one they'd given me at the hospital. Aris was indeed waiting for me, and as soon as he heard me pull up and saw I wasn't coming straight to the front door, he came out through the cat flap to greet me. I stroked him affectionately and told him I'd brought him a surprise. He responded by closing his eyes, enjoying being spoiled.

I put the black bag down in the corner of the kitchen and left the rest on the worktop. While I put away the shopping I tried to settle on a plan for the afternoon. There were several hours of daylight left – it was early summer and the days were especially long and mild. But the attic would have to wait today. I didn't feel up to facing any more of its secrets.

Once Aris had enthusiastically devoured my gift, we went to my bedroom and I read well into the evening. The thriller on my new Kindle was proving a good distraction, although it didn't even come close to my own tragic family history. I reflected that any writer would struggle to put my experiences down on paper and make the story credible. My phone rang a couple of times – the restaurant suppliers were used to dealing with me direct on our orders.

Before going to bed for the night, I made myself a salad and took a shower. The landline rang several times while I was in the shower. Whoever it was, they wanted to talk to me and hadn't checked the time before calling: it was almost eleven o'clock at night. Now in bed, with Aris at my feet, Neca at my side and the thriller on my Kindle in my hands, the phone rang again. Resignedly, I lifted the sheets and went off to look for the phone, breathing through my mouth to avoid the overpowering smell in the sitting room.

'Hello?' I said grumpily.

'Hello, Berta.'

I recognised her voice instantly, although her tone, lacking the sarcastic enthusiasm I remembered so well, sounded strange to my ears. It was Yolanda. I was so stunned I couldn't speak, and she asked: 'Berta? Berta, is that you?'

'Yes, it's me,' I managed to say, recovering a bit from my shock. My voice wavered and I started to smell my mother's perfume again.

'How is it being back home?'

'I don't know what to tell you . . . What do you want, Yolanda? Why are you calling?' I answered, trying to hide how upset I was to hear from her.

'I suppose the solicitor told you the terms I suggested regarding the inheritance—'

'Yes, I heard about it,' I interrupted.

'Good. Berta . . .' she said, and then there was an uncomfortable silence at the other end of the phone.

'I'm waiting. I'd like to go back to bed. I don't think you know what time it is here. Honestly, I'm not sure why you're calling at all.'

'Sell up and go back to London. I promise you, that's the best advice I can give you. Leave as soon as you can.'

'Leave . . . ? Funny, that sounds like a threat to me.' Despite how distraught I was, I found the strength to answer her. 'I have the strangest feeling that if you're wanting me to sell up and leave as soon as possible, it would somehow be to your advantage. I'll go when I bloody well feel like it. By the way, there's still time for you to claim your share.'

'Listen to me – get out of there! Goodbye, little sister.'

'I'm sorry to tell you that I won't be taking your advice. Goodbye.'

The pleasant drowsiness that had almost kept me from answering the phone had vanished.

◆ ◆ ◆

Except for those times when the intense smell of my mother's expensive perfume hit me and I briefly fell back into the agonising past, I'd pretty much managed to remember that fifteen years had gone by since I'd left. Even though I was living in the same setting as during the worst years of my life, I was constantly aware that my role in that macabre performance was more than over. But Yolanda's voice had now erased the line that separated logic from imagination. And then . . . it's not that I returned to the past per se, just that I had the horrifying feeling that I'd never left that goddamn house at all – as though the fifteen years I'd lived so far away were all an illusion. Knowing how vulnerable I was – that after all this time I was still a victim of Yolanda and my mother – was unbearable.

I went back to bed with Aris and Neca, my heart pounding in my chest. 'Sell up and go back to London', my older sister had dared to order me. What did it matter to her what I did with my inheritance and my life, since she'd never even cared about my existence at all? Previously, I'd suspected that she was heavily involved in Bodo's disappearance, but now I was sure of it. For some mysterious reason, my staying in our house in Madrid worried her enough that she had to make that absurd call. I'm sure she thought I was still the same foolish, naive person I used to be, the girl she could manipulate at will to get away with all her bad behaviour and lies, when just a few words from her would scare me into doing whatever she wanted. But she'd underestimated me: she didn't seem to have changed at all, but I had. I'd gained something valuable when I moved far away from her and Alberta.

I didn't fall asleep until my pulse had settled, and even then I didn't stay asleep for long.

Chapter 7

Tuesday, 17 June 2014

I had terrible nightmares that night. I should have got up to make myself some soothing camomile tea, but was too terrified. Just beyond my bedroom door, Alberta's spirit was wandering through her domain, waiting for me in every object, around every corner, in the very air contaminated with her ghastly scent. I squeezed my eyes tight shut and hugged Neca just like I did when I was a little girl, trying to tell myself I was in my flat in London, far away from this unhinged environment, or giving orders in my restaurant kitchen, but I was unable to calm myself until the first fingers of dawn had crept in through the bedroom curtains and cast out all the menacing shadows surrounding me.

After tidying myself up a bit, I went down into the kitchen. Teresa was there, slicing vegetables.

'Hi, Teresa.'

'Hello there, love. Every day you're getting up a little bit later! Did you sleep all right? You don't look so good.'

'No, I think it was one of the worst nights of my entire life, in fact.'

'Oh my goodness! Why?'

'Yolanda called last night.'

'You don't say!' Teresa exclaimed, stopping what she was doing to stare at me in surprise. 'Well, I'm glad she thought to call and talk to you. It's about time you two saw reason and let bygones be bygones, now that you're older.' She fussed on, trying to minimise what had happened years before, but she must have known it would not have been a pleasant call. 'Go on, sit down, love, and I'll make you some breakfast.'

'It was a very short conversation,' I told her, with no intention of sitting down yet.

'Well, at least it's a start.'

'She seemed very eager for me to get rid of everything and go back to London. Doesn't that strike you as a little odd?'

'Sweetheart, your sister's right – there's nothing to keep you here now.'

'Sure, but . . . what does it matter to her what I do with my life, especially since we haven't seen each other in fifteen years?'

'I'm sure she said it for your own good, because she knows how hard it is for you to be here after the way you left.'

'Oh please, Teresa!' I blurted out, raising my voice. Her words seemed more cynical than conciliatory, even though I knew that wasn't like her. 'She was trying to find something out. I'm not sure why, but I think for some reason she needed to know if I was planning on staying here, and she wasn't thinking about me, she was thinking of herself. I don't know what it's all about, but I do know that my being in Madrid is making her nervous. I didn't tell her much, as you might have guessed.'

'Oh dear, don't be so negative. It's been a long time, and people do change. Just look at you – you're like a different person.'

'I don't know if you're serious or if you're making fun of me. This is Yolanda we're talking about, remember? The Yolanda who married my father for money? No, Teresa, she hasn't changed, and neither did my mother. I don't know how you could have stood being around them year after year. I can't tell if you just didn't notice, or if you're a saint,' I said, knowing full well that she was the most perceptive person who'd ever set foot in this house.

'Your mother was always good to me, and you two were like my own daughters.'

Sitting down as Teresa served me breakfast, I noticed that the bag of my mother's personal items was still in the same place where I'd left it the day before.

'The hospital called me yesterday to pick up her things,' I said, looking at the black bag.

Teresa followed my gaze and asked: 'Do you want me to take care of it?'

'We'll do it together as soon as we finish breakfast.'

Once I'd finished my coffee and toast and fed Aris, I cleared the dishes and then placed the bag on the table. Teresa dried her hands and came over. There was no way to untie the knot.

'Would you mind fetching the scissors, Teresa?'

I cut the knot with one snip, and all of a sudden a terrible host of smells invaded my lungs. Once again I had to hold my nose and breathe through my mouth or I wouldn't have lasted a second.

A beige blouse and blue skirt told me that while I'd been gone Alberta had lost her perfect figure. Next I took out some black leather shoes, her pants and bra, and finally a smaller white bag, knotted as tightly as the outer one had been. Teresa was barely breathing in the effort to hold back her emotion, and I reflected briefly on the confusing strength of the ties that bound her to my mother. Once again I snipped through the knot, and an earring rolled to the ground. Teresa chased after it like a madwoman, then placed it next to the other items of jewellery we'd now found: the partner to the earring, a matching ring, her wedding ring demonstrating her false and eternal widowhood and a small key hanging from a golden chain.

Teresa gathered the clothing and shoes back into the black bag, visibly upset. 'I guess we could throw all this in the bin,' she said with a deep sigh, not taking her eyes off the little key.

'You guess right – get rid of it and as far away as possible,' I snapped, although instantly regretted using such a sharp tone when Teresa was so sensitive. I grabbed the key and, coiling up the thick chain, held it out for her to see. 'Look what we have here. What do you want to bet that I won't need to break the lock of the old drawer in the attic after all? If she was wearing the key around her neck, there has to be something important in there.'

'I'm glad you won't have to break into it – that chest of drawers is a beautiful antique,' she said, surely just to say something. It was obvious she was still shaken from seeing the clothes my mother had been wearing on the day she died.

'As soon as I figure out what's inside it, it's yours. I can't take it to London and I wouldn't like having it around anyway,' I answered, still stunned, staring at the key in my hand. 'What a twisted woman she was, Teresa. Have you ever known anyone who wore one key around their neck and hung another on their cat's collar to hide them away? Right, I'm going to pour myself a second cup of coffee and then head up to the attic. I simply have to know what she was trying so hard to keep hidden up there.'

'I'll make another pot of coffee, then I need to finish up my tasks for the day and go home. Darling . . .' She stopped, staring at the jewellery for a few seconds, like someone gazing in devotion at her favourite saint.

'Yes, Teresa?'

'Your sister's right. Sell up and go back to London – there's nothing for you here but bad memories.'

'You're wanting to get rid of me too? Of course I'm going to go back – there's no reason for me to stay. But I'll go when I've finished piecing this whole damn puzzle together – it just gets more and more weird and complicated by the day.'

Grabbing my second cup of coffee, I went to tidy things in my room for a while until Teresa had completed her tasks and left. I wanted to be alone in the house when I finally faced the mysterious old drawer.

◆ ◆ ◆

Just as I'd thought, the tiny golden key opened the drawer that had thwarted me on Sunday. Before looking inside, I swept the dust from the surface of the chest of drawers and wiped it clean, then sat Neca on it so she was right in front of me for support.

It was hard to get the drawer open because it was so crammed full of letters, which were sorted into bundles tied with all manner and colours of string and ribbon. Nothing new, it seemed. I'd already found a whole bunch of old letters up here – the postman might just as well have delivered them straight into the attic. Somehow though, because of how these ones had been locked away and so neatly organised, it made me think they had to be the most important items in the attic.

I grabbed a bundle and flicked through, reading the details on the envelopes: they all seemed to be addressed to my mother and to the very same house in which I now stood. Turning them over to see who they were from, I read the return address on the last envelope in the bunch: S.G.F., writing from the United States, and more specifically from the Olympic Peninsula of Washington State.

It wasn't terribly comfortable up there among all the mess and clutter. There was barely any light and the dust in the air made it hard to breathe, so I went over to an old basket I'd espied in the corner. Dumping out all the old dried flowers inside, I replaced them with the whole lot of letters from the drawer so they were easily transportable. I placed Neca carefully on top, but Aris would have to go down on his own. I was pretty sure he'd be all too glad to leave.

I headed out into the garden and, passing through the kitchen, saw my lunch laid out on the counter. It could wait another hour – I'd had breakfast quite late. The clock seems to stop ticking when there's nothing and no one waiting for you. Lying in the hammock, in the shade of the willow tree, I was ready to start reading.

◆ ◆ ◆

Taking a good look at the bundles of letters, I noticed two important details: firstly, that each bundle held all the correspondence from a particular year, and secondly, the odd fact that none of the letters had been opened. What kind of lunatic locks away dozens of letters without even reading them? All of a sudden my blood ran cold, in spite of the warm June afternoon. I would be the first person after all these years to read the contents of these letters from Washington State! I didn't want to rip something that now seemed so precious, so went back into the house on the hunt for a letter opener, anxious to start reading. I found one right away, having remembered seeing a silver one bearing my mother's monogram in the drawer of the sideboard in the hallway. Aris trotted along at my heels; his water bowl was empty, so I refilled it before returning to my hammock.

Before getting started, I sorted through the heaps of letters by year: twelve of them, in consecutive chronological order from 2002 to the current year. The first bundle held fifteen letters and the postmark of the earliest letter was dated 22 April 2002; it seemed like the obvious place to start. Carefully, I drew it out from the rest, and placed the others back in the basket. Not all of the letters were sealed after all: the first one had been opened, although so carefully it was barely noticeable. There was a second envelope inside; when I took it out, a note fell on to my lap. The first thing that caught my attention was its gorgeously unique handwriting. The shape of each consonant and vowel was identical – as if all the letters had been learning the same dance for years and were now linking to form words across a fine, straight sheet that acted as the dance floor. All in all, it exuded a wonderful sense of harmony and integrity. The script was written in black ballpoint pen.

> Dear Doña Alberta,
> I'm taking the liberty of writing to you to ask you a very important favour. It may not help my cause, but from now on you will receive regular letters like this one for your daughter Yolanda. Please, please help us to stay in touch by passing on my letters to her. As I told her, I had no other choice but to run away – it was either that or be wrongfully imprisoned. I can only hope this nightmare ends soon so I can explain myself and thank you in person.
> With warmest greetings,
> Saúl

I was dazed for a few seconds, but then understood immediately that the author of all these letters must be the young man accused of Bodo's disappearance, and that in his concern that Yolanda was being kept under observation, he had sent all his letters to my mother for her to pass on to his beloved. Alberta, not a person known for her curiosity, had only had to open one to know that they had nothing to do with her, but rather something connected with recent events not of her making, and so she had preferred to keep the lad at a distance and ignore him, while her daughter had clearly never received the correspondence. But why on earth would Alberta keep them locked up in the attic? My mother's motive for saving them even though she hadn't bothered to read them was – like everything else about my mother and my sister – quite beyond my understanding, at least for now.

The inner envelope said 'For Yolanda, from Saúl'. I put an end to my musings and opened the envelope.

> Olympic National Park
> 4 April 2002
>
> My beloved Yolanda, my life,
> How are you? It's only been three days since we said goodbye and already it feels like a lifetime. I don't know if we made the right decision in parting; I don't think I can bear it. The world has been so unfair to us . . . I refuse to endure this long exile to pay for a crime I didn't commit – unless love itself is a crime? Maybe we should wait a little longer and then fight for the truth until it's over. I would give my life to have you here with me for a moment, just a single moment in exchange for my whole life.
>
> You can't imagine how beautiful this landscape is. It's getting dark, and from the table where I'm writing, I'm watching as the day fades into an immense and silent lake. On the distant shore the sun is dipping behind an amazing forest that covers the whole of the mountain. A few steps from the door of the cabin, sinuous ripples

dance an eternal waltz on the water. If it weren't for how much I'm missing you, I'd swear that I'm in the middle of paradise. But no, paradise is being with you, my darling.

Yolanda . . . what happened to us? How could our love possibly have ended in this fatal trap? How briefly our happiness lasted . . . I can't believe there's a whole ocean stretching between us right now. I've gone over what happened in those months so many times that sometimes I think I'll go mad. But I will be a man and bear it, and when all this is over I will return to fulfil my promise to you. Hold on tight, my darling. If you can be strong, I can be too.

I hope you can find a way to send word to me, and that your mother takes pity on us and sends your letters on. This silence, this not hearing from you, is killing me.

I love you, my darling.

Saúl

Gripping the paper in my hands, nearly paralysed with emotion, I couldn't stop thinking about what I had just read. These were the words of a man deeply, even desperately in love. I had the strongest sense that he'd fallen victim to a vile deception, since here he was, pleading his innocence to the one woman who would have known everything and whom he couldn't deceive. Knowing Yolanda, this was far more than just a feeling. I seriously suspected that she was more to blame than he was. Even though Saúl's first letter didn't spell out what had happened in the previous few months, it seemed clear that he was referring to Bodo's death and the unbelievable fact that all the evidence suggested he was the killer.

I was shocked that someone could be so deeply enamoured of my sister. Maybe Saúl hadn't known her for very long and had left without happening to see her dark side, although that's assuming she even had a good side. The only thing I knew for sure was that this love-struck man had been yet another victim of the cold and heartless Yolanda. I snatched up the second letter from 2002 in excitement, and continued my exploration into the heart of this total stranger.

> Olympic National Park
> 28 April 2002
>
> Hello, my darling,
> I know you asked me to be patient, and warned me that I wouldn't hear from you until everything was sorted out and I was no longer a suspect, but this uncertainty is tearing me apart. I don't even know that you're getting my letters. If you're reading this, please answer me – there must be some way to get in touch and put me out of my misery. At times I've even been tempted to call you, but I promise I won't do that. I can hardly stand it.
>
> You can imagine how eternal the days are for me here. I'm living all but isolated from the world, and I don't care. I don't need anything except you. I was lucky Dylan offered to help me. Even though we've known each other since my childhood in Seattle, and we've stayed in touch by phone, we hadn't seen each other for the longest time. He's a great guy, you know. As well as giving me a cabin to live in, he's brought me everything I need so I can start painting and fill all these long

and lonely hours. I wish I could . . . No, I can't – I can't focus on that. Every day when I sit down in front of that blank canvas I freeze up. I think all my inspiration stayed over there where you are. Dylan also said it would be good for me to work, and he's offered to get me a job renting out canoes down by the dock. I just don't know how to motivate myself, when sometimes all I want is to die.

I see your eyes everywhere. I wake constantly in the night thinking I'm holding you in my arms, just to be plunged straight back into despair when I realise how far away you are. I know I have to pull myself together and start making money so I can survive, but I just don't have the strength, my love. I can't find it without you. Maybe if I just heard something from you . . . I need to know that you're all right so I can keep going and not lose hope. I pray every day that things get resolved so I can come back to you. You see, I'm appealing to the only one who can fix this for us, praying to Him like I used to when I was a boy. Before this, I don't think I'd prayed since the day of my first communion.

I pass the time by looking out over Lake Crescent, and all the while my mind races, trying to find an explanation for everything that happened after your husband disappeared – but I always come to a dead end. Who killed him and why did I get framed? It's completely mad.

I wonder how long it will be before I get a call from you, telling me that everything is finally over and I can come back – if, that is, I can get back to Spain at all on my fake passport. By the way,

> this may be a bad idea but I have to take the risk and give you my new phone number. I've noted it down for you at the bottom of this letter. I'll keep it plugged in while I'm sleeping, in case it rings.
>
> Darling, give me a sign to help me find the strength to keep going. I need to know what's happening over there in Spain and how the trial is progressing. I hope none of this brings you down yourself.
>
> Yours as always,
> Saúl

The world seemed terribly unfair to me just then. I was deeply envious of the passion that Saúl felt for my sister, a love that I'd dreamt of my whole life and had thought was impossible in reality. She didn't deserve it, wasn't sensitive enough to appreciate it.

I stayed out there in the garden for a long time, watching the breeze rippling the leaves of the willow tree, the letter on my chest, trying in vain to understand everything I'd found out since returning to this house with its dark and sinister secrets. I kept coming back to where I'd started: I hadn't returned only in order to receive my mother's inheritance. I was also here to untangle the tissue of lies surrounding Alberta and her elder daughter and, perhaps, to give this last victim back his freedom – all assuming that there'd been no more victims to follow. It wouldn't be easy and there was a lot left to untangle, but I was ready to tackle it. This time I wouldn't be taking the simple way out, if only to help this poor man who'd been waiting twelve years for an answer. For my mission to stand any chance of success, the first thing I'd need to do was hire the best detective in the country, even if I had to use up my entire inheritance along the way.

◆ ◆ ◆

After a light meal, I started work on finding a detective. I needed help with unravelling the mysteries around all the disappearances – Fabián, Bodo . . . and maybe I could even help Saúl, the man by the lake. I spent the whole afternoon researching online, hours going through page after page, forum after forum, and making calls. Something finally became crystal clear: the best detectives, according to the 'experts', had little or no web presence, or at least used third parties on their websites to filter potential clients. I don't know how many calls I made before I finally got somewhere. On the other end of the line I was apparently dealing with the secretary of a detective agency, a type of agency responsible for sorting calls and putting clients in touch with the best detective for each case.

'Associated Hispanic Investigators Agency. What can I do for you?' said the woman, very energetic and business-like, a touch aggressive.

'Hi, my name's Berta de Castro and I'd like to hire a detective,' I answered, not quite sure what to say.

'All right. Tell me a little about what you want to be investigated.'

'I'm sorry, but . . . shouldn't I give that information straight to the detective?' It didn't seem right. I didn't fancy telling my most intimate secrets to the secretary.

'I understand your misgivings, but I need to know so I can assess whether we have a private investigator in our agency suitable to handle your case. You don't need to tell me much; just the big picture will do.'

I didn't have much choice, and after hours of research was too tired to care whether this was right or not, so I gave in and told her. 'I need information about two disappearances: one thirty-five years ago and the other twenty-three years later. It's possible that they were both murdered—'

'OK,' she said, interrupting. She didn't seem at all burning with curiosity or even surprised at my words, which I found reassuring. 'I'll pass this along to my colleagues and you'll get a call back within twenty-four hours. Is this a good number on which to reach you?'

'Yes, yes, this number is fine. Is that all?'

'Yes. For the time being you'll just have to sit tight and wait. It's been a pleasure.'

'Thank you. Goodbye.'

After hanging up, I had a sinking feeling that I'd made a huge mistake. I didn't trust this girl on the phone who, after I'd told her something so important, had simply said, 'You'll get a call back within twenty-four hours.' I supposed to some extent it made sense that a detective agency would be extremely cautious, but I still felt dreadfully uneasy.

It wasn't quite eight o'clock yet so I decided to read a few more of Saúl's letters, and went back out to rest under the old willow tree. There was more than an hour of daylight left and the basket still lay there, waiting for me.

Olympic National Park
5 May 2002

My dear Yolanda,
It's raining like mad here in Olympic Park – you can hardly tell where the surface of the lake ends and the sky begins. Looking out through my window, there's a glorious landscape that only serves to emphasise my melancholy and how badly I'm yearning for you. I spend hours staring at this huge, dense, silvery curtain of grey, enchanted by the droplets that seem to rise from the water and

float up towards the mountains. It's like watching the flickering dancing of flames. It's easy to imagine all kinds of mythical creatures emerging at any moment – I can almost see the elves scampering and the fluttering of playful fairies. But only almost, because the vision of your face fills everything. I see it over the lake, in the rain, on the peaks of the tree-covered mountains . . . I live for my obsession with seeing you again, with ending this nightmare so we can finally realise our dream of being together, loving each other for all eternity. On days like this, when I'm forced to spend hours shut up indoors, I miss you even more.

I've started working down at the dock. Friday was my first day. The truth is that Dylan pays me very well for doing very little: in the three days I've been there I've only rented out four canoes, for an hour each. My cabin's right near the dock and next to the restaurant, so the customers just ask the waiters about the canoes and they call me – I'm practically working from home. Dylan has been such a huge support for me in my darkest moments. When he closes the restaurant for the day, he comes over to visit me, and we talk for a while. I don't know how he puts up with me . . . He says I should tell my mother that I'm back in Washington State, but no, I'm still not ready to tell her everything that's happened – that's assuming the police haven't already been in contact and told her their version. Poor thing . . . I'm sure she's worried because I'm not answering her calls and, if she already knows they're looking for me, I don't even want to think about what she must be going through. I'll go and see her soon, but for now the only thing I want is to be alone and have the time and space to think about you. I hope I don't go mad. I don't know how long I can last in this state.

Yolanda, write to me. Help me endure this dreadful punishment. Send me a sign that my words are reaching you.

With all my love,
Saúl

Until this third letter, I hadn't found an answer to any of my questions. It was as though Saúl cared about losing his beloved Yolanda above all else, even the grave accusation that had forced him to escape to the US. It frightened me to see how much he loved her, and to see how capricious and blind passion could be. She didn't deserve his love, especially not to this extreme.

I read one more letter before dinner. A photo fell on to my lap as I took it out of the envelope. It showed a young man sitting on a pier with his back to the camera, facing an enormous lake surrounded by lush forest. A note on the back read: 'Thinking of you always, darling.'

I liked the way he expressed his feelings, but was even more fascinated to see this figure in front of the lake. I couldn't see his face, only his body language, his posture in front of the vast landscape, as though he were one with his environment, his long hair blowing in the wind, his arms outstretched and leaning on the pier, infinite . . . That wonderful picture said so much about this man . . .

Olympic National Park
14 May 2002

My love,
How are you, my darling? Nothing has changed with me. It's as though my soul had stayed behind in your arms, forever in your arms, while my empty carcass wanders endlessly, aimlessly, on the interminable shore of this lake.

It's only about a month since we parted, and I still haven't heard from you, haven't heard how things are going in Spain, whether you've finally proved my innocence, found a way to free me . . . This whole situation is driving me mad – how could they not see that the evidence was all wrong? I'm so utterly miserable – I'm completely innocent, but apparently the only one paying for Bodo's disappearance. Today this waiting seems harder on me than ever. I can't stand it. There has to be some way for you to communicate with me.

Sometimes I think you're not getting my letters at all. This endless uncertainty is slow torture. But I've found a solution: Dylan has a friend in Boston who's agreed to create an email account you can write to without any direct link between the two of us. You just have to create a new account too, not using your real information, from an internet cafe, and then write to me through Dylan's friend. We can't talk using Dylan's laptop – who knows if the police will come here one day to interview him and search his computer, since we were neighbours as children, after all. There are no internet cafes here in Olympic Park, and no one else I can trust. Apparently it would be hard for the police to track your emails if we follow this route. If he hears from you, the friend in Boston will call Dylan. The email address is eagles5111115@hotmail.com. Please write to me, Yolanda – I desperately need to hear from you. It's been so long . . . and the more time passes, the more likely it becomes that you're not getting my letters. This is unbearable torment.

Last night I dreamt of the last time we made love. It was so vivid . . . I wouldn't have cared if I'd died right then between your breasts – that death would have been far better than waking up without you by my side. Do you remember it? It was on the morning of the day your husband disappeared. Who could have predicted, in the midst of so much joy, what was about to happen? While I think about it . . . a few days ago I found the ticket stubs for the movies I went to see that night – right when, according to the police's version, I was in the middle of killing your husband. How ironic is that? I didn't even bother looking for them at the time – I thought I'd thrown them away when I left the cinema, but it turns out they were there in my coat pocket the whole time. They came all the way with me to this lake as a reminder of that fateful day; here they are, right in front of me on the table . . . I guess it doesn't matter now – I'm on the run, and now I really have committed a serious offence and it would be crazy to go back. I shouldn't have left. I don't know why I listened to you, but you were just so scared, thinking they'd lock me up . . . You have no idea how much I regret that decision. Well, what does it matter in any case – I'm trapped in the worst of all prisons: my own mind.

Yolanda, forgive my insistence, darling, but if you are reading my letters, please write to me and give me hope.

I'm sending you a photo Dylan took of me a few days ago, so when you look at it you remember where I am and that I'm always thinking of you.

You are in my heart and thoughts every single moment of the day.

Saúl

I was deeply moved by the despair of this man from Washington State. What if I answered him? Why shouldn't I? Of course, a lot of time had passed since he'd written the letters I'd just read, but I knew he must be waiting for an answer or he wouldn't still be trying to reach Yolanda. After all, his most recent letters had arrived only a few weeks ago. Even if the response came from someone else and not from his beloved, I thought it would still be welcome news to him that someone had finally replied to his letters. I'd have to choose my words carefully. I didn't want him to know in my first letter that I was Yolanda's sister, because above all else I had no answers to the many questions I was sure he'd come up with. I could have called the phone number he'd sent, but, no, it would have been a lot harder for me to hide my identity that way.

17 June 2014

Hi Saúl,

I'm the new owner of the house that used to belong to Doña Alberta de Castro. This morning, I was having a look in the attic and found all the letters you sent to this address over the past twelve years. If it weren't for your last letter having been sent just a few weeks ago, I probably wouldn't have dared write back to you. I just wanted to let you know that I found them – almost all still sealed – and took the liberty of being the first person to open them. I read your second letter, the one you wrote on 28 April 2002, and couldn't resist contacting you to say that I mean to keep on reading them. I hope you'll be able to forgive me and that you won't think poorly of me. And please don't worry – I'll keep this to myself.

I hope also that it doesn't come as too much of a shock to learn that the first person to read your love letters is a stranger. Maybe you would have preferred not knowing, still thinking that Yolanda had received them. I'm so sorry, but I thought it was about time you had an answer, although I would much rather it was coming from her.

Lastly, I must tell you that with only four letters, you've shown me a side of the world I never knew existed – knowing that someone is capable of true love such as yours . . . It has been a complete revelation to me and has given me reason to hope. For that alone, I can assure you that it was worth your writing them, and I hope you don't stop. Thank you so much.

I sincerely hope that your pain passes quickly and you soon find the love you deserve. Maybe you already have.

Yours,

BC

I decided to use only my initials, guessing they wouldn't mean anything to him. I would sign it the same way on the return address – the address itself wouldn't be a problem, because I'd told him I was the new owner of the house where he'd sent all his letters. I'd send him my own address in London just as soon as I left.

I couldn't resist and went to my laptop to write an email with the same words I'd just written out by hand, advising the recipient that the email was meant for Saúl, the man living in Olympic Park. The internet was much faster, but I would still send the letter as well, in case the email account no longer existed or the friend in Boston was no longer bothering to check the inbox after such a long period with nothing coming in. I hesitated a moment before finally hitting the send button.

It was all too clear to me that Saúl was just another victim of the wicked Yolanda, one more name on her long list. This time my sister had really gone too far. She never could have guessed that Saúl's letters would fall into my hands so many years later, now that I was no longer the fearful, timid girl she used to threaten and scare. No, I wouldn't leave now until I'd won. It was plain to see from this last letter that Saúl had an alibi he hadn't been able to prove at the time: he'd been watching a double feature at the cinema at exactly the same time as he was supposed to have been murdering Bodo. And as he said, he'd gone to the US at my sister's insistence . . . Everything seemed so planned out, so Machiavellian and contemptible that it was hard to credit.

I sat reflecting on all of this for over an hour – it seemed to be turning into a habit. I realised I didn't actually know anything much at all about Bodo's disappearance, didn't have the least idea of the facts and didn't know where to start.

The photo showed a despondent young man, staring out at the immensity of nature, burdened with the anguish of endless waiting. Although sitting with his back turned to the camera, he was clearly tall and slim, with long hair below his shoulders; the snapshot had captured the ripples where it was ruffled gently by the breeze. I thought it was a sensational image.

Suddenly my heart lurched. I really liked this guy – his personality was starting to charm me and I felt an uncontrollable desire to save him from his undeserved troubles. The feeling was both strange and pleasant at the same time, albeit fleeting – the result, I'm sure, of my enforced isolation and period of loneliness. Besides, years had gone by since he'd written those letters . . . I didn't know if he'd be happy at this point in time to be rescued from the 'worst of all prisons: my own mind.'

I looked down at the basket and realised that unless I read his most recent letters, I wouldn't know if he'd finally overcome his pain and whether time had given him the chance to regain control of his life in that beautiful setting, or somewhere else, without Yolanda. He'd kept writing until a few weeks ago, however, which told me at least that his love hadn't been forgotten.

While I was mulling this over, my mobile rang.

'Hello?'

'Berta de Castro?' asked an unusually deep, hoarse male voice, with a slightly foreign accent.

'Yes, that's me. Who is this?'

'My name is Alfonso Salamanca, a private investigator with the Investigators Agency.'

'Oh! I'm so glad you called.'

The timing couldn't have been better.

'Thank you. I have a few hours free after one o'clock tomorrow afternoon. Would you like to meet for lunch to go over your case? In theory, I'm very interested in taking it . . .'

'That would be great. Where would you like to meet? Nowhere too difficult to get to – I don't know Madrid that well,' I said, to break the ice.

'Fair enough. How about the terrace of the El Espejo restaurant? It's on the Paseo de Recoletos – you can't miss it.'

'I'll be there.'

'Good. Don't bother looking for me – I'll find you.'

'All right. Well, see you tomorrow at one o'clock then.'

'One more thing: whatever happens, do not try to contact me. I'll call you if necessary.'

'OK, I understand.'

'See you tomorrow.' And he hung up.

It was a disturbing call. This Alfonso Salamanca seemed very mysterious – but then what else should I expect from a private detective? I was a bit wary meeting this unknown person, a man who almost certainly led a double life, but the important thing was that my plans were underway. We just needed to come to some agreement, and of course make sure he was well prepared for the delicate task that lay ahead.

It was almost completely dark out in the garden when I decided to go in and call it a day. My head spinning, I felt absolutely drained after sleeping so poorly the night before. I cooked an omelette for dinner, and sliced an apple for dessert. Finally in bed with Aris and Neca, I fell asleep almost instantly.

Chapter 8

Wednesday, 18 June 2014

Teresa had already gone for the day; the kitchen was tidy and the dirty clothes I'd worn since my arrival in Madrid were hung up in the laundry room. I had a feeling that for some reason she hadn't wanted to see me this morning. When I went out into the garden I found the photo and the letters I'd read the day before back in the basket, which she'd put on the table so it wouldn't get wet while she was watering. Teresa must have been as surprised to see them as I had been. Had she maybe even taken a peek at the letters that were already open? All these years later I was seeing a very different side to Teresa, which I'd never noticed over the nineteen years when I'd seen her every day. I don't know why exactly, but more and more I was noticing the similarities between her and the housekeepers who play such a prominent part in films about murder, mystery and suspense. The very idea of her having some connection with the shady activities of my mother and sister made my hair stand on end. On the other hand, it wasn't that far-fetched that the faithful servant knew much more than she let on – she'd spent her life under Alberta's command and had even lived with us for a time. And yet she always seemed so unaware of all the family conflicts . . .

If she wasn't, she was doing a terrific job at seeming to hold herself apart from any of her mistress's personal affairs.

I brought the basket of letters inside and had breakfast with Aris – coffee and little muffins for me, milk with no sugar or coffee for him, though he didn't turn down a small piece of muffin. Then I took a shower, got dressed, threw the letter I'd written in my bag and set off for my intriguing appointment.

◆ ◆ ◆

By half past twelve I'd left my car in the public car park on the Paseo de Recoletos, and five minutes later was seated on the terrace of El Espejo with a glass of beer in front of me.

The morning was fresh and warm. A few of the tables around me were occupied, mostly by well-dressed men and women who looked as though they'd just dropped by from work to snatch a quick bite. Two older ladies sat surrounded by shopping bags at a nearby table, shamelessly criticising their daughters-in-law, discussing intently how they weren't remotely worthy of their darling sons. I checked my watch constantly, every fifteen seconds at the most. Two minutes before one, I was startled to hear a familiar voice behind me.

'Berta de Castro?'

'Yes, that's me. You must be Alfonso Salamanca.'

'The very same. If I may?' he said, before taking the seat across from me and extending his hand.

The waiter came over at once, and my companion asked for a beer and the menu to find something to nibble on.

In all honesty, my initial reaction was one of disappointment. He must have been nearly fifty, around middle height for a man, and pretty overweight. His appearance was generally sloppy, with grubby jeans, a badly wrinkled checked shirt, and shoes that appeared never to have had the benefit of a good brush and polish. Though his hair was clean and shiny, he needed a good cut and seriously taking in hand. Thankfully, the shrewdness of his gaze and the clean smell of his expensive soap were a little more reassuring. In return, however, I noticed that he was pleasantly surprised at my own appearance. We women can sense these things.

He ordered a few tapas for us to share and launched straight into the conversation. 'OK, first of all you should know that my fee is five hundred euros a day for exclusive attention. That's how I work – it's a mistake to mix cases. As I said on the phone, I have two hours free for this meeting today. They're on the house, but after three o'clock you're paying.'

I was stunned. That was a lot of money. If this man, a total stranger, dragged the investigation out, he could deprive me of all my inheritance, my savings and even my restaurant.

'Did you say five hundred euros a day?' I asked, as though I hadn't heard him properly.

'That's right. And that's in addition to all the additional expenses resulting from the investigation, such as third-party services, travel, fees for documents, bribes . . . Naturally, I won't be able to give you a receipt for some of this. You need to understand that in my profession there are jobs I can't bill you for and you'll just have to trust me. You should also be aware that if I wanted to cheat you, it wouldn't be too hard for me to forge the receipts.'

I listened to him as he talked, more and more taken aback at it all, even speechless.

'Moreover, you should know that I am completely anonymous and independent in my work. I'm not on the National Business Register or recognised by the Home Office, so if this investigation ends in a trial, I couldn't stand as a witness, and some of the evidence I uncover might possibly not be admissible in court. I don't know if you understand . . .'

'More or less . . .' I answered, although in that moment I could make neither head nor tail of anything that might happen in the future.

'Well, that said, if you still want me to work for you, we can get straight down to business.'

'The truth is that I don't really know what to say . . . If the investigation goes on too long, I don't know if I could still pay you. It's not easy getting hold of that kind of money from the bank.'

'I can tell you from experience that if a detective can't get the information he's looking for in two to three weeks at the most, he'll probably never find it. Anyway, you're at liberty to call a halt to my services any time you want.'

'Well, in that case . . .'

'I forgot one very important detail: I work on a cash basis only, so every time we meet you'll have to pay me for the days I've worked up to that time. It's your choice.'

'But . . . I really don't know you at all. It's hard to make a decision like this so . . . so quickly . . .'

'Señorita de Castro, the information you need has nothing to do with me. In fact, I doubt that any detective with good judgement would let his client know more than the essentials about him. Let's meet again in two to three days' time so you can see whether you feel my services are worthwhile before you've committed too much money.'

I was surprised that he called me 'Señorita' so confidently, and so obviously took it for granted that I was single. 'Well, you've convinced me,' I said finally, staring him straight in the eye, trying to find in him all the confidence I needed. 'So . . . you have a deal, Señor Salamanca.'

'Great. I'm all ears – tell me your story and what you need me to find out. Tell me everything you remember, as clearly as possible.'

'I really don't know where to start.'

'How about at the beginning?'

'Well . . . all right. I came back to Madrid a week ago after living in London for fifteen years. My mother died on the ninth of this month – Monday of last week.'

'I'm so sorry for your loss,' he said politely.

'Thank you. The fact is, my mother's solicitor only needed me to be here to deal with her estate . . . The whole time I've been away, I haven't spoken with her once, nor with my only sister. I was nineteen when I left . . .'

'Go on. Why did you leave? Would you like another beer?'

'No thanks, I'd rather have a coffee.'

'Excuse me.' He called over the waiter, who was keeping an eye on the terrace from behind the restaurant door. 'Would you bring us another plate of salad, a small portion of omelette, a beer and a coffee? Go on, please.' He gestured, urging me to continue.

I was suddenly struck by the way he pronounced his Rs, almost with a German accent, that was somehow familiar to me.

'Do you have time? This could take all afternoon,' I asked him, remembering that we only had two hours; we'd already been out on the terrace for half of that.

'I'm completely at your disposal. I need to earn my first wages: two hundred and fifty euros for the half-day.'

For a moment I'd forgotten how expensive it would be to work with him, but swallowed hard and went on.

When I'd finally finished telling him my story, enough time had passed for the inquisitive detective to have four more beers and smoke half a pack of Chesterfields, while I had two cups of herbal tea after the coffee. Every now and then he interrupted to ask me a question or take notes in his little book.

'I think that's all of it,' I concluded. 'So what do you think about my crazy tale? I can imagine it seems far too bizarre to be true.'

'At this point in my life and after so many years in the business, I've seen and heard it all – more than most people could ever imagine. The only thing you haven't told me is why you want to look into all this now, after so many years.'

'When I came back to Spain to deal with my mother's estate . . .' I stopped short, wanting to be completely honest, especially with myself. 'Well, when I came back I was sure that the time and distance had wiped away all the pain of my past. I thought I'd been reborn – but the truth is that the fifteen years away were no more than a long intermission. I can't go on without knowing the full truth, not this time. And besides, the letters from that poor, love-struck man . . . I feel like I'm the only one who can free him from his torment. I'm sorry, maybe I'm explaining too much . . .' I apologised, realising that my confession was too personal to share with someone I'd only just met.

'Don't worry: on the contrary, all the information you can give will be useful. But just remember this – you've only read a few letters and still have several years left to get through. It's possible that after so much time, this person no longer wants to come back to Spain at all. In any case, he's a fugitive from justice and won't get off easy for that crime.'

'I can imagine . . . but his last letter was dated only a few weeks ago – that doesn't seem like he's forgotten what he left behind.'

'Berta, I . . . can I call you Berta?'

'Of course.'

'I need to see those letters as soon as possible,' he said, scratching his head with the cigarette between his fingers, making me nervous that his thick hair would catch on fire.

'I'll bring them next time we meet. But this guy left without knowing anything of what really happened – they're the letters of a heartbroken man who knew less of what was going on than anyone else involved.'

'I might be able to extract information that even he didn't see was important. It would be interesting, for example, to find out who helped him escape. If he was really under that much suspicion from the police, he wouldn't have been allowed to leave the country, so I imagine someone had to furnish him with a fake passport. In fact, he probably wouldn't have been able to leave the police station on his own, considering he was a primary suspect. Whoever helped him would have known he'd be recognised and they acted very fast – probably already had the documents ready as he left Spain the same day. He may have written something about this in his letters; it would be a good place to start if we want to get to the bottom of all this. If he really is innocent of everything and so naive, who helped him get out of the country?'

'I hadn't thought of that. It does seem like he must have been helped by someone who didn't want a trial to take place.'

'And you? Who do you suspect?' he asked me, obviously realising that in my mind Yolanda was behind everything.

'My sister.'

'I see. I think that's enough for today. I'll call you as soon as I have anything of interest. In the meantime, be discreet – don't tell anyone about this, not even your mother's housekeeper, OK?'

'OK. I'll wait for your call.'

We shook hands amicably and said goodbye. I think we got on well right from the start. Although I felt a little foolish for entrusting all my family secrets to a complete stranger, my instincts told me that despite his appearance he was an honourable man.

◆ ◆ ◆

I went to the grocer's next. My stay in Madrid was going to be longer than anticipated, and I needed to stock up the fridge and larder accordingly. I ended up buying completely random things, because my mind was absorbed in other matters. I couldn't stop thinking about the conversation I'd had with the detective. I went back and forth between feeling brave for finally telling someone all the things that my family had covered up for so long, and feeling completely stupid. In London I was a successful businesswoman with a comfortable life – why didn't I just forget all this and go home? But amid the jumble of my thoughts and doubts, something like a thrill ran through me: I wanted to go home and read more of Saúl's letters. He was winning my heart through his words, beyond the time and space that lay between us, or maybe it was just an avid need to know more, like when you're stuck into a really good novel and want to race on to the next chapter. I couldn't be entirely sure.

Back at home, I made a sandwich under Aris's watchful gaze, lucky to be able to count on his gentle, peaceful company in this house of mystery and intrigue, which was feeling so increasingly hostile. I ate my sandwich in two bites, impatient to get back to Saúl's letters. The basket was still in the kitchen where I had left it this morning, after finding them in the garden where Teresa had saved them from getting wet.

With a sudden jolt, I realised how easily my mother's employee came and went through what was now my house. Perhaps I'd underestimated her. Alfonso's advice made me think that possibly I trusted Teresa too much. After all, she'd been loyal to her mistress her whole life long, rather than to me – she cared for my sister and me as if we were her own daughters, but for some reason she worshipped my mother. Knowing how much I hated Alberta, must she not then see me as an enemy?

I decided to read in bed, so, after taking a cool shower, I grabbed the bundle of letters that remained for 2002, and went to my room with Aris and Neca.

> Olympic National Park
> 25 May 2002
>
> My love,
> How are you? I'm getting through as best I can. I try to distract myself, take long walks when there's time, play a little poker now and then with Dylan and his friends, and that's about it. Between this and my work at the dock, my days are passing and I endure your absence.
>
> There's still no word from you... Dylan says you haven't written to the email address I sent you. I simply don't know what to think, but I have a bad feeling that you're not getting my letters. Maybe your mother's keeping them from you, and I can't say I blame her. I can imagine how much she must hate me, considering all I stand accused of... I can't bear to think that you don't even know I'm writing – maybe you even think I've forgotten you? Never – you hear me? Never!
>
> I've finally started painting again. After facing that defiant blank canvas a hundred times, finally I picked up my brush and managed my first stroke of paint on the surface yesterday. For now, I've set myself the straightforward project of simply trying to capture what I see through my window, though I can hardly do justice to such

beauty. You cannot imagine how incredible the lake looks in springtime. I admit I find it hard to concentrate. I see you everywhere: emerging from the water like that afternoon we spent by the sea in Marbella, atop the mountains even, in the eternal grey skies . . . and you're the one and only thing that inspires me.

I've been obsessed with the idea of coming back. My life has no meaning without you. But Dylan is convincing, saying I wouldn't even get past the first security checkpoint at the airport with the fake passport I brought over from Spain, and reminding me that by now half the world is out looking for me. I remember all too well how abrupt it was, how your lawyer dragged me out of the police station after the line-up and less than three hours later we were saying our farewells at the airport . . . It was as though you'd known all along I would be identified by those witnesses, and everything was set up all ready for my flight . . . There has to be some way back.

This has all been so unfair and ridiculous . . . We were about to tell the whole world we were in love, were planning your divorce and a life together without having to hide from anyone, and right at that moment your husband disappeared. No matter how often I mull it over, I still can't understand how the police found evidence pointing to my having killed him. Sometimes I think it could all have been a warped plot on your husband's part, but . . . I don't know. Maybe he found out about us and took it as an opportunity to plan his own disappearance? I think I remember you telling me he had some legal issues with his business. Yolanda, think about it – it would have been a perfect move on his side, and I was an easy target. But maybe I just have too much time on my hands and too much time to think, and I'm starting to talk nonsense.

Write to me, Yolanda, for God's sake. Just end this uncertainty that's becoming the torture of my days and nights.

With all my love,
Saúl

It was a very revealing letter, full of love and despair like the others, but with two interesting facts: on the one hand, I was saddened to learn that Saúl couldn't return with the fake passport that had brought him to Washington State, which confirmed what the detective had guessed earlier that day. On the other, the notion that Bodo might fake his own death to escape the law was not that farfetched, though I really doubted Yolanda would have been in on something like that. Plus, knowing that she'd been the one who'd urged Saúl to leave and the one who'd made all the arrangements, she must have had a powerful reason.

No, this innocent and loving man couldn't hurt a fly. It was becoming more and more clear to me that he was the innocent victim of my sister's dark magic, and, who knows, maybe that of my own father. I shuddered – all this was lurid in its madness.

I read two more letters before switching off the light, both of them messages of despair, appeals for help. They were the cries of a lover torn apart by his grief.

I had never thought that this kind of passion could exist beyond fairy tales and the ramblings of mad poets. I was so sure that no one could ever reach such heights that I hadn't even bothered wishing for that kind of romance for myself. But knowing now of its existence, I realised that I'd forgotten that humans are a duality, that man does not live for bread alone and that falling in love can be far more intense than any material achievement. Perhaps I'd never experienced it precisely because I'd never believed in it. But what about Yolanda? Did she herself deserve that privilege? I understood now that loving someone without a soul was like playing music to a cockroach, and was convinced that my sister had never appreciated how from millions of other people she had been singled out to experience a love beyond all compare. The irony of fate and its capriciousness seemed overwhelming.

I picked up the photo from the lakeside and gazed at it until I fell asleep. I dreamt of him, of course; probably because he was the only masculine presence I had close to me right now, and I was still a young woman with unmet needs of my own.

Chapter 9

Thursday, 19 June 2014

A loud noise from the kitchen woke me. I tried to go back to sleep but the sun was streaming in through the window. Aris stirred restlessly at my feet, his movements threatening to crumple the letters that I'd read and left open on the bed the night before.

While getting washed and dressed in the bathroom, I felt slightly uneasy for the first time since my arrival, knowing that Teresa was roaming freely through the house. This morning I was not glad to know that I wasn't alone. The housekeeper who for nineteen years had seemed the epitome of tenderness and devotion suddenly cast shadows that disturbed me with how little I really knew of her – what she was thinking, what she did when she wasn't in the house, anything about her own life and home . . . but I was starting to suspect that she knew absolutely everything about the three of us, even more than I knew myself. I tried to shake off these dark thoughts and compose myself so I could greet her without acting suspiciously. I found her sweeping leaves on the terrace.

'Good morning, Teresa. What a beautiful, peaceful day. You're so lucky you get to enjoy this climate all year round.'

'Hello, darling. Did I wake you? I'm so sorry – I dropped a glass on the floor . . .'

'It's fine – I'm glad to be up a little earlier than over the last few days. Besides, I slept really well and it's worth it to see this lovely morning.'

'I'll have some breakfast ready for you in a minute,' she said, setting down the broom and getting ready to go in the house.

'You don't need to, Teresa, I can do it.'

'But I'd be so happy to—'

'Teresa, I can do it myself, OK?' I interrupted, more sharply this time.

She picked up the broom again to hide her unhappiness at my response.

I was sitting down in front of a bowl of cereal and a cup of coffee when she came into the kitchen to empty the dustpan.

'Put that down, Teresa. Sit and have a cup of coffee with me.'

'Sweetheart, I have so much work to do. I have the ironing waiting for me over at Carmen's house later on . . .'

'If you have all this work, I really don't know why you insist on coming here. There's no need – I don't have much for you to do while I'm here.'

'It's for the garden, really. I want to care for it until you sell the house. It won't make a good impression if it's—'

'Come on, it's still early,' I said, fetching her a coffee cup. Facing the worktop, with my back to her, I ventured a question, trying to find out a little more about her life. 'Do you live alone, Teresa?'

'Mostly. The son of my cousin lives with me, technically speaking. He's been paying me for years to rent a room, but he's out every day and when he comes home at night I'm usually asleep already. It's like living on my own. He doesn't give me any trouble or offer any company either. If it wasn't that I do his laundry . . .'

'Really? I had no idea,' I said in surprise, turning back to the table.

'He came to town as a student long after you'd left, so how could you have known? Anyway, he never completed his studies but he opened a car body repair shop with money that his parents left him. He's thirty-two years old and should really have moved out ages ago. I don't insist though. It helps, actually, to have the three hundred euros he pays for the room to cover my bills. He's a very solitary fellow.'

She broke off to take a sip of coffee. I was listening attentively, trying to catch any hidden meaning behind her words.

'He doesn't have a girlfriend? That's rare for a man of his age.'

'I think he was seeing a girl, but nothing serious. In all honesty, it's nice to have a man in the house at night, the way things are these days.'

'I can understand that. Teresa . . .'

'Yes, my dear?'

'Why did you leave to go and live on your own?'

'Well, you girls were getting older and you each needed your own room. When I lived here I slept in your room. Your mother didn't like it' – her gaze darkened with the memory – 'but it was just what I had to do. Anyway, I was always here at daybreak to wake you and I didn't leave until after you went to bed, if you remember. You two have always been my life. I clean and iron for three households, but . . . I don't know what I'll do with myself when you sell this house – I'm going to feel so lost . . .'

'Then it'll be your turn to rest, Teresa. It's high time for you to take more care of yourself.'

'Are you going to stay here much longer?' she asked, clearly wanting to know.

I had a feeling her interest in my answer lay far beyond her own feelings of loss at not being able to return to the house every day.

'I don't know yet. It depends on how long this whole process is going to take with winding up the estate. I'll most likely leave when everything's settled and the property's up for sale – in addition to taking care of certain other matters I didn't expect to find,' I added vaguely, although she knew instantly what I meant by 'certain other matters'. 'I guess I'll have to come back one more time to sign the papers, but it's possible I may not even have to stay the night in Madrid then.'

'The house in Marbella has been up for sale for years – I'm not sure if you knew. It's handled by an agency that takes care of the cleaning and gardening.'

'No, actually, I didn't know that.'

'I thought maybe the solicitor had told you. I'm sure he will the next time you see him. I don't even want to think what it would be like over there . . . After what happened to Bodo . . . He and your sister lived there almost all year round. In the end, your mother didn't like to go back there, as you can imagine. You know how she couldn't stand gossip. So, when your sister left, she decided to sell it, but in the current recession . . .'

Considering her usual discretion, she was mighty talkative this morning, so I took advantage of the moment, taking mental notes of everything she said. 'You know, I don't understand how they could have blamed the gardener for Bodo's murder if they never found the body. What grounds did the police have to accuse him?'

'I don't know much about that. When she was on her own again, your sister moved back in with your mother for a few months, but they never talked about it. All I know is that witnesses said they saw the lad taking the body out from the house in Marbella that night . . . And someone else claimed to have seen him down at the marina on Bodo's personal yacht. Everything pointed to him. Besides, if he were innocent, why would he go on the run like he did? But what do I know, darling? I only heard bits and pieces, and—'

'Maybe he just felt trapped – that must have been a really difficult situation for a young guy like him to handle.'

'I don't know about that . . .' she said in response, but I could tell she knew more than she was saying. Lying did not come naturally to Teresa, whatever my wider suspicions. 'If all the evidence the police collected pointed to him doing it . . . There had to be something to it, didn't there? You shouldn't pay so much attention to those letters.'

'What do you know about those letters? What do you mean?'

'Nothing, love, nothing. You know I've always been the one to take care of the post, that's all.'

'I know. In fact, you were always the one doing everything – all my mother did was watch television, read her magazines and go out with her friends. What kind of empty life was that,' I blurted out, unable to hold back my bitterness.

'That boy never stopped writing since he left; you probably saw from the dates on the letters. When your mother opened the first one and realised it was from him, she didn't bother opening the rest. It was only natural, considering what he'd done,' she explained, as if trying to downplay the importance of what was, to me, a crucial matter.

She seemed very nervous and kept fidgeting with the knot of her scarf.

'There's just something fishy about this whole business . . .' I shut my mouth abruptly, realising I was on the verge of voicing my suspicions to absolutely the worst person – someone who had blamed Saúl because she could never allow the implication that Alberta or Yolanda might have had something to do with this filthy affair. I could have told her that this was all nonsense, that it was absurd that my mother, if she'd known Saúl's whereabouts and truly believed he was guilty, would not then have informed the police. On the other hand, why wouldn't she have passed on the letters to Yolanda? I felt compassion for Teresa, recognising that her innocence and lack of awareness were leading her inadvertently to indicate the probable guilt of the women she was trying to protect. She stared at me now, increasingly anxious, waiting for me to finish my sentence.

'So if my mother and Yolanda didn't talk about it, which doesn't at all surprise me, how did you find out what happened?'

'People talk, they find out about things, and I think it also came out in the newspapers.'

'But you don't talk to people or read the newspaper?'

'My cousin's boy was already living with me when it happened . . . He told me about it.' I noticed that she regretted bringing up her relative again. 'I was interviewed too.'

'You too? Surely not . . .'

'Yes, but this all happened so long ago, my love. Why bother digging it all up again?'

'Well, for me it's like it only just happened. I've been completely oblivious of all this over the past however many years.'

'I have to get going. I was planning to make you something for lunch, but—'

'There's no need – Teresa, you really don't have to worry about me. I know how to take care of myself.'

'I know you do, but I don't mind doing it,' she replied, an unhappy look on her face. Then she stood up and started to clear the table.

I looked around but the basket was nowhere in sight. 'Where are the letters?'

'I took them to your room when I went to make your bed, while you were in the shower. I'll get all this cleaned up and then I'll have to go. There's so much ironing to do.'

Downing my second cup of coffee, I watched as she cleared the breakfast dishes away, realising that over the past few days the image I'd always had of our housekeeper as loving and humble had faded away. During the nineteen years I spent with her, I had never once had the slightest suspicion that her sweetness and devotion might be hiding a dark side. She always represented the light for me, the only truth among all the lies. The few happy memories I'd brought to London with me were all in connection with her. Maybe I'd just been deceiving myself because I desperately needed to believe that not everything around me was filthy and awful, and so my mind had protected itself by clinging on to an illusion in order to preserve my sanity. Teresa had always remained my final hope. Now I wondered if she'd just been the best part of a bad situation. Unless my instinct lay way off the mark, the new Teresa would end up as the real surprise of my return, but what if I was wrong? I felt terrible.

◆ ◆ ◆

I spent the whole day reading and thinking, letter after letter. I couldn't put my finger on why, but the more I came to know Saúl, the kindlier I felt towards the whole of humanity. That true love of his, his integrity, his unshakeable commitment to the woman he adored, even though she never answered him – it all seemed unutterably noble.

Over the course of the morning I read through the letters from June, July, August and September of 2002. All of them, one after the other, described an unwavering passion that seemed only to grow with time and absence. I pretended they were addressed to me, that I was his beloved. Right then my emotions were so raw and I was so desperate for love myself that I didn't mind picking at the leftover crumbs of the disastrous love affair he had shared with Yolanda.

It sounded as though the reason that had made him go into exile had now taken a back seat, and that the pain of having lost Yolanda far outweighed the torment of his delicate legal situation. In all of his letters he begged Yolanda over and over somehow to get in contact with him, to give him hope, a reason to go on living. Five months of writing to her, five months with no response, and this lad from Lake Crescent still held on to his fantasy as tightly as he had on the very first day.

After reading each letter I felt the burning desire to write again to the email address in Boston that his friend Dylan had arranged, but then I looked back in the basket and saw there were still eleven years of unknowns, and that his life might be completely different now, not to mention that I still hadn't had a response to my first email. He might be married, have children . . . Maybe he was even happy with his family, who knows, even if he had kept on fanning the flames of his youthful passion through his letters. Maybe he had fallen in love again but kept on writing to Yolanda out of mere habit. He must have grown up and matured. Surely he would be able to fall in love again – he might even love two women at the same time.

I checked my phone again to see if there was an email from Boston. Nothing.

Captivated by his letters, by this love that I had made my own, I even forgot to eat. It was Aris, wandering back and forth between my room and the kitchen, demanding his lunch, who finally broke the spell.

At half past three in the afternoon, before making myself a ham and cheese sandwich to give me strength, I read the first letter from October.

Olympic National Park
7 October 2002

Hello, my love,
As always, the first thing that comes to mind when I start a letter to you is to ask how you are, and why I haven't heard from you yet. You have no idea how my imagination runs wild when I think about that, nor how painful my thoughts are.

It's my birthday today. I'm twenty-one. I remember it not as the day on which I came into the world, but because exactly one year ago today I was reborn: it was the day we met. Do you remember? I do, perfectly, in every detail, as though it had just happened. I was hoping to hear from you today, but the hours have flown by and there's still no word from you.

My mother called me. Dylan gave her my number after much insistence on her part. Even though I asked her to give me time and space, and promised I'd visit when I felt ready and the police had stopped looking for me, she couldn't resist. I wonder if she, with the knowledge of everything that's happened to me, got in touch so I wouldn't feel so alone on a day like this? So what's going on with you? Has something happened that's stopping you? I don't even want to think about that. My mother's really worried about me – she's trying to convince me to turn myself in, sure that by now they must have found the real murderer and that, even if not, the two ticket stubs would clear me of all suspicion. But I made you a solemn promise – I swore I wouldn't come back until you yourself had told me everything was all right. Either way, crossing the Atlantic on a fake passport is in itself a very serious crime in this country. My mother has offered all her savings to hire a good lawyer; she's convinced that proving my innocence would be a lot easier than I think. She's also said it's been months since she stopped getting calls from the inspector in charge of the case. It seems like he's given up trying and no longer believes it's possible that I'm living in the US. Dylan dreams up much less orthodox ways of getting me back to Spain. He says I could go back the way I came, on a false identity, and that if I want he'll look into it for me. They're both worried – they can see I'm not happy.

I spoke with my mother for over an hour. She even bought a new phone to call me on, so no one could trace the call via her normal one. She's dying to know where I am and wants to come and visit me, but I'm afraid they're still watching her and might follow her. What torture it is, living this way, especially for the people who care about me. Because in reality I'm not tormented by my lack of freedom, but by not being able to be with you. I could live hidden away from the world for all eternity as long as I was with you.

I've spent most of today thinking about the morning we met. It was the best birthday gift I could ever have received. I rang your doorbell to offer my services as a gardener and you opened the door. You were wearing that sheer gossamer dress from Ibiza that showed off your golden skin and your long, glossy hair, with the hint of a tiny floral bikini peeking through the white fabric, and a body as beautiful as it was tantalising. I thought I'd died and gone to heaven. 'The garden is all yours,' you said before I'd even finished introducing myself. 'You can start work today.' You walked me through the garden, and my legs were trembling. It was love at first sight, for the first and only time in my life. That same morning we ended up making love in your bed, the bed that you shared with your husband. What madness – what wonderful, glorious madness! And how clumsy I felt, making love to a goddess like you.

I would give the rest of my life to relive that moment just once – I think I've told you that already. Nothing life can offer will ever compare with the six months of love that we shared. Fate has been so hateful and cruel to us . . .

Take care of yourself, my sweet darling, and in so doing you will be taking care of me.

Saúl

While I nibbled my sandwich in the kitchen, the six-month-long relationship between Saúl and my sister was becoming clearer. Yolanda had already decided to get rid of her husband when she opened the door to Saúl, who appeared at exactly the right moment. How had she managed to get him accused as the likely killer? It was something I was more than ready to find out.

Suddenly, a wave of fear washed over me. This house I was living in – this house that was now practically mine – had for forty years and until only a few days ago been the domain of the most evil woman I had ever known. For a few moments I seemed to sense her presence, which began with the scent of her perfume, floating on the air from the kitchen into the hallway and through into the garden. At first the gusts were far apart, slight, barely noticeable, but then they started to become more constant and more intense. Every hair on my body stood on end like never before, while my body shook violently from head to toe. The air started to cool and my temperature dropped to freezing. The thick smell, somewhat sweet and musty, that flooded the kitchen held an unmistakable warning that I had no trouble in understanding: *Stop prying into the past and snooping around in my house. I'm still here and I won't rest until you get out.* I knew she was there, watching me. The air became dense, unbreathable, as though her ghostly presence were infusing the whole space around me.

Sweat broke out as I started to panic, and drained of all energy I tossed my sandwich aside. Aris stared intently at the centre of the room, as if someone was standing there, right in front of him. Yes, the cat was looking at her and I swear I could see the hatred in his eyes. He stood rooted to the ground, defiant, ready to strike, as though he wanted to defend me. My sweat turned icy and I began to shiver.

As soon as I was able to move again I went back to my bedroom, terrified, sure that I'd just had a supernatural encounter like the ones you read about in books. I'd always been so sceptical about anything beyond the five senses. I'd even mocked people who believed in the paranormal, thinking they were con artists or folk who'd lost all touch with reality. Looking back, I no longer recall this particular event as a supernatural experience, but rather as something arising from my subconscious as a result of the powerful odours overwhelming my senses. The same goes for similar events I experienced over the following days. These episodes did however make me feel closer to all those people who talk about similar terrifying experiences, and I can now fully attest to how intense they can be.

Although the whole incident lasted no longer than ten minutes, it took a long time afterwards to recover and return to my senses. As soon as I was physically able, I logged on to my laptop to look up a hotel, so I could get out of this house before I lost all the confidence that I'd struggled to build up in myself over so many years in London. Just as my heartbeat was slowly returning to normal, my phone rang and I was finally wrenched out of my troubled state.

'Hello?'

'Berta, it's Alfonso,' he said, and I recognised again the strange way in which he pronounced his Rs.

'Hi, I'm so happy you called. How's it going, Alfonso?' The 'I'm so happy you called' was a tad too much, but he had just helped me come back into the here and now.

'Good, good, everything is underway. I called you to set up a meeting. How about tomorrow: same time, same place?'

'No problem. I don't really have anything fixed; I'm not staying long in Spain and the days seem interminable. Have you come across anything?'

'I've got access to some of the legal documents and I've made a few calls. I must admit, I'm intrigued. This is a very interesting case. I'm sorry – I suppose it's all rather sad for you.'

'I can't wait for you to tell me what you've found out. Wild horses couldn't keep me from our meeting tomorrow.'

'Great. Berta . . .'

'Yes?'

'Don't forget to bring the letters.'

'Oh, well . . . it's just that . . . there must be hundreds of them, and I've only read a small fraction so far.'

'That's fine. Bring me the ones you've read and we'll talk about the rest later.'

'OK, that sounds good.'

'One more thing – remember I only take cash. Sorry to be so mistrustful, but that's the business for you.'

'No problem. A day and a half – that's seven hundred and fifty euros, right?'

'Exactly. I have a few other small expenses, but nothing much. We'll take care of those next time. Until tomorrow then. Good night, Berta.'

'See you tomorrow, Alfonso.'

I knew I needed to get over my fright, and make use of the time until my meeting with the detective to read as many letters as I could. No one could appreciate them as much as I did, but I was sure Alfonso would discover a lot by reading between the lines, and they'd be more useful in his hands. Besides, time was against me, especially when it came to my bank account. But I still didn't want to give him the sealed letters – I wanted to be the first to know what they said, and what if he lost them or they were stolen? They were so valuable to me. By now I was opening them, in fact, as though they were addressed to me personally. In some ways they were: they had waited for years to be read, and I was the one to do it. It hurt to think I might miss a single word.

I decided to be organised and take notes, in case the letters weren't returned to me. Getting started gave me new energy, and I stopped brooding on the incident in the kitchen. I dug through my bag for a pen and the notebook I'd been carrying for months without ever using, and set down all the information I'd learned so far: Saúl's new phone number, the discovery of the two ticket stubs, the email address Dylan had provided, the call from his mother and his date of birth, which was the same day he'd first met Yolanda. Considering how many letters I'd read already, this wasn't a whole lot to go on. If these letters went missing, however, at least I had enough information to get in touch with him and offer clues to the investigation, though for now it was all filed away in my mind. Imagine if I could talk to him, or hear his voice . . . or what if he emailed me in return? My heart was suddenly racing.

And so I kept reading, this time paying close attention to any facts that might be useful for my investigation. I don't know if I was just so moved by his words of love for Yolanda and had lost my head, but I couldn't find much else that was helpful.

Tucked in the envelope of the letter dated 1 November, I found another note, this one addressed to my mother.

> Dear Doña Alberta,
> I have been sending these letters to your house for months, hoping that you were passing them on to your daughter Yolanda. Maybe you refuse to give them to her because you believe I'm a murderer. Well, I'm not – I had nothing at all to do with what happened to your son-in-law. I only ran because I was about to be arrested. My one crime in this world is loving your daughter more than life itself.
>
> Please, I'm begging you, *please* give her my letters if you can, because I need to hear from her.
>
> If on the other hand she herself is choosing not to respond to my letters of her own free will, please disregard this note and accept my warmest greetings.
> Saúl

His blind faith in Yolanda was such that he could find no explanation for her lack of response other than the potential blunder or fault of the intermediary. Objectively speaking, the truth was that he wasn't really wrong. What he could never have imagined though was that he had been used in the most contemptible way, and that even though the letters had arrived at their destination, no one had bothered to open them. Saúl mattered to Yolanda only as much as the rest of the world did: in other words, not at all.

Before reading the letter that went along with this note, I was plagued by doubts. What if I myself was simply obsessed, carried away by my own painful memories, and had lost all objectivity? Was I really cleverer than the police, who had spent months investigating the case? Of course I wasn't, but then – Yolanda . . . It takes years of practice to gain skill in any discipline, not to mention having been born with a certain predisposition, without any kind of title to certify it, and as far as manipulation and scheming were concerned, my sister had no rival – she was up there with the best of them. I was quite sure she was controlling this young man, the love-struck and naive Saúl, and that his guilt had seemed quite obvious to the police. It was natural I should have misgivings because this whole affair was just too crazy for words. Even so, I had an advantage over the police: I knew both mother and daughter all too well, and they couldn't hoodwink me as easily as they did the rest of the world.

Now that I'd conquered any doubt, I kept on with my reading.

> Olympic National Park
> 28 December 2002
>
> My dear Yolanda,
> If my letters are reaching you, you're almost certainly wondering why it's been so long since my last letter and you're probably concerned as to why. Believe me, I know how that feels. I've

been very sick, but don't worry, I'm feeling much better now. Apparently I caught some odd virus, which turned into bronchitis. Four weeks ago Dylan found me half-unconscious when he came to bring me my shopping. I had a terrible fever all that night, it seems. He didn't stop to think, but carted me off to the nearest hospital. I was forced to tell them the truth when they asked for my personal details, so I wouldn't be surprised if the police come for me any day now. I'm guessing Interpol has been on the hunt since I left Spain, but I'm not sure. I have no idea how widely they can search and how much of the world's data they have access to. In any case, it's done now.

I'm writing to you from Dylan's cabin – he and his girlfriend Carol have been taking care of me until today. The three days I was in hospital, my mother didn't once leave my side. Dylan called her, because at one point they feared the worst and he thought that nothing else mattered. But I came back from the brink of death – the doctors said it was a miracle. He didn't think it was a good idea for me to go back to my mother's house where I grew up, so he brought me to be looked after by him and Carol in their cabin. The police might still be keeping an eye on my mother's place, especially now that I'd revealed my true identity to the hospital. Anyway, it's been a long time since they bothered my mother. It's all speculation on our part, in any case, and the truth is we have no idea if they're still looking for me, or how the authorities might even handle a case like this.

I don't want you to fret, my darling, I'm fine now. Tomorrow I'm going back to my own cabin and I'll leave these two in peace. Anyway, in a few days they're going to Seattle to celebrate the New Year with friends. They insisted I go with them and I finally agreed. Although I'd rather stay here, I don't want to be a complete drag.

I don't know how I'm ever going to repay Dylan, and I don't just mean the hospital bill, but his constant generosity since I first came. He and Carol send their regards – they're right here in front of me making dinner. Dylan wants me to give you a message: 'Write to this poor bastard before he loses his mind.' You see the reputation I have here, and they still want to take me to a New Year's party? Don't worry, we're only joking around. I'd love for you to meet them, and they're really looking forward to seeing you over here. That day will surely come – there must be a reason for all this happening.

I love you, my precious girl. Happy New Year. I hope that all your dreams come true this year and that we can finally be together again!

Saúl

I wrote down in my notebook that Saúl was admitted to the hospital nearest to his cabin for three days between the end of November and the beginning of December in 2002. These details might just prove of some importance in the investigation.

Then, without having eaten dinner, I curled up in bed thinking about him. Saúl was the only thing of Yolanda's that, without her knowing it, I wanted to snatch away with all of my might. I wanted him so much more than I wanted Alberta's inheritance, which mattered very little to me just then, and only because it meant I could fund my investigation. I was beginning to like him so much it scared me. I dreamt of him that night, both awake and asleep, and he was always right beside me. I dreamt that all his words of love were meant for me. Just before I'd gone to bed, I marvelled again at the photo of him. Even though his back was to the camera, I could almost see his face. He didn't even know I existed but I felt like I knew him, and so much better than Yolanda had ever done. There was no doubt about it – I was falling in love with him.

What I felt that night was completely foreign, something from another world. A delightful tingling sensation ran through me from head to toe. It was such a complete feeling of joy that I'd have laughed in the face of death at that moment – I would have died of sheer happiness. Part of me knew we'd never actually get to meet, and that my love for him would remain hidden from the rest of the world, but that didn't make it any less real to me.

I knew it was crazy, but I didn't want to give it up for anything. I didn't want to lose that feeling but to experience it to the utmost, revel in it with every fibre of my being. I was willing even to risk all I'd achieved over many years of struggle. Nothing – not my work, not my independence, my flat in London, my friends . . . absolutely nothing in my life made me feel the way I did now, falling in love with Saúl. I never could have imagined I could feel this much. Without his letters, I would have lived my life in happy ignorance, convinced that I had everything I could possibly want. His words were a wake-up call, and suddenly they were the only things that mattered.

And so I fell asleep, finally touching true happiness.

Chapter 10

Friday, 20 June 2014

The muffled sounds running through the pipes told me that Teresa was out watering the garden. I was annoyed, my privacy invaded. She no longer felt like family, although I still wasn't sure exactly why my feelings for her had changed so much.

I peeked out through the curtains and there she was indeed, holding the hose, washing down the terrace as though it were hers. In all fairness though, it belonged more to her than it did to me, and maybe that's what bothered me so much: not even part of the family, Teresa had had my mother's respect and trust, and maybe even her affection – something I had never had. This house was more hers than mine because she had never left it, not even during the most difficult times. Beneath the apparent detachment she showed for what was legally now my property lurked a certain sense of possession that didn't go unnoticed, and that bothered me immensely. I'm not sure if the fifteen years apart had changed her or me, but she no longer seemed the same person as the one I remembered from my childhood.

I really wanted some coffee and toast and was starving from not having eaten in so long, but just didn't fancy her company this morning. I tidied my room a little and locked the door with some suspicion when I left. I took a while washing and dressing in the bathroom, giving her time to finish her work, but it was no good and finally I gave up. Emerging from the bathroom, I saw her heading across the hall to my room. She was about to turn the knob on the door when I spoke. 'Morning. Don't worry, Teresa, I've already straightened my room.'

'Oh dear, you quite startled me!' she exclaimed. She hadn't expected me to be right behind her. 'Good morning, darling. I was just going to change the sheets. You know we always change the sheets on Fridays in this house.'

'Yes, but the person who made the rules is gone. Don't worry about it. I've already made the bed and I'll change the sheets tomorrow,' I retorted with authority, wanting to make it crystal clear that I was in charge of the house now.

'But I have to load the washing machine with all the towels and—'

'I'll do it tomorrow, OK?' I interrupted decisively.

Her face changed instantly, noticing the coldness with which I was treating her. She let go of the knob at last and turned around. On her way to the kitchen, she took off her apron, ready to leave.

'I'm going to the market to buy some fresh fish in a little while. Do you want anything?'

'No, I'm fine. I'm not planning on eating here today. I have plans at El Espejo. Don't worry about me.'

'There's freshly made coffee ready,' she said, hanging her apron behind the kitchen door and picking up her bag.

'I can smell it. Thank you.'

'See you later, love.'

'Bye, Teresa. Have a good day.'

I didn't like her 'See you later'. I didn't want her to come back and rummage about in my house while I wasn't there, but I didn't have the guts to tell her not to return that day. I still wasn't completely sure whether my intuition about her was right, or whether the aversion I was starting to feel towards her was all in my mind.

I got fresh water and food for Aris and made myself a wonderful breakfast. Then, all ready, I began to read as much as I could before leaving. I wanted to bring Alfonso as many letters as possible. I went back to my room and, so I didn't waste time when handing over the letters, delved back into Saúl's past, specifically into 2003.

He was excited about his painting. The letter from 15 February had a photo with it of one of his pastel sketches showing the landscape as seen through his window, a view of the lake and the surrounding tree-covered mountains, but two things about it caught my eye. One, the artist had drawn himself working at the easel, once again with his back to me; two, a pair of beautiful eyes gazed up at him from the waters of the lake, full of passion and sweetness. They were Yolanda's eyes, only the sparkle and innocence they exuded were not at all like her; they were simply a product of the imagination of an artist in love.

Suddenly I had an almost uncontrollable urge to rip up the photo. The image was palpable proof of my sister's utter bewitchment of this innocent man. I was overcome with rage, helplessness, resentment, thoughts of revenge . . . It simply wasn't fair. Once again her cruel tricks had got her what I'd been searching for my entire life: someone to really, truly love me. When the maelstrom of emotion had subsided, I thought it over more carefully. Maybe I wanted Saúl because he had been hers, just like I'd always envied her clothes, her slender figure or the privileges my mother granted her.

His drawing was exquisite, magnificent. I imagined how powerfully seductive it must be in close-up. I fantasised about seeing the painter in the middle of his creative process, in his cabin, captivated by the lake. I could make him out better in this second photo: quite tall and slim, but strongly muscled. In his right hand you could see a stick of pastel moving towards the paper, which he'd fastened to a drawing board with pins. The hand was large, bony, slender, dark . . . noble. There in close-up you could see better his thick, straight, chestnut hair, which must have been cut because in this image it no longer fell below his shoulders.

I wished with all my strength that he would turn around. In a single second, with just one glance, I would have been able to learn so much . . .

> Olympic National Park
> 8 February 2003
>
> Hello, darling,
> It's almost Valentine's Day and I can't stop thinking about our time together, the only time fate has allowed us to enjoy. I don't know if you'll remember . . . I was mowing the lawn. That morning your husband (those two damn words kill me, 'your husband') decided to work from home and our plans were ruined. But you thought of something even better. I tremble at remembering the note you handed me while you were asking me how the rose bushes were doing, so he didn't suspect a thing. 'Today is Valentine's Day and no one can stop us from having our date. Meet me at the Don Carlos hotel in two hours. Tell the people at the front desk your name and they'll bring you to the room,' said the note. Word for word. You swore he hadn't, but I still think your husband saw us, and he was the person who took the note

from my sweatshirt when I took it off and left it on the table in the garden. It doesn't matter now. What does matter is that you gave me the best day of my entire life. I close my eyes and I can still see you . . . Jesus Christ, you were so beautiful! I still recall so vividly the touch of your skin, smell your perfume, see your smiles and hear your whispers of love and pleasure. A wonderful shiver just passed right through me, remembering every detail.

Today it is I who want to surprise you. Would you like to know what I've painted for you? It's your eyes. I don't need to look at photos of you to paint them – I see them everywhere, constantly. I can't forget them, I can't, and I don't know if I want to. Forgive me, my love, but this isn't a day for sadness.

The owner of the local art gallery, a friend of Dylan's, came over a few days ago to look at my paintings. You won't believe it – he bought one! I've sold my first work! It seems quite incredible to me. It's been like a breath of fresh air and a reason to endure the long, cold days of this winter, which feels eternal. He asked how much I wanted for the one I painted for you, but I told him it was a gift for someone and he picked a different one.

When he got me alone, Dylan told me that if he asked me how much I'd like to sell them for, I could name my price without any worries. It seems this man is not just an amateur collector – he knows very well if something is really worth it. He gave me five hundred dollars for one with

> ducks in the foreground and the lake in the distance. Well, actually the lake's in the background to everything I've painted so far.
>
> I think Dylan told him I'm on the run from justice, because before he left he said he'd have a think as to how to get round my situation so he could show my work in his gallery. He seemed really interested. I'm so excited, Yolanda. I'm sure you can tell by my words. Knowing my work is appreciated helps to ease the pain of your absence.
>
> Happy Valentine's Day, my love!
> Saúl

It filled me with joy to see that he had recovered some hope at least; because he deserved it, because in some way he was already part of my life, and especially because it meant that not everything was lost and Yolanda hadn't managed to break him after all. I was sure that over time the wound would heal, and Saúl would waken from his impossible dream. My sister was not the woman he believed her to be, and even if he went back to Yolanda, their life together would not in any way resemble what he'd imagined.

Another interesting fact had emerged in that letter – it was likely that Bodo knew about his wife's affair with the gardener. I admit I wasn't at all surprised. My sister's husband, my father, loved neither himself nor anyone else. Making money was his only true and enduring passion, and hardly sustained by the most honourable means. I don't think the knowledge that his wife was sleeping with Saúl would have caused him any real upset, just as I don't think it would have made him leave either. So why would her lover have needed to kill him? It was all so absurd . . . What I couldn't know was whether this detail would help Saúl or hurt him, in case he ever had to prove his innocence.

I wrote this down in my notebook and kept on reading, knowing I'd need to head off soon to meet Alfonso.

The last letter I read before setting off was dated 23 March. It was similar in tone: between words of love, confidences and pleas for her to reply, the news was still fairly positive. He was kept hopeful by the possibility of showing his art and the arrival of spring, which would soon let him start painting in oils again.

He'd continued seeing the group of people he'd met on New Year's Eve and spoke especially fondly of Nadia, a girl who had tried to seduce him. According to him, they had a lot in common – they were of similar age and both lonely, she loved art and often visited exhibitions when she had the funds, sometimes travelling interstate to see them. She was finishing her fine arts degree in Seattle, although she wasn't a painter herself; she wanted to study the history of American art. The best thing of all, Saúl said, was that she was passionate about her work.

I felt a little jealous, although also relieved to learn that Saúl's heart was at least a bit freer. I wanted to believe that, because there was honestly not a single letter so far where he didn't declare his undying love for Yolanda.

Before I left, the phone rang. It was the solicitor's secretary. 'Señor Soler wants you to know that everything is going well, but it might be a few weeks until we have all the paperwork ready for you to sign.' The firm obviously cared about its clients and took pains to keep them informed. I guess that was included in their fees.

When I finally left, I was running a little late. Driving down the street, I passed Teresa holding the keys to the house. She was beginning to get on my nerves. Why had she come back? Was she waiting for me to leave so she could snoop about? Was it just me, or did my sensible housekeeper really have something to hide?

Either way, I'd been suspicious enough to take the letters I hadn't read yet out of the basket and hide them in my wardrobe. I'd left a little scrap of paper between two of the bundles, and another in the doorframe to my room. If Teresa came in and touched the letters, I would know. As soon as I signed all the legal documents and put the house up for sale, I would ask her for the keys. It was amazing that I could have gone from love to utter rejection in a mere matter of days. I might be wrong, but deep down I felt that Teresa knew so much more than she was telling me, spending so much time coming to the house every day . . .

◆ ◆ ◆

I made it to the restaurant at five past one, out of breath, but not too late thanks to my familiarity with the nearby car parks and the fact that there wasn't much traffic.

Alfonso was waiting for me, at the same table as before.

'I'm sorry I'm a bit late,' I told him, taking a seat.

'Me too,' he answered. Clearly he didn't like to wait around, as he looked a little annoyed. He pulled his chair in closer and leaned towards me, appearing absorbed in showing me something on the tablet that lay on the table between us.

'Don't move, don't turn around. Act like I'm showing you something,' he whispered. 'Someone behind you seems very interested in listening in on our conversation. I think the man to our right is watching us.'

I couldn't help trying to snatch a glance.

'Don't look.'

'Sorry,' I apologised, staring hard down at the screen.

'Listen, order a beer and stay for twenty minutes or so. Act like we've known each other all our lives, smile once in a while and make small talk, loud enough so he can hear you. Then call the car rental place where you hired the vehicle and tell them where it's parked so they can come and pick it up. If that man finds out what car you're driving, he'll follow you.'

'How do you know . . . ?'

'Shh . . . talk more quietly and look at the screen like you're interested.'

'I'm sorry, I just feel so ridiculous . . .'

'Look, after you've made that call, take a taxi. I'll wait for you on the terrace of another restaurant, Loft 39. It's on Velásquez Street, on the corner of Hermosilla, just fifteen minutes away. Don't try walking – it would be too easy for him to follow you. One last thing: don't take the letters out of your bag while you're here.'

A chill ran down my spine. This sounded dangerous – we were being watched! I was sitting with a spy who was being spied on. But who was following us and why? I was starting to feel scared.

Alfonso turned off the device, leaned back in his seat, ordered me a beer and started a trivial conversation, a little more loudly than his normal tone. 'I think this is the perfect spot – my sister will love it! She's going to get such a surprise.'

I was amazed at his imagination and what a natural he was. It was up to me now to continue the conversation. He'd made it easy for me. 'You said it – she's going to be totally lost for words. Did you buy the present yet?' I was even surprised by my own performance – I'd never thought I was that good an actor.

And so we went on, playing the part of a couple organising a surprise birthday party for his sister. Twenty minutes had passed when, bang on schedule, my phone rang. It was Brandon, wanting to go over a few questions and to ask when I was coming back. It was great timing, although the poor dear didn't understand a thing I said, much less my Spanish.

'Hey, Susana! I've been waiting for you to call,' I screeched into the phone, waiting a few moments, while Brandon asked over and over what I was talking about. 'OK, great – I'm on my way!'

Alfonso stared at me, not bothering to conceal his own amazement at my performance; if it had been possible, I reckon he'd have clapped. When I was safely in the back of a cab, I'd call my chef back and explain the situation, though I had no idea quite what I'd say.

'I have to go,' I announced to Alfonso after hanging up. 'I'll call you later.'

'See you later then,' he said in return.

He got up to say goodbye and we kissed on both cheeks, as though we knew each other well. Turning around to leave, I glanced in passing at the man Alfonso thought was watching us. He must have been under thirty-five, reasonably tall, of medium build and well dressed. He seemed very focused on the book he was reading. I didn't have time to notice many details, and couldn't really even see his face. My legs were trembling as I walked past. What kind of unholy mess had I got myself into? Well, whatever, if this man really was spying on us then my suspicions were justified, though of course I'd never have known if Alfonso hadn't warned me.

I called the car rental place and did as instructed, though I'd need to stop by later to hand in the keys.

Shortly after I got to the terrace of Loft 39, Alfonso himself arrived.

'What a morning!' he exclaimed, pulling out his chair. 'These last-minute setbacks get to me increasingly. Did you make that call?'

'Yes, it's all arranged.'

'Marvellous. It's not a good idea for you to be seen in your car – it would be way too easy to follow you.'

The waiter came over right away, and my companion ordered a couple of beers and a few different tapas.

'I have the letters in my bag. Is now a good time?' I asked before I forgot, still thinking about the man who'd made us move to a different restaurant.

'Perfect. If you'd be so kind as to pass them over.'

'Here you go, and your money's in this envelope. Tell me what your expenses come to . . .'

'Not much, just one hundred and eight euros.'

I gave him the money. 'Right, well, tell me what you've found out.'

'I've got access to the legal proceedings and it's one big load of nonsense. The evidence against Saúl Guillén doesn't hold up in the slightest, the witness statements are problematic to say the least, and, worst of all, the judge in charge of the case retired three weeks ago and the police commissioner has moved on to another job.'

'Of course, and how very convenient. It seems like everyone involved has disappeared – Bodo, my sister, the people handling the case . . . even Saúl. Doesn't it all just seem a bit too tidy to you?'

'It looks like it. We don't even have your mother.'

'You wouldn't have got anything out of her, I can promise you that. So what evidence do they hold against Saúl?'

'Three witnesses, that's all. Two of them stated that they saw him leaving the Marbella house, and that he'd been pushing a large bundle in a wheelbarrow towards a rented van. The third witness swore that he saw Saúl arrive at the dock in the same vehicle, get out the bundle wrapped in a big black bag, and take it in the wheelbarrow over to the yacht belonging to Bodo and your sister. Then he set sail and was gone for over an hour. Supposedly that's all the time he needed to get away, throw the body in the sea and come back.'

'But how could they know it was Saúl? Did the witnesses know him?'

'Two of the witnesses identified him in the line-up.'

'Of course, I should have known . . .'

'What I don't know is how they managed to get him out of the police station after the witnesses had identified him. He must have had a really clever lawyer who knew he'd have to get him out of the country on a fake passport right away, naturally against a hefty bail – just one more corrupt official to add to the list. But it's too soon to . . . Take all this with a pinch of salt, Berta. I still don't have enough to prove any of this, and it's all only conjecture. By the way, the lawyer is also on the missing list: he moved to Venezuela soon after the trial.'

'I can tell this won't be an easy case,' I remarked, seeing how hard it would be to find information without any informants.

'The funny thing is that before the line-up, all three witnesses stated that it was too dark to see his face, and moreover that he'd pulled up the hood of his sweatshirt.'

'Yes, suspicious, isn't it, that they were able to recognise him quite so easily after that . . .'

'Remember, all three gave matching physical descriptions of Saúl as tall, young, thin . . .'

'I don't know, it all seems so rehearsed . . .'

'This, along with the fact that the accused couldn't prove he was at the cinema when this all took place, made him the prime suspect. The trial notes only say that he claimed to be at the cinema and that he didn't have his ticket stubs – basically saying he didn't have an alibi.'

'He only found those ticket stubs once he was in Washington State, in the pocket of the coat he was wearing that day. He thought he'd thrown them out, so he'd never bothered looking for them – that's what he told Yolanda in one of his letters.'

'I bet you don't know who gave him the tickets?' Alfonso asked me.

'My sister,' I answered confidently.

'It's all very strange . . . I can't explain how they could have botched the investigation so badly. Then there's the statement of the girl from the van rental company . . .'

'What statement?'

'She describes him perfectly, just like someone told her exactly what to say. We need to find her – I reckon they paid her off.'

'I can't believe this. I knew there was something fishy about it all, but I had no idea just quite how fishy it was. I'm getting more and more confused.'

'Did you know that Bodo Kraser was in the middle of some serious financial trouble when he disappeared? He was a sly old bugger, I tell you. Or, should I say, he *is* a sly old bugger, because I'm beginning to doubt he was ever killed at all.'

'Meaning?'

He must have noticed the change in my face, because he asked immediately, 'Do you know something about Bodo you're not telling me?'

'He was my father, although he never acknowledged paternity. I found out when I was nine . . . How did you know?'

'In this line of work you have to be a bit of a psychologist. To a large extent, the success of any investigation depends on how you interpret the information beyond what you're told at face value. You should have mentioned this right at the start – that's very significant.'

'I moved to London after learning that my sister was going to marry him. As you can see, our family was exactly the same as anyone else's . . .'

'So you say . . . but I'm actually thinking twice now about carrying on working for you. Do you realise that all the men who get involved with the women in your family disappear into thin air?' he said, exhaling a cloud of smoke.

From his hint of a smile, I suspected that he'd only said this to lighten the mood, seeing me so troubled and taken aback, but I wasn't entirely sure.

'Are you going to leave me now?'

'I'm only joking. It's just that you looked sad and . . . well, I'm not too good with my little stabs at humour.'

'That's all right then. I've never really thought too much about it, but it's true: none of the men in my family have lasted very long.'

'Fabián de Castro, Bodo Kraser, Saúl Guillén . . . It can't just be a coincidence.'

'Have you found out anything about Fabián?'

'Nothing – it seems he was literally swallowed up by the earth. Everything else aside, I think his is the strangest disappearance of all.'

'What's the next step?'

'Give me a few days. I want to talk to a few contacts who might be able to track down the name of the person who made the fake passport for Saúl. That would be a good place to start unravelling this mystery. Apart from that, I need to read the letters – they may contain more information.'

'I've read them and they just show that he's innocent. He did send a couple of photos . . .'

'You weren't going to show them to me?'

'Well, I didn't think—'

'Berta, let me do the thinking. I need to see them.'

I took them out of my bag and handed them over.

'He's a really good artist,' he said, looking at the photo of the pastel sketch.

He examined it for quite a while, including the reverse, then picked up the one of the lake scene and spent another few minutes over it, smoking while he thought. When he was finished with his perusal and had taken pictures of the photos with his phone, he handed them back.

'No, keep them,' I said. 'You can return them to me along with the letters when you're done. You need them more than I do.'

'That won't be necessary. If there's one thing we detectives specialise in, it's a photographic memory. The pictures I've taken will be enough for me.'

'If you like,' I answered, relieved.

'You like this guy, right?'

His question knocked me off balance and it took a few seconds for me to respond.

'Don't be silly! I don't even know him. I just . . . well . . .'

'Right.'

'Tell me something. How are you so sure that man was watching us?' I asked, changing the subject completely.

'I'm not sure, but nobody arrives at a restaurant straight after you do, chooses the empty table closest to yours, and doesn't turn the page of his book for half an hour. He's an amateur, but he did manage to find us – though I don't know how he found out about our meeting. You didn't tell anyone, did you?'

'No, I didn't tell a soul I was meeting you. Except . . .' I remembered then that I'd told Teresa I had an appointment at El Espejo. Alfonso guessed who I'd told; he seemed to be reading my mind.

'Tell me about the woman who's been working in your house all these years.' He clearly had not brought her up out of the blue.

'There's not much to say. She started working for my mother and Fabián when they got married; she's always been very loyal and sensible; she practically raised my sister and me to the point that I think of her as my real mother. She lived with us when we were little, before she bought her house in Leganés. She told me she still lives there with a cousin once removed – the son of her cousin – who came to Madrid for his education about twelve years ago.'

'And?' he asked. He was waiting for more.

'And that's it. When I left she was the one person I missed – you can't even imagine how much.'

'Go on,' he insisted. He wanted to know what I was feeling right now, what lay behind my words, and I don't know if it was simply in his role as an investigator. He was a very smart man.

'Over the past few days, ever since I came back – I don't know . . . she just doesn't seem the same to me. I can't put my finger on what it is. I think she knows more than she's saying, maybe even hiding information from me. She has the keys to my house, she's always had them, and she comes and goes at will, which is suddenly starting to bother me. I don't know – maybe I'm the one who's changed in the last fifteen years.'

'I see. Would you like another beer?'

'I'd rather have a coffee.'

'Waiter, two coffees, please,' he said to the lad serving the table next to ours. 'What can you tell me about your sister?'

'We're five years apart, and she's the older one . . . I don't really know what else to tell you. We've never got along. Ever since I can remember, I felt that she and my mother were part of a world that I just didn't fit into. At home I was the odd one out, the fool, the only one never in the picture. I think I really isolated myself as a way of surviving around so much treachery. I was the Cinderella of the story.'

'What did they tell you about your sister's father?'

'First, that he died of a brain tumour, or that's what our mother said . . . I mean, that's what she always told her friends and her daughters. Then I found out that he'd wandered off – that he'd slowly been losing his faculties and one day he just went out and never came back, according to the official version at least. But then a few days ago I found a letter from Fabián's mother that she'd sent to my mother after his disappearance . . . She was convinced that her son had had no mental problems and that he would never have abandoned his pregnant wife and daughter. I don't think he had any idea that he wasn't my father and that his wife was cheating on him.'

'But the fact is, he didn't come back. Do you think your mother could have been capable of—?'

'Yes, I do,' I said without hesitation, and then I swallowed hard. 'But I have no proof of anything and my opinion might not be the most objective.'

'Tell me, what do you think really happened?'

'That she "over-medicated" or rather poisoned him until he lost his mind, and that's what maybe made him go . . . Alfonso, I have absolutely no idea what really happened. All I can say is that my mother invented a version of her life that didn't match reality in any way. Remember that everyone thought and still thinks to this day that I was Fabián's daughter. I found out the truth when I was nine years old and wasn't allowed to tell a single person. I still use Fabián's last name, in fact. You can imagine how scared I was of her . . .'

'But a man in that condition, if he was that disorientated, could not have made it very far, and they never found the body. It's not that easy to hide a body.'

'I'm just telling you my personal opinion. I don't have any answers and that's why I hired you. The truth is, it's hard to believe any of this . . . Sometimes I wonder if I'm not just imagining it all . . . I don't have proof for any of it – not for my mother having an affair with Bodo, not even for the claim that he was my father,' I explained tensely, uncomfortable at the way he was making me confess my innermost thoughts. 'I don't like what I just told you, because it probably makes me sound unbalanced. It's not exactly normal for a daughter to presume that her mother has committed murder.'

'I'm not judging you, I'm just trying to get as much information as I can. I think it's time to go now. I'll call you when I come up with anything significant,' he said, leaning a little closer as he said my name, his face kind and understanding. 'Berta, I think that sooner or later we'll get to the bottom of all this and find the guilty parties. We'll get Saúl his freedom back and find you some answers about your past.'

'Oh, I hope so,' I said, somewhat more relaxed. 'We just need solid evidence so we can get the case reopened.'

'Finding the evidence is my job, but convincing a judge to listen to all this stuff will have to be yours.'

We said goodbye until the next time.

On my way back I headed to the Corte Inglés, the only shopping centre I knew here, to go to the post office and send my letter to Washington State before I changed my mind. After my talk with Alfonso, I was stricken with endless doubts, no longer sure if it was such a great idea to communicate with Saúl, even though he couldn't know who I was. Having addressed the envelope, I was about to shove the letter back in my bag and leave when I suddenly thought of the email I'd already sent to Boston. Hesitantly I handed it over to the girl at the counter. She smiled reassuringly, as though she knew it contained something troubling. How wonderful to get a smile in such moments of terrible indecision!

Next I dropped the key off at the car rental company and returned home in a taxi. When I opened the front door it was already past eight o'clock.

Aris was waiting for me again. I was so comforted by his steady gaze, finding him right there by the door, and leaned down to pet his soft fur . . . The heavy smell of my mother's perfume was also there to greet me.

I made myself a salad and rewarded my friend with a tasty tin of cat food.

Despite having Aris and Neca with me – more company than on any night in my flat in London – I don't think I've ever felt as lonely as I did that evening, sitting at the kitchen table in front of some lettuce and a few tomatoes. All three of us were gloomy. Even my doll seemed to have lost her look of surprise. Very slowly, a tear ran down my cheek, then another and another . . . It had been so long since I'd cried that a part of me was delighted. When the tears reached my lips, I caught them with my tongue and, ironically, the salt of my loneliness made me feel more alive than ever. Yes, I was sad, but so utterly alive.

In the last few days alone a torrent of emotions I'd never known existed had been coursing through me. True, almost all of them were painful, but they had roused me from my numb existence and, above all, were leading me to a love I had never thought I'd find. It was the most platonic love possible, and the chances that we would even get to talk to each other were almost zero. Well, so what? Did that mean my feelings were any less genuine than those of anyone else? Did the fact that I could not shout my love to the world nullify the truth of its existence? No, it did not! What I felt for Saúl was more real than tonight's crescent moon. His letters had won me over so completely that right now I would have given up everything I'd struggled for over so many years simply to have him at my side for one moment – just as he would have given everything for Yolanda. I felt the most profound understanding for the man by the lake through our shared experience – what Saúl felt for Yolanda was the same thing I felt for him. An outrageous foolishness for someone as rational as myself.

Time passed and my salad sat untouched, and still the tears trickled slowly down my cheeks. I had a thousand reasons to cry, but the water that filled my eyes came only from Lake Crescent. I don't know how long I stayed this way, imagining the wonderful possibility of meeting him, while Aris and Neca watched compassionately from the chairs on the other side of the table, as if they knew how I felt.

Between tears and sighs, I gave the kitchen a deep clean. When I'd got home I'd found that while I was gone, Teresa had tidied away the remains of the breakfast things, and I'd promised myself that I wouldn't give her any more reason to come and go as she did. I washed my face, made myself comfortable and then shut myself in my room with my two companions and Saúl's letters.

The piece of paper I'd left between the door of the wardrobe and its frame was on the floor, along with the one I'd placed between the bundles of letters. At first I was furious, and then concerned: I hadn't counted the letters I still had to read – what if Teresa had taken one? She might be reading them now – she was both skilled and careful and might have opened them and resealed them without my noticing. I was becoming quite paranoid. I took each one out and examined it carefully. At first glance, it didn't look as though any had been opened. There were a lot, so I first took the bundle from the most recent year, all the letters from 2014. There were eleven of them, and the latest three definitely showed signs of the seal having been tampered with. I opened the last one and discovered that the envelope had indeed been messed with. Before putting it back in the basket, I noticed that the return address was different from all the letters I'd been reading thus far. This letter, along with all the others in this bundle, as well as those from several years prior, came from Seattle, something I hadn't spotted until now. In fact, had my suspicions not led me to inspect them, I would certainly have missed this detail, and that someone had opened the envelope. I felt an almost uncontrollable urge to read the letter inside, concerning the most recent parts of Saúl's life, but then stopped myself, more out of fear that on the other side of the world he already had a new love or a family than from not wanting to break the chronological order. Finally, I focused on one question:

what about these letters could possibly interest Teresa? The situation was beginning to run away from me – so much mystery, so many doubts and lies, would have been too much for anyone. At this moment I felt too vulnerable to go on. I thought again about leaving and going back to my safe, routine life in London, to my tidy flat, to my successful restaurant and my satisfying sexual encounters with Harry. Until just a few days ago, everything I could have dreamt of was there, but now I felt trapped in a parallel reality that not even Alfred Hitchcock could have imagined. The path of my return had become full of obstacles, and the further I went, the more doubts I had, and the more treachery and secrets I uncovered.

That night my strength and resolve failed and I wanted only to be whisked back home – to my real home. I decided on a whisky, hoping it would relax me. As I walked down the hall, I once more sensed my mother's presence and shuddered, my legs wooden and unresponsive, but I kept moving onwards. Deep down I knew it was just another trap, laid not by her but by my own mind. Alberta was dead, and she couldn't hurt me any more. It was my own emotional weakness playing tricks on me. I managed to make it to the kitchen, albeit with damp temples and ice-cold hands, clammy and pale with my panic. This time I had won.

I poured myself a slug of whisky and took the bottle out into the garden. Aris followed me discreetly, as though he were escorting me. I lay down in my usual spot under the old willow. The air was perfectly clear, and the myriad stars flashed with unusual intensity against the indigo sky, cloaking the darkness in an unearthly celebration. That night I really needed to switch off. It didn't take long for me to fall unconscious, rocked off to sleep by the soft music a neighbour was playing. At some point I must have woken up and gone back to my room.

Chapter 11

Saturday, 21 June 2014

I hadn't even opened my eyes yet when my mind formed the question, *Will she have come?* I remembered that the night before I'd left my glass and the almost empty bottle of whisky out in the garden. I'd lost all trust in her, and no longer wanted to share my fears and doubts with Teresa as I did as a child. I listened carefully, not even getting out of bed yet, trying to hear any sound that might mean she was there. Finally I concluded that she wasn't, although I wasn't a hundred per cent certain. My phone told me that it was almost nine o'clock, so maybe she'd already left. Before going to the bathroom, I was reassured: she hadn't been here, as the little thread that I'd torn off my scarf the previous evening was still caught between the door frame and the door. *This is all so sad*, I thought. *How could I have come to this?* Watching the one person who loved me most, distrustful to the point of spying on her.

As I was tidying up, I remembered that it was Saturday and that I had a whole weekend ahead of me with no plans, no appointments and nothing to do. I'd been longing for a weekend like this for years, but now I felt as though I were suffocating. I'd never liked crowds or parties, or gatherings of more than four people. I have a natural tendency to isolate myself, but solitude to this extent was beginning to take its toll on me. I would have loved to have seen Mary right now, to go shopping and then for lunch in some restaurant on Carnaby Street, and listen to her say over and over that she shouldn't have spent so much money on clothes she might never wear. I needed her to distract me with her exuberance and chatter, to witter on with her trivialities and explain to me, all over again, how to be stylish and glamorous. After lunch, we'd probably go back to Harrods to return some of what she'd bought, in order to ease her conscience. I was missing her so much this particular Saturday. Back in my fantasy, I would almost certainly get a call from Harry in the evening . . . It was odd, but over the last few days I'd stopped missing that part of my Saturdays in London. I guess Harry was already part of the past. When I went home he'd have to get used to being a friend without benefits. Did I simply not feel like sleeping with him any more because of Saúl?

I had a quiet breakfast in the garden with Aris and Neca. What a pair of friends I had here though! I was embarrassed at the thought that some neighbour might happen to glance from a window and see me looking like a madwoman, seated at the garden table in the company of a cat and a rag doll. Once I'd finished, I tidied up the kitchen and my bedroom meticulously and turned on the washing machine, then took the bundle of letters still left to read from 2003 and laid myself down beneath the willow tree.

>Olympic National Park
>7 April 2003
>
>My beloved Yolanda,
>How are you? Sometimes I feel as though my questions go blowing into the wind. It's so easy for me to see your eyes and imagine you reading

my letters – you know how artists can go without food, but not imagination . . .

Some days I fear I'm going mad. Let me tell you what crazy thoughts I've been having, and how far from reality I've wandered. I feel like a puppet in the hands of love, someone nurturing an imaginary romance through his letters, writing to the wind, and that time, fickle as it is, may carry them on its breeze to someday make their way into the hands of a perfect stranger. In some ways, I'm consoled by the thought that my love isn't going into the void and that even though you may have forgotten me, my letters may bring love to someone else lost in time and space like myself. Somehow there is no more tragic possibility than the madness of thinking that my words of love will roam eternally through the heavens, looking for a recipient who never existed.

I'm sorry, my darling, today is a bad day. Even crazy romantics like me sometimes need tangible proof that our dreams can come true. And it's been so long without hearing from you! I can't help but think that you've forgotten me, or worse, that you never even loved me at all.

Forgive me for doubting you. I'm sorry . . .

I'll leave it at that for today. I don't think I'm very good company right now.

The eternal lover,

Saúl

Without realising it, my eyes had welled up for the second day in a row and I had to stop reading. Saúl's words were like a premonition:

eleven years earlier he had already thought of the possibility that his letters might end up with someone very distant from himself in space and time. It was as though he sensed my existence, as though somehow he was writing to me. I was his second choice, the one to provide comfort in a desperate situation. Right then I would have given all that I owned and more to be with him.

For me it was a letter full of hope, even though he seemed so depressed. For the first time he seemed conscious that his dreams might not be realistic, and even his farewell was revealing: 'The eternal lover' was light years away from 'Forever yours' or 'I adore you'. It was an unusual ending, lacking the involvement with the object of his affection that was so evident in the other letters. He could have written 'Your eternal lover' but, as he said himself in the letter, he no longer knew whether he was having an affair with Yolanda, the wind, or with someone else he had never even met. The 'the' in that sign-off indicated that he felt like a man in love, but was no longer sure with whom or why, and was beginning to glimpse the notion that he had been bewitched by a fantasy. In effect, he was saying something along the lines of, 'That's right, my dear: loving you has not all been in vain – it has given birth to a whole ocean of feeling within me that I had never thought possible.'

I sat for a long time imagining that his letters were addressed to me, and that maybe the real purpose of so many years of correspondence was to allow two people to meet who understood love in the same way. Somehow, that was exactly what had happened.

I remembered that the photos were still in my bag, hanging on the hook in the hall, so I went to fetch them, then went back to thinking about the man from Lake Crescent, I don't know for how long. I think I memorised every plank of the dock, every soft ripple of the waters around it, every curve of the mountains that cut across the sky . . . even the eyes of the man with his back to me.

Just then, the landline started to ring.

'Hello?'

And whoever it was hung up.

I stood motionless in the sitting room, rooted to the spot next to the side table with the phone, then went to perch on the sofa, in the exact same spot where my mother used to sit. As my weight compressed the foam, the cushions released the scent saturated in each fibre over forty years. The essence of her dark spirit engulfed me so completely that I felt her hanging over me, drowning me, suffocating me. I experienced the agonising episode with such intensity that I lost consciousness for a few minutes. First I felt my stomach turn over, then I had difficulty breathing, and finally dizziness ended up robbing me of my senses. I woke up soaked in sweat, frozen and with drenched jeans; I had wet myself.

Limp as a rag doll, I collapsed along the length of the sofa, my head ending up against the arm, and knocking the handset on to the floor. I lay there on my back and waited to feel better. It took me a while to recover and remember why I had fainted, while my eyes remained locked on the harsh glitter of the Bohemian crystal lamp, inducing a sort of visual hallucination. Cutting through my dreamlike state came a desperate voice I was slowly starting to recognise.

'Oh, sweetheart! What's wrong, my darling? What happened? Oh my love, oh dear, oh dear . . .'

Countless times in the past I had been overjoyed to hear Teresa's words of comfort, but never as much as I was now. All alone, I had gazed upon the face of death. Teresa began to mop at my face with a towel. She stopped once in a while to take my pulse and rest her hand on my forehead to check my temperature.

'I think I blacked out, Teresa,' I was finally able to mumble.

'Oh, my darling, I was so scared! I thought you were dead, my love. What happened?' she asked, her voice trembling. She really was frightened.

'It's that smell . . .'

'Shh, shh, easy now, don't think about it,' she said, picking the phone up from the floor and placing it back on the table. 'You shouldn't stay here on your own, darling. It was lucky I came by . . .'

'I think I need to take a shower.'

'You just sit there nice and quiet while I fetch you some clean clothes.'

Before she left the room I called out to her, 'Teresa . . .'

'Yes?' she answered, turning around. Her face was pale with shock and worry.

'You don't know how much it hurts me that things have changed so much between us. I'm so sorry that I can't trust you like I used to. I'm so sorry . . .'

She left the room without answering.

◆ ◆ ◆

Following my shower, I found Teresa in the garden with two cups of lime blossom tea on the table.

'A nice cup of tea will do us both good,' she said, looking at me with affection and sympathy.

I walked over and took a seat while smoothing down my hair, hoping it would dry fast in the warm air. From where I was sitting I could see the basket of letters and photos on the hammock beneath the willow, a mere five metres away. I thought Teresa must surely have seen them too and felt invaded, scrutinised to the very core of my being. Neca sat in a third chair, as if she were a participant in the conversation, and Aris, seeing that I'd emerged from the bathroom, had come out for a stroll in the garden.

'Are you going to tell me what happened?' Teresa asked gently.

'I told you, it's that smell . . . I went to answer the phone and suddenly I felt dizzy, that's all.'

'It seems like there was something more. You're hiding something from me, my love.'

'That's funny, coming from you,' I retorted, not bothering to hide my sarcasm, after a small sip of tea.

She accepted my refusal to talk about it and moved on to something else.

'The wind's picking up a little. You'd better gather together . . . your papers.'

Blown by the wind, the photograph of Saúl began to swirl in circles about the lawn. I jumped out of my seat to snatch it up and once I had it safe I turned around to find Teresa holding the last letter I'd read that morning.

'Stop that, I'll do it!' I yelled, startled.

'I'm sorry,' she answered, visibly wounded and almost in tears. 'It's just . . . it was flying past, and I caught it before it went over the ivy and into the neighbours' garden.'

She handed me the letter, still in its envelope. I picked up the rest of them along with the photo, then piled them on the corner of the kitchen counter. When I went back out to the garden, Teresa was finishing her tea, clearly nervous.

'What do you know about these letters?' I ventured.

It was time to get to the bottom of this.

'Me? Nothing. How would I know about your things, if you don't tell me?'

I knew she was lying, but couldn't figure out why. 'Well, it's strange because someone's taken the trouble to search my wardrobe and open some of the other letters.'

'What's got into you? I would never do a thing like that. How could you possibly think I might go through your things . . . ?'

'They've been opened, Teresa, and you're the only one besides me with keys to this place.'

'You're wrong, dear – it wasn't me!' she answered somewhat aggressively, truly offended at my accusation. 'I saved all those letters from the postbox for years, with plenty of time to read them, but I would never – do you hear me? – never have put my nose somewhere it didn't belong, nor would your mother have tolerated it. If someone really has opened your letters, you're going to have to look for some other explanation.'

'OK, OK, I'm sorry if I insulted you. It's just that . . . This is all so peculiar . . . Do you know who wrote them?'

'I don't have to know, but I can imagine. My powers of deduction would have to be pretty limited not to . . .'

I tried to change tack and get her on my side. I needed answers. 'Why didn't my mother ever give them to Yolanda? I guess you know he was writing to her.'

'Yes, I know they're addressed to your sister, though I don't have the slightest idea why your mother never passed them on . . . But I'll tell you one thing – after that boy left, your sister never wanted to hear his name again, and neither did your mother. It was as though he'd never existed.'

'Of course – just like with all the other men in their miserable lives . . .' I answered, thinking of Fabián and Bodo. 'The crazy thing is that she hung on to them. Now why would she do a thing like that?'

'I saved them – it was me – and I'm certainly regretting it now.'

I was puzzled – so my mother didn't know that Teresa had been keeping and sorting the letters for years.

'That just doesn't add up. Think about it – the day she died she had the key to that drawer hanging around her neck, and Aris had the key to the attic hidden in his collar.'

'I can explain that . . .'

'You can? OK, go ahead then.'

'When the first letter came and your mother knew it was from the lad who was accused of . . . Well, she was furious – you can't even imagine . . . She ordered me to burn it, burn everything that came from him. I told her she should give it to the police because it had a return address, but she, like a total madwoman, completely beside herself, screamed at me again to burn it . . .'

'Go on, please, Teresa.'

'It's not easy for me to remember what happened that day. I thought she just wanted to forget everything rather than go through the ordeal of continuing the investigation, considering how hard it had all been on her—'

'Yes, yes, I understand,' I interrupted, unable to hold back a malicious smile.

'I think she wanted to put everything behind her rather than give that boy what he deserved. But I kept the letters in the attic, like so many other things . . .' She looked at Neca. 'You know that she never went up there. So then I did the same with all the other letters that kept on arriving.' She began toying with the knot of her scarf. 'Two weeks before you came back, I went into the sitting room with the latest bundle of mail in my hand and she asked if there was a letter from Washington State. I froze, looked through the stack I'd just taken from the postbox, and there was indeed one. She made me give it to her, and said that from that moment on she would take care of burning them herself. When I had the opportunity, I went up to the attic to see if the letters were still in the chest of drawers, and found it locked. After that, I didn't dare ask for the key. You know how she was, always more inclined to action rather than words, so if someone disobeyed her she'd deal with it without any discussion. I thought she must have been up there and seen the others, along with all the other things I'd been saving ever since I started working in this house. I don't know . . . I just couldn't bear to throw away things that might have some sentimental value for you girls. I kept thinking that maybe when you were older . . . Everything she asked of me I did, except for this one thing . . . What I didn't know was that she still hadn't burned the letters: she was waiting for the right moment or something, I don't know.'

'Yes, probably. She wouldn't have saved them in any case – she detested keepsakes.'

'Anyway, the fact is that she hid the keys just to make me ask for them every time I wanted to go up there. I had to do it the very next day, to put away some old blankets, and she let me have the one to the attic door, but the drawer was locked. I didn't know if the letters were in there or not, and I never thought to ask.'

I sat still for a few moments, processing what I'd just heard. I believed her, believed everything she'd told me, but still sensed she was holding back something important.

'Berta . . .'

'Yes?'

'Maybe she was the one who opened them.'

'It's possible. But then who went through my wardrobe, rummaging through the letters?'

'I think it might have been me. I did move them to hang up some of your shirts . . .'

'I'm sorry, Teresa, I hadn't thought of that.'

I was devastated. I'd assumed that Teresa had been searching my wardrobe and reading my letters, but now I knew that I'd been carried away by my obsession. I was so glad we'd had this talk and felt so much more relaxed, with my trust in her renewed.

'Oh my goodness, look at the time!' Teresa exclaimed suddenly, checking her watch. 'I hate to leave you here on your own, but—'

'Don't worry, I'm perfectly fine now. It did me wonders to chat with you, and with Neca keeping us company,' I assured her, looking at my doll.

'Well then, I'll just peg out your washing on the clothes line and I'll go.'

'Leave it to me. You're so busy with everything, honestly.'

'I'll ring you later to see how you're feeling, darling.'

'I'll be here.'

As she was leaving, she turned back to look at the garden. 'I almost forgot – I left you some cherries in the kitchen. I saw them at the market and remembered how much you used to like them. That's why I came back.'

'Thank you, Teresa,' I replied warmly.

I felt confused, overwhelmed and guilty. Although I was sure Teresa was still hiding something, I was convinced of her innocence when it came to the letters. No, she hadn't read them, but there had to be some reason she'd been saving them for years that she hadn't wanted to tell me.

The wind was strong, spoiling the normal tranquillity of the garden, so I hung out the damp washing and decided to move into the kitchen, where I made myself a cup of coffee. Aris was curled up in his basket; he hadn't wanted to be outside either.

◆ ◆ ◆

>Olympic National Park
>18 April 2003

>Hi, Yolanda,

(I liked the opening line of this letter; not 'my darling', 'my love', 'my beloved' . . .)

>>It's just over a year since I left, since I saw you for the last time, since I gave you that one last

kiss... One year already... I'm starting to think of our time together as the fantasies of a madman – it must be my mind protecting itself from so much pain, archiving certain memories in the musty corners of my imagination. I have suffered, and still suffer so much from your absence... Sometimes I comfort myself by saying I'm a lucky man, because most people never know that love such as ours can even exist. But then, of course, they don't know either how very much it hurts to lose it.

I nearly sold another painting a few days ago. Nadia, the girl I met at New Year's, is in love with one of my pastels – the one with a close-up of a duck on the lake, staring at everyone who stops to look at him. She said she wanted it because it had a magical gaze. When I told her they were your eyes, she put the painting back. She says that the first painting I do without thinking of you will be the one for her. It's very hard on her.

Take care, Yolanda.

Saúl

Each letter was colder than the last. The year he'd spent alone without hearing from Yolanda was taking its toll. As he said himself, it was a matter of mental health – survive or die.

It was such a relief to know that he was beginning to accept his loss to some extent, and have a life of his own separate from the one she'd destroyed. It seemed that little by little he was allowing himself some leverage to breathe without pain, without remembering. I could understand Nadia perfectly – what woman in love would hang a painting of her rival in her own home? Even so, it bothered me to know that she was getting this close to Saúl, but I had to accept that I wasn't part of the space in which he lived, and not even part of his memories.

I kept on reading. The next three letters were all composed in the same vein. In one of them he sounded excited because the weather was warmer and he could finally open the door and the window to paint: he'd taken up his oils again, once more able to use his favourite means of self-expression. He reported that the lake in springtime had a different kind of light – full of colours. The good weather was allowing him to spend many hours out of doors, painting in the fresh air. His energies were renewed and he was excited about his new projects. In all three letters his tone when he addressed Yolanda was very different from that of his early letters, when he seemed completely torn apart by his loss. It was as though he had resigned himself to it, and that although he hadn't forgotten her in any way, his letters and messages of love seemed more like a means of release, like someone keeping a diary for therapeutic reasons.

◆ ◆ ◆

I was thoroughly immersed in my stranger's life when the landline rang again. My heart lurched in my chest and then seemed to stop beating – as I walked to the sitting room it started thumping again, faster by the second. I decided to hold my nose and breathe through my mouth. I didn't think I could bear the strong smell again that emanated from the area near the phone. I shuddered at the sight of the damp patch on the sofa from my collapse after the last call.

'Hello?' I asked, frightened.

'Berta?' said a voice I recognised, and I felt a little calmer.

'Speaking?'

'Good afternoon, this is Ramón Soler. I'm calling because I need a few documents regarding your mother's two properties. You know – deeds, building regulations certificates, floor plans . . . I'll send someone over to do the valuations as soon as I receive the documents.'

'OK, that's fine, but I'll have to track them down. I've no idea where my mother would have kept such things.'

'I'll need them as soon as possible. We won't be able to move forward with settling probate until then.'

'Of course, not to worry. I'll drop them into the office as soon as they've turned up.'

'Perfect. Well, that was all I had to discuss.'

'How is everything going?' I asked him before he could hang up. I needed to know how long it would be before all this was settled. Not so much because I wanted to leave as soon as I signed the papers, but more because now I was thinking about how much money I was paying Alfonso each day.

'Good: everything is underway. I hope to have it all settled in a fortnight or so. Don't forget those documents.'

'I won't.'

'Goodbye, Berta.'

After hanging up, I seemed to see my mother sitting there, watching me with the cold expression of a cruel tyrant, right on top of the damp outline where I'd wet myself. I left the sitting room fast, not wanting to risk another attack like the one that morning. Aris followed close at my heels.

It was lunchtime. I sautéed some frozen vegetables and paired them with a few turkey slices, salivating at the thought of the rich mushroom risotto we served at my restaurant in London.

I felt quite agitated as I ate, thinking that I would soon need to brave going into my mother's bedroom to find those bloody papers; they had to be in there. In the end it wasn't necessary after all: while I was brushing my teeth Teresa came in, worried about me.

'I'm sorry, my love, I don't mean to bother you, but . . . I called you and the line was busy. I kept picturing you collapsed on the sofa with the phone hanging down to the floor . . .'

'It's OK. I'm really glad you came. Do you know where the documents relating to the two houses are? Ramón asked me for them.'

'I think so. Hold on.'

It didn't take her long to track them down. She was back in five minutes and spread them out on the kitchen table.

'I think this is the lot. They were in the bottom drawer of the wardrobe – I put them there myself a few days ago after finding them on the bed.'

'That's right, I remember now – I saw them when I arrived . . . I thought you must have taken them out. It's weird that she was looking at these very papers just before she died,' I said, untying the knot of the ribbons that bound one of the files.

'Maybe she needed some of it for the sale of the house in Marbella?' she answered, then held out her hand. 'Here, I also found this key. I think it opens one of the drawers in her chest of drawers.'

'Another key, eh? Do you reckon Alberta was a housekeeper herself in a past life or something? She had such an obsession with keeping things locked up, even though she lived on her own.'

'I think it's where she kept her jewellery.'

'Thank you, Teresa,' I said, placing the key next to the bowl of cherries. 'I think I know what I'm having for dinner tonight – these look amazing!'

'Good, I can tell you're feeling better. If you don't need me any earlier, I'll stop by next on Monday, if that's all right with you.'

'Of course. I'll see you on Monday,' I answered affectionately.

I went through the files again, concluding that everything necessary for the legal proceedings was in there for Ramón. In one of them I found the architects' drawings of the two houses. 'Good,' I said to myself, 'seems like it's all here.' I retied the ribbons and went on to more exciting reading material, intending to drop the documents off at the law firm on Monday.

The first letter had the same tone as the ones before: Saúl was exuberant about all the possibilities in Olympic Park with the great weather they were having. According to him, he went outside to paint at dawn, taking his materials and a picnic, and only went back to the cabin at sundown. With each expression of joy, my heart rejoiced along with him.

I thought about our human fascination with twinkling stars that have been dead for endless millennia – that was a perfect parallel to how I felt when I read Saúl's letters. Right now I was living vicariously through situations lost in time for many years, and yet they felt as real to me in their clarity and brilliance as those stars that illuminate our summer nights, even though they no longer exist. Right now, time itself seemed such a cruel and hellish entrapment.

Before going to my bedroom with my two little friends, I called Brandon to ask how everything was going with the restaurant, and to tell him that I still didn't know how long I'd be staying in Spain. This made him rather nervous, as he was getting close to leaving on the holiday he'd had booked in for ages. I insisted that he shouldn't cancel his trip, and also asked him to move five thousand pounds from the restaurant account into my personal account, which made him even more concerned.

Brandon wasn't a man to pry and he never asked more than was absolutely necessary. His was the classic English mentality – restraint above all else. But this time he couldn't hold back and asked if there was anything wrong, to which I answered nothing that didn't have a solution, although not very convincingly.

When I'd put down the phone, I lay on the bed with Neca and Aris at my feet, and continued my journey through space and time.

Olympic National Park
2 June 2003

Dear Yolanda,

How's it going over there? Sorry, I feel more and more ridiculous when I ask how you are. I hope you can understand that – it's like trying to have a conversation with empty space.

I've just come back to the cabin after spending all day searching for fresh landscapes to paint: new perspectives on the lake mostly. It was cloudy this morning, but then it cleared and the day gave me five hours of incredible light. Later, around three o'clock, it started raining so I went over to Dylan's restaurant for a bit of a chat.

It was a quiet afternoon for him, and we had such a long and interesting conversation. Dylan is a great guy. I'll never have enough time or money to pay him back for everything he's done for me.

I think he was waiting for the right moment to talk to me about my situation, even though free time is exactly what he doesn't have much of to spare. He says it's about time for me to leave the past behind and start to build the future that I deserve as an artist, from scratch. He thinks I've got used to hiding away out of mere cowardice, but that there are other options for me and I just have to try. Dylan thinks my legal situation can be sorted, and has offered to hire a good lawyer. He's convinced that as soon as my paintings become known, people will pay top dollar for my work and I can pay back everything he's invested in me. His offer really touched me. I know he doesn't have a lot of cash and that he's always having trouble paying his bills. But what lawyer could defend me from the accusation of having entered this country on a fake passport, even if all the other charges do get dropped? I don't think I realised at the time quite what a risk I was taking. Anyway, I'm starting to resign myself to it . . . What would I be going back for anyway? Judging by your silence, it's obvious that there's nothing waiting for me in Spain. I explained it all to him and . . . well, he thinks that it wasn't you who made me lose my head, but what I felt when I was with you. To me those are one and the same, but he insisted that I'm confusing the two. He said that the emotions I felt when I was with you could have been possible, and in fact are still possible, with any other woman. He says I fell in love with love itself, and you just gave that love a name. I think he's been speaking to Nadia. Ever since I introduced her to him and his girlfriend, they've been hanging out a lot and they've become good friends. I don't know – this might be presumptuous on my part – but my guess is that Nadia's trying to convince me through Dylan to forget about you and me. I don't want to hurt her, if she feels the same way for me that I feel about you . . . But no, that can't be possible.

Dylan also told me that Martin Baker, the owner of the local art gallery, is very interested in showing my work, but that won't be possible either until I get my legal situation resolved. Sometimes

> I think my friend is even more naive than I am – he's not fully aware that I'm accused of murder and have fled from justice. If Mr Baker wants my paintings, he'll have to buy them for his personal collection or find a way to sell them without his clients knowing who I am, maybe even accept that I'll have to sign them with a pseudonym. As a painter, I am Yosa Degui. Get it? Yes, those are the first syllables of both of our first and last names.
>
> But I don't want to get distracted with these matters that don't yet have a solution. I'm just excited right this minute by trying to capture the light as it filters through the trees in the forest. It's fantastic and I'm amazed by it. You can't imagine how difficult it is to paint the spirit of these forests from within. Of course, you're in these paintings too – you always are, or maybe, as Dylan says, it's the love I felt at your side. It makes no difference.
>
> A kiss.
>
> Saúl

I struggled to fall asleep, the wind raging outside the house, making all kinds of strange sounds . . . Sometimes I thought I heard ominous, threatening messages whispered in my ears, along with repeated, muffled thuds – which stopped when I closed the bathroom window.

I dozed fitfully, tucked in tight with the covers pulled over my head.

Chapter 12

Sunday, 22 June 2014

The wind was still whipping through the garden. Its heavy, laboured whistling was really getting to me; it had got inside my head and was giving me a mild headache. I remembered how much I liked the wind in London on those afternoons when I'd leave the restaurant and cross over Lambeth Bridge. Between five and six o'clock in the evening, macs and neckties would fly about wildly as people crossed the waters of the Thames. Everyone in a hurry to get home – maybe that was what made the breezes blow so fiercely. But no one was running about in my garden here, so what was causing this damn relentless wind?

I had a big breakfast – it was almost lunchtime for me – then continued prying in Saúl's life, annoyed that I couldn't go out in the garden. The kitchen wasn't the most comfortable place in which to read and it seemed too early to go back to bed – there was no way, of course, that I'd consider the rest of the house, particularly not the sitting room. Every time I passed it to go to my bedroom or the bathroom, an eerie chill ran through me, through every fibre of my being, just like people say when they talk about haunted houses. I tried to convince myself that it was all in my mind, but the fact is, it was real; it happened over and over again: first came the smell, then the cold chill . . .

The kitchen was slowly turning into an office: my laptop, the files, the folder from the law firm, the letters, my notebook, the Kindle . . . Aris was curled up in the chair on my left and Neca was sitting in the one facing me, the two of them offering all the company I needed.

It was almost half past twelve by the time I started reading, and I didn't look up from the letters until seven o'clock in the evening, only taking breaks once in a while to go to the loo. I think I read around thirty letters, making careful notes based on insubstantial data in my little book. By six o'clock I was already travelling alongside Saúl through 2005.

Burying myself in a year and a half of the life of the man from Lake Crescent, with no interruption, gave me the opportunity to see his personal and professional life from a broader, clearer perspective and, above all, it was like having a front-row seat to his blossoming relationship with Nadia. Before he ever realised it, I already knew that he'd get involved with her, or, to put it another way, that she would live out her love story and he would allow himself to be loved, more out of appreciation for her than on the advice of Dylan and his girlfriend Carol. Saúl hadn't quite decided – he wasn't yet ready to love again, but she was.

He told Yolanda everything with perfect honesty, though reminding her again and again that his love and passion had stayed with her in Spain, and he was completely sincere in this. He was twenty-three years old now, and whenever he went out it was with Dylan, Carol and Nadia. Everyone who knew him assumed that Nadia was his girlfriend, and she didn't bother to correct them. On the contrary, she approached Saúl in public with excessive familiarity, just in case anyone had any doubts. In one of his letters he said, 'You know what, Yolanda? I've realised that most things that happen to us in life have little to do with our own decisions. I can't have the one thing I desire, but something I never wanted or looked for flies right into my lap.' He told her that he had been completely honest with Nadia – he'd warned her that he would never be able to love her as much as she deserved and that he was still in love with the woman he had left behind in Madrid; his muse, the one who inspired his art, the owner of his desires and sleepless nights. But she wanted to give it a go, sure that he would come to love her. I envied Nadia for her confidence and because she was so very much closer to getting him than I was. The things that separated me from Saúl made it quite impossible for my dream to come true.

The letter from 20 January 2005 pierced my heart.

> Olympic National Park
> 20 January 2005
>
> Forgive me, my love.
> I'm sorry, Yolanda, but yesterday I was with Nadia. Her car wouldn't start and Dylan and Carol weren't home. I offered for her to spend the night in my cabin – what else could a gentleman do? It happened, that's all I can say. Kisses led to holding each other and that led to . . . But I couldn't – I just couldn't do it! My mind flew far away; it crossed the ocean and anchored itself back in the first time with you. She swallowed her wounded pride, her desire, her passion and her grief, and I wanted to die – because of Nadia, because of you, and because of my damn bad luck.
>
> In spite of everything, even though I couldn't do it then, I'm sorry. Because I'm going to keep on trying. Even though I know I'll never love her

in the same way I love you, in some ways I do love her, and that's more than I could have hoped for a year ago. I wonder if a few paltry crumbs of love will be enough for her. We surrendered to my impotence and slept together, locked in embrace, after we'd both wept bitter tears for our thwarted loves: she for me, and me for you. Nadia says she's in no hurry, that we'll take it slow. I'm not in a hurry either.

She's a smart girl, talented, pretty and sweet, and, as Dylan says, I really don't deserve such luck. I'm sure there are many men who would fall head over heels with just one look at her gorgeous green eyes. No, I don't deserve her affection, but fate has presented it to me. Love is fickle like that, and no one knows that better than I do. If you fall under its spell but your love is not reciprocated, the resulting emotional damage can last your whole life long. How I envy Dylan and Carol . . . Loving and being loved in equal measure must be heaven on earth indeed.

If you're reading this letter I can imagine your distress, and I don't even want to think about how I would feel if you told me something like this.

I'll stop for now. I'm having a bad day. And, besides, I'm meeting my friends for dinner.

Despite everything, yours.

Saúl

What Saúl couldn't imagine was that his words would make a woman who lived in the future fall in love with him. Yes, love is unpredictable. I felt conflicting emotions as I read: on the one hand, jealousy, rage, helplessness at not being able to stop it because it had already happened and because I was only a spectator; and, on the other, tremendous compassion for Nadia. How was it possible for me to feel so close to someone who simultaneously caused me so much frustration and envy? I was beginning to be a stranger to myself.

My back hurt and my eyes stung. I needed to stop this, go outside and breathe some fresh air. A notification popped up on my laptop, telling me that Brandon had sent me a private message on Facebook: he was reminding me that his flight to Egypt was booked for 1 August. I didn't feel like answering him; his problem seemed so trivial to me right now.

I needed to get some exercise and clear my head, so I showered, then put on comfortable clothes and went for a walk through the neighbourhood. The wind was still raging, the gusts whipping me in the face and blowing my hair about violently. I walked for half an hour, thinking about him the whole way, imagining the scene a thousand times over of the two of us holding hands by the lake, my stomach full of butterflies like that of a teenager.

A shock awaited me on my return home – on hearing me open the front gate, someone ran off through the garden behind the house, leaping over the bougainvillea to get away. I froze, petrified, under the arch of the gate. When I was finally able to react, my heart pounding, I wondered if I should call the police before going in, or check for myself first to see if they'd taken anything from inside. I thought about Alfonso, but he'd been very clear that I should never try to contact him. The screen always came up with 'Unknown caller' when he rang me, and it didn't seem wise to ring the office of the detective agency to pass on a message like this, especially since they were almost certainly closed. I decided not to call the police either, and while I still stood there, indecisive and rooted to the spot between the pavement and the garden, a neighbour passed by with a bag, heading for the bins.

'Evening – everything OK?'

I must have looked pathetic. The man noticed that something was wrong straight away. I'm sure my shocked expression as I stood there under the lamppost was plain enough for anyone with eyes to see.

'Yes, yes, I'm fine. Thank you. Good evening,' I said, trying to end the conversation, because I wanted to be alone even more than I wanted to ask for help.

'You must be Alberta's daughter. I'm so sorry about your mother.'

'Thanks – yes, I'm Berta.'

'I'm Arturo – your next-door neighbour. If you need anything, don't hesitate to ask,' he offered kindly, putting his free hand in his trouser pocket and taking out a card. 'Here, this has my number. There have been a lot of burglaries in the neighbourhood lately . . . Do call if you need anything, won't you? Enjoy your evening then.'

'Nice to meet you and thanks very much,' I answered, taking the card with some misgivings.

At that point I didn't trust my own shadow.

As soon as he turned away, I hurried through the gate, clicking it shut behind me. Even out in the garden, I had the feeling that my legs couldn't support my weight. I searched clumsily, looking for the keys to the front door among the dozen or so on my key ring before realising that I didn't need them: the door was standing wide open. I walked down the garden path as though propelled along by the wind, scarcely in control of my own limbs. Once inside the hallway, I peeked my head around the corner towards the kitchen and saw that the basket of letters was standing empty. Horrified, one hand flew to my chest and the other to cover the gaping O of my mouth. The door to the garden was also open, creaking as it swung in the wind. It could only be opened from the inside. Whoever had stolen the letters had come in through the front door with their own key, and then left via the kitchen and run all the way through to the bougainvillea hedge and the street behind. I followed the trail he'd left: the lawn was strewn with letters, dancing in the wind like mad white butterflies. Seeing 'my' letters scattered all over the garden, at the mercy of this macabre and jerky dance, threw me into immediate action. I grabbed the basket and started after them, catching them one by one, battling the wind, which mockingly swirled eddies of abandoned letters wherever it pleased.

It took a while to gather them all. When I was done I searched every nook and cranny with the utmost care, especially those areas that were less well lit – it was dark by now and the light from the street lamps didn't extend to the whole garden. I could hardly see a thing out there, so I fetched a torch from the kitchen and then headed back out to hunt under bushes and in the most shadowy corners. Once I was sure there were no more letters left to find, I went back in the house with the torch under my arm, the basket in one hand and a few letters that had threatened to drift out from the top in the other. I cursed myself then for not having counted how many there were before setting about reading them, because I wouldn't now know if the thief had got away with any. Most of them had fallen out of their organised bundles, so I would need to spend some time reordering them. But that would have to wait, because right then I stumbled upon my second dreadful shock of the night.

Seeing Neca with that knife in her chest, still sitting in the same spot where I'd left her . . . I could have sworn she was even bleeding. I dropped the basket on the floor, and quickly searched around for Aris. In all the confusion of collecting the letters I hadn't even noticed if he was still in the house or not. I saw him down by my feet, looking up at me, feeling my grief along with me. I picked him up in my arms, sat down facing my childhood friend and cried like a little girl, my face buried in his furry back. He let me hug him as much as I wanted, until I felt calmer.

I picked Neca up carefully as though she might shatter, as though she really were injured and I was afraid she would bleed out or die in my arms. My whole body shaking, I drew the weapon out slowly, one more tear plopping on to her nose. The intruder had coldly and calculatingly stabbed her in the chest for maximum effect – this was personal and they must somehow be aware of her importance to me. I went to fetch the sewing kit from the sideboard in the hall and, trembling, set myself to the delicate task of stitching up Neca's chest and dress. The slash to her chest was so deep that the knife had nearly come out the other side through her back. I took my time, wanting her to be perfect, and, despite my heart pounding with emotion, I did a neat job. I checked every stitch, calculating where and how to place the next one, mending the single most beautiful thing from my past – Neca and what she represented in terms of friendship, warmth and forbearance, even in the hardest moments. It was a miracle she had survived until now, waiting in the attic for fifteen long years to tell me that it hadn't all been so bad and that, if I clung to the good times, I could win through in the battle ahead. She was my icon, and when I looked at her I remembered why I was there – she gave me the confidence to face the difficult task that awaited me. Her little face seemed to say, *We overcame so much suffering together when you were small, so we can do it again now.* She was my lucky charm – one of those talismans in which people confide when we think all is lost. We talk to them, carry them with us at all times, protect them . . . convinced they can keep us from harm.

Next I mended her dress with blue thread, taking the utmost care, passing the needle first from right to left, and then from left to right, securing the threads of the fabric one at a time, up and down, as Teresa had taught me. I don't think anyone else could have done it so well. Pleased with my progress, I relaxed a little, and began to embroider her name over the stab wound. While I concentrated on this task, I couldn't help thinking that whoever had hurt Neca and thrown my letters to the four winds, all around the garden, must be someone I knew, someone who knew how to hurt me. I think Aris had been spared because he'd belonged to my mother and that was why he hadn't been the object of the break-in – or else he'd simply known where to hide from this unknown bastard.

My precious work done, I sat my friend down in her chair and went on to my next task: sorting the letters back into their years and sequence of dates.

Once they were all in order, I made myself something to eat, mulling over everything that had happened. Who was the stranger I'd seen jumping over the hedge in the garden? Could it be the same man who'd been spying on Alfonso and me at the restaurant, the same one who'd phoned me and then hung up without saying a word? Why did he want the letters? Suddenly I became aware of how vulnerable I was living alone in this house and started to panic. I left the beaten eggs in the bowl and the frying pan on the stove and, before making the omelette, went through the house making sure that all the doors and windows were locked. When I came back, the kitchen was full of smoke and that was the final straw – I broke down.

I turned off the stove, sat down in the fug of smoke and burst into tears again, this time in true despair. I felt quite overwhelmed at the series of events over the past few days, sobbing out my sadness, rage, helplessness, panic . . . and because of that damn wind which had almost taken my letters and was driving me mad. There is nothing more tragic than crying alone. Normally when we open the floodgates, we seek out company to comfort us and share our pain, as though the act of weeping on one's own would be pointless.

When our eyes fill up without someone close by to care for us, it's because we simply can't take any more.

I don't know how long I sat there with the tears streaming, pouring out my frustrations into the smoke; I only know that I caught sight of Aris gazing up at me with seeming compassion. Well, no, I guess I hadn't been crying alone after all then. I picked him up and rocked him like a baby; both of us had had so little affection in our lives . . . 'We have to clean all this up and eat, otherwise I'll end up being the next victim of this madness,' I told him.

I cleaned the kitchen and at nearly one o'clock in the morning finally sat facing an omelette and salad, this time without incident – it was perfect and delicious.

I took another shower to get rid of the smell of burning, but under the stream of water it felt as though I was being watched, more naked than ever. Through the frosted pane of the window I seemed to see shadows crossing the garden, and wasn't sure it was just the branches of the willow blowing in the wind. That was the fastest shower of my life. I tried calling Teresa but she didn't answer – it was too late. Exhausted, I crawled into bed with my companions.

Chapter 13

Monday, 23 June 2014

I woke with a start – I had an important appointment scheduled with the solicitor this morning, who was waiting for the documents he'd requested. I'd been too scared and it had been too late to wash the smell of burnt cooking oil from my hair during my rushed shower the previous night. It was twenty to nine now, according to my phone, and I still had time, so after feeding and petting Aris the first thing I did was take another shower, then I had breakfast and left. No sign of Teresa, which surprised me, but I didn't have time to think about it.

It was a hassle being without a car again and I had to take a bus to the metro station, but at least the wind had subsided and it was a beautiful morning. Grabbing the files I needed, which weighed a bloody ton, I headed out for the law firm with my hair still wet. I bumped into Teresa on my way to the station.

'Morning, dear.'

'Hi, Teresa.'

'I'm so glad to see you. I called yesterday but you didn't answer – I was worried about you. I hurried over as soon as I was done at the doctor's.'

'Oh, I don't know, maybe I was in the shower. That's funny – I called you too, but I think it was too late in the evening.'

'You know I've always liked going to bed early.'

'Well, as you can see, I'm OK. We'll talk tomorrow.'

'I brought you some fruit and chicken in sauce—'

'Oh hell, there's my bus. See you later.'

When I got out of the metro, Madrid seemed more gorgeous and alive than ever before. Being among so many people was invigorating.

◆ ◆ ◆

I had to wait for over an hour. I wished I had my Kindle on me so I had something to look at. I felt so exposed in front of all the clients and lawyers passing by . . . Feeling spooked, I saw my stalker in every man.

At last, the married couple who had the appointment before mine emerged and the secretary invited me in.

'Hello, Señorita de Castro,' said the solicitor, holding out his hand. 'Did you bring what I asked for?'

'Hello. Yes, I think I have it all – everything related to the two properties at least,' I answered, putting the files down on the lavish office desk.

'I see, I see,' said the solicitor, gazing down at the thick files. 'If you want, I'll return anything that's not necessary, but you'll need to wait for Julia to review all the paperwork.'

Julia peered over the top of her glasses to look at the hours of slog awaiting her, and said, 'These other files will keep me busy for a while, and I won't be able to look over your ones until I'm done—'

'That's OK,' I said, interrupting. 'I'll pick it all up next time I'm here. I don't think I'm going to need anything from the files if I haven't missed it over the last fifteen years . . . I know you'd asked me to look out for specific documents, but I didn't know precisely what you might need. I'm sorry.'

'Well, I do hope you're less trusting with the rest of the world,' Julia noted. 'If you say you don't even know what's among these papers . . .'

She was right – I should really have some vague notion of what I was handing over to the lawyer representing my sister.

'Perfect,' Ramón said, intervening to make sure I didn't have any change of mind. He looked to be in a hurry. 'We'll send someone to value the house in Madrid this week, and give you plenty of notice. We don't need a new valuation for the house in Marbella – it was done recently when the sale was reviewed. I hope to have everything sorted out by next week, or the week after that at the latest, all depending on how your sister's lawyer gets on,' he said to wind up the conversation. He rose to his feet and held out his hand, unable to hide his air of urgency.

'Until next time then, Señor Soler.'

I felt somewhat disappointed – I'd given up an entire morning, only to deliver two files. I had hoped to get some information, sign some paperwork, something. Although on second thought, if I had anything right now, it was plenty of time on my hands.

The episode from the previous night was weighing heavily on my mind. I didn't want to go home, and still shuddered at the memory of that man's shadowy form running across the garden. The normal thing would have been to tell the police, but I didn't want to jeopardise my own investigation. If I'd called the police, I might have been forced to tell them that I'd hired a private detective and then I'd have had to answer a thousand more questions. No, I wanted to keep moving ahead with my own inquiry, and on my own terms. I decided to take a long walk through town and wandered about as though in a dream, completely absorbed, looking for answers. At one point I had the feeling that someone was following me. Even if I couldn't say who it was, I was too terrified to turn around and see my pursuer. I didn't dare take the metro, so I called a cab and went home. I didn't even know if anyone was really there.

◆ ◆ ◆

The simple act of unlocking the front gate was not just routine but starting to require all my courage. I had never felt safe in this house, and now I felt even less so. I focused on Aris, hoping with all my might that he would be waiting for me. And there he was – he never failed me. What a relief to see his green eyes as I opened the front door.

'Hello, handsome! Hey there,' I said in greeting, hugging him gently. He purred loudly in appreciation. 'I love it that you wait for me. Did you take good care of the house while I was gone?' I asked as if he could understand.

No matter the content of what I said, I knew he liked the affectionate tone of my voice. He let himself be petted as he nuzzled his head against my neck over and over.

'My God, you're a weight! I don't know much about cats, but I reckon you're a little bit on the heavy side. I'm going to have to talk to Teresa – I think we're both feeding you every day.'

I decided to make myself comfortable, fetch my dry laundry in from the clothes line and carry on with my reading. The second task wasn't necessary after all, because I found the sheets and towels ironed and folded with incredible precision and lying on my bed. It was only to be expected from someone who had worked for Alberta for so many years.

Alfonso came into my thoughts while I was changing and taking off my make-up. I hadn't heard from him since Friday, and suddenly it occurred to me that something terrible might have happened. Investigating Bodo's disappearance was becoming a far more dangerous activity than I had anticipated. I got the chills thinking that we were both being watched and that the house wasn't safe. I'd have to change the locks or leave, because the situation was affecting my state of mind.

I was heading out to the garden when a WhatsApp message pinged through to my phone. It was Brandon, letting me know that the money was now in my account. It was very curt, without even a basic greeting – his own particular means of expressing his irritation.

The afternoon was perfect for relaxing under the willow tree.

> Olympic National Park
> 2 February 2005
>
> My beautiful Yolanda,
> I have to tell you, it's official now: Nadia and I are dating. I don't think it's likely to end well – one person can't build a relationship all on their own. I'm a clear example of that, chained by a love that exists only in my imagination, just like with Nadia. Or are you there after all? Tell me! Tell me before I move forward with a relationship that will just hurt everyone.

(I wanted to shout at him, *Yes, I'm here, but my name is Berta!*)

> When she and I are together, I try to let myself be loved, although that's really hard for me. I think I let myself go because I know how it feels and I don't want her to suffer over me the way I suffer over you. I think I would also be OK with you allowing yourself to be loved by me this way, if I

could share part of my days with you. That would be so much more hopeful than this absurd and empty waiting. I'm satisfied with so little . . . She has infinitely more than I do.

She's a very patient girl. I know she's dying for me to hug her occasionally or whisper 'I love you'. She says she'll wait for as long as it takes . . . I don't know – I'm sure she's telling the truth but it's also true that time changes everything in its path and she'll end up hardening her heart. I expect to hear from you less and less each day. The hopelessness that's growing slowly within me also makes me feel a suffocating guilt. What if you can't answer my calls for help? What if you've disappeared, just like your husband? Do you know how it feels to have one part of me that blames you and the other part that sees you as a victim? Not knowing is the worst torture of all. Still, I'm trapped in the love that you and I shared – it's as though the days we spent together leave every other emotion in the shadows. It was all so intense . . . If only I could give Nadia a tiny piece of what I felt when I was with you . . . But no, I've been too badly damaged and I think I'm incapable of loving again. The fact you're no longer in my life only makes whatever's wrong with me worse.

It's already night and the soft lighting in the cabin is enveloping the paintings around me with a magical glow. It's enveloping you – all my works have your essence in them.

> I have to leave you now – the group is waiting for me at the restaurant. At this time of year we have the whole place to ourselves.
> A kiss, if you want it, from,
> Saúl

I felt like an invisible part of a bizarre romantic quartet, an intruder in that love triangle where love flowed in only one direction, imprisoning some without allowing them the possibility of being loved back. I too had tried the hallucinogenic potion and was trapped, but felt so much more alone than the others. I was the only one they didn't even know about.

Part of me felt close to Nadia. I understood her better with each letter and wanted her to be loved in return, for her own sake and also because it would mean that Saúl had finally escaped from Yolanda's clutches and could be happy – although I was also bitterly jealous of her closeness with the man by the lake. I wanted him to be happy, of course, but I also wanted him for myself.

I was coming to realise that the winters accentuated Saúl's natural melancholy. He couldn't use his oils and brushes to express his creativity because the fumes meant he needed ventilation, and the cold prevented him from throwing open the windows. Also he was deprived of his long rambles through the lush forests that surrounded him, which further increased his endless anguish with life.

In the last letter he told me . . . he told Yolanda that he still couldn't make love to Nadia. 'I can't – I still can't love her like a man should love a woman, and she needs more than just affection,' he told her, after blaming himself for having ever allowed the relationship to begin in the first place. He seemed so honest and so true to himself . . . so sincere!

In the same letter he sent a photograph of Dylan, Carol, Nadia and himself sitting at a restaurant table, next to a huge window that framed Lake Crescent. The light from outside washed out the picture and I couldn't see their faces, especially that of Saúl. I could tell that Dylan was mixed race and well built, and that Carol was blonde and slender. I could barely see Nadia next to Saúl, who was in the foreground, the two of them completely in shadow. The direction of light through the window scarcely hit the right-hand side of Dylan's profile. But one detail was easy to make out: everyone was smiling except for Saúl.

When Harry asked me why I'd never been able to fall in love in my life, I'd always answered that I hadn't yet found the man with enough of a sense of humour to balance out my own reserve, and that it would be hard to find a man like that in London, where the inhabitants usually mix this trait with an irony I could never understand. But I was lying – Harry had a great sense of humour and contagious optimism. What's more, Saúl had many qualities I'd fallen in love with, but he didn't seem very happy. Nonetheless, he had won my heart purely through the words he had written.

I went back into the house as dusk fell, feeling like a sitting duck out there in the garden, protected only by the light of the street lamps, and all the more so after what had happened the night before. I gathered up the letters, meaning to keep on reading after dinner.

Teresa's chicken was sensational. I finished it even though I wasn't hungry just so I could savour every bite, though I did share a small scrap with Aris. I was enjoying the last delicious mouthful when the entryphone rang – the first time I'd heard it since coming home. I jumped so violently that the morsel of chicken flew right out of my mouth. I picked up the entryphone by the front door, my nerves in tatters.

'Who is it?'

'It's Alfonso Salamanca. I know it's late . . .'

'Just a minute.'

I didn't dare buzz him in straight away because his voice had come through distorted via the speaker, and the camera showed only a sinister-looking shadow. Instead I went out and walked over to the front gate, which had a small barred window I could look through, just to be on the safe side.

'Alfonso . . . what are you doing here?'

'Can we talk?'

'Sure, of course,' I answered firmly, opening the gate at last. 'Come on in. You don't know the fright you gave me.'

'I can imagine. I'm sorry.'

'Shall we sit out?' I asked, still flustered, leading him towards the central area of the garden.

'Sounds perfect – it's a beautiful night. Ah, I see you were having dinner, and in good company too,' he said when we passed through the kitchen, seeing the leftovers of my meal and Neca sitting at the head of the table. Aris trotted close on our heels. 'Sorry to interrupt.'

'That's all right, I'd just finished. You should have come ten minutes earlier in fact – I ate way too much. Would you like something to eat? I don't have much in, but—'

'No, thank you, I also dined rather well. A nice little snifter might be just the thing to aid the digestion and relax me, however. It's been quite a day.'

'Sounds good. Take a seat and I'll be right back.'

From the kitchen, as I was preparing the drinks, I glanced out at Alfonso, bathed in the artificial light of the garden. He was not hugely good-looking and rather unkempt, reeking of tobacco and expensive hair gel, though in his favour it was obvious that he showered regularly and kept his nails clean and trimmed. Everything in his round face looked too small: his eyes, nose and mouth had too much space around them somehow, as though nature had made a mistake and given him the features of a child. Maybe that's why he looked both innocent and wise at the same time.

His face was sad and he seemed bowed down with constant worry, exuding loneliness while simultaneously coming across as trustworthy. That was all at superficial level, because as soon as you got close to him and talked with him a bit, he turned into a man with a certain attraction, wise and experienced, and his gestures and smooth movements hinted at a certain polished education. He held a cigarette in one hand and petted Aris tenderly with the other.

'Here we are,' I said, putting a tray down on the table with two generous glasses of Jack Daniel's, along with ice, nuts and an ashtray. I was dying of curiosity.

'This is a real invasion of your privacy, I know, but I needed to talk to you.'

'Why not on the phone? Sorry if that sounded rude – I didn't mean it that way. Actually, I'm glad of a little company . . .'

'I needed to show you something and ask your opinion, but I wanted to do it in person. You remember the guy who followed us to the restaurant?'

'How could I forget? Ever since then I can't shake off the feeling that he's somewhere behind me, even if I couldn't catch sight of his face.'

'I ran into him this afternoon in the lobby of my hotel. He had his back to me and was reading a newspaper – well, he was pretending to read a newspaper at least – but I recognised him all right. He didn't see me and I managed to take a photo of him. Can you show me the one you have of the guy from the letters?'

'Sure, it's in the kitchen.'

I went into the house and he followed me.

'There's better light in here,' he said, fishing out his mobile. The photograph of Saúl in one hand and his phone in the other, he said, 'Tell me – what do you see?'

'Well . . . two men with their backs to the camera, one sitting by a lake and the other one reading a newspaper,' I answered, though I had a sneaking suspicion what he was on about.

'I believe it's possible that they're the same person. Look . . . they're the same height, just the right age difference, identical complexion, hair colour,' he said, listing the qualities, holding the pictures closer to my face, urging me to analyse them.

I was stunned. Yes, at first glance they did look like the same person with a few years between them – more than ten years to be exact.

'But . . . that's impossible,' I managed to say, after taking the phone and the photograph from him and studying the images more closely.

'It doesn't seem so impossible to me. When did the last letter arrive? Think about it – we're a two-day trip at most from Washington.'

'A couple of weeks before I came back, I think. Wait, I'll look at the date – the letters are in this basket here.'

I went straight to the smallest bundle at the bottom of the basket, which only had three letters in it, and took out the last one.

'Right, according to the postmark it was sent on 27 May of this year, a little less than a month ago.'

'That's more than enough time for him to have come back. I need to read that letter, if you don't mind.'

I handed it to him, full of doubts. 'If it's not relevant and the letter doesn't say anything to help our investigation, I'd rather you don't tell me what it says. I'd like to keep reading them in chronological order.'

'If you say so,' he answered, curiosity registering on his face. 'Is there something you haven't told me that I should know?'

'No, nothing like that!' I exclaimed irritably. 'It's just a compulsion of mine to always follow a logical order in everything I do.'

'Good, I hope so. Berta . . .'

'Yes?'

'You can trust me completely – everything you tell me will be in strictest confidence. If there's anything you think I should know, tell me.'

'I've answered all your questions with total honesty. I don't think I've held anything important back.'

'Great.'

He didn't believe me, but he also didn't seem to care that much, as if he knew that my not wanting to know the content of the letter was on purely sentimental grounds without any bearing on the case. He probably suspected that I was attracted to the man writing the letters and that I wanted to live his story like a novel, with the last page saved to be read at the end.

Taking the letter from him, I snatched up the letter opener, which I kept always close at hand, sliced open the envelope and drew out another from inside, noticing once again with these two that they appeared to have been carefully resealed after opening. The second envelope, which had been inside the first, I opened with the same level of caution, handling them both like rare manuscripts of historic importance, taking the utmost care even in the way in which I cut the paper. Alfonso looked on patiently but with mounting surprise. I handed him the two envelopes without extracting the letters within.

'I think it's this one. If you look at the return address you'll see it came from Seattle. I guess he must have moved at some point.'

'Interesting.'

'By the way, I do also have something really important to tell you,' I said, remembering the letter thief and doll assassin.

'We'll talk about it in a minute, but let me read this letter first. May I?' he asked, pointing to one of the kitchen chairs.

'Certainly,' I answered, and sat facing him expectantly.

He seemed very focused in his concentration and for a moment, when he turned the page over, I had the impression that he was moved by what he had read. When he'd finished, he slipped the sheet back in its envelope and handed it to me.

'Well?' I asked, disappointed by his silence.

'Well, what? Didn't you tell me you didn't want to know anything about it until you read it in order?'

'Yes, but . . . did the letter confirm your suspicions that Saúl might be in Madrid?'

'It didn't confirm it, but it's still a possibility, and in fact it seems even more likely now than it did before I read it. I need to track down a contact who can settle this for me, although he doesn't exactly work for free.'

Oh . . . how tempting it was right now to read that last letter! But no, still no.

'That reminds me, I owe you two thousand euros, plus the extra expenses.'

'Forget about the extra expenses for the moment.'

'Well, you'll have to forget about the two thousand too, at least for the moment. I wasn't expecting you.'

'Don't worry, I didn't come here for that.'

'I have another photograph, but I don't think it'll help you much. It's backlit and much too dark.'

I found it among the letters on the counter and showed it to him. While he was looking at it, I got together all the letters I'd read since the last time I saw him and spoke to him again.

'I've read these already, so don't forget them.'

'Wonderful,' he said, handing back the photo. 'You're right, this one isn't very helpful. Who are the other people?'

'That's Dylan – he's in charge of the restaurant and, I think, of the local resort; he also rents out the cabins and canoes on the lake. He's Saúl's best friend – his only friend, apparently. Next to him is Carol, his girlfriend, and behind Saúl, that's Nadia, the girl he's dating.'

'*Was* dating, Berta: this happened over nine years ago now.'

I wondered if this clarification was taking into account the last letter he'd read. If it was obvious in that letter that he was still with Nadia, he wouldn't have made that comment. *Maybe he's with someone else now, or maybe he's back with Yolanda – why not? He could be in Madrid with her*, I thought. I was really upset at this possibility, and Alfonso noticed it.

'Shall we go back out into the garden?' I asked him.

'Terrific.'

'It's nice and cool out, and the wind's dropped at last. You don't know how welcome this climate is after living in London for the last fifteen years.'

'Berta, do you know where your sister is?'

'According to what Teresa told me, she's in Australia, and it seems our solicitor believes that too, since they're handling her part of the inheritance by proxy. But I can't be sure – with Yolanda you can never be certain of anything. A few days ago, after years without us talking at all, she called me here at the house to warn me to leave as soon as possible.'

'What number did she call from?'

'There was no number to recognise – lately everybody's been coming up as an unknown caller. I assumed she was phoning from Australia.'

'Well, I believe she's in Spain, possibly even in the vicinity of Madrid, or at least she has been for the last few days.'

'She can't be . . . What makes you think that?'

'I told you, I have my contacts.'

'But if . . . The paperwork for the inheritance is being delayed because she's delegated her powers to an attorney, claiming she can't travel . . . That would be too twisted, though I guess nothing would surprise me any more . . .'

'Yes, she definitely has ceded all powers to a lawyer, but I don't think she did it from Australia. What's more, I could swear that she's never lived on that continent at all, although the strange thing is that she travels out there a lot.'

'How do you know?'

'I can't tell you how – this type of information . . . I don't exactly get it legally.'

'So you think both Saúl and Yolanda could be here?'

'It's a possibility, but I can't give you any solid facts at the moment. I need to talk to Teresa. Could you convince her to come with you to our next meeting?'

'I don't know. She doesn't even know you exist.'

'Tell her, but don't give her more information than is absolutely necessary. It's important that I ask her some questions.'

'Since you came I've been wanting to tell you something that I can't get out of my head.'

'OK, surprise me.'

'Yesterday, about eight in the evening, I went to take a walk around the neighbourhood and on my return scared a man in the house who, when he heard me come in, got away over the hedge at the back. He came for the letters because I found them scattered all over the lawn; I don't know if he managed to get away with any. I also found Neca, my doll, with a knife through her chest. I think whoever it was knew very well which things are most precious to me – someone must have fed him information. Fortunately he didn't do anything to Aris. Maybe he didn't have time or it wasn't what he came for.'

'What did he look like? Did you see his face?'

'It was really dark and it all happened so fast, I could barely make out his silhouette when he was running away . . .'

'Try to remember; this is very important.'

'Tall, thin, around forty years old, quite agile . . .' Suddenly I realised that my description fitted perfectly with the man who'd followed us to the restaurant, as well as matching Saúl.

Alfonso took his phone back out and showed me the picture of our suspect. 'Look at him more closely – could it have been him?'

'I don't know,' I answered suspiciously. I refused to believe that the letter thief, the man who'd been watching us, and Saúl were the same person, but then I reconsidered and answered honestly. 'Yes, it could have been.'

He downed the rest of his whisky and put his phone back in his pocket.

'Alfonso,' I said, trying to get his attention, because just then I saw him watching Aris walking slowly across the lawn.

'Yes?'

'You have to find out where Saúl is. He can't be the one who broke in here yesterday.'

'He could be the very same.'

'No, it's not him, I'm sure of it. Find him and you'll see.'

'I don't know if you're being objective enough. It seems to me that that boy has won you over through his letters. Either way, I don't see him in the same light myself, although nothing really surprises me any more.'

'It's not him. Something tells me this is another trap.'

'We'll find him in the end, don't you worry. Mind if I have another?' he asked, holding up his empty glass. 'Only a finger. It's about time for me to be going.'

I poured him more whisky as he gazed up at the stars, smoking slowly as he stroked Aris. He was clearly enjoying the moment.

'You may be right,' he spoke again, setting his glass down on the table without taking his eyes off the sky. 'Someone may have hired that young man to give false evidence at the trial. It's possible that the man following us is the guy the witnesses thought was Saúl that night Bodo disappeared. But . . .'

'But what?' His half-explanations made me anxious.

'I don't know, that last letter . . . I have to go,' he said, after finishing the rest of his whisky in one swallow and putting out his cigarette. 'I parked quite a distance away to make sure they didn't follow me. Though from what you told me, I'm not sure it matters – our man seems to know everything about you, even what you had for last night's dinner. By the way,' he said, standing up now, 'rent yourself another car – living out here you're going to need it. Besides, you never know when you might want to make a quick getaway. Sorry, I didn't mean to alarm you,' he said, seeing the change in my expression. 'I'll call you soon.'

I handed over the letters, walked him to the door and we said goodbye. Immediately after that, I went to gather things up from the garden table and locked myself back in the house. When at last I climbed into bed with Neca, Aris and the rest of the letters, it was almost midnight.

> Olympic National Park
> 4 May 2005
>
> My dear Yolanda,
> Spring has finally arrived in Olympic Park. Today it was sunny all the way through from dawn to sundown – such a luxury for me. I'm sure you can imagine what I did with so many hours of light.

Nadia came along. She made lunch and grabbed the chance to sunbathe while I painted. I don't really get why she sticks with me, just like she doesn't understand why I keep on with my letters to you.

Well, I have good news: Mr Baker bought another three of my paintings. This time he paid me twenty-five hundred dollars. The news is spreading throughout Washington State that there's an anonymous painter who lives alone in Olympic Park, whose works always conceal the eyes of a mysterious girl. I'm beginning to make some real money and this, along with the arrival of good weather, has properly lifted my spirits. He told me again that he'd love to organise a show of my work, but I just don't see how it's possible, considering my legal situation.

I asked Nadia to drive me over to Ruby Beach tomorrow. I'll have to get up really early as it's two hours away, but I desperately want to paint the incredible beaches of this peninsula. You cannot imagine the stunning contrasts of blue and green where the Pacific meets the forest. You would adore these landscapes . . .

I'll keep telling you about it all, lovely Yolanda.

Saúl

What I wouldn't give for one of Saúl's paintings . . . all the inheritance money I was about to receive and more. And as for taking him to that Pacific beach . . . I would give my life itself for one day by his side.

So that's where my reading stopped for the night. The words of the last letter had sparked all sorts of wonderful fantasies and managed to disconnect me from my sorrows. It was the perfect moment to surrender myself to the world of dreams, so I put the envelope aside, turned out the light and let myself be carried away to Ruby Beach, to stroll with Saúl by the edge of the Pacific as its foaming tides washed up on the sands, and he sought to capture the beautiful scenery of Olympic Park.

We walked hand in hand, barefoot, taking our time as our feet sank into the sparkling froth of the surf that polished the sand, revelling in the warmth of the sun and the cool, rejuvenating breeze. The melodious back-and-forth swishing of the peaceful waves was the soundtrack to our story. We didn't speak – no words could have been a thousand times more eloquent than how we felt in each other's company. That's all there was to it – we walked down the beach holding hands, like in those ads for home insurance that I liked so much, which managed to convey in seconds everything I wanted and would never have, neither with insurance nor without it.

Imagination is a powerful thing: in your lowest moments it's the best refuge, where everything happens exactly the way you want it to, and you can travel through space and time in a heartbeat to be wherever you want and with whomever you want. For so many years gone past, I'd hardly given myself any time at all in which to feel lonely, always chasing after my next goal. Coming back to Spain, with no work pressure and so little to do, I realised finally that when we are born we get two lives. One of them tests us and measures us constantly against other people, demanding we do more than simply survive: it urges us to fight for the betterment of humankind until our dying breath. But there's a parallel life in which everything is possible without the slightest effort, quite as real and vibrant as the other. You only have to give yourself a minute to enter the portal with your most cherished dream or fantasy to let the magic happen. What I felt for Saúl was so strong and every bit as real as my imagination allowed, to the point where I shivered with joy holding hands with him despite the fact that I happened to be in the single most hostile environment to love: my mother's house. It was an extraordinary situation. In my teenage years, I used to lie dreaming in this very bed that I was the beloved princess from a fairy tale, the heroine of a thousand happy endings, but these yearnings had no real foothold in my mind because of the extreme depths of my anxiety. If there was one thing I'd learned over the years, it was sometimes to slam the door on all my fears and surrender myself completely to the world of my imagination. And so I fell sound asleep, right through till the following morning.

Chapter 14

Tuesday, 24 June 2014

Someone opened the front door and my heart lurched with dread, because I knew now that another person besides Teresa and me had keys to the house. I'd have to call a locksmith first thing. I could ask Teresa to do it, but, no, this was my chance to start afresh so she would have to call me to get access to the house. Besides, I didn't know if the letter thief had got the keys from her – not that she would necessarily have given them to him on purpose, but he might have taken them from her without her noticing. It was also possible that this was all some twisted plot of my sister's, fearing she'd get the blame for her husband's disappearance; maybe she'd hired the criminal to scare me and to make sure I didn't read the letters. I had completely rejected the idea that Saúl had anything to do with it – he simply wasn't capable of something like this. The proof was that not even the expert manipulator, my sister Yolanda, had dared ask him to kill Bodo, knowing that he just wasn't cut out for that kind of crime. It was only the very start of the day and already I was plagued by doubts and questions.

Coming out of the bathroom, I noted the welcoming smell of freshly brewed coffee wafting along the corridor. Having Teresa around certainly did have its advantages, I had to admit. I found her in the kitchen, washing up the whisky glasses. It seemed like a good opportunity to bring up the matter of Alfonso and ask her to come with me to our next meeting.

I stared down at the glasses, the water streaming off them into the sink, and kicked off the conversation. 'I had someone over last night.'

'It seems like it was well needed. I'm so glad – you spend far too much time alone,' she answered, wiping down the worktop.

She seemed a little nervous, but not at all interested in who'd come over. Actually, Teresa never seemed much interested in the private lives of those she lived with – it was one of the many virtues that had kept her working for my mother for so many years. Either way, I was going to tell her. 'His name's Alfonso Salamanca. He's the detective I hired.'

She stopped what she was doing to look me straight in the eye. She didn't appear altogether surprised at the news. 'So what's all that about then?'

'Well, I just really need to know the truth. I'm not planning on leaving until I've figured it all out.'

'It happened a long time ago, my dear . . .'

'Precisely, and now it's time to straighten everything out and move on with our lives,' I replied casually, pouring cat food into Aris's dish. 'By the way, we're going to have to agree on which of us gets to feed this chubby little fluffball. I reckon he's gained weight since I've been here.'

'Oh my, you're right,' she declared, looking at him. 'Well, I'll leave it to you then. I can see you two have been getting on well.'

'Teresa . . .'

'Yes?' she said, turning back to her cleaning.

'Alfonso, the detective – he wants a chat with you. Would you mind coming along with me next time we meet?'

'Come on, darling, what on earth would I have to say to a man like that?'

'Please, Teresa. What would be the harm in it? If you say no, I'm going to think all my suspicions were justified,' I begged her, distractedly smearing butter on my toast.

'I'll do it for you, if you really want me to . . . But I can tell you right now that I have absolutely nothing to say that you don't already know.'

'Thank you. I'll let you know when we've got something arranged.'

She seemed uncomfortable, restless even. I was more and more convinced that she was hiding something important from me, though I couldn't see her being guilty of anything per se. Maybe in an effort to help the family, she'd lied about something or held back information that was critical to the case. I could rather believe in her potential complicity than in her own guilt, based on her inclination to protect those she cared about at all cost. Sometimes I thought she had some secret motive for coming to the house every day, besides helping me out and keeping me company. But then, on the other hand, I had no doubt that her love for me was sincere. I was so confused. It would be good to see her with Alfonso, and find out how she'd hold up against his questioning; he was very experienced at this type of thing. I was sure he'd be able to draw something out of her that I would never have managed on my own.

◆ ◆ ◆

While she was busy sweeping the outdoor terrace, I checked online for the nearest locksmith, one who was prepared to come to the house sometime after four o'clock to change the locks on the outer doors of the house, and the front and rear gates. Afterwards I checked to see if there were any messages from Boston, and then answered some work emails. I also sent private messages to Mary, Emily, Brandon and Harry via Facebook. I didn't tell them much, just that I was all right and that as of now I didn't know when I would be returning, due to some official business keeping me out here. Mary replied instantly, saying that if she could come to stay, she'd love to spend a few days in Spain so I could show her Madrid. I logged off without answering, to think about what I might say to her. I could only respond with a kind but reasonable refusal without giving too much away; for the time being, my past was mine alone.

Going into my room to put a few things away, I noticed through the window a mass of heavy clouds threatening to cover the sun. I was looking forward to reading more of the letters, but for this I wanted the utmost privacy, which meant waiting for Teresa to leave. I placed Neca on the pillow when I made the bed, showing her fresh scar. I was afraid Teresa would come in and notice it, so I tucked her between the sheets as if she were a sick little girl and then smiled to myself – because in a way she was.

I didn't have long to wait before Teresa's departure. I was just folding the letter that I'd fallen asleep with the night before when she popped her head round the door.

'OK, sweetheart, I'm on my way to my next job,' she said, glancing across at Neca.

'All right, Teresa – well then, have a nice day.'

'Look how snugly you've tucked her in . . . I bet she's lovely and cosy.'

'Well, I saw the clouds moving in,' I said, trying hard to smile and play along with her little joke. 'I'll call you to set up our meeting with Alfonso.'

'See you tomorrow.' She left, obviously displeased by my parting words.

I was about to sit down in the kitchen in front of my second cup of coffee for the day and a few more of the unread letters when the landline rang. Why hadn't the lady of the house ever invested in a darned cordless phone, considering how big this place was?

I picked up the receiver, standing as far away from the sofa as the cord would allow. A clap of thunder rattled the windows, along with my insides. Very timely.

It was Julia, the lawyer from Ramón's firm. I let out my breath when I heard her voice, recognising it right away because it was strangely husky for a woman. She wanted to know if I was home this morning, because the person doing the house valuation had had a cancellation and wanted to come by at noon. Thank goodness – there were still two hours ahead of peace and tranquillity.

◆ ◆ ◆

In the next two letters, Saúl told Yolanda (or rather, he told me) how beautiful the beaches were in springtime, fringing the forests of Olympic Park down towards the Pacific. Exhilarated, he said that the good weather had allowed him to steal away part of the incredible beauty of that landscape, to capture it on canvas. 'Seeing the wonders of this vast land all around me almost feels like the first time I held you in my arms, with the same burning desire to stop the clock, to live or die forever, irrespective of which, out of pure unalloyed joy. It's so gloriously different, wanting to die from sheer happiness, from wanting to die solely in order to end the suffering,' he said.

Destiny is so crude and unfair, shunting us humans hither and thither according to its whims, pointlessly, mercilessly, into futile situations, far from the true path that could afford us genuine happiness. Right then nothing seemed as excruciating to me as envy – the scorching desire for something that another person possesses but fails to appreciate. Yolanda had inspired a depth of love and passion that most women can only dream of, but she didn't have the sense to appreciate such a gift. I, on the other hand, who had wanted nothing more in my entire life than a little affection, had to settle for experiencing it through love letters addressed to another woman and thus prove, burning with jealousy, that it exists – although not for me. I was almost thirty-five years old and my dream was drifting further and further away, as though dragged off by some ghastly and invisible current.

The letter from 5 June plunged me into the depths of despair.

> Olympic National Park
> 5 June 2005
>
> Hi, Yolanda,
> Well, it's happened: I finally slept with Nadia.
>
> Maybe I shouldn't tell you that, but the thing is I just can't any longer imagine that you're actually reading my letters: I've lost any expectation of that and don't sense you at all on the other side. The paper I'm writing on acts as a confessional where I can pour out my fears, my hopes and my sins without thinking about who might be reading – or rather, I'm supposing there's no one there to make me do penance to absolve my guilt. This way I don't have the shame of having someone actually listen to my ramblings – it's like writing to myself and sorting my life out at the same time. What utter rubbish – of course, I'm getting my comeuppance for whatever I'm supposed to have done. Is there any greater torture for a sinner than to know true love but then lose it forever before even waking up? I don't think so.

> It happened when we were down on the beach ... I was consumed in my latest painting and she was frolicking in the waves. Suddenly, she slipped into my field of vision, and right on to my canvas. I can't say why, but I simply couldn't stop looking at her. The sight of her moved me, possessed me. And what she'd been trying to get from me with her endless caresses, entreaties and light touches, suddenly rose as if by enchantment. (Darling, if you're reading this and it hurts, please don't read on.)

(Yes, someone who loved him was indeed reading and hurting, but that someone kept right on.)

> Worn out from all her running and leaping through the crashing surf, she lay down in the sun. I hadn't noticed until that moment but her skin tone was a perfect match to that of the fine-grained sand on the glorious beach. Lying there under the intensely blue sky, she looked as though she was etched into the very fabric of the earth, the faintly drawn outline of a promising design, as gentle and modest as she was sublime. She had no idea that the man who had been sleepwalking for the last three years was finally growing aroused at the mere sight of her.
>
> Knowing she was quite unaware, oblivious to how her beauty enhanced the whole scenery, I became more and more excited and let myself be carried away by the moment. She barely moved, letting me do exactly as I pleased. On her part,

she simply trembled, moaned, sighed and panted, and finally released her tears into the undertow of the sea. She told me she had woken up so many times from similar dreams that she had dreaded breaking the spell.

I don't know. I think it must feel a little similar to the relief at finally paying off part of a debt, not to mention the joy at being able to make someone happy, even if it was just the one time, as well as proving that my manhood is still intact. On the long trip home Nadia didn't speak once; she just drove, nothing more, and sometimes her eyes glistened with the dampness of the ocean. I know why she remained silent – a single word would have been the start of a conversation that would remind her, once again, that it had all been just a beautiful fantasy.

I would give anything to be able to love her in the way that I love you, but then she would have to be you, or at least the woman I believed you to be.

Yours, held fast forever in the love that we shared,
Saúl

This letter was hard for me. On the one hand, I fully identified with Nadia. I *was* her, I was on that beach, in that dream, and I felt the same agony that it would all collapse in a single breath like a castle built on dry sand. I too would have let him take his pleasure, lying there as still as a statue, my whole body on fire but fearful of putting him off. On the other hand, it seemed so wrong that Saúl should feel burdened with such guilt for the simple fact of having given himself to a woman who loved him so greatly . . . I could have screamed until my throat was burning. Of course I wished him all the happiness in the world with that girl – I preferred her a thousand times over my sister and he deserved to be happy with her – but my jealousy lay like burning coals in my chest, and their relationship meant the end of any hope where I was concerned. When Saúl fell in love, it was forever – although anything was better than him living out his days trapped in the treacherous clutches of my sister Yolanda. Imagining the two of them in that landscape racked my heart with pain.

I was still on that beach in my imagination when the entryphone rang.

The man who arrived to value the house was a brusque fellow, quite unpleasant even. His impeccable dark-grey summer suit looked made to measure, teamed with a gleaming pair of expensive leather shoes. He was good-looking and no doubt very photogenic. Polite but rather sour, he made me feel as though he were doing me a huge favour at his own expense.

I showed him around the property, from attic to garden. He measured everything with his laser meter, examined the walls, doors, windows . . . taking notes of it all on his tablet, completely ignoring my presence as though he were annoyed I was there. For some reason, he didn't ask a single question, as though he were quite capable of finding everything out on his own and wouldn't in any case lay any worth on my answers. Satisfied eventually that he had all the information needed for each room, he then went out to inspect the exterior of the house in great detail, again taking measurements with his laser meter and recording copious notes. He finished his painstaking assessment at last and turned off his device.

'That's it, ma'am. Goodbye,' was all he said.

Despite his speed and efficiency, it was after one o'clock by the time he left and getting on for lunchtime, which today was a pasta salad and fruit. The cupboards were nearly bare and I'd have to do another food shop.

After the meal, I decided I was ready to unlock the chest of drawers in Alberta's bedroom. The key had been staring me in the face from a small bowl on the kitchen counter for some days now, but each time I saw it I told myself it wasn't the right time. Not that I wasn't curious – the problem was my actually daring to go into her room.

Crossing into her territory was like entering a dangerous and forbidden place. Even stepping across the threshold, I felt as though she were watching me, her gaze scrutinising my every movement, hovering, cold and spectral, over each object and in every corner. And that goddamn smell . . . It was as if she were breathing her very soul into me, taking over my entire being. I reverted back to the girl who would sometimes peek into her mother's room with absolutely no intention of actually going in, only to take a quick look from the outside – the girl who had stood in this very same corridor, breathless with fear. I was never someone to pry, and in that I was like her and Teresa, never in need of going to places that were off limits. I only did it once, but that was at Yolanda's instigation. I myself never had any interest in my mother's secrets – the one thing I wanted from her was some small sign of real affection, towards me or any other person. I simply wanted some form of evidence to convince me that she was a normal mother. It wasn't hard for me to respect her privacy, and I was never tempted to cross into what I saw as the very gates of hell itself. But I was no longer a child and she was not here, and this was not a matter of idle curiosity but an act of bravery on the part of a mature adult. I decided to breathe through my mouth and that did the trick.

The key Teresa had found did indeed open the drawer. As it slid open and I saw what was inside, I let out an inadvertent cry: 'Oh my God, it's the treasure of Ali Baba!' Before my eyes lay a booty that even the most hardened pirate would have coveted, the delight of any treasure hunter. Of normal size for such a drawer, the interior was divided into five compartments of various dimensions: one for watches, another for pendants and necklaces, while the next one was full of bracelets, and then two smaller ones for rings and earrings, respectively.

I didn't touch a thing – I couldn't: fingering those jewels would have been like plunging my hand right into her heart and resurrecting the monster. This treasure was cursed, accumulated over decades through the most contemptible feats of betrayal and artifice. Besides, my stunted sense of curiosity hadn't grown over the past years. I slammed the drawer shut, locked it and left the room as fast as though it were ablaze. Only then could I finally breathe through my nose, and I went to rinse out my mouth, which felt as stale and dry as her jewels.

Having poured myself a glass of water and washed my face and hands most thoroughly, I made a pot of coffee to get me through the rest of the afternoon. My thoughts kept turning to Teresa. I didn't know how much she had been involved in the wicked acts of my mother and sister, or why, but I did know that her unwavering integrity was more than proven: it would have been so easy for her to empty out that drawer and live like a queen for the rest of her life. She could have left the items of jewellery that Yolanda and I would have recognised and we would never have known that anything else was missing. So, if it wasn't for personal ambition, what other reason might she have to stay silent? I was tired of all this deception, of all the secrets and lies, and disappointed that even Teresa was somehow tangled up in my mother's unscrupulous doings. I hoped to high heaven that Alfonso could find the source of her motivation and, if possible, before I'd had to pay him the entire inheritance I hadn't even got my hands on yet.

Suddenly it dawned on me that I would also need to get a valuation for all the jewels in the drawer, and then notify Ramón so he could pass it on to my sister's proxy. I was sure it hadn't been accounted for in the negotiations, and I shared the quality of integrity with the loyal Teresa. I would have to tell them about it. All of a sudden I felt quite overwhelmed again – there were too many surprises, too many unknowns, and I would far rather spend my time getting to know Saúl better.

The letter from 25 July came with a gift – a photo of Saúl at Ruby Beach, standing in front of the sea with his arms spread wide, as though he were trying to touch the only cloud in the sky above him. The breeze ruffled his long hair, which seemed to dance on the glossy paper. His only item of clothing was some loose-fitting jeans, which barely hugged him around the middle. His long, slender and muscular torso . . . Oh, he was so young and lovely . . . Once again, I was unable to see his face – it was as though he would rather show Yolanda his relationship with the world than himself. God, I fancied him! It had been nine years since that photo was taken; he must be thirty-two by now. I fantasised about being with him.

In the letter he came across as remorseful and guilty for staying in a relationship where Nadia gave everything and he only allowed himself to be loved. He said that Dylan had noticed his aloofness towards her and had had words with him about it, but that everything was pointless. He ended his letter by saying that he had to meet the others for dinner, and that he was going to treat them because he had sold seven more paintings. I didn't have time to open another letter as the doorbell rang for the second time that day.

The locksmith was a young guy, every bit as efficient as the man who had valued the house, but so much nicer. In half an hour he had changed the locks on both the garden gates, the front door and the kitchen door. He charged me one hundred and twenty euros for labour and materials, gave me two copies of each key and left.

The empty afternoon stretched ahead, so I went out to rent another car and do some shopping.

By seven o'clock in the evening I was driving a brand-new blue Volkswagen Passat and heading into the heart of the city. I did my supermarket run and a few other errands in the only shopping centre I still recognised, and with the provisions safely stashed in the boot, bought myself a ticket to the movies at the local cinema.

I took in a far-fetched romantic comedy, which seemed better suited to a lazy afternoon on the sofa by the TV than to the big screen. Even so, the film cleared my head and let me forget everything for a whole hour and a half.

Saúl popped straight back into my mind as I was leaving the cinema. I was starting to be so obsessed with him that in spite of all the bombshells that had hit me since my return to Spain, each more upsetting than the last, most of my thoughts were taken up with him and him alone. A handful of letters, written in a different time and location, had achieved what only a few days before I would have sworn was impossible with any man I could meet in person: I had fallen so deeply in love that I'd forgotten all about my life in London, and everything I had built up over so many years and with so much effort – in fact, everything I'd been so proud of to that date. My restaurant, my independence, my flat in the city, my friends . . . it all now seemed so bland and trivial . . . It's true what they say, that everything else fades into the distance, the closer you come to true love. And yet this love of mine was forcibly platonic and anachronistic in the strangest of situations, which broke every mould – and I was already almost thirty-five years old.

When I got home, Aris was waiting right behind the door. I loved this feeling of having someone there for me, of not being alone, particularly in this house, which became more menacing than ever at night. I had to figure out how to bring him back to London with me – we needed each other. He followed at my heels as I unloaded the shopping from the car into the house, and then sat patiently in the kitchen until I'd put everything away, as if guarding my purchases. It seemed that Aris too was grateful for my company.

Before going to bed, I went out to make sure that both garden gates were firmly locked, and spotted a sheet of paper on the ground by the front gate that I hadn't seen earlier in all the bustle of bringing in the shopping. It said: 'I came by and couldn't open the gate – you must have changed the locks already. I'll come back tomorrow after ten so I don't wake you. Teresa.'

Maybe it wasn't such a good idea not to give her a key. I'd talk to her about it the next day.

Taking the three photographs with me, along with my two best friends and the bundle of unread letters still left from 2005, I crawled into bed. Going on my phone to set the alarm so Teresa wouldn't find me asleep the next day, I found a voicemail from my detective: 'I tried calling a couple of times, but you didn't answer. I'll pick you and Teresa up from your house tomorrow. I'll call you in advance to confirm. Alfonso.'

In actual fact, I had not two but three missed calls, one from Harry. They must have tried calling while I was in the shopping centre, where the music over the loudspeakers was especially loud, or while I was in the cinema. It was a good feeling to end the day on, knowing that at least I had a plan for the next morning, and that Alfonso was still busy with the investigation. As per usual, no email from Boston in my inbox – it seemed increasingly clear that no one was using that account any more.

Before drifting off into sleep I thought of all the things I would say to him if I were answering his letters, revealing my identity and how much I felt for him. So very many things . . .

Chapter 15

Wednesday, 25 June 2014

Teresa didn't come the next morning. By eleven o'clock I was starting to get twitchy, because when Teresa said she was going to do something, she would do it, come hell or high water. I ran through all the possible reasons in my mind while making my bed and picking up my dirty clothing, strolling through the garden with Aris, drinking two cups of coffee . . . By noon I was really starting to properly worry that something bad had happened to her. Above all else, Teresa was a woman of her word and it was highly unusual for her not even to contact me to explain. Soon afterwards there was a call from Alfonso.

'Hello, Berta.'

'Hi, Alfonso.'

'Can I come and pick you up around five o'clock—'

'I think something's happened to Teresa,' I said, interrupting his flow.

'What makes you say that?'

'She came by yesterday while I was out shopping and slipped me a note under the gate . . . She couldn't get in because I'd had all the locks changed.'

'Well done. What did her note say?' he asked in a hurried tone, like someone with not a lot of time to spare.

'That she'd come back after ten o'clock today – but she's still not here.'

'There could be any number of reasons for that. What makes you think the worst?'

'Because she always, always does what she says. I just know something serious must have stopped her from coming when she promised – I'm absolutely convinced of it.'

'I see . . . Look, I'll come to your house at five and we'll talk then.'

'OK, see you later.'

I realised I needed to go to the bank for cash to pay Alfonso, and they were closing soon. I called Teresa's mobile for the second time to let her know I'd be out over the next hour, but she didn't answer.

When I got back, there was no note to say she'd been here while I was gone. I called her again and still she didn't answer. Not in the mood to prepare a proper meal, I made myself a tuna sandwich, only to keep body and soul together. I was worried. After lunch I went out in the garden with Aris.

It didn't feel right to keep reading Saúl's letters, so I got out my Kindle but couldn't concentrate. I was more and more taken with the idea that something really terrible must have happened to Teresa and I couldn't get it out of my head. Thinking it over, I came to the conclusion that my beloved housekeeper couldn't be as alone in the world as it seemed. She had to have told someone about our forthcoming meeting with the detective, and that simply had to be why she was missing. Had she been talking to Yolanda? Did this have anything to do with the letter thief of the other night?

Anxious to share my suspicions with him, I waited two hours in the garden for Alfonso. The time seemed to drag on for ever. At quarter to five, the entryphone rang at last. I picked up and buzzed him through.

'I know I'm early. I'll wait for you to finish getting ready,' he said once he was inside, seeing me without make-up and standing there in my slippers. I didn't have to be a genius to realise that my appearance was quite a bit different from that on previous occasions when we'd met.

'Do we have to go out? I'm not exactly in the mood to sit still in traffic.'

'Well, no, not if you don't want to . . .'

'Let's sit out in the garden then – we'll be much more comfortable and it's a whole lot more private.'

'I only meant to come and pick you up . . . I didn't think you'd hired another car yet, but I can see I was wrong . . . To tell the truth, it's not customary for me to hold meetings in my clients' homes – it seems like such an imposition on their privacy.'

'Don't worry about it – can I tempt you with some coffee?'

'That would be great,' he answered, obviously delighted by the prospect of staying. 'Did you say that this house is on the market?'

'Yes, or at least it will be as soon as the deed has been made over to me,' I responded, already in the kitchen.

'Would you mind showing me around quickly while the coffee's brewing?'

'Are you interested?' I asked in surprise. It would never have occurred to me that a man like him, seemingly such a loner, might have plans for a permanent base.

'Could be. Technically I have a house in Germany, a little place my parents left me, but the truth is I'm hardly there for months at a time. I travel too much, live out of hotels – usually whatever's most convenient for the local airport where I'm working on a particular job – and sometimes in rented flats, but lately almost all the work I do is out of Madrid. I like this neighbourhood; it seems very quiet.'

'Too quiet for me, having lived in London for fifteen years. Listen . . . if you do go for it, it might not be such a bad idea for us to deduct the five hundred euros a day that you're charging from the house price, because if the investigation goes on for much longer and my solicitor doesn't sign over my inheritance soon, I don't know if I'm going to be able to pay you,' I said jokingly, although there was some truth to my words.

'That's really not a bad idea,' he said, smiling – for the first time in my presence, I think, 'but don't you worry, I wouldn't abandon this case just because of the money. I'm sure we could come to some arrangement if necessary. When I start on an investigation it's like starting on a puzzle – I can't leave it until I fit all the pieces together. Each case ends up as a personal challenge for me. It wouldn't be the first time a client canned me before the job was done and I kept working on it for my own satisfaction.'

'Wow, that's not what I expected. All right then, I'll show you the house while the coffee's on.'

It was a very quick tour, though I was sure that not a single detail had escaped his keen observation. When we were looking around the main sitting room, he commented, 'You ought to open the window and air this room out. It has a wonderful grille over the opening – I doubt even Aris could get through there.'

'You smell it too? It's horrible – it smells as though my mother's sitting right there.'

'I have a good nose despite being a smoker, but I wouldn't need one to smell this: it's an overpowering blend of expensive perfume and urine.'

I was terribly embarrassed at not having cleaned the upholstery on the sofa, but took his advice, raised the blinds and threw the window open. Straight away the sunshine came streaming into the room.

'That's better with the sun in here, otherwise it's a very cold and chilly room.'

'Yes, it is . . . I thought I was the only one to notice that.'

A little later on the grand tour, we passed the door to my mother's room. 'And this is the master suite – or rather the queen's chambers – which were my mother's quarters. Be my guest,' I added, gesturing for him to take a look around, although I wasn't going in myself.

'Why doesn't this room have a window?' came his voice from the little private sitting room that connected with the bedroom. 'Unless I'm mistaken, this wall faces on to the garden.'

'Ah, that's just one of the secrets my crazy mother took with her to the grave,' I answered, without stepping into the room, raising my voice a little too loudly and breathing in and out through my mouth. I was starting to feel giddy.

'It's just that this would make the perfect office if you added a nice window. You could also turn it into a dressing room, though I don't need one myself.'

After a quick look at the attic, we sat down in the garden with our coffee.

Alfonso was a touch more smartly dressed this afternoon – he'd taken care to smooth down his hair for once, maybe even with a dab of product, and his shirt looked freshly pressed. For a fleeting moment I wondered if he was starting to like me, if he had done all this for my benefit, and felt flattered.

'I suppose you haven't heard yet from Teresa . . . ?'

'Not a word, and she hasn't answered my calls either. I'm genuinely very concerned about her.'

'Calm down, she'll be all right.'

'Well, how do you know? Oh, that's a foolish question – it's your job to know.'

'At twenty past two this afternoon I saw her entering her house with two shopping bags and a young girl, about eleven or twelve years old, I would guess. I'm not particularly good at estimating ages where children are concerned.'

'I'm so relieved to know she's all right, but now I . . . I don't understand. Maybe she had to take care of a neighbour's daughter . . .'

'Just hold on, I'm getting to the good part,' he said, and then fell silent for a moment while he lit a cigarette. 'The girl lives with her, and so does that crook who followed us to the restaurant.'

'Are you sure?' I asked, dumbfounded, leaning in close to emphasise my question.

'Positive. I've been tailing her for two days. That's why I asked you to bring her to our meeting, because her life just doesn't seem to fit what she's been telling you.'

'That can't be right . . .' I couldn't get over my surprise. 'When I asked if she lived alone, she told me that—'

'I know, I know, you told me. She lied, and it seems she has two good reasons: this bloke who's her cousin, and the girl.'

'I just can't believe it . . .'

'The guy's name is Pedro Vidal, and yes, he's the son of Teresa's cousin. He doesn't have a job as far as I could tell, other than watching us and frequenting brothels and dodgy bars. His standard of living doesn't match his situation – he's been unemployed for a long time.'

'But . . . I remember Teresa telling me that he ran a car body repair shop.'

'You're right there – he shares the business with two other partners, but never actually goes, and I doubt very much that this one suburban repair shop makes enough money to finance all his extravagant habits. I reckon he's the one who impersonated Saúl to incriminate him; in fact I'd bet my life on it. I'm planning to visit the witness who said he recognised him this weekend.'

'You're going to Marbella?'

'Yes. You want to come?'

'Just a second.' I held my hand up, palm out. 'One step at a time. I'm a bit stunned. You're telling me that this relative of Teresa's was the one who carried Bodo's body out of the house, put it in a van, brought it to the harbour and loaded it on the yacht to dump it in the ocean?'

'I think that's exactly what happened,' he said, slowly blowing out a cloud of smoke.

'But . . . why? What on earth would Teresa's relative have to do with all of this?'

'I'd venture to say that someone who knew both him and Saúl noticed the resemblance, and that besides being an idiot he's also a scoundrel. It must have been easy enough to persuade him to do it in return for a nice wad of cash.'

'So you think he killed Bodo and that he's coming after me because he's afraid I'll find out what he did?'

'No, no, nothing of the sort. What happened before Pedro Vidal took the body out of the house where your sister and her husband lived is a completely different matter. And, what's more, I don't think his part in all this went any further than leaving the house with the bundle and putting it on the yacht.'

'Hang on. Let me see if I've got this straight – so it could have been my sister who killed Bodo and paid this guy who happens to look like Saúl to get rid of the body, so the witnesses and police would think that . . . ? That just seems so . . . so . . . warped and evil . . .'

'Berta, this version of the facts makes the most sense, but we can't jump to conclusions. It's just as possible that it happened the way you thought. However, I have a feeling we'll run into a few more surprises yet. Do you want to know the name of the young girl who lives with Teresa and her cousin?'

'Go on, surprise me – although that might be hard right at this minute.'

'Well, we'll see. The young lady's name is María Teresa Kraser de Castro.'

Yes, that took me by surprise all right. It took me a moment to understand exactly what her name signified. Alfonso waited patiently for me to work it out in my own time. He lit another cigarette and stared off into the darkness of the garden, as if respecting my privacy. At last I drew myself together. 'I think I need a drink. Is this a good time?'

'It's a perfect time.'

Within minutes, our coffee cups had been replaced by two glasses of whisky and ice.

'So, as if by magic, I have a new sister who is also my niece. Who could possibly top that?' I murmured at last.

'That certainly seems to be the most logical hypothesis. She's attended the same school all the way through since nursery – a private school very close to Teresa's home, which means that—'

'That she raised her,' I answered. 'That's what she's been hiding from me – she's been keeping quiet to protect this child . . .'

'That, and the fact that her cousin's mixed up in this whole shady business – she must surely know about that. The guy found out first-hand that you were back in Madrid and started following you, and it's possible his aunt even told him about my wanting to meet with her and he's been threatening her. The chap's a bit slow in the brain department, frankly. It's been all too easy to check into his miserable life, and he's a lousy spy, an alcoholic and who knows what else. He spends all day away from home so we can visit Teresa any time we want. I don't think it would be too difficult to get the information we need from her. She's the key to cracking this case wide open, though she's also a victim and we don't know exactly how much she knows about what's happened.'

'I'd really like to find out why my sister decided to leave her daughter with Teresa.'

'Yes, but it would be even better to find out who bribed Teresa's cousin into impersonating Saúl. That's much more relevant to our ongoing investigation.'

'Listen, this is all really tough for me. There's no time to recover from one blow before I get hit by the next, and then the next. We're talking about my family here. I had really thought that nothing connected with my mother and sister could hurt me any more, but I'm finding it hard to keep my distance. I only meant to come here for a few days max, and I was so sure of being strong, so confident I was a brand-new woman . . .'

'Of course – I do have sympathy, Berta. I'm sorry if I seem insensitive, it's just that I'm not very good with emotions. Besides, it's my job to keep my own head clear and calm, not let myself get carried away by supposition; objectivity is essential in any investigation. So will you be coming to Marbella?'

'Let me think about it. I don't know if I'm up for any more surprises. And . . . going back to that house . . .'

'Whatever you want. You don't have to come with me – it was just a suggestion.'

'Wait, doesn't it seem a little unprofessional for your client to tag along on a trip related to the investigation?' I asked. I'd suddenly twigged that his insistence here went beyond his passion for the job.

He also realised that he'd been too obvious and quickly changed the subject. 'I brought your letters back,' he said, taking them out of his folder.

'I'll give you the ones I've read since I saw you last.'

'No need. I don't think I'll find anything there to help – it's quite obvious that guy had no idea what happened. I'm sure if you come across anything important, you'll let me know.'

'If you say so,' I responded, taking the letters and setting them down in a neat pile on the table. 'If I find anything of interest, of course I'll tell you. Would you like another tot?'

'No, I think it's better that I leave,' he said a little curtly before getting up, as if embarrassed by having made subtle advances to me.

'Wait, don't go without your money – it's in the kitchen. Tell me what I owe you for the extra expenses.'

'Nothing. Don't worry about it – it's hardly anything at all.'

I went into the kitchen and he followed, ready to leave.

'Berta . . .'

'Yes?'

'You're a smart and sensitive woman, as well as very attractive . . . I'm sorry, this is awkward. It's . . . it's this damned loneliness.'

'There's nothing at all to apologise for, Alfonso. If I change my mind, I'll let you know. As a matter of fact, right now I'm thinking it would do me good to get away from this house for a few hours, though it's not exactly the kind of trip I was hoping for.'

'The invitation still stands, but no pressure. I'm good at working on my own.'

'I have no doubt.'

After he left, I felt mildly guilty. I think he regretted having apologised, putting his awkwardness down to loneliness and eliciting my sympathy, because he left with his tail between his legs, clearly upset that he'd let me see his vulnerable side.

No, Alfonso was not my regular type; he just made me feel . . . a combination of compassion, fondness and respect – akin to what a girl feels for her father or towards an old professor. Nothing that could compare with the tide of emotions I felt on reading Saúl's letters, or even with the fleeting passion that had taken hold of me in the early days with Harry, which had been more out of need and physical attraction than anything else. If I hadn't read Saúl's words, I might possibly have considered a fling with the detective – he did have a morose sort of appeal, bless him. At this stage, however, it was completely out of the question and my thirst could only be quenched by true love.

During the period in which I'd lived in London, I'd instinctively built up a thick protective shell, not through any conscious process, but simply because I'd abandoned any notion of affection in my new life, convinced that this was the only way to find the independence and personal identity I sought so badly. I think that had made me reset my needs as if I were reborn, but here and now I'd suddenly been gripped once more with the same urgent need I had felt as a girl to love and be loved.

Either way, Alfonso's interest in me was just one more revelation in an afternoon full of unexpected shocks and surprises. I simply could not believe that my sister – someone who cared only about her own dreams and desires – had given birth to a daughter by Bodo . . . There must have been some reason other than to satisfy a woman's natural maternal instincts, and it had to involve money. But then, on the other hand, why would she give up a large portion of her inheritance? Would she turn down the jewellery as well, when the solicitor told her about it? Did she have a motive even more powerful than money? Yes – it had to be a path to even greater riches. Teresa's hypothesis that day at the restaurant now made a lot of sense. And where was Yolanda right now? Why would she decide to go ahead with her pregnancy, but then hand her daughter over to be raised and educated by Teresa? Putting the lives of the women in my family under the microscope was like delving into an endless underground network of interminable twisting passageways, where each step led to the maw of another gallery full of mysteries. The deeper I went, the darker it became and the more lost I felt. Every answer brought with it ten more questions, each more perplexing than the last.

I was once again overcome with the desire to run as far as I possibly could, identical to the impulse that had driven me to London in the first place. The women in my family and everything connected with them led towards a dark and tainted realm, most terrifying to a person with a gentle and trusting heart. But I had lost my innocence now, along with any belief in heaven and places free from pain and deceit. I knew that happiness was a state of mind that could only be reached without shortcuts or running away from the task. I had left this house once already, thinking that the path I had taken would always propel me onwards, but now it turned out I was right back where I'd started. I knew now that there was no heaven to be found and that you had to make it for yourself, from the inside. Leaving again would add yet another defeat to my life, and perhaps the final blow to any hope of future happiness. I made a conscious decision to pull myself together and face things head-on – this time there'd be no easy way out to avoid the pain.

I laid myself down in the hammock with Aris and Neca, needing to hug and touch someone or something that wouldn't present me with an invoice. The cat's easy presence comforted me. I envied him his simple life, with nothing to sort out and no goals to achieve beyond allowing himself to be petted. He purred with joy and curled up in my arms, leaving all the problems of the world down to me. And there we stayed until darkness fell.

◆ ◆ ◆

A shower, sausages and a fried egg perked me up. I was getting a little concerned at my eating habits these days, on top of my current sedentary lifestyle – I was well on the way to losing my figure and risking a heart attack. It was a fleeting thought, because then

I got excited by the prospect of being alone again with the man by the lake. I made sure all the doors and windows were locked, and curled up with my letters and my friends.

> Olympic National Park
> 14 July 2005
>
> Dear Yolanda,
> I feel the summer in my veins. My God, this amazing light, which exposes every leaf of the trees, every drop of water in this paradise, every feather of the birds, every line of the clouds in the sky... I'd forgotten the wonderful crudeness and insolence of the colours of nature. The paintbrush never leaves my side – it controls me and forces me to reflect on my canvas everything that catches my eye.
>
> I'm heartbroken that this season is all but over and I haven't yet managed to capture half of its radiance. Since losing you I have trouble enjoying things that make me happy without thinking about when they will end. Once upon a time I thought I had something for all eternity, but losing it taught me a painful and valuable lesson. I rejoice in the knowledge that the seasons will come round again, and will always cycle back through the tapestry of our lives, leaving us hope for tomorrow as they fade. Whereas you, on the other hand...
>
> Tomorrow I'll go down to the dock. I want to paint that meeting between nature and something man-made with its blend of artificial and natural

colours: the people waiting for the ferry with their faces full of anticipation, and their emotions as they arrive and depart; the kids on deck playing in the wind ... I want to paint how the sea breezes dance in their soft hair. Everything tempts my brushes so long as this light remains. I feel so fortunate this summer – painting opens a door to me through which many of my sorrows can escape. I have two great loves now: the one I met in Marbella, and my art. I would paint in any case – it's become an obsession for me, an uncontrollable passion – but I know I'm lucky to be able to make a living out of something I enjoy so much.

Mr Baker is almost as enthusiastic as I am – he comes by the cabin two to three times a week to see what I'm working on, and slowly but surely he's buying up all my paintings. According to him, Yosa Degui is starting to be known, and apparently the word is spreading among the art collectors of Washington State that there's a reclusive artist who paints wonders. They're already talking about a new artistic trend: the 'flickering' style – how the light vibrates in the outlines of each element in my paintings. Doesn't this all sound so wonderful, Yolanda? Are you happy for me? Who knows – maybe this mad hobby of mine where I put all my feelings down on canvas will open up a new path back to you. I like to imagine so, anyway. My happiness would be complete if you would answer this letter, if only to congratulate me, although I'd prefer a kiss. I'm so dying to kiss you one last time – just one more time would be heaven on earth.

Things aren't going so well with Nadia. She's starting to despair of me, and I can't say I blame her. She's suffering the burnout of someone who gives so much, yet gets so little in return. At least I can say that I never lied to her – I never promised I could love her – but that doesn't make her feel any better, rather the contrary. She says that she would give anything if I only showed her a little love, even if it were just a pretence, even if it were just one time. All she wants is the tiniest demonstration that all her devotion has been worthwhile. That's how miserable she feels – that even a white lie would be enough to bring her comfort. It pains me to see her suffer so, but it's just not in my power to ease the agony of her heartache.

The flickering painter,
Saúl

I felt an urgent need to write to him again, to congratulate him and send him that kiss he wanted so badly. So I did it. I got out my notebook where I'd been taking notes, and wrote my next message.

25 June 2014

Hello again, Saúl,
Another letter from me – sorry for taking over your postbox one more time. I wanted to tell you that I've just been reading another of your letters and couldn't resist the temptation to answer it.

I don't know anything about art. I never gave myself the time to enjoy it, and I'm sure if I were to see your paintings I would lack the knowledge or sensitivity to fully appreciate them. But your excitement has rubbed off on me from reading your words, and that I can certainly value. I thought, *Why not? What's wrong with congratulating this man who's so in love with nature and with . . . with love, who lives so far away from me in time and in space.* Maybe, as you've said yourself many times before, I'm writing into a void or to a complete stranger. It's been many years since you sent these words to Yolanda: 'My happiness would be complete if you would answer this letter, if only to congratulate me.' I know an answer from me won't bring you the 'complete happiness' that you longed for so much in those moments, and I'm not her, and I don't even live in your past; even so, I wanted to congratulate you, if you'll let me. I'm so very happy to know that the 'flickering painter' is beginning to savour the richness of life at last – I just wanted you to know that.

Thank you for writing all these letters. You have restored my faith in humanity.

Sincerely yours,
BC

I ripped the page out of the notebook, folded it carefully and put it on the bedside table, ready to post the following day. So long as he didn't answer, asking me to stop writing to him . . .

I drifted off into sleep, wrapped in dreams of walking hand in hand with the love of my life.

Chapter 16

Thursday, 26 June 2014

There was still no sign of Teresa. Impatient for his morning feed, Aris roused me rather than my alarm. The house was just as she had left it, though after a mere couple of days it was already getting messy. I'd have to make a decision soon – either hire a new housekeeper or take care of the chores myself – but for now it could wait.

Just as I was taking my first sip of coffee my mobile rang; as usual, an unknown caller.

'Alfonso?'

'You got it. Hi, Berta.'

'Hello.'

'Listen, pack up your things immediately and find a hotel.'

'What?'

'It's important you get out as soon as possible. I don't have time to explain right now.'

'But . . . just like that, without even telling me the reason why . . .'

'Do you want me to book you a room in my hotel?'

'Well, OK . . . if I have to go to a hotel . . .'

'Great. Head directly to the Hilton, a few minutes from the airport on the Avenida de la Hispanidad – you can't miss it. On arrival, there'll be a room booked in your name. We'll talk tonight at dinner, as soon as I get back from taking care of something.'

'OK...' I said uncertainly. I had so many questions, but it was obvious he was in a hurry.

'I've got to go. Don't leave it too long.' He hung up before I could say goodbye.

I looked at Aris. 'And what do I do with you?' I said to him.

I called Teresa again, but nothing. No response. Naturally I couldn't leave my friend and companion all on his own. Suddenly I thought of the neighbour who'd given me his card when he was taking out the rubbish, and remembered it was still in the pocket of the jeans I'd been wearing, so I left my coffee and toast and went straight to my bedroom. Yes, it was still there in the pocket.

The name of the kindly neighbour was Arturo Caballero Iglesias, and he was a historian, indeed a professor, at the university. I rang him without any further hesitation – I was out of time and options here.

'Hello?'

'Arturo Caballero?'

'Yes, speaking. Who's this?'

'Hi, it's Berta de Castro – your neighbour? You gave me your card the other night...'

'Ah yes, I remember. How are you?'

'Yes, fine, thanks,' I answered, not wanting to go into detail, although in all honesty I was not fine in any way, shape or form. 'It's just that, I've had something... unexpected come up, and I have to leave for a few days, and... Well, I can't take Aris, my cat...'

'Aristotle, yes, he's a friend of the family. Don't worry, he'll be fine.'

'Are you sure?'

'Completely. You can lock up and leave without any worries. He's a very clever cat and he knows us as his second home. Where do you think he goes when you're not there?'

'You don't know what a relief that is. Can I call you from time to time to check on him? I don't know how long I'll be gone and I'd like to—'

'Call whenever you want. It'll be a pleasure to have Aris here for a while – don't you worry about a thing.'

'Thank you so much.'

'Think nothing of it. See you soon.'

'Bye.'

I didn't waste a moment after that, but quickly cleared away the breakfast things, packed my bags and left as fast as my nerves would let me. I was sure Alfonso had every good reason for warning me to leave as soon as possible.

It was hard to abandon Aris, but I had the feeling he understood. I waved goodbye to him from the gate. I'd brought all the letters with me, of course, including the one I'd written, as well as Neca, who I now saw as my talisman, my lucky charm, as she didn't take up too much space in my suitcase.

Once away from the house, I hoped I was out of danger, so I went first to send my letter off at the post office in the Corte Inglés before heading to my new residence. Alfonso was right; I found the Hilton with no problems. My detective had good taste – the hotel was magnificent, not to mention just a step away from anywhere in the world.

Sure enough, there was a room reserved in my name, and it took only fifteen minutes to settle in. By quarter past twelve, I was in the restaurant looking at the lunch menu. Right then my priority was food.

I was becoming obsessed with the idea, or maybe I was just starting to realise, that my life was in danger and that they could be spying on me from anywhere in the hotel, so I watched everyone around me from the corner of my eye: the people next to me in the lift, in the corridors, in the lobby . . . Any one of them could be a potential killer and out for my blood. On arrival at the restaurant I took a moment to scope it out: it was located in a large inner atrium, with galleries running around the sides above ground-floor level, and the rooms leading directly off these. Corridors led away to further areas of the hotel from the corners of the galleries on each level. The majority of the tables could be seen by any passing guest or employee. Everything from the decor to the building itself was exquisitely timeless and elegant, while at the same time contemporary, but it wasn't perhaps the best place in which to hide out. Partially hidden beneath the main gallery, I chose an empty table from which I could scan most of the room, but as soon as I was seated I thought it probably hadn't been a good idea to eat there. I felt so on display for anyone harbouring evil intentions towards me . . . This time, however, my hunger won out and I ordered a salad and a grilled sirloin steak, which I gobbled down so I could get out of there as soon as possible. I don't think I'd ever bolted my food that rapidly in my life, but I felt vulnerable, watched by a thousand malevolent eyes. It wasn't all just in my head; I had enough reason to suspect that Teresa's cousin could be out there somewhere, lurking among the staff and hotel guests. On the other hand, any one of us in the restaurant could also be seen from above, though I was probably the only person in any real danger. Every now and then I might be in the sightline when a guest poked his or her head out over the railing of the gallery above to look at the view, and in those moments I couldn't help gulping down my mouthful without even chewing. After a cup of coffee, I made my way back up to my room.

Inside the room – spotless, quiet and classy – I found extensive information about the hotel facilities. I was tempted by the pool.

It was a beautiful day outside, even starting to get hot, but I didn't have a swimsuit. Besides, it seemed sensible to keep a low profile until I could talk to Alfonso.

Before continuing with my reading, I logged on to the internet to check my email and Facebook messages. There was an email from Brandon, who greeted me tersely, attaching an Excel document of the expenses and earnings of the restaurant for the first two weeks of the month. I thanked him and asked him to be patient with me, promising that I'd let him know in a few days' time when I was coming back. Next I read the vast number of messages left by Mary on my Facebook page. She was hopeless and really did seem more Latin than English in character: passionate and impulsive to a fault, in addition to having a bombproof sense of humour. I really should call her. When I did, she confessed that she'd slept with Harry. Oh, Mary . . .

Once I was done with work and friends, and after checking that Dylan's contact hadn't looked at the email account he'd created for Saúl, I made myself comfortable and returned to my reading. The first letter was written only seven days after the last one, as though the young painter was impatient to be in touch with Yolanda again.

It was a letter brimming with excitement. Martin had offered him five thousand dollars for his last piece of work. He was thrilled with the financial freedom that the sale of his paintings gave him, and the summer that invigorated him so much. 'I needed to tell you that – you or whoever is reading my letters, if indeed anyone is opening them,' he said. How could he have imagined then that Yolanda's sister would end up reading them? He also said that Nadia was insisting they move in together to formalise their relationship, but that he had refused. He admitted that he felt bad, that he was tormented by the idea that he might still be going out with her just so she would drive him to the places he wanted to paint, ease his loneliness and satisfy his urges as a man.

Infected by his enthusiasm, I wanted again to answer him, to tell him to go ahead, that a woman he didn't know was making sure the false charges against him would be dropped, and was doing her best to discover the identity of the real culprits of the crime. However, I knew that the smarter thing to do was to wait until I heard from him – if that ever happened. On the other hand, knowing his sensitivity and the incredible attachment he had to the love he had shared with Yolanda, I wondered what it would mean to him to know that 'his beloved' was at the very least directly involved in Bodo's disappearance. Now that he was so excited with his work and had recovered his will to live . . . No, he deserved to enjoy the happiness he had found after suffering for so long. Reflecting on his euphoric state, I realised that many years had gone past since the time of his writing, that this was no longer the moment in which he had felt so moved. It was so hard for me to separate his time from mine.

I kept reading until my phone pinged loudly with a message from Alfonso: 'I left Marbella two hours ago. I'll meet you tonight at eight o'clock in the hotel restaurant. Important: delete all my messages.'

I followed his warning, a chill running down my spine. If Alfonso was afraid someone might read the messages on my phone, he could hardly be feeling certain that I was a hundred per cent safe at the Hilton.

I was surprised he'd left for Marbella so early. I'd almost decided to go with him for the weekend, even though I was hoping to go to the coast independently of our mission. In any case, the important thing right now was whether he'd found the information he was looking for and if this would all be over soon, because I sensed the danger drawing ever closer, growing ever more active.

I kept reading for a while, although it was hard to concentrate. I felt like someone being held hostage, and was dying for more coffee but didn't dare set foot outside my room, at least not until I'd talked to Alfonso.

In the last letter I read, Saúl was back to feeling depressed again.

I felt his gloominess as if it were my own, and when I reached the last word it was as though my splendid afternoon had been plunged into the melancholy mists of Lake Crescent, the mists that Saúl was unable to capture from behind his window. Winter had arrived in Olympic Park and the cold weather was forcing him to work inside the cabin. The smell of the turpentine from his paints was giving him bad headaches. I shared his helplessness when he tried to capture the colours and lines between all the greys of the landscape. I wanted to close the curtains and dream that my head was nestled on his chest. I also wanted to wait with him for the winter to pass and for the light to return. And so I did. Until another intrusive sound from my phone alerted me to a new message: 'I'm at the hotel. Meet you in the restaurant in one hour.'

It was after seven so I got moving, put together an outfit from the suitcase I hadn't unpacked yet and took a shower.

Facing the mirror while putting on my make-up, I found myself looking at a stranger. In the space of a few short weeks my fresh and defiant face with its slightly confrontational expression had vanished. My eyelids now drooped listlessly over my dull gaze, as though far too exhausted to take the world in fully, and in spite of the sunny climate my skin was pale and wan. My face was a true reflection of the melancholy that had seized me, and also of his. 'Berta,' I said to the mirror, 'forget everything that happened almost nine years ago. You're losing track of time and space. Right now it's time to go and have dinner with your detective.'

I tried to return to the present and to revive myself, without much success. Right now what mattered was finding the real culprits in Bodo's disappearance and giving Saúl his liberty back, along with discovering the truth.

◆ ◆ ◆

On entering the restaurant atrium, I found Alfonso at the exact same table I'd sat at for lunch a few hours earlier. Maybe I had potential as a detective myself, I thought, smiling at the irony.

Alfonso had been so busy handling my affairs with such painstaking care that I felt an immense rush of tenderness for him, because in spite of everything he looked tired – as tired of it all as I was. He stood up as soon as he saw me.

'How are you, Berta?' he said in greeting, forcing an energy that he couldn't possibly still be feeling after his long, hard day. 'Are you comfortable enough in this hotel?'

'I don't think I've felt comfortable anywhere since this all started, but, yes, the hotel is wonderful, thank you. And how are you? How was the trip? I can't wait to hear all about it.'

'Exhausting. But first things first, let's order something to eat. I haven't eaten since breakfast and can't think straight.'

'I'll have a salad. I had a feast fit for a queen at this very table at lunchtime, but I think I ate way too fast. Eating here was like showering in the middle of a football stadium with everyone looking on.'

'That's true,' he said, glancing around us, 'but don't you think that's an advantage at the moment? Who on earth would dare attack you here?'

He called over a waiter and ordered without thinking, without even looking at the menu – pork chops for him and a salad for me. I had the feeling this wasn't the first time he'd dined here. He then took out his phone and started typing on it.

'Well? Aren't you going to tell me what happened in Marbella?'

'Sorry, I just had to answer this message,' he replied, looking up from the screen. 'I've been talking to the eyewitness who identified Saúl in the line-up . . .'

'And?' I asked impatiently as he went back to his small screen.

'Just a minute, I have to send something. I'm almost there.'

'Thanks,' I said sarcastically.

I waited. Two minutes later he was ready. 'OK, I'm all yours,' he said, putting his phone back in his pocket. 'When I showed him the photos, the guy tried to justify his hesitation and bad memory, citing the passage of years, blah blah, but finally he made up his mind that, yes, Teresa's cousin could definitely be the man he saw on the dock loading that bundle on to Bodo's yacht that night. I think they pressured him somehow, but I couldn't get him to say who. Getting the case reopened is not going to be easy, and the time that's passed is not exactly in our favour.'

'Yes, I do realise.'

'Look, even if they did call this witness back to testify, we can't be sure he wouldn't stand by his previous statement in court.'

'I can't believe it was so easy to change facts that would be so obvious to anyone . . .'

'I recorded the conversation . . . Berta . . .'

'What?' I said, urging him to continue because he'd stopped, looking as though he were considering his next words.

'I told you already when we first started working together that as a personal investigator I'm not allowed to testify. Any information I find can only help you shed light on your past; any evidence I collect over the course of my investigation is something separate. Am I making sense?'

'Sort of. So what about the recording?'

'It all depends on the judge. I'll send you the audio file later. Once you've saved it to your computer, erase it from your phone.'

The waitress brought our food over and we fell silent. Meanwhile, Alfonso used the opportunity to cast an eye around the dining room.

'Are you finally going to tell me why I had to pack my bags at a moment's notice and come to the Hilton?' I asked when the girl had left.

'Last night when I left your house, I saw his car parked down the street.'

'The car belonging to Teresa's cousin?'

'Yeah. I think he was watching us from somewhere in the garden . . .'

'What? You should have told me!'

'Take it easy. I waited outside until he left. It didn't take long and I was sure he wouldn't come back the same night, because everything else goes out of his head when he goes off to his blessed bars and brothels. The guy's desperate and I don't know what he's capable of. What I do know is that he works alone and that he's a total loser. Most probably he was paid a lot of money that night to pass himself off as Saúl.'

'So what's the next step? What do we do now?' I asked him, feeling like we'd reached a dead end.

'We talk to Teresa – she has to know more about all this, besides having kept quiet about being the guardian of your sister's daughter.'

'Not to mention the daughter of my father . . .' I said, thinking hard as I forked in my salad. 'And how are we going to talk to Teresa?'

'Easy – by going to her home, of course. We'll visit tomorrow. She's normally alone after nine or so. That cousin of hers, besides being a crook, is also a total freeloader.'

'OK. Well, let's hope it's worth it . . . I admit I'm really nervous about meeting my sister – or my niece, I guess. What a family!'

'You may not believe it, but I have seen worse.'

Alfonso looked genuinely troubled when he said this. I was certain he was thinking of his own family and wanted to know more about this man who was still such a stranger to me.

'Am I allowed to ask a personal question of a detective?'

'Yes, of course, although you can never trust the answer.'

'Where are you from? Your accent is familiar, but it's not precisely Castilian Spanish either.'

'I was born in Barcelona, but I've lived all over the world.'

'Because of work?'

'Among other reasons,' he answered, looking down at his plate, as if implying he wasn't interested in the conversation.

'Are you married? Any kids?'

'You're very inquisitive all of a sudden,' he said, looking at me again. 'I was married, I don't even remember when. Are you really interested in my life? If I go on any further, you'll probably dispense with my services.'

'I'm sorry, it's just that . . . Well, I don't know if you've realised but for the last few days you're the only company I've had, and I mean company that knows how to talk, so Aris and Neca don't count. It's not even curiosity as such. I've never been someone to probe into other people's lives – I just like to observe . . . I guess I just don't know anything about your life, but you know everything about mine and I feel a little at a disadvantage.'

'That's not true. There's a lot I don't know about your life. Why did you only live with Harry Lee for a few months, for example?'

I was stunned. He'd been looking into my life in London! 'Excuse me? What do you know about Harry?'

'Don't worry,' he said with a slight smile, 'I only know his name and about the period when you lived in the flat on Trebovir Road.'

'You investigated me?' I felt that he'd violated my privacy and I didn't like it.

'What kind of detective doesn't start his job by checking out his client to begin with? Do you have any idea how many people hire a detective so they can manipulate him and lead him to false evidence? You can't trust a single person in this world. But, go on, you haven't answered my question.'

His words were terribly reassuring. Somehow, he seemed even more professional, given that he'd been so meticulous.

'Oh, he's a bit of a layabout really. He's a far better friend than a boyfriend.'

'That's so often the case. Do you fancy dessert?' he asked, changing the subject completely. Apparently, he was starting to feel uncomfortable.

'I could do with some tea – I'm a little nervous. Not even knowing where you live is hard to get used to.'

'Make that two teas. I'm also a little on edge. I'm like a child: the more tired I am, the harder it is for me to fall asleep. I might get a real drink later – that helps too.'

'I think I'll join you.'

We drank our tea and talked of insignificant things, such as how modern and impressive the hotel was, or how hot it was in Madrid in summer, which put us both at ease and gave us more of a break from our worries than the tea did. With our drinks in front of us, however, we returned to the subject that had brought us together.

'I can't stop wondering whether Teresa will tell us the whole truth when she finds out we know about the girl. I guess it won't make sense for her to stay quiet any longer, because I'm sure the only thing holding her back is that girl. I can imagine how much she loves her – she adored us. I keep picturing the look on her face when she sees us on the doorstep . . .'

'The most important thing is to get the lowdown on Pedro Vidal. The girl is irrelevant for now, although I understand the emotional connection you have with the subject and I know it's hard for you to keep your personal feelings out of the investigation. We have to find out to what extent Teresa's cousin was involved with Bodo Kraser's disappearance, and get Teresa onside so that when the time is right she'll be ready to testify. A witness like her would be extremely valuable in getting the case reopened. It's possible of course that she's been threatened, and it may not be that easy to get her to talk. It may even be that they've told her they'd take away your . . . niece.'

'Yes, and I can just imagine who'd be responsible for that. Have you found out anything about my sister Yolanda? Do you know where she is now?'

'The message I got just as you arrived was from my contact with information on her. According to him, it's true that she's been travelling back and forth to Australia for seven years, popping in and out like someone going off to the shops, but actually she spends most of her time here. She has a house in Aranjuez and although she's not registered as a resident in the town, that is where she's living. That's all I know for now, but I wouldn't rule out any more surprises. She sounds like a very slippery customer.'

'Are you sure? But . . . that doesn't make any sense,' I responded, incredulous. It seemed impossible that, finding her just a few kilometres from Madrid, she wasn't involved in all this somehow.

'Well, that's what my contact told me and he's not generally wrong. I don't know all the ins and outs, only the ones I've told you, but that's basically it: she splits her time between two continents that couldn't be any further apart.'

'It's ridiculous that she hired a proxy to deal with all the legal matters of the inheritance if she's living so near by. How did your contact find out that Yolanda's living in Aranjuez?'

'He has his sources. People leave traces via credit cards, buying properties, calling home insurance to fix a leak . . .'

'She has a house in her name?'

'No, it appears to be in someone else's name – someone with whom she has a joint bank account, and it's not Bodo, of course. A fairly inept arrangement for someone wanting to hide – superficially it works well enough, but it all quickly comes to light with a little digging. I have the address and plan to drop by there tomorrow. I'd invite you along, but for now I think it's best she doesn't suspect you know where she lives. I'm guessing she'll be in touch with Teresa and this cousin, and she'll be aware that you've hired a detective, but she doesn't need to know anything more than that. In fact, as far as we're concerned, the less she knows the better.'

'So it's possible she's living with someone?'

'I hope to find that out tomorrow. You'll have to be patient – these things take time . . .'

'I never thought I'd be dealing with all this when I came back. I could have gone home and simply flown over to sign the papers and collect my inheritance. To be honest, I'd stopped caring about my mother and my sister long before I moved to London, but . . .'

'It's because of Saúl, isn't it? His letters?'

'At first it was just needing to get closure on my past. I went through a lot of hardship during my first few years in London, and after that I thought I'd overcome everything and become this new woman, and that I'd actually come through OK after everything I'd suffered in Spain. When they told me my mother had died, I felt absolutely nothing – maybe just annoyance at the inconvenience, which made me feel proud, thinking I'd managed to get over all that. But then as soon as I set foot in the house I grew up in . . .'

'I understand.'

'It all came right back, you know? It was like being transported straight back to those days without love, always anxious, terrified that I hadn't followed her orders precisely to the letter . . . You can't imagine how hard it was growing up in that house.'

'No, I can imagine,' he said again, implying that his own childhood hadn't been happy either.

'Anyway, when I realised that the wound hadn't healed and that the simple act of walking into that house had ripped it wide open again . . .' I began to get emotional and he leaned in close, affectionate. 'Well, I started to realise that the old Berta was still alive and kicking, and that, besides the paperwork relating to the inheritance, I needed to take care of some more complex issues before I left. I have to admit, I've almost quit Spain again a couple of times – it's all too painful for me. I put it behind me once, and I could do the same again. But those letters . . . Knowing there's an innocent person out there, still waiting for justice after so many years and that I'm the only one who can help . . .'

'I have the feeling there's more to it than that,' he said, making it quite obvious that he could sense what I wasn't saying.

'How do you mean?'

'Just my gut instinct as a detective. Actually, you don't need to be a genius to notice. I knew just from how you looked at that photograph. You women, your eyes light up when you feel those butterflies in your stomach.'

'You must think I'm completely ridiculous. It's totally absurd to be attracted to someone just on the strength of their letters.'

'Well, I think you're a little naive, but I don't think your feelings are absurd – far from it.'

'Alfonso, have you ever been in love?' Even I was surprised at my question. It must have been the alcohol.

'Several times – too many, if you ask me. Falling in love is a right bastard. Sorry, I've never found a more apt expression than that.'

'I couldn't have said it better myself,' I reassured him. He looked a little embarrassed and I couldn't tell if it was because of the swear word or because of his confession.

He drained his glass and signalled to the nearest waiter to refill it, and I finished mine as well to join him in a new glass.

'The worst is when you find out all over again that love doesn't last. Every single time leaves you more wrecked and hurt.'

'At least you've experienced it.'

'More than that, it's given me bad indigestion. In my experience, love is to be savoured while you have it – right then the feeling is all yours, pure, unpolluted and eternal. The best love stories are the ones that end just in the nick of time, like in all those fairy tales.' He stopped for a moment to sip the drink the waiter had just served him. 'The prince and his beloved live happily ever after because the author cleverly cuts off the story at just the right time, thereby shunting the reality of all the arguments and accusations off into the rosy future. I don't think too many romances can withstand that second part – apparently they exist, but I haven't come across one for myself. We all work so hard in the early days to put out the most fabulous and desirable version of ourselves, hardly able to recognise our own features in the mirror at times, but then later on, exhausted with the colossal effort, we start to let ourselves go . . . The only love that will truly stand the test of time is platonic.'

'That may be so, but it's hard to accept that the person you love will never be within your reach,' I told him, lost in thought, musing over my own feelings.

'I swear to you that it's nothing compared with the pain from knowing with absolute clarity that the other person doesn't share your feelings. I need a smoke. Fancy heading out to the terrace?'

Outside we found half a dozen tables occupied by couples and groups of friends enjoying the balmy evening over their drinks. It was a little after ten by now. Once we were sitting down, with a good amount of alcohol now coursing through our veins, we continued with our forensic examination of love and its complications.

'Love is like a mischievous little imp roaming the world and causing havoc all over the place. The bastard's always ready, wins the game every time and no one escapes unscathed from his perverse clutches. He's certainly been lurking in the background of most of the disasters in human history.' He spoke slowly while he thought it over, drawing on his inevitable cigarette. 'Look around – Saúl, you, me . . .'

'Alfonso,' I said, interrupting to force him out of his reverie and to pay attention to me, 'I'm almost thirty-five years old . . .'

'No one would guess that,' he said flirtatiously. He hadn't given up on me, and I felt sorry for him.

'It's all happened over the last few weeks . . . Well, I've always believed that love was the invention of poets and department stores. I know that for many years this conviction allowed me to focus on myself so I could build an independent life and a future, but it's only now that I feel so incredibly alive and have this new insight into every step I've taken in my life. Recognising that I'm so much more than just a work in progress has been a total revelation for me.'

'Maybe that's just because it's the first time . . .'

'Yeah, well, I know it's a love well outside the bounds of reality . . .'

'They all are.'

'You can't even imagine what's it's meant to me to prove that I'm capable of loving someone, anyone, besides myself. Until now I've only felt resentment or indifference towards other people, maybe something like friendship at the most. I've been on the run for fifteen years, stressed out, not allowing myself a single moment for reflection, because I knew the painful emptiness I would find and that I'd be unable to fill it. And yet all of a sudden, nothing could make me happier than looking into my own heart and reflecting.'

'I tell you now, that mischievous little imp could very well be strolling through Olympic Park in Washington State to tell that boy what you feel for him. I wonder how long your heart will put up with it, this feeling of yours not being reciprocated.'

'I don't know, but right now I'm very conscious of what I have because I've felt it so deeply – for me, living through it has been worthwhile and I've never seen things so clearly before. Reading Saúl's letters has felt like being reborn. It's madness, utter nonsense, I know that, but I can't help it, and I don't want to. To think that if I'd found these letters in London while I was buried in the frenzy of my job . . . No, it wouldn't have been the same: going through this period of loneliness and waiting has been crucial for me. Life truly is full of the strangest surprises.'

He sat for a long while ruminating while he finished his drink and his last cigarette, until finally he decided it was time to go. His face looked tired and worn.

We said goodnight as something more than investigator and client: we'd started to build a friendship and on his side it was something a little stronger. When I got back to my room the world seemed just as unfair and arbitrary as before, but now a bit friendlier. I undressed and climbed into bed without even thinking about where I was, and a pleasant drowsiness lulled me into sleep.

Chapter 17

Friday, 27 June 2014

I ordered room service for breakfast. Another day with nothing to do and I was thrilled to think that I could spend the morning immersed in Saúl's past. If not for the marvellous discovery of his letters, I would simply not have been able to cope with the string of tragedies I had found waiting for me here on my return from London. The words of the man from Lake Crescent had been a most effective anaesthetic – as soon as I went back to them, the pain and the weight on my shoulders disappeared completely.

I missed Aris so much that as soon as I had finished breakfast I called the neighbour who had so kindly offered to take care of him. He told me that Aris was a delight, and that at that moment he was lying next to him as he read. I envied him the soothing company.

I started reading without further ado and found a few letters with no more than a hundred words each. Saúl had fallen sick from the cold, down to his passion for capturing the mist, from the paint fumes and the depression he'd been prey to for years. His illness was as much mental as physical, obsessed with painting what lay hidden in the fog that oozed from the waters of the lake. In addition, his headaches were getting worse.

Dismayed, my eyes welling with tears, I quickly picked up the next letter, hoping that Saúl had overcome this terrible crisis. My hands were shaking so much it was hard to open the envelope. It had been almost twenty days until he'd written again.

>Olympic National Park
>1 November 2005
>
>Dear Yolanda,
>At last, after a gap of nearly three weeks, I've finally found the strength to get out of bed and write to you. In between I ended up seriously ill, both physically and mentally. I don't recall, but Dylan tells me that one night a married couple in the area went to fetch him, because they'd heard strange loud noises from my cabin. He found me lying unconscious on the floor, my forehead bleeding from where I'd banged it. I was straight away taken to hospital where I regained consciousness within a few hours.
>
>It's funny because I'm starting to feel like your name is synonymous with 'journal'.
>
>The headaches have gone away too, and I don't need the pills to help me sleep any more, but I'm devastated.
>
>The day I came home from hospital I had a difficult talk with Dylan. We'd barely crossed the threshold when I noticed that my oils, canvases, brushes, and of course my paints, were gone. I looked at him, furious, and asked why. 'I'm sorry, mate,' he said, 'but you have to wait until the summer to go back to painting in oils. The doctor

was very clear on that. The fumes from the turpentine are really damaging your health.' I told him he had no right to do that to me and who was he to take the liberty of getting rid of all my materials? Dylan reminded me that, however isolated I felt, I was not alone – that he, Nadia and Carol had been at my side throughout, taking care of me when I was raving from fever, and that I still had my mother too. That hurt me a lot . . . I don't really know what I said but I ended up shoving him out of the cabin like he was nothing to me.

I feel gutted about it and I've gone every day to the restaurant to ask his forgiveness, but he won't speak to me – he's really angry and hurt, of that I'm sure. No one's been to visit me since then. And the mist is still out there, watching me, waiting for me. I know this will seem terribly selfish to you, but the truth is I don't know if I'm hurting so much because I can't paint or because I've lost my friend.

I've asked one of the forest rangers to take me to the dock tomorrow so I can catch the ferry and go into Seattle to buy materials, because if I go on like this, shut up in my cabin, all alone and without my brushes . . . I'm sorry – I can't stand this loneliness before the mist rises again.

I'll write back soon.

Saúl

I would have run to the lake without rest to stop him, convince him that he needed to wait until spring and to keep him company and offer the comfort he needed so badly. I was tormented by the thought that he might have got sick again with the headaches and the madness that the turpentine had caused, and that they had taken him to hospital unconscious.

My empathy for this man who was not only a stranger, but who had lived another nine years following on from this incident and who was probably a very different person now, was like being gripped by a madness parallel to his own. The more letters I read, the better I understood him, and the more I loved him the greater became my desperation to break down the barrier of time and space that kept us apart. I remembered what Alfonso had said the night before: 'I wonder how long your heart will put up with this feeling not being reciprocated.' I was starting to wonder myself.

My phone pinged while thinking about this, Saúl's most recent confession in my hands. It was the audio file Alfonso had promised to send. I took a deep breath to clear my thoughts and pressed play. It was only part of the conversation, the part he thought would interest me, I guess. It confirmed what the detective had told me: at first the witness was against going on record because of how many years had passed, but finally he concluded that the man in the photograph could easily be the one who had put the body on the yacht that night. What Alfonso hadn't told me was that he had withheld the information that the guy in the photograph was not the same person the witness had identified in the police line-up, which would have proved without a doubt that he had meant to entrap him. If he had made it plain that the guy in the photo was not the same man, the witness would almost certainly have denied the resemblance. His statement was likely to be ruled inadmissible in any potential court proceedings because of Alfonso's little subterfuge.

Suddenly the danger that surrounded me became all too real again. I was meddling in a matter completely shrouded in lies, blackmail, unexplained disappearances, maybe even murder . . .

with the involvement of people known for their lack of any heart or scruples. I must have posed a considerable threat to them and knew they'd not hesitate to resort to any method to shut me up. But somehow I also felt strong in my determination to fight the battle, sure in the knowledge that my very vulnerability would serve to protect me and keep me vigilant.

Yes, I had changed all right during my time in London. No one remains the same after fifteen years – the passing of every single day moulds and shapes us, leaving its mark on our mind and body. The young girl who left Madrid in 1999 would have been terrified in a situation of such great peril. She'd have kept herself out of sight, holed up all alone in her room with only Neca for comfort, until she could no longer stand it and ran away. With her mind all in pieces, she certainly wouldn't have had the capacity to fall in love. Whether it was indeed the power of love that had given me strength or the isolation forced on me by this chaste passion, it did not rule out the possibility that the man by the lake had stolen away at least part of my common sense. Well, it's true, is it not, that the greatest achievements come from people labelled as nothing better than idle dreamers? Isn't it the irrational obsession with a fantasy that helps turn it into reality? I thought of Saúl's preoccupation with capturing the very soul of the mist, and his readiness to follow his vision even to the detriment of his own health. Judging from the heap of letters still waiting to be read, he was still alive and must finally have succeeded somehow in distilling the essence of the fog in his paintings.

I was sure that every day of my thirty-four years had led me towards falling in love to this degree, and even if it proved nothing more than a wild dream, who was I to care? If I hadn't fallen so hard, right now I'd have been seeing to the running of my restaurant – the place was always booked out on Fridays. *Poor Brandon*, I thought, *he must be completely overwhelmed, dishing out the orders left, right and centre in both dining room and kitchen.* It also struck me that being the owner of a thriving business, albeit one so popular with its clients, was simply no longer the central goal of my life. What now occupied my thoughts was whether Saúl had found the patience to wait for the return of good weather to start painting in oils again – or I suppose I should say, whether nine years ago he had managed to find that patience. What a nonsense it all was – I still had trouble comprehending that his letters came from a time dead and past.

I settled down to read one more before heading out for lunch.

Olympic National Park
18 November 2005

Yolanda, my dear confessor,
It's been tough but I'm resisting temptation. Dylan found out that I'd gone to Seattle to buy materials for my painting, and swallowed his wounded pride to come and talk with me to dissuade me from ever doing something so stupid again. That same night he came over with everything he'd taken away while I was sick. He made one thing very clear: that if I so much as took the lid off a tube of paint before the fine weather came and I could paint outdoors, there'd be no more second chances – I would lose his friendship and that of the others for good. He was so firm and determined, more than ready to carry out this threat. I tried to impress on him the cruelty of what he was asking, that I could only be free from my obsession when I had conquered the mist of

the lake and put it on the canvas, but he grabbed me by the arm and forced me over to the window.

'Take a good look out there – what do you see?' he asked me.

I answered, 'That same unrelenting mist. It's like an impenetrable brick wall . . .'

'No, mate, what you see is only in your mind. It's been clear for days and the sun is shining, just like it was in the days before you passed out. Do you see now why you can't go back to painting in oils or open a single tube of paint till you get better and the spring comes? You're hallucinating, Saúl. You can't trust your mind right now.'

I didn't want to believe him; I wanted to think it was all simply a lie said to convince me, but at the same time I knew he had never once lied to me before.

The mist is still out there, but now I don't know if it's real and I'm plagued by the doubt. I call Dylan constantly to ask if he can see the mist. Today he told me that, yes, it really is there outside my window.

In hospital they prescribed me some psychiatric drugs that I stopped taking the day I got back to the cabin; they made me too sleepy, in a constant state of drowsiness. Recently I've started taking them again – maybe that's why I can better resist the temptation to go back to my brushes. Sometimes I draw and sketch with my pastels so I can partly soothe this itch, which more and more feels like a slow and deadly poison.

Nadia is distant with me. She comes to visit, brings food and we chat a bit, but never about us, because she doesn't want to talk about that. Tonight we're meeting Dylan and Carol for dinner at the restaurant... I don't know if it's a good idea. Things aren't like they were before and it could be upsetting for everyone.

Today I woke up wondering what's been happening in your life. I think my mind is clearer with having so many hours and not a lot to do, and so I've started thinking of something other than the mist. I hope you're happy, and that the love we shared hasn't made you a prisoner like it has me.

So long, Yolanda.

Saúl

Consumed with unhappiness, I looked again at his photos and then, still sitting on the bed, stared at myself in the mirror on the wall. Was I also trapped in that endless meandering labyrinth where unrequited lovers are doomed to wander? I could already mark the passing of time in the fine lines starting to form around my lips and my eyes. 'The best years of your life are passing you by, Berta – it's now or never,' I told myself. I took a deep breath and started to get myself ready for lunch.

A group of people stood waiting to go up to their rooms as I stepped out of the lift, Alfonso among them. He was so lost in thought that he didn't even notice me. I called out to him before he followed the rest of them into the lift. 'Hey, Alfonso!'

'Hi, Berta, how's your morning going?'

'Lonely. I'm going to have a bite to eat – want to join me?'

The lift doors closed behind him and he remained in the hallway, but then immediately pressed the button to call it back again.

'Thanks, but I've already eaten. I need some time out . . .'

'You're not going to fill me in on the latest?'

'Sorry, but we'll have to talk another time. I need a rest. I'll text you this afternoon, OK? I can tell you right now that there's not much news.'

'OK, well, I'll see you later then,' I said, a little disappointed.

Before stepping into the lift, he called back to me. 'Berta.'

'Yes?'

'You should eat out today. See you later.'

And the doors shut behind him. My melancholy over Saúl's last letter gave way to anxiety. Had Teresa's cousin found us again? Was he watching me from around the corner at this very moment? One of the other lifts opened and I hurried into it, pressing the button to take me down to the underground car park.

After ten minutes of aimless driving, I stopped at the first service station with a restaurant, where I chose a pasta salad and pastry, and then went back to the till for a coffee.

I must have presented a pretty pathetic picture: a thirty-something woman, all alone, drinking coffee in a roadside diner, surrounded by coarse lorry drivers who made no effort to hide their looks of lechery. I managed to hold back until after I'd paid the bill, but burst into tears as soon as I'd found shelter back in the car. There was a whole legion of reasons why I might feel so miserable, but right then I couldn't have explained precisely why. I was simply overwhelmed by fear, uncertainty, sadness, loneliness . . . and the painful joy and longing of my love. There was no concrete reason in my mind, only the need to release all the pent-up emotions that had been building over the past few weeks. I'd felt completely ridiculous sitting with that cup of coffee in the midst of sweaty men thirsty for female company, but quite honestly that was only one of the clouds that caused the storm.

Looking up, I saw a group of lorry drivers swagger past. They glanced back at me and talked among themselves, although this time they seemed a little more respectful – maybe softened by my tears.

I stayed parked in front of the restaurant for fifteen minutes at least, until I felt a bit better and the ringing of my phone finally rescued me. 'Hello,' I answered weakly.

'Hi, Berta, it's Alfonso. Are you all right?' he asked immediately. He'd probably noticed the tone of my voice.

'Yes, yes, I'm all right. What's up?'

'Where are you?'

'To tell you the truth, I've no idea. I'm at a service station a short way from the airport.'

'How about we meet in half an hour near the exit of the hotel car park and pay a visit to Teresa?'

'Sounds great,' I said, suddenly more lively, which I'm sure he also noticed. 'I'll be there.'

He wasn't there when I drove by because I was a little early, so I found a parking bay, then headed off to the rendezvous point where I spotted him in his car to one side of the entrance. He saw me and got out to open the passenger door. Quite the gentleman.

Sitting in the passenger seat, I flipped open the mirror in the overhead sun visor; my somewhat blurry gaze blinked back at me in the reflection. My tears had made my mascara run and my eyes looked like two black holes. Suddenly I felt embarrassed. He looked at me in sympathy.

'Tough day, huh?'

'It hasn't been the best of my life. I ought to go up to my room and fix my make-up.'

'You can do that right here. I'm sure you have everything you need in your bag – you ladies all do. I'll step out and have a smoke while you're busy.'

He got out of the car and leaned back against the driver's-side window. It didn't take long for me to wipe the make-up from under my eyes, touch up my eyeliner, powder my face and slick on some lip gloss. Then it was my turn to wait until he'd finished his cigarette.

Finally he got back into the driving seat. 'Better now?'

'Much better. Are you going to tell me about Aranjuez?'

He pulled out of the car park and started telling me about his morning as we drove along.

'That's where she lives all right, when she's in Spain. It was hard to be certain – seems like no one in the area knows her, and her postbox only says Señora Kraser. I didn't actually catch sight of her, nor was I able to confirm whether she's currently in Madrid. It's all very peculiar.'

'Just like everything else about my family, quite honestly. Alfonso, what do you reckon happened? I'm sure you've come to your own conclusions and you have a theory.'

'Sure, I've got my own theory, but it's better to wait in situations like these, even more so in a case as complicated as this one. It's true that instinct can be a big help, but it's also true that preconceptions cloud your ability to see clearly, and it's important to be open to any possibility until you know all the facts. But I am absolutely sure that the people involved have a big stake in all this – there's a lot of money wrapped up in it.'

'It's clear to me that Teresa's cousin is the one who killed Bodo, and that my sister paid him to do it.'

'Well, I'm not so sure. That would be the simplest interpretation, but . . .'

'But all the evidence points to him . . .'

'I don't know – it's still too soon and we're missing a lot of information. Shall we get a coffee before we see Teresa?' he asked, slowing down to stop at a cafe beside the next exit.

'If you want.'

When we were sitting at the table, I asked him, 'What are we going to do? Just go right up and knock on the door?'

'Yeah, we don't have a lot of options. I don't think her cousin will be home at this hour, because when he gets up he's out until dawn. It's possible he's looking for us right now.'

'I'm kind of nervous . . .'

'I know. Don't worry, you're with a survivor.'

'So far, but you have to die sometime,' I said, trying to make a joke.

After spending some time reading texts and typing on his phone, while I stirred my empty cup over and over, he said, 'Sorry, the person I have watching Teresa's house was messaging me . . .'

'You have someone watching Teresa's house?'

'Something's happened. I'm so very sorry to have to tell you this: Teresa is dead.'

I couldn't speak for a few seconds, taking in what he'd said. Teresa . . . In the blink of an eye my beloved nanny and housekeeper no longer existed . . . Suddenly I could hardly breathe and my heart was pounding in my chest, but for a few seconds I was unable to cry. I just couldn't react because it was too great a shock. Teresa . . . the closest thing to a mother I had ever known . . . I couldn't speak because of the utter despair bearing down on my chest and suffocating me.

'Jesus Christ, Alfonso!' I cried finally. And then the tears slowly started to flow, between choking sobs. 'That's horrible . . .'

'I'm so sorry,' he repeated, unable to find any other words to ease my pain right now.

'How? What happened?'

'I don't know yet. All I can say is that the police are at her house right now . . .'

'The police? Why? Teresa . . . my darling Teresa . . .'

Burying my face in my hands, I was getting more and more upset by the minute. All the happy memories with Teresa from my childhood began to flash through my mind like images on a carousel: those days full of laughter on the beach, the stories and goodnight kisses, the special smile she gave us when she came to pick my sister and me up from school, the winter afternoons playing ludo . . . Without her I never would have survived my childhood, and my life in London would never have happened; the strength I'd needed to face those awful years had come from her. I remembered the sheer relief that came from knowing I had her complicity and her company among all the day-to-day punishments, reproaches and coldness. Teresa . . . I felt her loss so deeply. I broke down fully at last in a storm of tears and sobbing.

Alfonso took hold of my hands and waited, quiet and patient. After several minutes I was able to pull myself together enough to speak. 'I should have listened to her and not gone digging up the past – maybe my obsession had something to do with her death . . . She warned me about it in her own way . . . It's all my fault . . . my fault . . .' I mumbled between sobs, burying my face in my hands. A young couple stared at me from the bar and I discovered that I could still feel shame alongside my grief.

I stopped and looked for a tissue in my bag so I could blow my nose and wipe away my tears, but my hands were shaking so badly that I couldn't even open the zip. Alfonso took a handkerchief out of his own pocket and gently dried my cheeks with it.

'Don't torture yourself with that now, Berta. None of this is your fault, especially not Teresa's death. We still don't know what happened – there could be a thousand reasons why she died. Maybe it was an accident or a heart condition . . . who knows?'

I assumed that he had basically ruled out a natural cause of death. It would have been too great a coincidence – for a woman who until a few hours earlier had never shown any sign of a health problem to meet her end straight after we had scheduled a meeting in order to ask a few questions . . .

'I need to know what happened – I want to go and see her.'

'Of course, I'll take you. But give yourself a few minutes first and order some tea. You need to calm down.'

My tears continued to flow as I drank the tea, my body still trembling with the shock. Sip after sip I mourned her loss with short, heartfelt words. Alfonso waited until he saw me a little more composed.

'Are you going to be able to go to her house?' he asked me.

'I think so.'

'All right then, let's go,' he said, holding out his hand to help me to my feet.

On the way to Teresa's house, my tears fell steadily, dripping slowly down my cheeks. I couldn't even think. I was too shocked, and sadder than I'd ever been in my whole life.

I'd lived with both of them throughout my childhood. I'd spent the same amount of time with each of them – the same number of days with the woman who had brought me into the world, my mother, as I had with Teresa. How could it be that the death of the first was nothing more than an inconvenience, and yet the death of the second broke my heart? It's not that I was incapable of feeling; it was just impossible to love the woman who had given me life.

Alfonso parked on the street next to Teresa's.

'Ready? We don't know what we're going to find in there, and I need you to remain as calm as possible,' he cautioned me before we got out of the car.

'I'm ready,' I said without conviction, without even being sure where I was or what I was doing.

Still in the car, he took his handkerchief out of his pocket, dried my tears carefully and, taking my face tenderly in his hands, said, 'Berta, you don't have to do this if you're not up to it. Stay here if you'd rather. I won't be long.'

'I can do it,' I said, fishing for my make-up bag to repair the damage for the second time that day.

The narrow cul de sac looked to be part of a humble housing complex. When we got there we found it crowded with people, who swarmed around two police cars and the front door of one of the buildings. My heart knocked harder in my chest and I looked up at Alfonso, feeling dizzy.

'Listen carefully,' he said, raising my chin so I would look at him. 'You're going to go up to those officers and introduce yourself for who you are: Berta, the daughter of Teresa's employer for forty years. You've come here because she hasn't been to the house in a few days or answered your calls. That's it – understand? You have to do it alone and they can't see me with you. If you go to the police and tell them who you are, they may take you in for questioning. We can't risk them asking who I am and what my relationship is with you. You started this investigation outside the law and it might turn out poorly if they discover certain information, like your not handing over the letters or that someone broke into your house and you didn't report it – you might end up as a suspect yourself. I'll stay here and look around, try to figure things out.'

'OK,' I said, drawing in a deep breath to gather my strength.

'You'll do great – you're doing this for Saúl. Remember: you know absolutely nothing. You're as shocked and surprised as all the neighbours,' he finished, giving my shoulder a light shove to move me forward.

I had a hard time getting near the police, because there were so many nosy onlookers packed around them that I could hardly get through, but I finally made my way past the crowd and approached one of the officers. Inhaling deeply, I tried to hide my overwhelming grief and sadness.

'Hello, officer, my name is Berta de Castro,' I said by way of introduction, when at last I caught his attention. 'I've here to visit someone who lives on this block.'

'And who might that be?'

'Teresa. Teresa Ros,' I answered, saying her name as though I had to drag it from the depths.

'I'm sorry to have to inform you, but this woman was found dead in her home this afternoon. Her house is under guard.'

'But . . . how? What happened?' I was still so shocked by the news that it wasn't hard to act surprised.

'We don't have any information for the moment. They took the body away half an hour ago. How did you know Teresa Ros?'

Hearing the officer talk about my recently deceased nanny with such coldness made the tears flow freely once again. I gathered all my remaining strength to go on and introduce myself.

'I'm the daughter of the woman Teresa worked for for forty years.' I paused to take a breath. 'I'm sorry, I'm in a state of shock. She was . . . I came because she hasn't come by the house for a few days or answered any of my calls,' I managed to tell him, following Alfonso's instructions.

'I see. I'm sorry for your loss. I need your name and phone number. We may have to contact you.'

I gave him my details, and he wrote them down in his notebook before excusing himself and going to talk with one of the neighbours. Two women stared at me and whispered as I wept, unable to hold back the bitter tears of my pain any longer. Perhaps they were surprised at the grief etched so clearly on my face.

I stayed there a while to listen to what the neighbours were saying. According to one lady, who looked very upset, the little girl, tired of waiting for her aunt to pick her up from her dance class, had come home alone. When no one answered the door, she went over to the neighbour's house to get the keys, and then they found her dead in the sitting room.

'The little girl came to my door, so upset. Just imagine, the poor dear . . .'

The officer interrupted her account, apparently not that interested in what had happened; the young man just wanted to do his job and clear the area. 'Have any of my colleagues taken your statement?'

'Er, yes, a little while ago, when they first arrived. I told them that . . .' answered the woman.

'All right, ma'am. We'll call you if we need anything – you can return home now. It's time to clear the street, people!' said the policeman to the rest of the crowd.

Before leaving, I got him to answer one last question. 'Can I go in to see the girl who was living with her?'

'She's with social services now, ma'am.'

Depressed, demoralised, completely destroyed, I retraced my steps in search of Alfonso's car. Teresa was dead . . . The only person who had ever really loved me. In some way I did still feel responsible – ever since I came back I hadn't been able to put myself in her place for a single moment. I'd thought only about myself, about finding out what she was hiding from me, sure that she was doing it to protect herself. Now I realised that perhaps, as always, she was just taking care of the people she loved. I was so lost in thought and so miserable that I almost walked right past the car.

'Berta. Berta!' Alfonso raised his voice from inside the car when he saw how distracted I was.

'Sorry,' I said finally, 'I was—'

'Come on, get in – let's get out of here.'

I obeyed.

'Poor Teresa, poor Teresa . . .' was all I could manage to stammer, crying inconsolably.

'I'm so sorry, Berta,' he said, trying to offer me his shoulder from his seat.

He had all the patience in the world, waiting silently while he timidly stroked my back and my make-up stained his shirt as I cried on his shoulder.

'What a day, huh?' he commented when I regained my composure. 'I think we should go back to the hotel. We could both do with a stiff drink. My assumption is that they're not watching us – that bastard's too busy trying to stay out of the way for now. He won't bother us for a while.'

I lifted my head to look at him, not thinking about what my face must look like so close to his after I'd cried so much.

'What do you mean? Have you figured something out?' I asked him.

'I hate to be the one who has to tell you this . . . They killed her, Berta; they beat her to death. The person I had watching her house saw her cousin come out, covered in blood like a madman, and then my man managed to talk to a neighbour later, who told him how the police had found her. There's no doubt it was Pedro Vidal. My contact can't find him in any of his usual bars. Right now he's highly dangerous. I think he's off his head, and he's involved in everything . . . We need to get to the bottom of all this as soon as possible.'

'Oh my God . . . Please no! I simply can't believe it . . . It's just too awful! But how are we going to end it, if the further we go on, the more death and destruction we find? Oh sweet Jesus, that my gentle Teresa should have met with such a horrific death . . . I can't believe this is really happening.'

'I don't know what to tell you. I feel your pain, but you have to be stronger than ever now if you want these bastards to pay once and for all.'

'But how?'

'I don't know. Right now I can't tell you what our next step is, but I do know that it's about time for you to go to the police and tell them everything that's happened so far.'

'And what would I say?'

'What you know and what you suspect – everything you can think of.'

'I will, but I'd still like to help Saúl, make sure he's not thrown in jail. I'm afraid they might find the letters. He's a fugitive from justice so he's not completely innocent. I'm so confused.'

'Sooner or later he'll have to show his face if he wants to prove his innocence, and he'll also have to pay for his escape: the two go hand in hand. Anyway, they'll probably call on you to testify and you will have to tell the truth.'

'I will tell the truth. I don't think the police would ask me about some letters that they don't even know exist.'

I was silent the whole way back, sighing now and then and feeling terrible for the way I had acted towards Teresa in her last days.

Before we went to our respective rooms to freshen up, we arranged to meet an hour later in the hotel bar. That night I needed company more than ever before in my life. I showered in minutes. In times as hard as these, I couldn't bear the loneliness of this place, so cold and strange to me, so far from all my friends, from the people I'm sure would have comforted me.

It was after ten on a Friday night, so the bar was really crowded, but with a great atmosphere. A nicely chosen playlist was playing ballads from the eighties at just the right volume, not too quiet, not too loud. A few couples swayed slowly on the dance floor.

We hadn't eaten, so the first drink had an immediate effect, and the second was decisive.

We drank in silence, staring at the dance floor, both of us envying the couples in love who were holding each other tight, seeing up close the prelude to a long night of love. A bit drunk, my sadness and feelings of guilt were diminishing. I thought about Saúl and Alfonso thought about me.

'Shall we dance?' he asked.

I turned around to stare at him, not sure I'd heard him right. 'What?'

'I asked if you want to dance. I love this song.'

Diana Ross and Lionel Richie were singing 'Endless Love'.

'I'll be a pretty sad partner, since I'll be thinking of someone else.'

'Don't worry. I'm an expert at dancing with girls who are in love with someone else.'

'In that case, yes, let's dance to this beautiful song.'

I was tired and dizzy, and I needed affection badly. Tonight I needed to forget more than ever, perhaps as much as he did.

Two adults, both completely alone, deprived of all ties of affection, single, needy, tipsy from the alcohol, locked in each other's arms at the mercy of a beautiful love song . . . Right then each of us was the only kindness that could be seen on the desolate horizon.

We forgot about everything – we needed this break to be able to move forward. For a few hours all my desires and nightmares seemed no more than a pleasant, far-off dream and I could be myself, living in the present and in reality, rather than in some fantasy. The past and the future were cast aside for now: my mother, my sister, her violent deeds, Teresa's death, my niece, Saúl . . . They all had to wait. I was hungry for affection and Alfonso had so much to give.

At first it was a little awkward with our bodies so close together, but it passed. I rested my head on his shoulder and let myself be transported by the music and by his arms. I felt loved; I liked it, and . . . his shirt smelled so good! We danced to three songs in a row and then had a third drink before going up to his room. He grabbed me around my waist, as though I had always been his.

We barely spoke, both knowing this was a fragile thing and that the slightest breeze could break it.

Before sliding his key card through the door, he looked at me for a moment, gathering his courage to ask me the necessary question. 'Berta, are you sure?'

'You're a wonderful man, Alfonso, and it takes a whole lot of guts to ask me that and risk missing out on a night of sex and passion. Yes, I am absolutely sure,' I said in honest answer, because out of all the options open to me right this minute, he was the best – by a long shot.

I got even more than I'd been hoping for: tenderness, patience, understanding, generosity and the most enormous pleasure. I think he did too. It was a revelation. Until now my experience with men had been limited, reduced to a couple of sporadic and unsatisfactory encounters, and to Harry, who couldn't disassociate from his ego, even in bed. Alfonso was a good lover, skilled and selfless. At three in the morning I fell asleep on his bare chest, crying again over the tragic death of my beloved housekeeper and thinking about the strange anaesthetic effect sex had had on my pain. Before I drifted off to sleep, I remembered my friend Mary once scandalising me by confessing that she had never had better sex with her boyfriend than on the day she buried her father. Now I finally understood.

Chapter 18

Saturday, 28 June 2014

The room was in shadows. Still groggy, I reached out my arm and realised Alfonso wasn't there. I turned on the lamp and looked around: his tablet was gone, as well as his wallet and suitcase . . . The chest of drawers was open and the drawers inside were completely empty. As I sat up, about to get out of bed, I found a handwritten note on the bedside table, next to the phone.

> Hi, Berta,
> Last night, with you sleeping in my arms, I knew it was time to put some distance between us. We can't go on like this. I found happiness with you and that is what I'm taking away with me. I couldn't stand seeing another look of regret when you wake up.
>
> Don't worry, this won't affect our professional relationship. I'll keep working for you and call when I have news, just like last night never happened. I hope you'll be able to do the same.
>
> Oh, and I think it's safe for you to go back home now.
> Alfonso

He was right. If he'd been at my side in the morning, the first thing he'd have seen would have been the regret on my face, along with an apologetic 'Good morning' – not for myself but for the harm I might have caused him. I could taste the bitter guilt right now, in fact. I'd let myself be carried away by my own need for male company, despite knowing how much more it meant to him than to me. I remembered the usual warning against mixing business with pleasure.

This was all too much to take in just now – too many thoughts swirling around in my brain, begging for order and coffee. Brushing my hair in front of the mirror, I told myself, 'Stupid, stupid, stupid . . . now you're even more alone than you were before, and all for a little bit of fun.' I missed him – Alfonso was a good guy, a terrific companion and, above all else, a magnificent detective. Right now he was the only person in Spain who was on my side. Yes, I'd been really, really stupid.

I had a quick breakfast in the cafeteria before stopping by my room, having decided to go home.

I took a shower and then packed my clothes and the letters in my suitcase, looking forward to reading more of them – the only thing that could give me any comfort right now.

At the front desk, I found to my surprise that the bill had already been settled. I remembered then that I still owed Alfonso at least two thousand euros and that I wasn't sure I had that much in my bank account. I'd have to take out a large chunk of my savings; the investigation and my stay in Madrid were dragging on far too long.

Before heading home, I went shopping at the supermarket, where I spent almost two hours to avoid the rush hour, and because it was the day before a holiday. Then I stopped by the bank, which was fortunately open on Saturdays. There wasn't too much time to brood, nor could I afford it: traffic jams, queues everywhere, the heat... although a persistent bitterness followed me the whole day long. I had so many loose ends in my life... so many problems to solve and so much grief and loss.

◆ ◆ ◆

The entryphone rang just as I was about to stretch out in my favourite spot beneath the willow tree to get my thoughts straight and continue reading Saúl's letters. It was Arturo, the kind neighbour, the only one I knew. He just wanted to make sure I was home, having noticed around lunchtime that Aris had left, and to offer his condolences on Teresa's death.

'I heard what happened to the woman who worked for your mother. I'm so sorry. She was a lovely woman and my wife was terribly fond of her. We're coming to her funeral tomorrow to bid our farewells.'

'It was such a tragedy,' I answered. 'I only found out by accident... Do you know what time the funeral is? I don't actually know anyone else in her life...'

'It's at four o'clock in the parish church of El Salvador in Leganés – my wife found out through one of her neighbours. They were friends of a sort... they'd exchange plants and talk about gardening. Teresa has been so kind to us since we moved here ten years ago. It's a real pity.' He was polite and discreet and didn't stay long.

I lay down under the willow tree and my first thought was for Teresa. Imagining how terrible her death must have been with the pain of the beating she had endured, I was shaken to my core and felt my heart break in two all over again. I blamed myself for having thought badly of her, for having judged her without knowing what was going on in her private life, for my lack of insight, for not having given her the benefit of the doubt . . . I realised that, as always, her only motive had been to protect the most innocent. She had surely raised my niece as a daughter. She had done so much good in her life, but the best of all had been to give love where it was missing.

It was all so grim and far-fetched that it seemed impossible to believe. True, my sister was devious and unimaginably selfish, but, even so, the fact that she had endured nine months of pregnancy, knowing how much she valued her body and her independence, and then gave her daughter away like unwanted goods . . . She must have had a powerful reason. Alfonso must be right – there had to be a lot of money at stake.

I would have liked to see the girl, to talk with her, tell her that she was not alone, that I was her aunt as well as her sister . . . Well, maybe I could leave that last bit until later. I wasn't sure if with her tender years she was ready to take in news like that, remembering how hard it had been for me to take in, even at my age. Or maybe I was underestimating the situation, and the girl knew who she was better than I did. In any case, I'd have liked to tell her that she could count on me. And I would, as soon as I found out where she was and after a few days had passed. Now was not a good time to show my involvement in Teresa's life or with the girl – the murderer might be on the lookout. Besides, I needed Alfonso's help with that.

I missed my detective a lot; how easy he was to be with, his confidence, the feeling of knowing that I was with someone who had experience with cases like mine . . . I hoped there was no actual 'curse' as such on the women in my family like the one he'd referred to, and that he wasn't going to disappear like all the other men any time soon. Right now I had no one else in Madrid who I could trust. I remembered last night and thought that, in spite of the sad circumstances, it hadn't been nothing; it hadn't been bad. It was such a shame that Alfonso had come into my life after I'd started reading the letters; if I'd known him before, maybe a romance between us could have been possible.

They say everything happens for a reason, but I was sure the opposite was true: there's no reason for anything that happens. It's all chance, and the thing you want most hardly ever happens at the right time. I think most of us are constantly trying to adapt to adversity; sometimes we manage, but in most cases we settle for imagining shapes in the clouds and limit ourselves to simply making the best of whatever comes along.

I barely knew him and yet I missed him as though he'd been a huge part of my life. He had given me so much love in just a few hours . . . I knew it was a selfish feeling, born out of loneliness and vulnerability. Since first leaving Spain fifteen years ago, I'd never needed so much reassurance and support as now, not even when I first hit the streets of London, where the language, people, climate and my financial struggles had made me feel helpless in a city that is ruthless with its weak.

They say the home we're born into is always linked with feelings of love, trust and protection – with happiness. For me it was the reverse: it only ever made me experience fear and desolation, just like with the word 'Mummy'. Besides feeling bereft, I was also deeply sad and disappointed: not one single thing I'd achieved in all my years of work and effort had any value to me right then. I think what hurt the most was recognising quite how exposed and friendless I actually was – quite unable to help my situation. All I could do was wait for things to develop and maybe then come to a decision.

This whole affair filled me with a vast emptiness and anguish, and suddenly I was no longer in the mood to read any more of

Saúl's letters. I just couldn't stop thinking about Teresa, memories of our past times together and the grisly way in which she had met her end. By eight o'clock in the evening, I was thoroughly exhausted. The sun shone as brightly as ever, but it was black as night in my soul and I was physically and emotionally drained. I made myself a cup of tea and went to bed, to grieve over my troubles and my recent loss until I fell asleep.

Chapter 19

Sunday, 29 June 2014

It was getting light outside, but I stayed in bed another hour. I was feeling ill, aching in my head and my soul. Aris was patient and waited for me.

After a long and refreshing hot bath and a cup of coffee, I felt a little better. I was trying to figure out how to turn on the sprinklers and which plants needed to be watered by hand when the entryphone rang.

It was a couple of police officers, who had come to ask me a few questions. They looked too young to be wearing their uniforms, a clear sign that I was no longer a girl.

Once in the garden, the taller one started to explain. 'We came to ask you some questions about Teresa Ros Villanueva. According to the report, you were at her house yesterday a few hours after her death and passed your details to an officer.'

'That's correct,' I confirmed, starting to tremble from head to toe. What scared me most was that they might ask me something that would jeopardise Saúl. I remembered that, the day before, Alfonso had advised me to tell the truth, but I wasn't so sure. The officer continued, while his partner stayed silent and watched.

'How did you know Teresa Ros?'

'She worked here for my mother for forty years – she was like one of the family.'

'When did you see her last?'

'Three or four days ago. She came every day and it was really unusual for her not to come for two days in a row, so I went to her house . . .' Suddenly I couldn't speak, remembering that moment, and I tried to hide it, but the tears sprang to my eyes.

'I see. Did you notice any strange behaviour in her in the days prior?'

'No, nothing that made me suspect anything like this . . .'

All their questions were strictly according to protocol with none of them requiring me to compromise anyone, nor did they even ask me about my personal life. They were only interested in my address in London and why I had come back to Spain. They were surprised at how close together the deaths of my mother and Teresa had been, but didn't ask about it in any more detail. When they were done, I signed their forms and they left. I had a terrible feeling that I'd committed a serious crime of omission that might come back to haunt me in the event that they reopened the case of Bodo's disappearance. Actually, if the young officer had delved further, I would have answered him truthfully.

I spent the rest of the afternoon wandering through the garden, followed a few steps behind by Aris. Being close to the jasmine, the bougainvillea, the lilies . . . It was like being close to Teresa. It seemed almost cruel to me that these flowers could sparkle with such defiant strength and beauty, while the person who had tended them with such care and diligence lay in her coffin awaiting burial. Dragging the hose behind me, I watered here and there as I walked, barely conscious of what I was doing, thinking back on the questions the young officer had asked me and pouring yet more tears of sadness and despair over the lush vegetation.

Around half past two I prepared a veal steak and salad, and just after three I looked up the address for the church of El Salvador and went to pay my final respects to my dearest nanny and housekeeper, Teresa.

◆ ◆ ◆

I'd chosen a discreet outfit of black trousers and a blue shirt, tied my hair back and put on some large dark sunglasses, appropriate for the warm sunny day. I arrived a little early and, after a five-minute walk from my parking spot, found the church almost empty, so took a pew near the rear to wait for the rest of the congregation.

The hearse arrived a few minutes later, and then my darling Teresa was borne on her final ceremonial journey down the aisle towards the altar. My heart was in tatters. I presumed that the four strong men bearing the coffin were undertakers from the funeral home, as none of them had a similar appearance to her cousin, and he would hardly have dared to appear. Around twenty people followed on behind, and there she was among them suddenly, my niece who was also my sister – a beautiful little girl, quite inconsolable and the very picture of grief, walking unsteadily behind the coffin of the woman who, I was sure, had cared for her like her own daughter. The urge to go up to her and comfort her was unbearable, but it wasn't the right time. What would I say to her – that I was her aunt but also her sister? I could have simply introduced myself as her aunt from London – surely Teresa must have occasionally mentioned me to her – but I just didn't feel strong enough. As an aunt, I didn't know what she might expect of me and I wasn't in any position to offer concrete help to her.

I was barely able to follow the sermon of the priest who was officiating at the Mass. From behind the shield of my dark sunglasses, I could scarcely take my eyes off the coffin that held Teresa's body. It just didn't seem credible that she was lying there, lifeless, covered in terrible bruises and the sutures from the autopsy. It seemed hardly any time since we were drinking coffee in the kitchen, Teresa with her watering can out in the garden, or cooking chicken and rice for me . . . Only a few days ago I could have prevented her tragic death, when she asked me to leave matters well alone, and I could have changed things so this pretty little girl was not now left grieving and abandoned. Tears of sadness and guilt flowed, lonely and silent, in the corner where I sat. If only, if only I could go back in time and change things . . .

I said a prayer for Teresa's soul and left quietly before the ceremony was over. It wasn't even five yet when I got back home.

Having changed my clothes, I took refuge under the old willow tree again with Saúl's letters, unable to stop thinking about Teresa, who had been so genuinely kind and good, and, above all, about the lovely young girl who had followed her coffin, crying, her heart broken just as mine was. Her face hadn't been clearly visible to me, but I'd seen enough of her slim figure and long, straight waist-length hair to recognise her resemblance to her mother – hopefully only in the physical sense. Fearing my spirits would sink even lower, I forced myself to stop thinking about her and opened the first letter of the day.

> Olympic National Park
> 2 December 2005
>
> Beautiful Yolanda,
> This winter feels especially hard. I don't even know how many days I've been shut up in this cabin. Every now and then I'll open the door a crack to throw food out to the ducks. I'm terrified of the cold. I don't know if it's because I'm too weak or

because of the medication, but I'm always freezing. Dylan tries to make me feel better by telling me this is in fact one of the coldest winters he can remember in Olympic Park. It could be . . . I just wish spring would come so I could open the window again.

At least I can still use my pastels. Mr Baker says that all my artworks have the same magic, no matter what technique I use. I think I hear Dylan's voice behind his words, because both the gallery owner and my good friend are trying their hardest to encourage me to forget about painting in oils for the moment so my recovery continues. In any case, he buys all my works and, as he says, they are all getting bought.

I have good news for you: I've finally managed to capture the mist! At last I've been able to drag it out of the lake and bring it to the other side of my window – only with pastels and paper, mind you, but I've done it and have now recreated it seven times. Mr Baker says my pictures are causing a lot of excitement on his website, and that everyone's wanting a view of the mist from the lake – he insists that I should sell the lot when I've finished the series. He wants a whole collection on the theme. A whole series . . . But I still don't know when this grey fog will clear from my mind.

I stopped reading. Martin Baker had a website where he exhibited and sold Saúl's paintings!

Naturally, I set up my laptop on the kitchen table to start searching for the website. When I turned it on, I was bombarded with messages and emails, none of them the one I'd been waiting for so eagerly, so I went straight to Google and typed in the name of the gallery. There were more than two million results for my search – endless possibilities. Without even thinking, I clicked on the first link, as nervous as a love-struck teenager going on her first date. One of the tabs I found had a list of the painters represented on the website. My fingers were shaking. I clicked on it and scrolled through the list until I came across Yosa Degui! Next to his pseudonym, in small letters, it named him as 'The Flickering Painter'.

A photograph of his back, sitting on the dock, very similar to the one I had, was on the left-hand side of the page, and on the right a list of all the thematic collections of the artist: 'The Forest', 'The Lake', 'The Dock', 'The Harbour', 'The Mist', 'The Spring' and . . . 'Yolanda'. The last collection turned the magic of the moment into rage, but only for an instant; I was so emotional . . . At the bottom of the screen a banner announced: 'An exhibition of the works of Yosa Degui in Paris, 30 June–20 July 2014'.

I had to stop a minute to reorient myself. 'OK, take it easy now,' I told myself, after a few deep breaths. 'You're not reading about the past any more. His exhibition has this year's date on it and it's taking place tomorrow. I could get there if I set off now.' I took another deep breath. The landline rang in the sitting room, but it would have to wait. I clicked on the announcement to get more information.

> From 30 June to 20 July, the final collection of Yosa Degui will be shown at the Atelier des Lumières in Paris. Twenty-two works in pastel and thirty-one in oils complete the series 'Letters to a Stranger', a journey through his artistic career. Visitors should note that the artist is unable to attend the opening or subsequent days of the show in person. Martin Baker will represent the artist and act on his behalf with interested clients.

I was paralysed, I don't know for how long, staring blankly at the tiles of the kitchen floor. Was fate playing some kind of game with me? An exhibition of his final collection would be opening the next day, mere hours from where I was now, and it was called 'Letters to a Stranger'. I got up and went out into the garden, pacing up and down to get some air and clear my head. Was I living in the real world or in fantasy land? It wasn't possible for someone to live untroubled for fifteen years, and then suddenly have to deal with so many shocks, one on top of the other. It even struck me that this might all be some strange kind of dream, and that any minute now I'd be waking in my own bed in London. I drifted aimlessly here and there, locked in my own little world like a madwoman.

I could all too easily imagine that there wasn't much left of that naive young man who'd left for the United States, his heart and soul in pieces. Nevertheless, it was clear that he had never forgotten Yolanda, or at least still treasured the love he had known. The feelings he had experienced with the first woman he had loved seemed to have transported him to such a degree of extrasensory intensity that the trauma of losing her had left him severely impaired. It was as though the cascade of endorphins that had once invaded his body had been so strong and powerful that nothing else could stimulate his senses in the same way. His only desire was to be with her.

Maybe in the letters I hadn't read yet from subsequent years, he'd managed to let go of the past and fall in love again. He was a very successful artist, and the thrill of fame and glory can change a person. The point is that he had survived Yolanda's spell, and, at least in the professional world, he was doing quite well.

Slowly but surely I was coming back to myself and facing reality. I had a car parked outside and enough time and desire. If this were all a dream, I was ready to enjoy it.

The phone kept ringing and then my mobile beeped, telling me I had new messages. This was not the moment to deal with anyone else, nor was I willing to let the next development here in Madrid or in London ruin my most immediate project. What was stopping me? It was a little after five in the afternoon; I could be on the road in an hour and I could be in Paris before dawn. I had no other plans for the weekend, but, even if I had, I wouldn't have given up the chance to be so close to the love of my life for anything in the world.

I would have stayed online a while longer and memorised every word written about Saúl and his work if I hadn't been in such a rush, so I just prepared for my trip and booked a hotel in Paris. My mind got to work quickly – this was no time for distractions and I didn't give myself a second to reconsider. I still hadn't unpacked my suitcase from the hotel, so just took out the dirty clothes and tossed in an elegant dress to wear to the opening, along with a couple of shirts. My hair still stood on end every time I realised that in just a few hours I would be so close to his art, perhaps as close as I could ever be to him.

I called Arturo to tell him I had to leave again for a few days. Luckily, he and his wife had just got home from Teresa's funeral. I'd been so wrapped up in my own grief that I hadn't even noticed them there. He very kindly told me not to worry about Aris and wished me a pleasant trip.

◆ ◆ ◆

By six o'clock I was out of the house and ready to leave for Paris, more excited than I'd ever been in my life. I felt like a schoolgirl about to take her first trip – at least, that's what I thought it must be like, because Alberta had actually never let us go on any school trip that lasted more than a day; she had always invented some reason to punish us so we'd have to stay home. Just another one of the mysteries she took with her to the grave.

As I pulled the front gate to, I went back over everything I might need. I still had time. Suddenly a little uncertain, I locked the door. In the passenger seat my phone was ringing again – someone was trying their darnedest to get hold of me, calling over and over at what was a bad time. I wasn't planning on checking my messages or missed calls until I got to Irún. I didn't want to hear a thing until I was already far away, so that nothing important could call me back to Madrid. No! I felt I had to follow my instinct and not miss that exhibition for anything in the world, even if it cost me my life. It was the first time I'd ever thrown caution to the wind and followed my heart, and it was a feeling beyond compare. But I was guessing it was Alfonso – he was due to call around now. I decided to answer before getting underway; I didn't want to drive off not knowing it was something important, especially if I was in danger. Sure enough, it was Alfonso.

'Hello?'

'Hi, Berta. Are you all right? I've been calling your mobile and your house phone. I was really worried.'

'I'm sorry, I was just getting ready for a last-minute trip.'

'A trip? Where are you going?'

'Paris. I found out online that they're opening an exhibition of Saúl's art tomorrow and I want to be there.'

'In Paris? But . . . Saúl won't be there . . .'

I was surprised that he'd said this with such utter certainty.

'How do you know?'

'I read the last letter, remember? He talked about this exhibition in it, and how his legal situation prevented him from leaving America. He wasn't even writing to your sister any more – it looked more like an entry from a journal than it did a letter.'

'What else did it say?'

'That it would be Yosa Degui's farewell, and that Saúl would die in Paris. That he was starting a new life with a new identity, and he had taken up sculpting. That there was nothing left of that broken boy desperate to return to Yolanda; he's a grown man now, excited about his future.'

'I want to be there for that farewell. I need to say goodbye to Saúl.'

'That's crazy – it's madness . . .'

'Crazy, huh . . . Does anything really make sense in my life lately?'

'Hmm . . . Are you driving?'

'Yes, I didn't even look at flights. I have a car and enough time on my hands.'

'But it's not a great moment to leave. I have news about—'

'No, Alfonso, not right now,' I interrupted, afraid that any update on recent events would lead to a conversation that I didn't want and didn't have time for.

'Berta, I'm still on your side. What happened between us the other night didn't change anything.'

'I'm so happy I can still count on you. Look, I need to get going, Alfonso – we'll talk when I get back.'

'OK. Be careful, Berta.'

'I will. Goodbye, Alfonso.'

'Have a good trip.'

◆ ◆ ◆

I drove resolutely and with a certain calm in spite of the situation, knowing that I still had many hours left to go and that I needed to conserve my strength. Before leaving I'd looked up the route online, and mentally planned out all the rest stops I would make and when I would arrive. During the trip, I went over and over in my mind the conversation I'd had with Alfonso just before leaving, wondering what he'd meant by having some news on the case. I hadn't wanted to hear it – I was afraid it would be something that would force me to stay. Either way, I was sure it was nothing that couldn't wait for my return. But more than anything, I thought about what the last letter might mean, the one Alfonso had read. Saúl was no longer that same melancholy guy wrecked by a lost love: he had changed and he was hopeful for the future. He was now a mature man who had finally turned the page of his life. He had even changed the way he expressed himself artistically, moving on to sculpting. Who knows – maybe he had a family, a wife and kids who filled his life with love? Yosa Degui, the Flickering Painter, Saúl – they would die in Paris and I was on the way to their funeral. I thought about how the passage of time changes everything and about the snare I'd been caught in, trapping me in a moment that no longer existed.

Paying attention to the road, but mired in my reflections, almost hopeful, only now and then was I sometimes interrupted by the image of Teresa's face, barely conscious of the hours passing. Before midnight I was crossing the Pyrenees. I was lucky not to be stopped, since I hadn't paid for the additional coverage required for a rental car to cross the border.

Chapter 20

Monday, 30 June 2014

I could sense the beauty of the landscape surrounding me, but the darkness of the night forced me to focus only on the headlights of the other cars and the immediate section of road lit up by my own lights. Surprisingly, I wasn't too tired. The car had Bluetooth, a technological wonder that gave me the ability to play music from my phone, which had stopped beeping shortly before midnight, thank God.

Just then 'Hotel California' by the Eagles came on, followed by Tina Turner, and then Eros Ramazzotti burst through the noise of the road with '*Cose della vita*' ('Things in Life') . . . I'd chosen my 'medium' playlist – not too high in energy but also not too soothing. Maybe when I started getting drowsy I'd put on my 'fast' playlist. For the moment, I was wide awake.

I imagined what it might mean to Saúl for his works to be exhibited so far from where he lived, in a city iconic for its art, and not to be able to witness such an important event – it would surely equal not being able to go to your child's graduation. Months of work and passion, during which I knew his health had suffered tremendously, for his paintings to then be transported across a vast ocean and be shown somewhere unfamiliar, looked at by complete strangers, people he would never meet, never speak to. It must in fact be even worse than not being able to attend a graduation: it would be more like losing one's beloved child forever and never hearing back from them again.

The title he had given to this last collection was brazenly evocative to me: 'Letters to a Stranger' . . . I assumed that after so many years of writing with no response, Yolanda had indeed become a stranger to him. My most recent information regarding his feelings for her went back some eight and a half years – the last letter I'd read was from December 2005. I hadn't finished it, excited at the news that Martin Baker had a website where he sold his paintings. All the rest were still at the house, waiting for my return. In the almost three years of letters I had read so far, the romance had been evolving – for Saúl at least, who had gone through various stages: the desperation and upheaval of the first months of loneliness, then helplessness and melancholy, and finally resignation.

I was dying to know what his last paintings were like. Would he still be obsessively working Yolanda's eyes into every one of his scenes? As I drew closer to Bordeaux, I imagined what he might look like right now, if he still had his long hair and good looks, and I dreamt of the same thing over and over: him and me by the lake, surrounded by the mist that had tortured him so much, our arms around each other's waists, shivering with love and happiness.

Even if my desires were realised, the actual reality would probably never be as magical as what I'd imagined. The most beautiful love affair has to be the one in your dreams, the one that relies completely on yourself, constructed from your own needs and desires, with no contradiction or any obligation to fulfil the wishes of the other party. And that is quite different from what actually happens, when you're subject to someone else's opinions, to the normal trials and tribulations of life, and to the necessity of surviving as sensitive souls in a harsh world. I pondered then that if I'd already been so intensely happy loving the ideal man and tasting the fruits of paradise all by myself, what more could I possibly want out of life? I was convinced that this unique romance with Saúl would be eternal and incorruptible so long as it remained mine and mine alone. Was that true, or was I just consoling myself because I was as obsessed in my own way as he was, and had no alternative? Did I harbour some deep and long-buried fear of facing life as a couple because of the bizarrely consistent absence of a stable male figure while I was growing up at home?

Sitting at the wheel, crossing national frontiers in the middle of the night to fulfil a desire all of my own, I felt like one of those princesses I'd read about, believing myself to be more in love than anyone else in the whole wide world – except that no prince would come to rescue me, because my story existed only in my head. Yes, I felt important, proud of my actions, of having for once been capable of doing what I really wanted – me – with nobody's say-so or by-your-leave. It gave me an incredible sense of satisfaction to serve as the eyes of my beloved in a place where the law prevented him from going and, who knows, maybe when I got back to Madrid I would dare to write and tell him all the things I'd seen and felt. Above all else, however, the most powerful thing driving me forward that night on that black and lonely road was the knowledge that I was getting closer and closer to his final paintings.

Leaving Bordeaux, I stopped at the first service station I found open at that hour. I will admit that getting out of the car in that desolate lunar landscape, all my resolve regarding my decision and the bravery I'd been feeling since I left home quite deserted me, along with my confidence and sense of pride. Noting the unusual cold and solitude, I debated with myself as to whether I should continue, suddenly aware of how crazy this all was, and how vulnerable a woman alone could be in a place this empty in the early hours around dawn. Whatever the case, I needed to refuel, get some coffee and buy water and something to eat for the rest of the trip, as well as go to the loo and stretch my legs.

I went into the shop just beyond the pumps, and picked out the necessary items: bottles of ready-made coffee and water and a bag of dried fruit. The drowsy lad at the till knew a bit of Spanish and charged me for the items as well as fifty euros for the petrol to fill my tank – it was too early for him to leave the shop at this hour and serve me out there himself. Going to the loo, however, seemed like a mission too far. It was one of those service stations where you have to ask for the key to the loo, which I reckoned was probably tucked away behind the building – and my courage only went so far. I was going to have to find somewhere else to go.

As I left, I noticed a BMW parked a few metres away with the driver inside, smoking, as though he was waiting for something or someone. But why? Who on earth might he be waiting for at this hour and in such an inhospitable place . . . ? My body tingled with pins and needles as I walked back to my car. I started filling up with my fifty euros' worth of petrol, shaking so much I could barely hold the apparatus; if the nozzle hadn't been so firmly pressed into the opening to the tank, the potent mix of fuel vapours and the cigarette of the man in the BMW could have spelled disaster. I stared fixedly at the meter, trying to hide my terror – the digits had never clicked through so slowly in my life. Around me was the night, as black as pitch.

I didn't wait for the whole fifty euros' worth to go in; my ears buzzed with the sense of danger. The smartest thing to do would be to get out of there as fast as possible. As I pulled out of the exit, the BMW started its engine. I'd planned my route to Paris, but, seeing him in my rear-view mirror, I pressed my foot down hard on the accelerator and, as soon as possible, pulled between two huge lorries in the slow lane up ahead, hoping to obscure myself from view. We were driving through a densely wooded area, and a string of signs came up ahead, pointing to side roads. Veering off sharply down a single-track lane that seemed particularly tucked away and obscure, I wondered at the same time if I'd just taken a path that would lead straight to my death – at least on the main road my pursuer hadn't dared approach me any closer without putting his own life in danger or risking another driver calling the police. I was sure he hadn't seen me exit, however, and hoped this little track would lead to some house with a turning space so I could head back to the main road. If I hadn't managed to shake him off, we'd otherwise end up face to face. This lane was barely wide enough for a single car.

The narrow route did indeed lead towards an old farmhouse, where the crunch of the tyres on the gravel and the headlights shining on the puddles must have alerted the owner, because before I could turn the car on the small patch of flattened earth in front of me, a man in shorts and a T-shirt appeared at the front door, pointing a shotgun in my direction. Now even my mind was quivering with fear.

I had two choices: get out and explain to the farmer that I'd taken his road by mistake, or speed up and turn around, and likely come face to face with my pursuer. It was like having to choose between death by gunshot or torture at the hands of a psychopath. Impulsively, I chose the first option, without even thinking – there wasn't time for it. I rolled down the window and put my hand up in a gesture of peace, repeating over and over, 'I'm sorry, I'm sorry, I'm sorry . . .' At that moment, a woman stormed out and snatched the gun away from the man with obvious anger. She came up to the car, looking quite friendly.

'*Ça va?*' she asked me in French – was I all right?

'I'm sorry, I'm sorry,' I kept saying, as if I couldn't remember any other words from the dictionary. 'I took the wrong turning . . .'

'You are Spanish?' she asked this time.

'Yes, from Madrid,' I answered, a little calmer now, seeing that she understood me.

'Spanish and very brave. What is a woman like you doing at this hour on these roads?' she said in heavily accented Spanish, although I could understand her all right. 'Come on, you need something to drink. What a scare this husband of mine gave you. He sleeps with that shotgun since he was mugged two years ago – and don't worry, it's not loaded,' she explained with a small smile.

'Well, thank you very much, but . . . I don't know if I should . . .'

'Come on, come in for a moment and relax. You're in no condition to keep driving now anyway.'

I couldn't help wondering whether the car that was in pursuit of me would be waiting around some bend in the road, although not, of course, too close . . . Or maybe it would be lying hidden among the trees with the headlights off? I decided it would be a good idea to accept the kind woman's invitation.

Stepping out of the car, my legs could barely support my weight. Instead of looking at my hostess, I kept my head twisted back towards the road, scanning the darkness in vain. She seemed to understand that I was on the run from someone.

'*Bernard!*' she yelled, calling her husband so loudly that in the silence of the night its echo resounded to the heavens. I could only assume that the driver of the BMW would have heard it too.

'*Oui?*' came her husband's voice from inside the house.

'*Va voir sur le chemin s'il y a une voiture.*'

I understood what she'd told him: to go down the lane and check if there was a car. This woman certainly had her head screwed on.

Her husband did as she asked and, while the good woman made me tea on a stove that looked like something out of the Middle Ages, along with everything else here, he went to check out the path that connected his house with the main road.

I was trembling so much in my chair that, amid the silence and with no one else around, it made a rather irritating non-stop rapid knocking. The woman folded a piece of paper and stuck it under the shortest leg of my chair.

'I'm sorry, I—'

'Shh . . . Don't you worry – calm yourself, you're safe here. There's a loaded shotgun in the cupboard,' she said, trying to reassure me. She introduced herself over the cooling but unidentifiable tea. 'I'm Alice, and you are?'

'Berta,' I managed to say.

'So what happened to you, Berta?'

'Someone's been following me since I left the petrol station where I tanked up a while ago. All I could think of doing was to get between two lorries to hide from him and then take the first exit off.'

'Are you sure you were being followed?'

'Yes, I wasn't imagining it. So, anyway, I took the road that led here, to your house. Are you sure your husband hasn't been gone for too long?'

'Don't worry, *ma chère*, he knows how to take care of himself. You'll see – he'll be back in no time,' she answered, not very convincingly.

Unless I was wrong, he had in fact been gone for a while now. The little lane wasn't that much of a stretch off the main road, and, however slowly you were going, it surely couldn't take more than ten minutes to get to the end and come back? It had already been over a quarter of an hour. We both started to worry now, so Alice decided to join me in a relaxing cup of tea and we sat quietly for a couple of minutes, until finally we heard the sound of an engine against the racket of the dawn chorus. Alice let out a deep breath after peering through the window.

The two of them talked for a while in French and then Alice explained that her husband had indeed found a car hidden along the road in a clearing among the forest brambles. It was facing the road with its lights off, waiting. The driver got the fright of his life seeing Bernard get out of the truck with his shotgun pointing at him, scowling. According to him, the man left in a hurry, pulling out of his hiding spot so fast that he almost ran him over. Apparently he was bouncing about like mad because of the ruggedness of the terrain, and his paintwork must have suffered because he didn't even try to avoid the brambles and branches of trees that overran the path on all sides. Bernard followed him on to the main road and for quite a way further, to make sure he wasn't coming back. That was what had taken him so long.

After hearing the woman's translation, I told her, 'I have to go. He knows I'm here and he'll definitely be back.'

'Do you know this man?' Alice asked me in bewilderment and curiosity, realising that there might be a background to everything I'd been through.

'I'm not sure, but he could be a . . . Could you ask your husband what he looked like, please?'

I understood Bernard's description before Alice had even translated: tall, thin and under forty.

'Oh yes,' I murmured, after hearing the account of his general appearance. 'I know who he is all right.'

'Well, you'd have to be either mad or desperate to follow someone in the middle of the night all the way here from Madrid. We women really ought to lock ourselves away and have a long hard think before accepting any man's offer of marriage,' she declared, assuming this fellow was my husband. I didn't correct her: this wasn't the time to get into a long, drawn-out conversation.

'I'm sorry, but I really have to go. The longer I wait before setting off, the more time he'll have to turn around and come and find me.'

'You're right – it's best you go as soon as possible.'

The husband interrupted our conversation to say something to her and then Alice told me, 'Bernard will guide you to a different road – follow it to the end until you get back to the main road, just over an hour away.'

'Thank you – thank you so much. You saved my life, both of you, and I don't know how I can ever thank you enough . . .'

'Hurry up. No time for that now.'

'Can I go to the loo first?' I asked, a bit calmer now. Feeling more reassured now that I knew I was going to be escorted on to a different route, I finally realised that my bladder was fit to burst.

I drove behind Bernard for an hour and a quarter along a narrow road. When we got back to the A10 he stopped to say goodbye and wish me '*bonne chance*'. All I could say was '*merci*', over and over.

It was getting light now. If my strength didn't fail me and I didn't run into any other setbacks, I would only make a quick stop in Tours to get petrol and then drive on all the way to Paris without resting.

The highway was getting busier (more light, so more people) and I felt much safer, although I didn't let my guard down and constantly checked in my rear-view mirror for the BMW. Sometimes I even relaxed a little, remembering my reasons the day before for setting off on this trip.

It was nearly eleven thirty in the morning by the time I arrived in Paris, and an hour later I'd checked into a room at the Hotel Albert. I collapsed in bed with the feeling that I'd made a very stupid mistake that could cost me dearly, but after a while I was able to think more clearly. Now at my destination and apparently out of danger, I could see with sudden clarity what had brought me here. Only twenty days had passed since my life had been turned upside down – nothing at all compared with the thirty-four years I'd already lived. It had taken a mere twenty days to transform me into someone I hardly even recognised, all starting with Teresa's call on the ninth of this month. Ah, my beloved Teresa . . . How could I have known then that just a few weeks later I would stand grieving at her funeral? 'Berta, my love, it's so wonderful to talk to you again. Darling, I'm so sorry to have to tell you this but your mother has passed away . . .' My heart had skipped a beat, but not from the news of Alberta's death. I'd contemplated my mother's demise many times in fact without the slightest tremor – fifteen years away with no contact can help a lot. No, it was more to do with my emotion at hearing the voice of my sweet nanny and family housekeeper.

Since my arrival in Madrid, the secrets of my mother's and sister's lives had begun to reveal themselves to me day after day, as though I were trapped in the pages of a mystery novel – one where the suspense had been ratcheting up to my increasing dismay and disquiet the further I had gone along with the story. I started to understand that the independent and frivolous Berta had been living an enormous lie over a fifteen-year respite. My past had been waiting for me patiently all along. Coming back had been total catharsis in just three weeks – a liberation, a powerful rebirth – after confronting the Berta who had been hidden away under lock and key in the attic of my mind, under the false conviction that she would suffocate and wither in there. Exactly as my mother had locked away those letters at the end, with the same absurd certainty that no one would read them and that Saúl would continue to be the only party found guilty in the dark plan hatched by her favourite daughter.

It's funny how a handful of words can hit their mark to such great effect: they just need to be written from the heart and reach the right person at the right time. The years that had passed since they were written were irrelevant, and nor did it matter that Saúl had a new life now, full of hope and expectation. I was the one who had gathered up the sincere love he had felt and the profound pain he had suffered. It was the Berta I'd hidden away in the past who needed to read his letters in the right place and time. Only three weeks had been enough to make me realise that, of all the lies of the past, the most ridiculous had been the one I'd told myself – the one that had turned me into a robot with no feelings, something I would never have understood without the letters of that man from Lake Crescent. I was here now to prove it, that what I had felt when I read his letters was not some mirage. I had travelled all the way here to meet him, the Saúl who had awakened me to the world of emotions, who had taught me that to live without feelings is no more than mere survival.

This fresh emotion made me forget everything I'd been through the night before and finally realise how long I'd gone without food or checking my phone. I'd decided to put it on silent when its pinging woke me in the morning, and went out now to find a decent cafe. I ended up walking for miles, because all I could find near the hotel and gallery were clothing and shoe shops.

It was a gorgeous morning, so I picked a table on an outdoor terrace and ordered a delicious sandwich and a Coca-Cola.

I had eleven missed calls on my phone, all from an unknown caller, probably Alfonso, along with eighteen WhatsApp messages from a number I didn't recognise, and twenty-seven emails. None of them from Boston. I logged on to the cafe's Wi-Fi to start with the messages – all from my detective: 'Berta, the police have proof that Pedro Vidal killed Teresa and they're looking for him. Know what that means? They're opening an investigation. If they go down that road, it'll lead to Bodo.'

That was the first of many.

'Call me on this number when you can. We need to talk.'

The next: 'Berta, I'm starting to worry – you're not answering my calls. Tell me where you are and I'll come and find you right away.'

They were all like that. He'd left the first message before our conversation – that was the news about the case that I hadn't let him tell me. I was hugely happy that the authorities had finally discovered what a villain Pedro Vidal was: this man who had beaten my beautiful Teresa to death so viciously – the aunt on whose goodwill he had relied for so many years. I only hoped they'd be able to arrest him as soon as possible. It was wonderful news, but didn't require my presence in Madrid, at least for now, which was reassuring. The other messages had been sent a few hours after I'd left – he must really have wanted to know how I was doing. He did seem anxious at not hearing from me, so I decided to call to put him at his ease.

'Oh, Berta, I'm mighty relieved to hear from you! Where are you? Are you all right?' He didn't even give me time to say hello. When he saw my name on the display he just picked up and started firing questions at me.

'I'm safe and sound in Paris – calm down, everything is fine. You don't need to worry about a thing.'

'Berta, please be careful. Pedro Vidal is still on the loose and he's desperate . . .'

'Honestly, don't worry, I'm perfectly fine. I'll see you when I get back.'

'OK. Take care of yourself.'

I didn't read the emails; it looked like most of them were about my restaurant. I'd already had enough for today. The police investigation was underway and that was fabulous news. I kept that in mind and concentrated on my visit to Paris.

I had time to rest at the hotel for a few hours. Although I couldn't sleep, the truth is it did relax me a little and allow me to get my bearings before focusing on the upcoming event.

Given that I was within walking distance of the gallery, I wouldn't need to leave until half past five, giving me plenty of time to get ready and then make my way there. As the time drew closer, I got more and more excited. I should have been exhausted from the lack of sleep and stress of the past few days, especially with all the terrors of the night before, but somehow I wasn't – I felt radiant and ready to enjoy myself. Whichever way I looked at it, this was a crazy situation that not even the impetuous Mary would have understood. I'd driven many hours overnight, and been chased by someone out to get me, all to attend the opening of an artist I only knew through a clutch of letters written many years before – meanwhile turning my back on a thousand serious matters needing my attention in Madrid . . . It was utterly reckless and totally unbecoming for a woman who had always been led by her overweening common sense and notion of what was right and proper. But then Mary would have said, 'You're in love? That's fantastic – go get him, Berta!' I had no doubt that she would have cheered me on all the way in pursuit of my love.

I was so close now to these final works of the man from Lake Crescent, and my joy was infinitely the greater at hearing from Alfonso that the police knew at last that Teresa's cousin was the killer – the beginning of the end of this whole sorry saga. But I would savour that glorious news later: the best surprises should be enjoyed one at a time.

My outfit, face and hair as I wanted them, I looked at myself in the mirror over the chest of drawers and told myself truthfully, 'Berta, no one would know how many hours you've been driving with no sleep – you look sensational! No make-up on earth can match the glow of a woman in love.' I'd put on a very flattering white dress that enhanced my best features: my skin tone and the glint of my russet-brown hair. Mary had coached me well in the art of choosing the best clothes to complement my complexion and natural colouring. The boat neck sat perfectly, showing off my collarbones and upper shoulders, and making my neck look long and slender. The seductive wisps and tendrils escaping from my artfully twisted bun were exactly where I wanted them. Putting my hair up was the right choice with that dress, highlighting my delicate cheekbones and sexy little chin. Fair enough – I needed cheering up. It was like getting ready all on my own for a prom or graduation ball, and I wanted to feel confident in my appearance. Finally I stepped into a pair of silver heels and picked up my matching bag before applying a spritz of scent for the finishing touch.

I was off to meet the man of my dreams and wanted every detail to be perfect, decking myself out with him in mind. Here and now was where dreams and reality would shortly intersect, and I'd perhaps be the closest to Saúl I would ever manage in my life.

The city unfurled beneath my feet with pleasure, as I proudly glided along the red carpet like a queen – the whole of Paris was mine that evening. I walked down the avenue in total happiness, feeling proud and triumphant . . . To arrive there on my personal crusade, I had had to overcome the most challenging of tests. I was in that beautiful city for nothing and no one other than love, which had finally come knocking at my door – and I had thrown that door wide open to welcome it in. Right from the beginning I had accepted that the other person in my romance had no awareness of my feelings. I was all dressed up to celebrate the fact that, through loving him, I was capable of doing so much more than on my own. I was welcoming here this new Berta who could feel, who could love, and was more proud of myself with every step.

When I arrived at the gallery and saw my reflection in the window, I congratulated myself again.

It was two minutes to seven and the place was already busy. Diverse groups of people clustered around the entrance, each quite distinct from the other. To the right stood a married couple and a single man, all three very elegant and clearly very rich. A few metres away were three girls and two guys in their thirties, somewhat bohemian, dressed in distinctive one-off vintage clothing – probably artists interested in the work of the Flickering Painter. To the left, meanwhile, stood two Nordic-looking men, possibly patrons from other galleries, collectors or investors, but they certainly didn't look French.

I climbed the small staircase that led inside and, looking through the window, understood why some of the guests had come back out: there was barely room in there for me.

Chapter 21

7 p.m., Monday 30 June 2014

I pushed open the door to find a kind-looking man of around sixty seated behind a table. Against the deafening babble of guests with their glasses of wine, he rose to his feet to greet me, pronouncing his words with care so I could understand the French. Did I have an invitation? he asked, and when I said no, answered that such a beautiful young woman should not miss the opening ceremony for the famous painter Yosa Degui. He winked and let me go through. It's funny, those extraordinary moments in life sometimes, when we come away from an encounter with someone, not even knowing the other person's name, but filled with a warm glow of gratitude that human beings can be so wonderful.

Every corner, every face, every single moment . . . Absolutely every detail was registering in my brain as though on to a hard drive. I felt so unbelievably alive, with all my nerve endings tingling, and didn't want to miss a thing. It felt like my first date . . . Actually, it was my first date, although somewhat belated.

I walked through the large group that crowded about the entrance and threw myself completely into his world, the fascinating, melancholy and enigmatic world of Saúl. In the showroom, which was huge, I could see his paintings over the heads of the audience, calling me, as if they had only one reason for being there: me, and me alone. 'Breathe, Berta, look at them in sequence and take all the time you need, from right to left,' I told myself, letting out a deep sigh.

I would have liked to have been there all alone and didn't appreciate seeing these crowds of people scrutinising every brushstroke of the canvases that Saúl had covered with fragments of his own life. Slipping between the other visitors as stealthily and discreetly as I could, given my height and the colour of my dress, I finally made my way through to the first painting. I managed to stand back at an acceptable distance with no distraction in my eye line, although even further back would have been perfect to view it with the best perspective.

It showed a landscape where the main subject was the trees of the forest overlooking the lake. Every branch was represented by a phrase joined to the trunk at one end. These were overlapping and it was hard to make out all the disjointed words in Spanish: 'Dear Muse, always yours, today I feel alone, I love you, nothing without you, loneliness, romance . . .' I had the inner satisfaction of knowing that I was most certainly the only person here able to understand the message in all aspects because I knew the frustrated past of the artist. I couldn't say whether the landscape came to me or whether I came to it – all I know is that I was intoxicated by the profound emotion I found captured among the phrases, which seemed to droop out of pure misery, waiting to sink once and for all in the waters of the lake.

I was so caught up in it that I lost all sense of space and time, just like when I read his letters. My distraction and total stillness must have drawn the attention of the people around me, since one girl was bold enough to come up and drag me out of my rapture.

'Are you all right?' she asked, tapping my shoulder lightly.

'Yes, yes, I'm fine, thanks. It's just . . . this painting is so incredible!' I answered, still captivated, my eyes glued to the rhythm of the brushstrokes.

The girl seemed to understand and was moved. 'It really is – it's a marvellous work,' she responded, looking at the landscape, almost as drawn by it as I was. But only almost.

Still wrapped in enchantment, I moved on to the next canvas. I think the people gave way to let me pass when they saw my fascination, which must have been contagious. They even covertly cleared an area with enough space for me to enjoy the painting with some perspective. The words kept dancing on the motifs that filled the landscape. This time the pier had the leading role. It was extraordinary! After two paintings of the dock, one from the pier and another that looked as though it had been painted from the deck of the ferry, I found the one that struck me most of all so far: in the doorway of a wooden cabin stood a tall, thin man, fairly unkempt, with seven ducks at his feet, pecking at the words that he crumbled with his slender fingers. To the right of the figure was a window through which you could see the easel and the work that was waiting. It must have been a grey day, because the light was sad and it was drawn in pastels.

I felt uniquely privileged among this crowd. However much they stared at the paintings, searching for answers, only I knew that this figure in the painting was Saúl Guillén, the Flickering Painter, also known as Yosa Degui. The red sticker on the corner of the frame told visitors that it was not for sale. I would have given all my inheritance money to have it with me for the rest of my life.

On the wall facing the entrance hung the most outstanding artwork of the exhibition: a large oil painting of Ruby Beach, with a somewhat disturbing cast of light. Everywhere in the gallery led to this inviting virgin beach, which seduced your line of vision towards the immensity of the sea. The undertow of the waves lapping at the white sand was at eye level for any spectator of normal height. Little ripples in stark white reached out from the image in my direction. My legs went weak and my feet would no longer support me, while a cold sweat broke out on my forehead from sheer emotion. Those snowy white crests spoke to me, each curl a letter, each connected to the next to form words; every wave, a word; the shoreline, a sentence about to be washed up on the sand.

Someone noticed the state I was in and offered me a glass of wine, which I accepted without taking my eyes off the foaming waves. It probably wasn't very sociable of me, but my heart and mind belonged completely to the bubbling of this beach, while my gaze ran over it again and again, from left to right, reading, 'Dear sweet and patient stranger, let us drink to all the bitter words you have imbibed from my letters.'

As if I were completely alone on that beach, I lifted my glass, approached its sacred waters and then drank the ambrosial nectar in mystical ecstasy. I savoured each sip until it was absorbed and there was nothing left. Then an angel must have brushed against my shoulder to break my enchantment and make me turn my face towards the exit. There in the shadows stood a tall man with a very white smile, watching me with his own glass raised, holding it out to me. It was Saúl.

In the heart of the gallery a circular bench was set around a central table covered with leaflets on the show. Depending on where a visitor sat, it faced any given area of the room. Two people, I don't even remember what gender, led me to the bench while everyone else stared at me in eager surprise. Sitting next to me was a man who remained silent for a moment as he took my glass, and that calmed down the bystanders, who slowly wandered off to enjoy the other paintings.

When the man saw that I was more receptive, he leaned in and said right into my ear, in a fairly acceptable Spanish accent, 'He came for you. He risked his freedom to meet his new muse.'

'Martin Baker?' I managed to ask.

'The very same. Saúl got your email and it meant so much to him that he decided to take the risk of coming to Paris. His paintings were already in the gallery and he felt the need to leave you a personal message in his most symbolic work. He arrived seven days ago, and he's been working ever since on that painting,' he said, pointing to the landscape of the beach that hung over the room, 'the final painting of the exhibition. He painted it in record time – look at its meaning, the title and the texture: it's all still fresh. I think that he sensed you would be here today. He also wants you to know how much it's changed his life to know now that his stranger has a name, and that she's you. It's funny – looking at you I realise that he hasn't painted those other eyes in years, and that can't be a coincidence.'

'He came for me . . . ?'

'It's a pleasure to meet you, Miss – you've been a total surprise. I do hope that destiny allows us to meet again,' he answered, standing up and giving me a slight bow by way of farewell.

'I hope so too, Mr Baker.'

With that he left, leaving me alone and full of questions, among a crowd that had finally chosen to ignore the madwoman dressed in white.

I couldn't leave the bench, where I still sat contemplating that beach, quite mesmerised. There were many more paintings to enjoy and messages to decipher, but I'd had enough for today; I would come back tomorrow. Right now I just wanted to feel the wonder of loving and feeling loved for the first time in my life. I was so dazed that I couldn't even be sure if it had really happened, if Saúl really had been there, travelling vast distances and risking what little freedom he had left in life just to raise a glass to me . . . His face, turned towards me, smiling, happy, with his glass lifted . . . It had been like an apparition, a wonderful dream.

It was all over, and Yolanda was in the past. The paintings hanging in the Atelier des Lumières were an ode to Saúl having managed to start on a new path, having shed the heavy weight of his painful memories. Jesus, he had come out of hiding to celebrate with me! Not in my wildest dreams had I imagined such happiness. I never thought you could reach such a magical, seductive world from this one.

Little by little, people were drifting out of the gallery. By nine fifteen I was the only one to remain, still seated on the central bench in front of the Pacific Ocean, bound to the words that ran along its shore.

'Mademoiselle.' A kind voice brought me back to the harsh reality. It was all over.

'Yes?'

The gallery owner – the same kind gentleman who had allowed me in at the start – was standing in front of me, holding his hand out to invite me to stand up at last, probably with the intention of guiding me to the exit. Just then all the lights that brought the paintings of the man by the lake to life were switched off, and night fell on the beach.

Only the faintest gleam around their corners stopped the timid silhouettes from dying on the walls.

'Marie, turn the lights back on, please!'

The ocean shone once more beneath the sun.

'Thank you,' I said, rising to my feet.

'It doesn't seem as though you've quite finished with the exhibition. Take your time to savour the paintings on your own.'

Silence accompanied me as I walked through the gallery, seeing all the paintings still waiting for me, all of them brimming with thrilling messages, with beauty, with brushstrokes as tremulous as my soul. I didn't feel able, however, to delight in them for quite as long as I would have liked, thinking of that nameless man from the gallery who had twice been so kind and patient with me. And so I said goodbye to the final painting, leaving behind the one thing that had been fully worthwhile in my nearly thirty-five years of life. It was a painting of the lake shrouded in mist, that very mist that had tortured him so much, but between the wisps of vapour shone a radiant stream of light, a torrent of words of hope. This was what the brief message I had sent him by email had inspired in him: that there was new hope in his life, and it came from me.

I left the big room slowly, utterly stunned, followed out by my patient, silent guide.

Before I left, I asked the kind gentleman why the paintings were not for sale. He told me that they all already had a buyer, and that the exhibition had been a complete success. I was devastated, ashamed that this had not been obvious to me. But he was holding back something special for me: the painting of the man feeding the ducks.

'The artist kept this for you,' he said, taking it off the wall to place it in my hands. I couldn't believe it – it was mine . . . 'If you want, you can leave your address and we'll send it on to your home,' he commented, as I stared at the painting with the awe and wonder of a girl who had just been granted the one gift she had always longed for.

'If it's all right, I'd rather take it with me now.'

◆ ◆ ◆

I walked on air the whole way back to the hotel. I don't know if it was Saúl's painting, which was like carrying a kite pushed along by a gentle breeze, or if it was all in my mind, but I was no longer in the mortal world. I remember only that I didn't once seem to tread on the surface of the pavement that led from the gallery to my hotel, but rather that it seemed transformed into a pathway of clouds. All the shops appeared to be shut, and the only light that evening streamed out from what I was carrying in my hands. No, I have no real memory of that walk, which I must have taken, because I ended up back at the hotel lobby.

The pair of receptionists at the front desk greeted me as I wafted in from the street.

'You are Señorita de Castro?' one of them asked.

'Yes, that's me.'

'Someone asked for you – he's waiting in the lounge off to the right.'

'For me? Are you sure? Did he give his name?' I asked, suddenly frightened and fearing the worst, that maybe Pedro Vidal had finally found me.

'Yes, his name is . . .' She looked down at her notes for a second. 'His name is Saúl Guillén.'

'Oh . . . thank you! Thank you so very much.'

I walked towards the room, my heart thumping painfully with emotion.

Sofas separated off a number of seating areas, some of them occupied. A man rose to his feet at the back of the room when he saw me come in. It was him.

Overwhelmed and in shock, I covered the distance between us, his painting in my hands.

'Hello, Berta,' he said in greeting, a gentle smile on his lips.

'Saúl . . . you're here . . .'

Trembling, I took his hand as he guided me to my seat, exploring the slender and delicate fingers of the man who fed ducks.

My eyes never once left his face – he was more attractive than I'd imagined, and taller, stronger, more manly and . . . he had a beard now, thick and neatly trimmed, from beneath which flashed his gentle white smile. His hair was tied back, very dark still but with a few strands of grey these days, and the brown warmth of his eyes and natural tan of his skin stood out against his white coat with its mandarin collar. He seemed somewhat older than his true age, or maybe just more mature in his outlook and experience.

'I came here to meet you, and you don't know how happy I am. I could not have forgiven myself if I'd left without thanking you for everything you've done for me.'

That easy smile, tender and kind, stayed on his face as he spoke, matching the glow in his eyes.

'How do you know . . . ?'

'A mutual friend told me about you. Berta, I don't have much time; I shouldn't be here at all.'

'I understand,' I said with deep regret.

'I came to tell you that I'm starting a new life and I don't want you to suffer on my behalf any longer – I've left behind all of my difficulties and moved on. I came today to say goodbye to Saúl forever and I want you to do the same.'

'You can't ask that of me. I don't think I could ever forget you. You have no idea what your letters have meant to me.'

A tear ran down my face. He leaned in and wiped it away, stroking his thumb very slowly across my cheek. He smelled like the lake, like the forest in winter and turpentine – like his paintings. I couldn't help putting my hand over his to hold it there just a little longer.

'You're freezing . . .' I whispered.

'It's this feeling of loss that makes me cold: you know that.'

He drew a little closer and pressed his lips to mine. I closed my eyes and the tears flowed freely down my cheeks as we kissed, and I trembled more violently than ever.

Then he pulled away to say goodbye.

'You're so much more beautiful than I'd imagined. It's time for me to go now, Berta.'

He stood up and a man on the other side of the room rose to his feet at the same time. It was Martin Baker.

My beloved painter was almost at the door when the urge to see him one last time got the better of me. Still seated, I called out to him, 'Saúl!'

He turned his head for a moment while Martin continued walking to the door.

'Thank you for the painting.'

'Goodbye, Berta,' he said, and smiled again.

I got into the lift, my mind far away, the touch of his lips still on mine, savouring that one fleeting kiss. As I opened the door to my room, the sight of Alfonso pulled me out of my wonderful reverie. He sat in the shadows on a low chair, smoking. I could barely recognise him.

'What are you doing here?'

'Don't fuck with me, Berta. What do you think I'm doing here? Pedro Vidal is still out there, and your life has been in danger ever since you left Madrid. I couldn't just do nothing. I drove like mad to get here . . . I don't know what I was thinking.'

'I'm sorry – I'm really sorry, Alfonso, but . . . I just had to be in Paris today.'

'Right . . . you know it's a miracle you're still alive, don't you?'

'Yes, I know. Teresa's cousin followed me all the way out of Bordeaux yesterday . . .'

'No, Berta, he followed you all the way to this hotel. If I hadn't decided to come, you'd be in the same position as your darling Teresa right now. I think I need a drink from the minibar.'

I leaned the painting against the wall, sat on the bed and switched on the lamp on the bedside table, still in my dreamlike state, still intoxicated from the intense moment I had just experienced, and unable to fathom why Alfonso was in my room.

He poured himself a tot of something strong, then went on, a little more in control of himself. 'Berta, if I hadn't come to alert the gendarmes, you'd be dead right now. Pedro Vidal was arrested minutes before you left the hotel to go to the gallery. He was waiting for you and he was armed. The situation would have been a lot easier and less dangerous for everybody, even Saúl, if you hadn't come.'

'I'm so glad I came before you could stop me... Alfonso, I saw him – he came all the way here. I just left him.'

'I know. I was raising a glass to you both all on my own up here, and I know he was waiting for you in the hotel lounge.'

'You were at the exhibition? You saw him? Did you talk to him?'

'Yes, but only for a few minutes. It was complicated, but that doesn't matter now...'

'What do you mean it doesn't matter? What do you know about Saúl? What are you hiding?'

'Nothing – I don't know anything that you don't know. I said hello to him and Martin Baker because I was at the exhibition just like you, and I know he was waiting for you because I ran into him at the entrance to the hotel. That's all.

'Listen, Berta, in a few hours Saúl will be flying back to the US. He came here on a fake passport, and we couldn't risk —'

'No, Saúl's not going back to the US. He's left everything behind to start a new life,' I said, lost in thought.

'I'm very happy for him,' he replied, and then took a long, pensive drag of his cigarette, 'and I'm so very sorry for you.'

'I'm happy for him too, but you don't know how desperately it hurts to know that I'll never see him again.' Grief overwhelmed me and the tears started to flow.

Alfonso didn't speak until I was a little more collected. 'Would you like to get something to eat while I fill you in on everything that's happened while you've been away? I know a sensational restaurant a short walk from here.'

I forced a wavering smile and accepted his invitation.

◆ ◆ ◆

It was a lovely night and we sat outdoors on the terrace of a typical Parisian restaurant. Deep within, I felt torn to shreds, holding back the tears with the feeling that nothing would ever be the same again, the bittersweet taste of his farewell kiss still lingering on my skin: he had said goodbye to me forever. From that moment on, he had shut the door on his past and set off down a road full of fresh possibilities, but left behind a woman who felt newly forged from the fire, and enormously fortunate to have touched the soul of the man from Lake Crescent – softening a little the grief of that goodbye. Since my departure from London, the hand of fate had once again intervened to condense such a mixed bag of emotions into one place and time that part of me nonetheless remained anxious to hear the news that Alfonso was waiting to tell me.

He ordered the best wine on the menu. We clinked our glasses beneath the myriad twinkling stars and began to talk.

'So tell me, what's been happening?'

Just as I was doing, he pulled himself together as much as he was able and said, 'We're almost at the finishing line. It's only a matter of days until it's all over. In case something happened to her, Teresa left a written statement exposing the involvement of her cousin and your sister in Bodo's disappearance, as well as her fear that Pedro Vidal might attack her or your niece.'

'Teresa . . . All the suffering and secrets she took with her to the grave . . .' I murmured, after downing my glass of wine in one.

'Yolanda has been arrested. She made her statement this morning . . .'

'She was in Madrid?'

This news was so startling that it finally succeeded in capturing my attention.

'So it seems. I also found out that . . .' He hesitated, as though searching for the best way to say something without causing me too much pain.

'What?' I pressed, sensing that I wasn't going to like what he was about to say.

'Do you know why your mother's little sitting room next to her bedroom doesn't have a window?'

He waited for my response. I could think of only one possible reason and it was so dark I couldn't even say it out loud. In the meantime, he drained his wine and refilled the glass. Our meal still lay untouched on our plates.

'In the cavity beyond that wall facing the garden . . . Well, according to Yolanda's statement, that's where Fabián's body is. She defended herself by blaming your mother for all the crimes and exposing all her dirty laundry, as if she were merely another victim. Fabián is walled up in your mother's sitting room. I expect the police will have found the body by now.'

'But that's ghastly . . . I can't believe I grew up in that house . . . How could my mother have spent hours in that room every night before going to sleep? What kind of human being brought me into this world? It's horrible . . . I understand it all now – I guess that was the bargaining chip my sister used to get whatever she wanted from Alberta . . . I need water . . .' I whispered, feeling sick with the shock.

Alfonso poured the water from the carafe and handed me the glass. 'Easy now, Berta, all of that happened a long time ago. There's no need to torture yourself with it now.'

'Oh my God . . . All these days, alone, sleeping with a dead body just down the hall . . . What a cold-hearted bitch she was . . . What about my sister then – why did they arrest her? What did Teresa's letter say?'

'That Yolanda was the one who paid Pedro Vidal to fake the death of her husband. It's a very detailed statement in which she explains that Yolanda's real intention was to kill him herself and frame Saúl, but Bodo found out about her plan and made a deal with her: he gave her more money than she'd be entitled to as his widow and could carry on with her life, with the caveat that she'd let him go and thereby escape his own financial difficulties, along with all the suspicions the police were starting to come up with over his dodgy business dealings. I'd say those two were pretty well matched.'

'So . . . he's alive. My father is alive.'

'Very likely, it seems. They've already issued an arrest warrant.'

'Do you realise that I'm the daughter of two totally unscrupulous criminals?' I asked him, and turned my face away, hiding my shame and the tears that I could no longer hold back.

'Berta, look at me,' he said tenderly. I turned back towards him, my gaze still lowered. 'Look at me,' he repeated, and finally I did. 'You are nothing like them. Ever since you were young you've been yourself, and you rebelled in your own way against everything around you. You aren't anything like your sister either – you never went along with her fun and games and you never, ever stopped striving to live with integrity. You've even been able to fall in love with a guy just from reading his letters. In what way is that being anything like them?'

'I can't go back to that house, I just can't. This is all too much for me.'

'You have to be strong and be there to defend what's yours: your house and your past. Besides, you owe it to the most innocent people in all of this: Saúl and Teresa.'

'It's funny – at one point I got suspicious of Teresa, and in the end it turned out she was the bravest person I knew. She was by our side all of our lives only to lose her own life in such a dreadful way . . . And what will happen to Saúl now?'

Alfonso reached across the table to take my hands. His hands were as cold as Saúl's had been when he dried my tears. It must have been the same thing happening to him: that dreadful feeling of loss . . . 'Don't you worry, we'll get him back his freedom; I'll help you. But right now you need to return to Madrid to help with the investigation. This nightmare will be over very soon, I promise you.'

'It won't be easy to get over these last few weeks. I know I'll never be the same again,' I answered, very conscious of how much it hurt him that we'd met under such unhappy circumstances.

'It's a pity you're sad on a beautiful night like this.'

'It's a pity the stars dare to shine so brightly on such a sad night; it should be mourning the loss of the man by the lake,' I answered.

'It's bloody hard, I know . . . Do you realise how stunning you look tonight? I've never met a woman so well suited to grieving.'

In his own way, he too was saying goodbye to an affair of the heart that would never meet its potential.

I was overpowered by a deep compassion for the pair of us – right now we were both feeling the pain of a love that could not be. It seemed so unfair that we hadn't met at another time when things were right . . . Alfonso loved me with all his heart and would have given anything to have me in his life, just as I would have done for Saúl. I remembered our night together at the Hilton, his tenderness and generosity, and how honestly and bravely he had borne the harsh disappointment of my loving someone else. Just like Saúl, he too had gone on a dangerous journey for my sake, in order to save my life. He deserved my love, but I had already given myself to another. Right now we were two warriors defeated in battle, having given everything we had. We had so much in common . . . We had bet everything on love and both of us had lost.

'What's going to become of us once all this is over?'

'Well, we'll always have Paris.'

ACKNOWLEDGMENTS

With thanks to you, most generous reader, for reaching this final page. You have stood by me since my first story and supported me every step along the way – without you my literary career would not have been possible.

ABOUT THE AUTHOR

Mercedes Pinto Maldonado was born in Granada, though she now lives in Málaga, Spain. She studied medicine, but left the field to devote herself to literature. She is currently working full-time on writing, reading, and creating novels. She is considered a humanist writer who can use any genre as the framework for her stories. Her website is www.mercedespinto.com.

ABOUT THE TRANSLATOR

Photo © 2018, Michelle Gray Photography

Jennie Erikson graduated from the University of Washington in Seattle with a BA in history and anthropology. She earned an MA in medieval archaeology from the University of York in England and has worked on excavation sites on Easter Island, in Jordan, England and the western United States.

Jennie lives in Colorado with her husband, where she reviews history books for her website (www.historybookreviews.com) and reads voraciously on every historical subject she can find.